ALLY OF THE CROWN

THE HEIRS OF WILLOW NORTH, BOOK ONE

MELISSA MCSHANE

Night Harbor Publishing

Night Harbor Publishing

www.nightharborpublishing.com

Cover design by Jay R. Villalobos www.coversbyjuan.com

North sign and shield designed by Erin Dinnell Bjorn

First Printing
10 9 8 7 6 5 4 3 2 1

For Jacob,
who understands romance better than I do

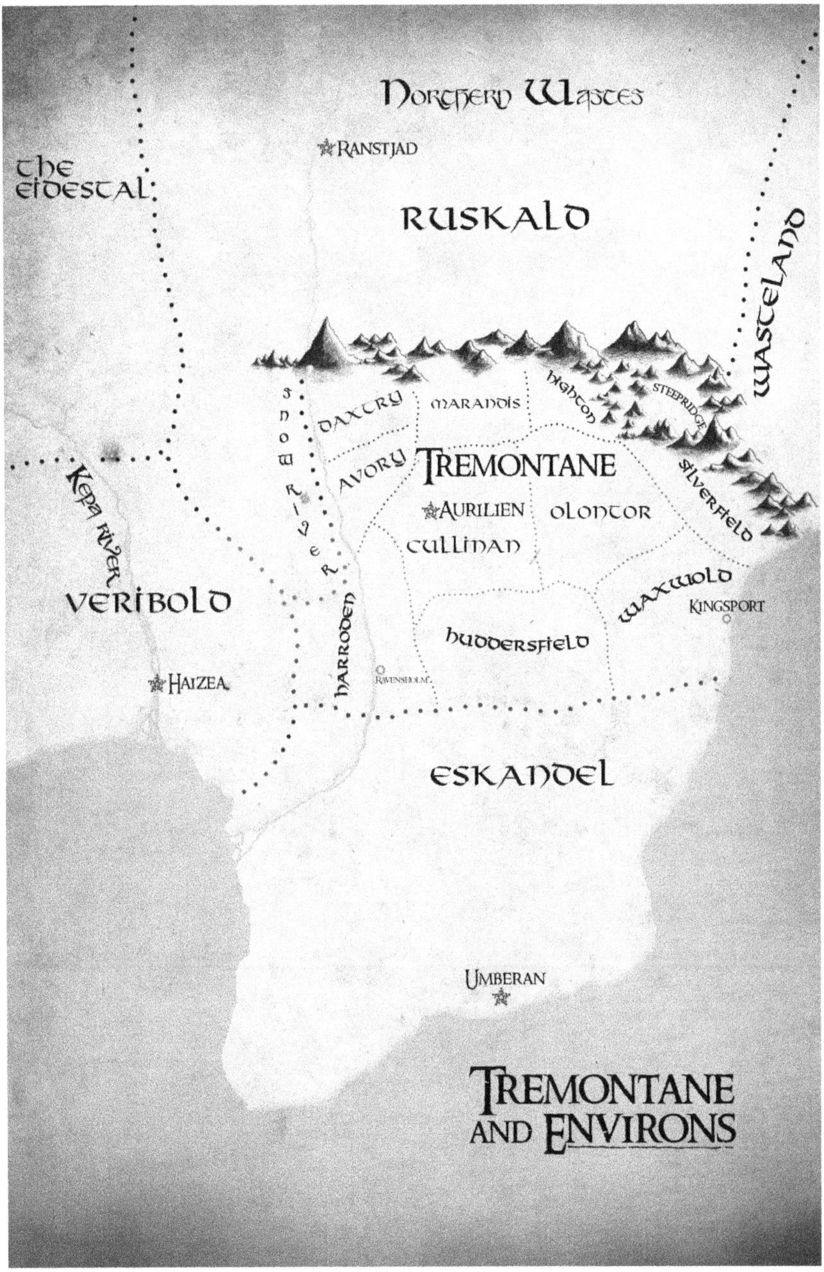

Northern Wastes

☆ Ranstjad

RUSKALD

The Eidestal

WASTELAND

Snow River

DAXTRY

MARANDIS

HIGHTON

STEEPRIDGE

AVORY

TREMONTANE

SILVERFIELD

☆ AURILIEN   OLONTOR

CULLINAN

Kepa River

VERIBOLD

HARRODEN

WAXWOLD

KINGSPORT

HUDDERSFIELD

RAVENSHOLM

☆ HAIZEA

ESKANDEL

UMBERAN
☆

TREMONTANE
AND ENVIRONS

---

*F*iona had stayed at so many inns over the last month all their taprooms had started to look alike. Low ceilings with fat square beams painted black or dark brown, planed oak floors worn smooth from generations of feet, round or square tables and ladderback chairs between the two. Either this was the ideal configuration for a successful taproom, or there was some carpenter somewhere who had a monopoly on the hospitality trade. This one was different in having chairs arranged in front of the fireplace, encouraging patrons to sit and enjoy a drink or five. It was a generous gesture Fiona appreciated.

The logs in the inn's long fireplace burned low, giving off scant heat against the cold of a Tremontanan winter. Fiona hitched her chair closer and thought about poking the fire into life, but the innkeeper, with his pinched, narrow face, had the look of someone for whom firewood was an extravagance.

She took a long pull from her mug and set it on the table at her elbow. Hot cider, not the alcoholic kind, and that order had earned her another skeptical look from the innkeeper. She never drank, not even new beer, not even when it was the only thing on offer. It had taken only one...accident...to teach her that lesson.

She stared at the flickering flames and felt her right palm itch with sympathy for them, denied their nature by the lack of fuel. If she had been alone, if this had been the fire in her own house, she might have rolled up her sleeve and taken hold of the log, made it blaze hot and bright and reveled in its joy at being freed. But doing so here would get her far more than skeptical looks from the innkeeper.

Having inherent magic wasn't illegal, not the way being an Ascendant was, but most people didn't care about the distinction. And fire-starting...it was a magic no one would make allowances for, not like healing. She'd be lucky to die quickly at the mob's hands. She closed her hand on the impulse and took another drink.

Someone dropped into a chair next to her. "What's a pretty lady like you doing sitting all alone?" the man said. Fiona managed not to roll her eyes.

"Enjoying the solitude," she said, hoping he'd heed the warning.

"What are you drinking? Let me buy you another." He was a big man with a heavy dark beard, but his smile was friendly, and she didn't get a sense of menace off him. Not that it mattered. Why did so many men think they could impose on a lone woman, even in a friendly way?

"Thanks, but this is my limit." She swigged down the last of her cider, made a face at swallowing the bitter dregs all at once, and stood.

"Oh, you're not leaving so soon? Come on, I just want to talk. You wouldn't leave old Jack here with nobody but the fire to talk to, would you?"

"Sorry. Maybe another time." This time tomorrow, she'd be somewhere else, probably fending off yet another too-friendly man. Too bad she no longer had a husband to dissuade them. She didn't want Roderick back in her life, but she had to admit being married to him hadn't been all bad. A husband-shaped shield, that's what she needed.

"If that's what you want, Fiona," the man said, turning his attention to the fire.

Fiona took two steps toward the taproom door and halted. She'd never said her name.

She returned to her chair and said, in a low voice, "I don't know who you are or what you want, but if you so much as think about interfering in my business, I'll make you wish we'd never met."

"You don't have anything to fear from me," Jack said. He stretched long legs toward the fire. "It's not much warmth, is it? Bet you could do something about that."

Chill dread filled her heart. "Who are you?"

"Someone like you. I told you, you don't have to fear me. I'd never give away another of us."

Fiona glanced at the innkeeper, placidly polishing glasses behind the bar. A few other patrons sat at the bar, and a young couple working their way toward serious inebriation laughed and groped each other at a table near one of the multi-paned windows. No one paid her and Jack any attention. "You have the wrong woman. I'm no one special."

"My inherent magic shows me the magic of others like us," Jack continued as if she hadn't spoken. "You're bright with fire, and not just because of the red hair. I asked the innkeeper your name. He's remarkably loose-lipped. You might want to move elsewhere tomorrow."

"I'm—" She closed her lips on *leaving town tomorrow*. "What do you want?"

"To warn you. There are hunters here in Maraston, and at least one of them has inherent sensory magic. They've already picked up a couple of hares, and I don't want them getting their hands on either of us."

Hares. Code for people whose inherent magic was harmless, the ability to sense lies or locate missing people. But to hunters, it didn't matter what magic you had; all of it made you potentially an Ascendant. Not that there was anyone left to teach Ascendant magic. Willow North had seen to that, eighty years ago. How those hunters justified using inherent magic to track down their victims, Fiona didn't know. But if they had someone—

3

Fiona stiffened. Suppose Jack were actually one of them? He could be there to keep her talking while the hunters moved in for the kill...

She stood again. "Thanks for the warning. I'll move on in the morning."

"There are three of them, two blond as Ruskalder, one dark-haired. He's got a scar on his cheek. Keep your eyes open."

Fiona nodded and walked unhurriedly to the taproom door, not looking to see if Jack was watching her. Once through the door into the chilly front room of the inn, she trotted up the stairs to her second floor room and immediately gathered her things. There wasn't much to gather; she traveled light these days. A change of clothes; a pair of lightweight shoes she was fond of, unsuitable for the winter weather; her journal. Most of her savings was sewn into the hem of her cloak, which was heavy and black and weighed several pounds even without the guilders it guarded. She wrapped it around herself and shouldered her bag. The room was paid for; all she had to do was find the back way out and hope it wasn't being watched.

The full moon cast shadows over the back yard of the inn, wan and pale compared to the sharp-edged darkness of a clear noon, but enough to confuse the eye and, Fiona hoped, conceal a woman. She stood in the scant shelter of the back door and surveyed the yard. It was a small square of hard earth where nothing grew. A roofed well hunched darkly to one side, and beyond the low fence was the stable yard. Men and women moved there despite the dark and cold, tending to patrons' horses. Fiona saw nothing to indicate any of them were watching the inn.

She slipped from the doorway and strolled along the back wall toward the road, keeping a careful watch on the moving figures. No one approached her. She flexed her bare fingers, wishing she had gloves. It was a bitingly cold, clear night, and she wrapped her cloak more closely around herself and let out a deep breath that turned instantly to a white cloud. When she was a child, she'd made a game of breathing out puffs of white condensation and racing around so they trailed after her. It had been a long time since she'd felt that carefree.

A few pedestrians trod the streets even at this hour, all of them bundled up against the cold and not paying any heed to anyone but themselves. Fiona turned right, away from the inn, and kept walking, though she had no destination in mind. Some other inn—

Behind her, she heard shouting. The man walking just ahead of her turned to look, so she did too. Three horses stood outside the inn, their reins held by a shivering young woman whose hair was bright gold even in the moonlight and the pale yellow glow from the inn's windows. As Fiona watched, a dark-haired man emerged from the inn's front door, followed by two others who were dragging someone between them. The fourth man fought and kicked, and even at this distance Fiona could tell it was Jack.

She stared, breathless, her mind a blur of terror. She should help him. She had no way to help him. She had to be touching something, or someone, to make it catch fire, and she only had two hands. Even if she could burn two of Jack's captors enough to incapacitate them, that still left the third free to capture or kill her. Probably kill her. But Jack had warned her. He might be in this position now because of that warning. She had to do *something*.

The two men threw Jack to the ground, where he lay for a moment before pushing himself up. Fiona saw the glint of moonlight on steel half a breath before the dark-haired man raised a pistol and shot Jack in the head. The spray of blood struck the girl, who flinched, but made no sound.

The man standing near her made a rush for the nearest building, where he vomited against its foundation. Fiona covered her mouth to hold in a scream. She took a step backward, then turned and hurried away as quickly as she could go without running. If one of those men had the ability to sense others with inherent magic, she couldn't risk drawing attention to herself. Heaven only knew how far that person's senses reached.

She turned the first corner she came to and ran, blindly, caroming off a wall as she turned another corner. Staying in Maraston tonight was stupid. She needed to put as much distance between herself and those hunters as possible. She ran until the stitch in her side had her bent double and gasping for breath, then she walked until she was out of the town's boundaries. Tiredness set in, making her bones ache, but she kept putting one foot in front of the other, following the frozen road westward. It was as good a direction as any.

She couldn't sleep outside unless she wanted it to be a sleep she never woke from, and she wasn't yet in that kind of despair. She consulted her mental map. Vanton was the next town west of Maraston, only a few miles. She would make it there before midnight, and if she was lucky, she'd find an inn still open. If not, she'd steal some sleep in a stable somewhere.

By heaven, it was cold. Fiona rubbed her hands together, then wrapped a fold of her cloak around them. She made herself think of other things, which didn't make her feel warm but at least distracted her. Those hunters hadn't even pretended they were interested in a legal trial to prove Jack intended to use his magic for evil, and worse, no one in authority was likely to care that they'd murdered a man in the middle of the street so long as they could prove he was a dangerous potential Ascendant. And Jack's magic could hurt no one. She cursed the hunters, running through a litany of profanity that distracted her further, then cursed the long-dead Ascendants for turning magic into something to be feared.

She hurried faster, hoping to stay warm. She was probably safe now that she was away. The hunters were opportunists rather than hunting her specifically. She'd been careful, ever since her inherent magic had manifested when she was thirteen, and no one had ever guessed she was anything but ordinary. Not even Roderick had known, which probably should have been her first clue that their marriage was a mistake. She'd always believed married people ought to be able to share one another's burdens, and inherent magic had to qualify. But every time she'd come close to revealing her secret, he'd done something that stopped her—they'd fought, or he'd ridiculed her, and she'd felt relieved that she had an excuse. Now that they were divorced, she was particularly grateful.

But even if those men weren't hunting her, they were close enough that she needed to be careful. She'd been traveling with no destination in mind, and that needed to change. But where could she go? Where did she *want* to go? That was a question with no answer. She didn't particularly *want* anything these days except a warm fire and no one prodding her to move on with her life. She'd adopted back into her birth family after the divorce, not wanting to be a singleton, and she loved her aunt and uncle and cousins, but they had a tendency to nag. Fiona wished her parents were still alive, but illness had taken her mother, and her father—she shut her eyes and stopped in the middle of the road, fighting off old memories. *It was an accident. Not your fault. Just an accident.*

She opened her eyes and kept walking. How far could she go? The Eidestal, or Ruskald? Neither the Kirkellan nor the Ruskalder were very welcoming of outsiders. Eskandel? Veribold? Or—a new thought struck her. There was that new country the Eskandelics had discovered, far across the southern ocean. Dineh-something. If she was worried about being followed, that was far enough away to dissuade even the most dedicated hunter. She knew nothing about the place, not even its name, but the idea gripped her. It was different. And it was at least a direction.

She walked more rapidly, wanting to get to her destination as quickly as possible. She'd need to take ship from Umberan in Eskandel, which meant going west to Ravensholm and then south. She could take the overland carriage from Vanton and be in Ravensholm in days. And maybe then she'd have some idea what she wanted to do with her life.

2

Five days later, Fiona strode through the streets of Ravensholm, her bag over her shoulder. The snow hadn't fallen here, so far south; instead filthy rainwater lay in the gutters and the depressions between the pavers. Leafless trees, the famous lindens lining Center Street, reached bony fingers toward the blue winter sky. The afternoon sun cast long gray shadows pointing Fiona's way down the street. She caught a whiff of hot roasted chestnuts and veered to one side to buy a paper cone full of the delicious nuts. She smiled at the woman ahead of her, who ducked into her coat collar and just shrugged in reply. Well, Fiona was in a good mood, and one sour woman wasn't enough to ruin that.

She accepted her cone with another smile and juggled a couple of chestnuts—too hot to eat, yet. Ahead, she saw a wooden sign with a spiky crown painted lopsidedly on it. The inn was tall and elderly, but its windows were clean and reflected the sky, and it didn't look very expensive. It was as good a place to stay as any.

Ten minutes later she sat on a lumpy bed in an interior, window-less room and took a deep breath, inhaling cool dampness the heating Device on the wall couldn't dispel. It had been the last room in the Crown Inn, but she'd opted not to look for someplace nicer. It wasn't as if she'd be there long. The wooden walls were stained dark brown and were bare of anything but a small oval mirror just big enough for Fiona to see her face. She scuffed the soles of her boots across the woven rug, streaked with marks that showed she wasn't the first to do so, and looked her reflection in the eye.

"I'm Fiona Cooper," she told herself. "I was Fiona Kent until I came to my senses." Though no one needed to know this. Divorce wasn't unheard of, but people did look at you funny if they knew your marriage was dissolved, like there was some flaw in you. The idea that a divorce might be best for everyone concerned seemed not to occur to some people.

She left her bag on the bed and went down the stairs, nearly running over a young woman coming up. "I beg your pardon," Fiona said. The young woman was dressed casually in trousers and a heavy knitted sweater, and her boots looked new, as if she'd only just bought them. She had hair nearly as red as Fiona's that she wore loose around her face, which was narrow and sharp-nosed. Fiona took a step to the right to get out of her way. The young woman nodded, not meeting Fiona's eyes, and hurried on up the stairs. Fiona shrugged and continued down the stairs. Someone here must know where she could buy a newspaper.

She put up the hood of her cloak against the rising wind and set out. This part of the city was old, and showed its age in its worn wooden walls, in the cracked paving stones and old-fashioned gutters, but everything was brightly painted and clean. It reminded her strongly of Kingsport, though the roofs here were shingled with wood and not slate. A handful of children rushed past her—on their way home from school, possibly? Or just racing the sun for a few more minutes of playtime.

She bought her paper from a grubby urchin on a street corner, then returned to the Crown Inn, took a seat in the taproom, and opened the newspaper. Nothing exciting was happening in the world. There were the usual tensions between Tremontane and Veribold, the usual gossip about people in the capital. Prince Douglas, youngest of Queen Genevieve North's four children, was once again the center of scandal, this time involving the daughter of the Count of Waxwold. How embarrassing for the Queen. At least he wasn't the heir to the throne, though by all reports Crown Prince Landon was as pleasure-loving as his youngest brother. How tiring to do nothing but have fun, all day long. Fiona had never been indolent and couldn't see the appeal.

She turned a page and ran her finger down the list of business announcements. There, a trading consortium was putting together an expedition to Dineh-Karit. They were looking for investors, but might be persuaded to accept simple labor. They were leaving in a week. Perfect.

"Do you mind if I sit with you?"

A young woman stood beside her table, her hands clasped tightly in front of her. After a second look, Fiona identified her as the woman she'd nearly run over coming down the stairs. The woman's red hair was tousled, as if she'd been outside and had it blown by the wind, but she was still only dressed in trousers and sweater and her cheeks lacked the ruddy look of someone who'd been standing in the cold for too long. Fiona glanced around the room. Most of the tables were unoccupied. "Crowds a bit much for you?" she said with a sidelong smile.

The woman flushed. "I just...don't want to be alone...and you looked...I thought you wouldn't mind."

The woman's embarrassment made Fiona feel bad about having been sarcastic, even gently. "I don't mind," she said. "Have a seat. I'm Fiona Cooper."

"Lucille," the young woman said. "Lucille Paget. Thanks ever so much." She waved over the serving girl and ordered the same meal Fiona had. It was the only thing on offer.

Fiona folded the newspaper and set it aside. "You passing through Ravensholm?"

"I'm on my way to Magrette. I have work there."

Magrette was the capital of Barony Silverfield. "Looks like you'll have fine weather for traveling tomorrow."

"Yes, but I wish I could move on right now!"

"You in a hurry?"

Lucille shook her head. "It's not that. I—" She shook her head. "It's not important. I just don't want to stay in Ravensholm any longer than I have to."

"I see." Fiona didn't see, but it didn't matter. Lucille struck her as one of those highly-strung young women for whom any small setback was a potential catastrophe. Or maybe Lucille had a good reason, and Fiona was just being insensitive. "You don't have to say anything more." She leaned back as the serving girl set a plate of roast pork loin and sautéed chunks of winter squash in front of her.

Lucille nodded, and waved at the barman to bring her a beer. "Do you want something? I'm buying," she said, and Fiona, after a moment's consideration of her plate, nodded and asked for fresh cider. They drank in silence, Lucille's attention darting in every direction. She squeaked and twitched every time the wind made the door rattle. Finally, Fiona's patience gave way.

"You seem worried about something," she said.

"What? Me? No, I'm not—" The door banged in its frame again, and Lucille gasped. "That is—"

"Why don't you just tell me?"

"Oh, I don't want to involve you!"

"Nothing says I have to be involved just because you've told me your problem. Go on. Maybe it'll help."

Lucille drew a deep breath. "I'm being followed," she whispered.

"By who?"

"Two men. They've been following me since I left Sharpesford. I thought I'd escaped them, but I saw them watching me when I went down the street to the shops."

"What do they want?"

"I don't know!" Lucille's voice went shrill, then dropped to a whisper again. "To rob me, I think. I'm carrying my whole savings so I can start over in Magrette." She patted the leg of her trousers, and Fiona heard the muffled clink of coin.

"Haven't you ever heard of banks?"

"My granfa' says not to trust them. Besides, I need some of it to pay my fare."

Fiona stifled a few choice comments about Lucille's granfa'. "Well, so long as you stay where lots of people are, you should be fine."

"I'm afraid because I have an outside room, though. They could get in easily."

"No one's going to break into the Crown Inn. It's in the middle of town."

"But they could!" Lucille was shrill again.

"Then ask for a different room."

"There aren't any free rooms."

Fiona sighed. Lucille was young, and dramatic, and oversensitive, but Fiona couldn't help feeling sorry for her—alone in a strange city, on her way to a new beginning. Or maybe it was envy she felt. "Why don't we switch rooms?" she said. "My room's on the inside and you should feel safer there."

Lucille blinked. "Would you? That would be so kind of you!"

"It's the least I can do," Fiona said drily. "Come, I'll show you where it is, and maybe then you can relax. But I really don't think you have anything to worry about."

Having stowed her bag in Lucille's room, which was a nice big one on the corner with plenty of windows, Fiona sat on the bed and wrote a few lines in her journal. *Not sure if L. is exaggerating, but it hurts no one to be kind. Something it took me far too long to learn.* She put the little book away in her bag, thought about going back to the taproom for more cider, then decided she was ready for the day to be over and a new one to begin.

She put on her nightdress and turned off the lamp, then curled up in the slightly damp bed. This room was warmer and drier than the one she'd given Lucille, but still chilly despite the heating Device she'd turned to full. Time for her nightly routine.

She closed her eyes and pictured a bonfire, blazing hotter than the noon sun at Midsummer, bare ends of logs sticking out all around like a fringe. In her mind's eye, she took hold of a log and pulled it away from the fire, smothering it and tossing it aside. The bonfire burned less brightly. She repeated the trick until the fire was no bigger than a breadbox, then embraced it, pulling it close to her and pinching off the flames until it was extinguished and all that was left was a head-sized lump of char. She pictured it dissolving in rain until nothing was left.

She didn't know if this ritual actually prevented her from igniting a fire in her dreams, or if it just calmed her mind enough not to sleep too deeply, but it had been over a year since she'd woken to the smell of smoke, and she was just superstitious enough not to break with tradition and forego the routine. The few times it had happened during her marriage, she'd had to do some fast talking to convince Roderick it had been the lamp. She dreaded the day she slept so soundly she burned the bed, the room, the house, and would have to explain walking unscathed from the conflagration.

Despite her mental exertion, she wasn't sleepy, but there wasn't anything else to do but go down to the taproom and not drink. She flexed her toes, then her ankles, and proceeded on up the length of her body, encouraging it to relax, and finally her active mind took the hint and drifted off to sleep.

She dreamed of doors lined up along an endless hallway, banging open and shut, until a final loud slam brought her awake. Confused and disoriented, she tried to sit up, but was restrained by hands gripping her arms. "What—" she began, but a hand went over her mouth, pressing her into the mattress.

She bucked and kicked, and her bare foot collided with something bundled in many layers of cloth. Someone grunted, and the grip around her arms tightened. The hand over her mouth was replaced by one holding a thick, wet cloth that stung her lips and smelled sour and bitingly cold. She sucked in another breath to scream, and the acrid stench filled her nostrils, dizzying her. Suddenly her limbs were too heavy to move, and a gray haze fogged her vision. She heard mumbling, tried to understand the words, and then unconsciousness claimed her.

3

She woke to rhythmic movement, a jostling, jouncing motion that nauseated her. She tried to raise her head, but it was too heavy for her to lift. Her cheek bounced off a smooth, hairy surface, warm and slightly yielding, and she inhaled the musky scent of a horse. Feeling began returning to her limbs, and she realized she was face down over the animal's withers, with heavy fabric, a coat or a cloak or something, flung over her upper body. Cold air blew across her legs and bare feet. The thudding of the horse's hooves echoed in her aching skull.

She thrashed, trying to sit up, and someone cuffed her hard across the back of the head. "Be still, or I will give you worse," an unfamiliar male voice said. Fiona lay still. It wasn't as if she could go anywhere.

So. Time to think, if she could manage that through the pain in her head. She remembered being assaulted in her bed, the biting smell of the cloth that had sent her unconscious. Kidnapped, but why?

Lucille. Those two men. Fiona closed her eyes and cursed silently. Apparently Lucille hadn't been exaggerating her danger. And Fiona had merrily put herself in Lucille's place. It would be funny if she weren't uncomfortable and being dragged away heaven knew where.

She let her head bounce against the horse's smooth, warm body. There had been two sets of hands when she was attacked, so at least two kidnappers, which matched what Lucille had said. They'd stop eventually, and discover they had the wrong woman, and then...what? They might just let her go, but they might decide leaving a witness was a bad idea. The ache in her head turned into a throbbing pain. She forced herself to breathe calmly. No sense borrowing trouble. Wait until they stopped, and see what happened next.

The jouncing went on for several minutes, as Fiona's toes grew colder and her stomach ached from being ground into the animal's spine. She couldn't see much beyond the horse's side and, if she turned her head, her kidnapper's thigh, but it was still dark, which told her it couldn't have been many hours since they'd taken her. Just as she had decided to grab hold of the man's leg and drag herself into a more comfortable position, and to hell with the consequences, the horse's gait slowed, and the darkness faded as lamplight bloomed around her. The rider came to a stop and dismounted, then hauled Fiona off the horse and set her on her feet, the cloak still tangled around her shoulders and head.

She wobbled, flung out her arms for balance, and kept from falling over. She fought free of the cloak's folds and dropped it on the hard, cold ground that felt gritty against her bare feet. "I don't know who you are," she said, "but you had better explain yourselves. *Now.*"

The man, who'd been about to speak, blinked at her. He was easily the tallest man she'd ever seen, tall and gaunt, with a face that looked like roughly modeled brown clay, and aside from the blink, he was completely expressionless. "Sir," he said.

"Sweet holy heaven," said his companion, coming around the horse to stand beside the gaunt man. "You're not Lucille."

Fiona transferred her attention to the newcomer. He looked dwarfish beside the gaunt giant, though he wasn't shorter than the average man, and he was handsome, with a square jaw and hazel eyes that looked as if they smiled a lot, from the faint lines at their corners. At the moment, they were wide and incredulous.

"I owe Lucille an apology," Fiona said. "I thought she was exaggerating about being watched."

The two men ignored her. "You said it was her room, Holt," the second man said.

"It was her room. I am nothing if not thorough, sir," the giant Holt said. "I apologize for my failure."

"It was her room before we traded," Fiona said.

The second man groaned. "You traded. Why the hell—excuse me —why would you do something so idiotic?"

"It's hardly idiotic when Lucille was clearly right about being in danger. I'd apologize for inconveniencing you, if I cared anything for your comfort."

"I suppose you also don't care that you've interfered with me retrieving my property, or that you may have indirectly cost someone his life?" The man took a few quick steps that put him almost nose to nose with Fiona; she was tall, but he was taller by a few inches. "You're incredibly brash for someone whose life is in jeopardy."

"You're not going to kill me."

"You don't know that."

"Then prove me wrong." Fiona stepped back and spread her arms wide, offering herself as a target. "You don't need me. I'm an inconvenience." She had to work hard to keep from trembling at the chill in the air. They were in a small barn, lit here and there by lamps, and it was warmer than outdoors, but not by much. Trembling would look like fear, and fear would ruin her gambit.

The man stared her down for a minute, then cursed and turned away. "This is a disaster," he said to Holt, who nodded. Fiona lowered her arms, then quickly bent to pick up the cloak—*her* cloak, she realized—and put it on. The chilly bare earth, packed hard by generations of horses and farmers, hurt her toes, but she refused to show discomfort, instead examining her surroundings.

There were two battered stalls against one wall, neither in use, and the back wall bore tracings of pieces of harness done in chalk by some past owner. Below the tracings, a couple of messy bales of hay were stacked in a way that suggested no one had much cared if they were orderly. A ladder led up to the hayloft, which was in shadow thanks to the lamps, but it looked empty. She couldn't count on anyone from a nearby farmhouse coming to her rescue.

The two men had withdrawn to the hay bales and were speaking quietly to each other. "Excuse me," Fiona said. They ignored her. "*Excuse me*," she repeated. The man Holt had addressed as Sir turned on her.

"Well?" he said irritably. "We're not going to kill you. I hope you're happy about that. Now, if you don't mind, we have plans to make."

"If they include going back to kidnap Lucille, I'll stop you," Fiona said, though she had no idea how she could do that.

"It's nearly dawn," Holt said. His voice was a mellow tenor unsuited to his inhuman face. "Lucille will be gone in an hour. Sooner, if our botched kidnapping is made public early."

"We don't have time to chase her down. We'll have to start over," Sir said.

"We don't have time to start over, sir."

"Do you have time to return me to the inn? I'm feeling a bit cold," Fiona said sarcastically.

"As if we'd do that, and have you turn us in as kidnappers," Sir said. "And we brought all your things. I *thought* we'd be traveling west today." He went to his horse and hauled Fiona's bag off it, tossed it in her direction, and said, "You can change into something warmer in one of those stalls."

Fiona snatched up her bag and strode to the stalls, which were splintered and rough and had gaps between the boards, but were shelter enough to satisfy her modesty. Though she didn't think either of her kidnappers was the type to peek. They didn't seem like hardened criminals at all.

Her boots were at the top of her bag, her journal was where she'd left it—they had been thorough in gathering her things. She dressed rapidly in trousers and a heavy shirt, tidied her nightdress away, then pushed open the door of the stall. She'd half-expected the men to be gone, but they were still talking at the back of the barn and gave her only the barest of glances when she emerged.

"I'm leaving," she said. "How much of a walk do I have ahead of me?"

"Wait," Sir said, and came toward her. "We'll take you back."

"Aren't you afraid I'll turn you in?"

"Weren't you afraid we'd kill you?" He smiled, a sardonic grin that dispelled the shadows from his eyes. "We'll leave you at the outskirts of town and let you make your way wherever you want to go. We're not criminals."

"Really? I thought kidnapping was a criminal offense. My mistake."

"Lucille Paget is the criminal. She stole a large sum of money from me and ran off."

"So have her arrested. The Crown looks dimly on vigilante justice." So long as it didn't involve potential Ascendants.

The smile went even more amused. "I have my reasons for not wanting to involve local law enforcement." He gestured at his horse. "If you're ready, we can leave now, and maybe I'll be able to salvage something of this day."

Fiona looked in Holt's direction. The giant was as expressionless as ever, but his stance was tense, and she was sure he wanted to remonstrate with his...master? But he said nothing, just came forward and mounted his horse. Sir did the same, then held out his hand to help Fiona. She'd ridden before. Once. She'd be lucky to remember how to stay facing forward. She let the man pull her up behind him, then wrapped her cloak more closely around herself as they headed back out into the night.

It wasn't true night anymore. The horizon to the right was limned with pale blue that grew brighter and warmer as they rode north across the endless plains—no, not endless, there was the sparkling hunch of Ravensholm, and beyond it the silver ribbon that was the Snow River. The indigo sky, star-filled except in the sun-faded east, promised another beautifully clear winter day. The horse's hooves crunched over the crust of frost, and that and the sound of five creatures breathing was all that interrupted the peaceful early morning.

"So Lucille stole from you," Fiona said, when the silence had gone on long enough to be tedious rather than pleasant. "And for some reason you couldn't just call for her to be brought up on a charge."

"All true."

"There has to be more to it than that."

"There is. But it's none of your business, Mistress Nosy."

"My name is Fiona Cooper. *Miss* Cooper."

"It's still none of your business."

"You kidnapped me. I think some of it is my business."

The man's hands on the reins drew in a little tighter. "I hired Lucille to perform certain services. She agreed, but then changed her mind and fled—taking my money with her."

"Distasteful services, no doubt."

The man chuckled. "If that's what you want to believe, Miss Cooper, go ahead."

"They must be at least a little immoral, if they won't allow you to go to the law."

"I just don't have time to involve them. There's a deadline. Which, thanks to Lucille, I'm now going to miss."

Fiona let out an exasperated breath. "Could you possibly be more cryptic? What is so secret that you can't just say it? You won't even tell me your name!"

"You didn't actually ask, Miss Cooper."

"Common courtesy says, if I give you my name, you should return the favor."

"Very well. You can call me Sebastian."

"What, no last name?"

"You don't need to know my family name. And the reason I'm being so cryptic is it's not entirely my secret to tell."

"Then tell me what you can."

It was Sebastian's turn to make an exasperated noise. "Fine, Miss Cooper," he said, "but only because I feel some small measure of guilt at having dragged you into this. I'm trying to prevent someone from suffering at the hands of a blackmailer."

"I see," Fiona said. "And going to the city guards or the Crown would only make the blackmailer carry out her threat. So how did Lucille fit into this?"

Sebastian was silent for a long moment. Just as Fiona was about to prod him for more information, he said, "The blackmailer's evidence is being held in the Jaixante. Do you know what that is?"

"Of course." Belatedly Fiona realized it wouldn't be "of course" for ninety percent of Tremontane's population. The Jaixante was the royal city of Veribold, a city within the capital city of Haizea, and no foreigners were allowed in. Even Fiona, in her travels with Roderick, had never been farther than its outer courts. "That is, I've heard it's very isolated."

"It is, except for seven days a year, when the Irantzen Festival is held, celebrating Haran's discovery of ungoverned heaven. Since Haran was at first acknowledged only by women, the festival is for women only—women and their attendants. So I hired Lucille to be my disguise, so to speak. Only I think I paid her too much, and she decided to leg it."

"How much?"

"Four thousand guilders."

"*Four thousand*—"

"I'd appreciate it if you didn't remind me how stupid that was. I should at least have paid her only half up front."

Fiona bit back a handful of other comments and came out with, "Can't you hire someone else?"

"The festival begins in four days. It will take nearly all of that time to reach Haizea. I'll just have to come up with another plan."

Fiona went silent. She wondered if Sebastian was thinking of an alternate plan right then. He still wasn't telling her everything, starting with who needed saving from the blackmailer. If the information were in the Jaixante, the blackmailer had to be someone high in the Veriboldan government, but would such a person care about blackmailing a Tremontanan? On the other hand, would Sebastian care about saving a Veriboldan? And Holt kept calling him "sir," which suggested Sebastian was wealthy enough to afford servants, as did that outrageous sum he'd given Lucille...there were just too many unknowns, and Fiona had never been good at ignoring puzzles when they came her way.

"What was Lucille supposed to do? Just attend the festival?" she said.

"Attend, and keep the Veriboldans' attention on her so they wouldn't notice Holt and me sneaking about," Sebastian said.

"Would they really let a Tremontanan woman in?"

"Haran's revelations proved we all go to the same heaven, and this festival is supposed to be a celebration of our similarities. I've heard. I only know a little about it."

"That's a terrible risk to take. Suppose you're wrong?"

"This is—was—the best chance I had. It was worth the risk."

"You could bribe a Veriboldan servant to find the information for you."

"That has its own set of problems, namely that Veriboldans don't always feel obligated to honor their agreements with non-Veriboldans. But it's my backup plan. Followed by assassinating the blackmailer, which I *really* don't want to do, aside from my qualms about taking a life. From what I know of the woman, she'll have safeguards to ensure the information comes out if she dies in a suspicious manner." Sebastian laughed, a short, mirthless bark. "Trust me, I've considered all the possibilities."

I bet he hasn't considered this one. "I'll do it," she said.

"Do what?"

"Get you into the Irantzen Festival."

Sebastian hauled on the reins so hard Fiona nearly lost her seat. "*What?*"

"You need a woman to attend the festival. I'll do it."

Holt drew up nearby. "Is something wrong, sir?"

"Aside from our mistake being completely out of her mind? Miss Cooper, you don't even know us! Why should you want to throw your fate in with ours?"

Fiona considered this. She had a plan already; she was going to Dineh-Karit. But after Sebastian's admittedly sketchy explanation, the idea of the mysterious southern continent didn't seem so appealing. *They're strangers, he hasn't told you everything, it's not your problem*, her inner voice whispered. "Because I think you can afford to pay another four thousand guilders, and I could use the money," she said.

It wasn't true. The truth was, this was a real adventure. Sneaking about the Jaixante looking for incriminating evidence, fooling the Veriboldans—a mere sea voyage to a distant, foreign country was trivial by comparison. "You don't have to pay me until I've gotten you inside," she added, "in case you're worried about being cheated again."

"This is a bad idea, sir," Holt said.

"It's a terrible idea," Sebastian said. "*I* don't know *you*. You could be a servant of G—of the blackmailer, sent to lead us astray, or put us in a compromising position."

"You can't seriously believe that."

"Miss Cooper, you have no idea what I've been through in the last two weeks. That possibility isn't even the least likely one I've considered."

"I don't even know who the blackmailer is or who's being blackmailed."

Holt said, "Lucille likely chose her because they are similar in appearance, sir. You know she would have anticipated being... retrieved. Miss Cooper is unlikely to be an associate of the blackmailer."

"Don't argue on her behalf, Holt. She hardly needs it." Sebastian closed his eyes and cursed. "Miss Cooper," he said, "I'm tired and hungry and desperate, or I'd argue with you further. As it is...I accept your proposal. Four thousand guilders, to be paid when Holt and I have access to the Jaixante."

"Do you really have that much money on you?"

Sebastian groaned. "It has just occurred to me," he said, "that you might be part of a ruthless gang of robbers, looking for a rich mark.

Holt, let's ride on. If we're about to be murdered for the contents of my money belt, I want to see if we can have a good breakfast first."

He heeled his horse around and set off westward. After a moment, Holt came up level with them. Fiona held on and watched the Snow River approach. She felt no regret about her hasty decision. *Choose, and bear the consequences, but never look back.* She'd learned that when her marriage was failing; you made the best decisions you could, and you lived with what happened. But she did feel a little light-headed, as if she were being swept along by the cold current she could see ahead of them. *Four thousand guilders is a lot of money,* she thought, *and who says you can't go south afterward?* But she had a feeling that whatever came of this adventure, a southern voyage still wouldn't seem exciting.

4

―――――――――

The sun rose as they reached the Snow River. At this time of year, its name was entirely appropriate; it ran sluggishly, and Fiona half expected to see chunks of ice bobbing along in its current. Clunky, foreshortened boats were pulled up along the shore, and as she and her companions approached one of them cast off its moorings and headed out into midstream. The Device that propelled it made a loud thumping sound, like a bass drum, and it echoed into the still winter morning like the heartbeat of a lost god.

Little sheds clustered at the river's edge, well-lit and smelling of hot bread and meat and coffee. The morning breeze wafted the tantalizing smells to Fiona's nose, and her stomach rumbled in response. Sebastian chuckled. "Food first, then the ferry," he said, "then we'll buy you a horse when we're across the river. No sense buying one on this side and paying for the extra passenger. I hope you can ride."

So do I, Fiona thought.

They dismounted near one of the sheds—they looked like dollhouses, with their fronts cut away. Fiona could see inside to the ovens and stovetops throwing off welcome heat that made their owners sweat in the chill morning air. Sebastian paid for hot rolls and coffee for the three of them, and Fiona stood next to his horse and ate and watched the distant city. Ravensholm, straddling the river a mile or so to the north, was just beginning to wake. Lights sparkling across it started to flicker and dim, and Fiona imagined she could hear it stretch and yawn, a giant bear turning over in its hibernation.

She wiped her mouth and handed back the empty coffee mug, chipped enameled tin that the coffee shed's owner tossed into a stack for washing, then followed Sebastian and Holt toward the river. The river, unlike the city, was fully alert, and more ships left their moorings as they approached the ferry, or one of the ferries. It was a broad, flat platform with a rail about three feet tall on both of its long sides. On its short sides, one of which pointed into the river, the other of which was nestled against the bank, were boxy glass and silver Devices. Fiona walked over to look at the nearer one. Gears and coils of metal were visible through the glass, and a greenish glow hovered over the entire Device.

"Miss Cooper," Sebastian called, "won't you join us?" He was standing a few feet away, next to a grizzled woman wearing a peaked cap and a heavy felted wool coat. "Mistress Clarence says we'll cast off in half an hour."

"And don't go messin' about the Devices," Mistress Clarence growled.

Fiona smiled politely and concealed her irritation. As if she'd hurt the things, anyway.

She followed Sebastian, who was leading his horse toward a spot marked off on the deck, then made way for Holt, who came up behind. The horses seemed not at all bothered by the motion of the wavelets slopping the sides of the ferry. Just to satisfy herself, Fiona went forward to look at the other Device. It was identical to the first, but glowed purple instead of green. She walked away before Mistress Clarence could make an issue of her "disobedience."

A few other horses came aboard, then a small family, well bundled against the cold. Fiona caught the eye of one of the three children, who was five or six years old, towheaded with a round, plump face. She smiled and winked, and the child turned away quickly the way children that age usually did with strangers. Good.

He wasn't too young to learn friendliness was no guarantee of trust-worthiness.

The ferry jolted, and the almost imperceptible hum of the Devices turned into an air-shattering roar that faded slightly, but was still uncomfortable. A noise-dampening canopy had been drawn across the place on the deck where the horses stood. *Good for Mistress Clarence*, Fiona thought. She winked at the small child again and grinned when he ducked away. A jolt, and the ferry swung free of the shore and made its way into the river with a barely perceptible movement.

Sebastian came forward to join her, but said nothing, merely leaned against the rail and bowed his head, apparently watching the river. Fiona settled in beside him and did the same. The roar of the nearby Device made conversation difficult, anyway.

Minutes passed, and she fell into a reverie in which her mind floated free of her body, bobbing along with the ferry like the rushing current that crossed its bow. Or was it really the bow, since when it came back across the river, it would become the stern?

Idly, she tapped the toe of her boot against the rail post. She was marginally aware of the other passengers, particularly the three children chasing each other around the deck and shrieking. Mistress Clarence shouted something that sounded like a command to get down off the gate, which had been latched across the stern to keep anyone from accidentally going overboard. The children seemed as unimpressed by Mistress Clarence's authority as Fiona had been. There she was again, shouting at the children to stop doing whatever it was. Where were those children's parents?

"It's children like those that make me grateful I don't have any," Sebastian said, pitching his voice to carry over the sound of the Device. "Though their parents don't seem to be trying very hard to control them, so I'm not sure where the fault lies."

"I was thinking much the same," Fiona said, matching his tone. "Though they're quiet now." The children had disappeared. It was probably too much to hope they'd gone overboard—no, that was uncharitable, since much of their bad behavior should be laid at their parents' door. She and Roderick had never had children. First, they'd been on the road, not a practical life to raise a family in, and then, when they'd settled in Kingsport, their marriage had been strained, with neither of them interested in adding the burden of children to it. Now Fiona wondered, as she occasionally did when she saw someone else's children, what her life would have been like if she had a couple of children to care for.

"Quiet might be dangerous," Sebastian said, casting his gaze over the ferry. "I just don't understand families like that. Letting their children turn out to be little monsters. My brother—" His lips snapped shut over more words.

"What about your brother?" Fiona asked, curious. Sebastian went back to looking at the water. "It's him, isn't it?" she said, inspired. "He's the one being blackmailed."

"My youngest brother, yes," Sebastian said reluctantly. "I shouldn't have mentioned it."

"It's not as if I know who your family is, Sebastian."

"No, but the less information I give you, the less likely you or anyone else is to figure it out."

Fiona wanted to prod for more, but Sebastian's face was grim and she concluded it would be a waste of time. "You sound as if you don't like him much."

"I don't. I know, he's my brother, I'm supposed to love him, but he makes it impossible. He's selfish and arrogant and if it wouldn't destroy my family, I'd leave him to hang."

"Not literally hang?" Something tickled her nose, and she sneezed.

"No, figuratively." A corner of Sebastian's mouth quirked up. "He's not a criminal, just stupid, and his reputation affects the rest of my family. Unfortunately."

"I'm sorry." She thought of her aunt and uncle and cousins, who weren't perfect, but were generous and kind. "It must be difficult to do all this on behalf of someone who it sounds like doesn't deserve it."

"It is, but—"

The biting tickle grew worse. Fiona realized she smelled smoke an instant before the high, terrified whinny of a frightened horse cut the crisp morning air. Sebastian's head whipped around, then he ran for the makeshift corral, Fiona hard on his heels. More screams joined the first, these human, some of them the high-pitched shrieks of children.

Straw covered the deck where the horses stood, and fire licked at it, making the horses lunge away and press against each other in their desperation to reach safety. One of the children cowered in the midst of them, jostled by their frantic movements. Sebastian swore and dove for the little boy. Fiona went for the fire.

It was small, thank heaven, but the light breeze fed it, and soon it would be out of control. Fiona whipped her cloak off and smothered the little fire, snatching the cloak away before it could burn. She stomped on what was left, wishing she were in a position to simply disassemble it with her hands, to cast the burning straw over the side of the ferry. The smell of scorched fabric joined the smell of smoke. Fiona scowled. If her cloak was ruined...

Sebastian had dragged the little boy away from the horses, leaving Mistress Clarence and her assistants free to care for the maddened animals. He set the boy on his feet and stepped back, allowing the child's distraught, shrieking mother to sweep him up in her arms. The boy screamed in pain, clutching his arm. "Holt," Sebastian said, "would you mind taking a look?"

Holt detached the child from his mother, making the boy scream more loudly. "Don't you touch my son!" the father shouted, grabbing Holt by the shoulder and pulling. He might as well have tried to lift the ferry. Holt ignored him.

"Holt has medical knowledge," Sebastian said to the father, prying the man's fingers off Holt's shoulder. "Let him work."

"Get your hands off me!"

Sebastian grabbed the man's wrist and twisted, spinning him around and taking his arm in a complicated-looking lock. "*Let him work*," he said.

"His arm is broken," Holt said. "It is not a bad break. I believe I can splint it, if someone will find me a length of board and some strips of cloth or short ropes."

The passengers, crowding around, made no move to help. Exasperated, Fiona went aft, searching for something Holt might use. The ferry was made of wood, and surely there were scraps of it lying around. She found, strapped to the rear of the ferry near the Device, a couple of oars that looked too large for a person to handle. She glanced around. No one was watching her; their attention was either on Holt, Sebastian, or the horses. With her back turned and her hands shielded by her cloak, she traced a fiery line around the oar where the blade met the handle, let it burn briefly, then smothered it with her hands. Setting the oar on the deck, she put her foot on it where she'd burned nearly through the wood and pulled up on the blade, snapping it off the handle neatly.

She was still unobserved. She traced another line of fire, this one lengthwise down the blade, then with considerable effort broke the blade in half. Kicking the oar handle overboard, she ran back to where Holt waited and offered him the pieces of wood. "Perfect, thank you, Miss Cooper," Holt said. One of Mistress Clarence's assistants handed him a coil of skinny rope and a knife. Silently and efficiently, Holt bound the boy's arm, keeping him pinioned as easily as if the boy were a half-drowned kitten, then released him to his sobbing mother.

Sebastian let the father go. The man took a few steps away, out of Sebastian's reach. "How dare you?" he shouted.

"I should ask you that question," Sebastian said coldly. "Your children were running around this boat like wild things, and you did nothing to stop them. Normally, I wouldn't care. But their behavior, and yours, put them in danger. As you realize."

The man recoiled. "How dare you criticize my children? Or me?"

"I dare because without me, you'd be mourning your son right now." Sebastian grabbed the man's hand again and slapped a matchlighter into it. "I ought to keep that, since I doubt you're any more careful with it than your children were."

"You—"

"The only thing I'm interested in hearing from you is an apology to Mistress Clarence," Sebastian said.

The father took a step closer. Sebastian shifted his weight, preparing to take a blow—or to throw one. He was taller than the other man by nearly a head, and Fiona noticed for the first time how he stood like someone who knew how to fight and wasn't afraid to do so. The father seemed to realize this as well. "Sorry," he said.

"Not to me." Sebastian stepped to one side.

The man swallowed. "I'm sorry, Mistress Clarence."

The captain glared at the man. "Take your family aft, and stay there," she growled. The man did as he was told. Fiona stepped out of his way as he passed her, not looking at her.

The crowd of passengers hadn't dispersed, though now they all stood awkwardly, like they didn't know where to go or where to look. They parted for Sebastian as he walked away toward the bow, followed by Holt. Fiona went after them. "Would you have fought that man?" she demanded.

Sebastian smiled crookedly at her. "Is that what you want to ask, Miss Nosy?"

"Would you?"

"If I had to. I hate making anyone look ridiculous in front of his children, but if he'd hit me, I wouldn't have let him do it twice. And I certainly couldn't let Holt do it."

"That's an odd way to put it. Why 'certainly'?"

Holt and Sebastian exchanged glances. "That truly is none of your business, and I'm sorry I mentioned it," Sebastian said. "Holt, would you gather our bags? I want off this ferry the moment its nose kisses earth."

"Of course, sir," Holt said, turning away.

Fiona waited until he was gone before saying, "You sound as if you're protecting him."

"What part of 'not your business' did you fail to understand?"

"I'm sorry." She was taken aback by the snarl in his voice, and clenched her fists against a memory of Roderick lashing out at her in just that way.

31

Sebastian blew out his breath. "No, I'm sorry, Miss Cooper," he said. "I'm on edge still from that encounter, and I spoke out of turn. It's Holt's privacy I'm protecting, not mine, and he would prefer not to talk about it. If you don't mind."

"I understand." She didn't, not fully, but she could appreciate a desire for privacy. *Roderick never apologized,* she thought irrelevantly.

"Where did the wood come from?"

"What?"

"The wood you gave Holt. There's not a spare scrap of wood on this boat, I looked. Where did you get it?"

Fear choked her briefly. "There was a broken oar near the back. I smashed it a little more to get pieces the right size."

"I see. You must be stronger than you look." Sebastian didn't look as if he believed her, but how under heaven could he possibly guess the truth? "That man should be grateful to you and Holt for helping his son. How does it feel to do a thankless task?"

"I'm used to doing things without being thanked." Roderick had been a master of turning achievement into inadequacy. Toward the end, he'd done almost nothing but heap recriminations upon her. In fairness, she hadn't been very generous with him, either.

"Well, you have *my* gratitude, for what it's worth. Though I doubt I'll be thanked for accomplishing this task myself."

"You mean the Irantzen Festival? Won't your brother be grateful?"

"I did mention he's self-centered and arrogant. He'll likely take it as a given that he deserves to be rescued. I just wish he'd learn from it."

"Maybe he doesn't deserve to be saved."

Sebastian shrugged. "Maybe. But he'll take innocents down with him, and it's for their sake I'm doing this."

"Then it's unfortunate you can't save them, and let him suffer."

"Unfortunate indeed." Sebastian pushed away from the rail. "We're about to land. Let's get the horses."

Moments later, the ferry bumped up against the shore. Fiona waited for Holt and Sebastian to free their horses from the makeshift corral. The little family trudged past her, their lack of eye contact clearly deliberate, though the little boy looked at her as they passed. She smiled, but her heart wasn't in it. If Sebastian hadn't been there... of course, if Sebastian hadn't been there, neither would she, and the whole drama would have played out to a completely different crowd.

They were the last ones off the ferry, and Fiona nodded cheerfully at Mistress Clarence, who scowled in return. Well, you couldn't be friends with everyone.

They rode a few miles westward until they came to a small town where they were able to buy a horse for Fiona. It was a pretty little piebald mare, black and white like a cat Fiona's friend Jessie had once owned. The cat, Mittens, had been disdainful of everyone, including Jessie, but the horse seemed pleasant enough, and Fiona mounted her with only a few reservations and a little help.

She curled her cold fingers around the reins and shrugged the folds of her cloak forward to cover her hands. The bright sun had no warmth in it, for all it melted what was left of the last snow. West of Ravensholm, County Harroden was all plains that turned into the desert hills of eastern Veribold, but that was miles in the distance. At the moment the land stretched out blank and empty to the horizon in all directions, with Ravensholm a faint bump to the east and the Snow River a fading glitter behind them. Fiona had last been there... five years ago, on that last trading journey with Roderick before they'd given up traveling and settled in Kingsport. Not such a long time, but she couldn't remember the landscape at all, whether it looked the same or not.

They traveled in silence all day, stopping briefly at a wayside inn at dinnertime to rest the horses and eat an unsatisfactory meal of dry meat and drier vegetables. Holt disappeared when they stopped, returning only when the horses were being saddled, but Sebastian didn't say anything about it and Fiona felt uncomfortable asking.

She spent the rest of the afternoon cursing herself for her whimsical decision. She was traveling to a foreign country with two strange men, and granted, she didn't think they intended her harm, but that didn't make her decision any less crazy. She didn't even know what she'd have to do at this festival. Suppose they got caught in their search; she would almost certainly be punished along with them. This was the stupidest thing she'd ever done.

Tilled and harvested fields, their stubble gray where the snow overlaid it, gave way to fallow ground that no one had ever cultivated. Tall weeds, dusty green and shadowed yellow, waved at Fiona and her companions as the wind moved them. The road was all hard-packed earth, dark brown and patchy where snow melt had stirred it up somewhat. To the north, storm clouds massed, purple and heavy with rain or snow. Rain, Fiona guessed, because the air was cold, but not freezing, and the storm was moving slowly enough it probably wouldn't reach them before nightfall.

Sebastian was a little less optimistic, because he urged his horse into a faster gait, and Fiona had to follow suit. Mittens—it wasn't a horse name, true, but the animal really did remind her of Jessie's cat —responded cheerfully to Fiona's inexpert prodding. Riding was growing easier, fortunately.

Behind her, Holt sped up as well. His horse was as tall as he was, but stocky, almost big enough to be a Kirkellan mount. Suppose you could match horses with riders like that? Sebastian was riding a bay gelding, but it was too short for him; he needed something leggy, something stubborn and secretive. And Fiona...her imagination came up short. How much of what she was was pretense, camouflage? Maybe Mittens was ideal for her, after all.

5

The storm was much closer when they rode into Demingham at nearly sunset. "We'll stay the night here," Sebastian told them, beckoning them close. "The border is only another ten miles away, but I'd rather come at it fresh in the morning."

"Very well, sir," Holt said. "If you will follow me, I will choose an inn that will meet your needs."

"Why does *he* get to pick?" Fiona said. It was whiny, but Holt's servility irritated her.

"Because Holt is trained to be security-minded," Sebastian said, "and it gives him pleasure to use his skills. And because I told him to. Unless you want the burden?"

"No," Fiona said, feeling more irritated at the back-handed chastisement. Her legs and back ached, she might have blisters where she didn't want blisters—this was definitely the stupidest idea she'd ever had. "I—" she began, but Sebastian had already moved off down the street after Holt, and Fiona prodded Mittens to follow.

The inn Holt found was the Silver Apple, a quiet three-story building down one of Demingham's side streets. Fiona gratefully relinquished Mittens' reins to the stable girl and, carrying her bag, went in the back door to find Sebastian and Holt had vanished. A round-cheeked woman in a cheerful floral dress greeted her with a smile and showed her the way up the stairs to a room that, for a miracle, she wouldn't have to share with anyone else. It was small, but comfortable, with a window that looked out over the quiet stable yard. Fiona could barely see Mittens' nose sticking out of her stall. It had a clothes press, and a bedside table with an elaborate lamp Device, and a wash stand with running hot and cold water. Apparently Sebastian's needs as anticipated by Holt involved a level of luxury Fiona had rarely experienced.

She sat on the bed, which had a brass frame and a patchwork quilt, and kicked her bag, which lay on the floor beside her. Briefly, she wondered if she'd made a mistake. It wasn't too late to tell Sebastian she'd changed her mind, was it? *No. I made him a promise and I intend to keep it.* She shoved her bag farther under the bed and left the room, locking the door behind her.

The dining room was rustic, with rough-hewn tables and chairs and a chandelier made from a wagon wheel. Yellow and orange flames in the large fireplace flickered wildly in the draft Fiona made when she entered. Sebastian was already seated near the middle of the room, and he looked up when she entered.

"Miss Cooper," he said, rising to hold her chair for her. "I hope your room is comfortable."

"It's nice," Fiona said. "Where's Holt?"

"Holt's eating elsewhere."

"You object to having him share a table with you?"

Sebastian gave her his wry smile. "Holt objects to eating with me," he said. "I've tried to insist that he's not my manservant anymore, that eating separately is ridiculous, but every time we're within spitting distance of civilization, he's back to eating in the kitchen. I've known the man twenty years, and he hasn't gotten any less stubborn the whole time."

"Your manservant?"

"I thought you weren't going to pry into my affairs, Miss Nosy."

"*You're* the one who brought it up. I hardly think that's prying."

Sebastian sighed. "My family hired Holt to look after me when I went away to school. It's not uncommon to bring a maid or a manservant if you're wealthy, which I'm sure you've worked out my family is. I like to think we're friends, when I can get Holt to break through that stiff-upper-lip thing he has. He's more correct than half my well-bred peers."

"You could always fire him, and make your relationship equal."

"I tried, when I left school, but it's my parents who hired him, so there's not much I can do about it." He leaned back as a serving girl set plates of food in front of them, pieces of oven-roasted chicken and boiled carrots seasoned with flecks of something green. Fiona didn't recognize the herb, but she wasn't much of a cook. Two mugs of beer came next. Sebastian picked up a drumstick and took a large bite, ignoring the grease that dripped down his fingers.

"So tell me," he said between bites, "why are you in a position to drop everything and travel with two strangers to Veribold's most closely guarded city within a city?"

"I don't think that's any of your business."

"Come now, Miss Nosy, I answered your questions. I think this is only fair."

Fiona shrugged and cut a carrot into bite-sized pieces. The green flecks gave it a fresh flavor, unexpected at this time of year. "I'd...quit my business and was looking for something different."

"What was your business?"

"My husband and I were traders."

"I didn't realize you were married."

"Emphasis on 'were.'" Fiona found it suddenly difficult to meet his eyes. "We divorced about three months ago."

"Oh. I...don't know whether to offer you condolences or congratulations."

"It was for the best, for both of us." He didn't sound judgmental, but you could never tell how people would react to the news that your marriage bond was dissolved.

"I see." Sebastian laid down the bare bone and went to work on another chicken leg. For a wealthy, presumably upper-class man, he had some appalling table manners. "And you had to leave the business? That seems unfair."

"I could have stayed, but I didn't want to." It had felt odd continuing to work with Roderick with the ashes of their marriage between them, like putting on filthy old clothes after a hot bath. "I adopted back into my birth family, stayed with my aunt and uncle for a while, then decided to travel."

Sebastian nodded. "And have you decided what you want to settle down to? Or is that too much prying?"

"No, I...haven't thought about it. Mostly I felt like traveling for a while. I was going to the southern continent before you sidetracked me."

"A polite way of putting it," Sebastian said with a grin. "Dineh-Karit's not known for being friendly to outsiders."

"You could say that of just about anywhere, except maybe Eskandel. There are always exceptions."

"True." Sebastian wiped his hands on his napkin—good, she'd half expected him to use his trouser leg—and took a long drink of his beer. "Is it not to your taste?" he asked, indicating her mug.

"No. I don't drink."

"You should have said something." He waved at the serving girl and asked her to replace the beer with something non-alcoholic. The girl gave him a funny look, probably wondering why anyone would come to a taproom if not to drink, but did as she was instructed. "Any particular reason?" Sebastian went on.

"Don't like the taste of alcohol," Fiona lied. "And you don't need to go to any trouble on my account."

"It's no trouble." Sebastian drained his mug and set it down, giving her a long, appraising look. "I'm having the hardest time not asking you more questions."

"Why? I'm not very interesting."

"Any woman willing to do what you've done is endlessly interesting. You do realize what I plan to do is dangerous, don't you? If the Veriboldans find out we've entered their royal city intent on theft, they won't be gentle with us."

"They won't be gentle with *you*, you mean. I will look like just one more woman attending the festival."

"You'd throw us to the wolves like that, Miss Cooper?"

She matched him smile for cynical smile. "I might beg for leniency on your behalf." He was right, they'd all be judged guilty if they were caught, and no one would let her off just because she was a woman. "I suppose we'll have to make sure we're not caught, then."

Sebastian nodded once, slowly. "I'm glad you're not Lucille," he said. "She wasn't nearly so interesting as you are." He pushed his chair back. "We'll need to make an early start, so I'm off to bed."

They walked up the stairs together as far as Fiona's room, where Sebastian bade her good night. Inside, Fiona undressed and folded her clothes away into her bag, preparing for that early start. She sat cross-legged on her bed in her nightgown and wrote in her journal. *S. intrigues me*, she wrote. *He's hiding everything about his identity—I'm not even sure Sebastian is his real name—but, surprisingly, it doesn't worry me. Probably because I'm not telling him everything either.*

It surprised her further to discover she wanted to tell him more. He had an air of quiet competence about him that inspired confidence. Not that she would tell him the truth about her inherent magic. That would be suicide. But he *listened* when she spoke, really listened in a way that said he cared about what she was saying. Roderick had always listened with half his mind engaged in what he was planning to say next. Sebastian's attention was...refreshing. *And he's handsome*, her irrelevant inner voice said, making her scowl. Handsome was well enough, but Roderick was handsome and she'd learned her lesson about being swayed by an attractive face and roguish eyes.

She put her journal away and turned out the light, but sleep eluded her despite her nightly routine. Finally she sat up in bed and amused herself by igniting tiny fires no bigger around than a ten-guilder piece on her palms, then closing her hands over them to extinguish them.

When she was young, when her magic had only just manifested, she'd tried to pretend she didn't have it. She'd resisted the urge to ignite fires, or touch existing ones, believing that might make it go away. But the urge to make fire only grew stronger, until the first night she'd ignited one in her sleep. No one had been hurt, though she'd been in a lot of trouble for "playing with matches" in her bed, but she'd realized that ignoring her magic gave her less control, not more. Now she indulged it as often as she dared, and spent her nights praying her efforts gave her the control she needed.

She played with the fire for nearly an hour while her body relaxed, then curled up under the blankets and listened to the wind rattling the window until she finally fell asleep.

THE STORM ARRIVED EARLY THE NEXT MORNING, WAKING FIONA BRIEFLY with the lashings of rain on her window. When the sky outside finally lightened and she left her room, the rain had faded to a persistent drizzle that seeped through the seams of her cloak and left her damp and uncomfortable. She huddled next to Mittens in the stable yard, under the scant shelter of the eaves, breathing in the smell of fresh hot bread from the nearby kitchen and wishing she'd eaten more heartily. Sebastian, checking his horse's tack, raised an eyebrow at her.

"You look sour this morning," he said. "I hope it's not the company."

"Just the weather."

"We'll be out of it soon."

"You're far too optimistic."

Holt, wearing a waterproof rain cape, came splashing toward them across the yard with a bundle in his arms. He handed Fiona a cape matching his and extended the other to Sebastian. "The rain is getting worse, sir," he said.

"Then we'd better get moving," Sebastian said, ignoring the irritated look Fiona sent his way.

The rain did worsen, but not by much, and the new cape kept Fiona mostly dry. Mittens tossed her head, shaking rain away from her face, and Fiona touched her wet, coarse mane and wished she could promise the animal a dry, warm bed soon.

It was hard not to look out over the rain-washed plains and wish for a dry, warm bed for herself. Dark clouds massed overhead, grayer to the east behind them, and ahead, to the west, they filled the sky until they seemed to touch the horizon, which was banded with purple and green. Fiona didn't know where the border was, but that horizon was certainly Veribold. She adjusted her cape and stroked Mittens' mane again, soaking her hand. Haizea was another two days' journey from the border. They would need to hurry if they meant to make it to the festival.

"Miss Cooper," Sebastian said, slowing to ride beside her, "when we reach customs, I'll do the talking if they'll let me. If they insist on talking with you directly, you're my sister Sharon and you're on your way to the Irantzen Festival. It's better not to complicate a lie."

You have no idea how well I know that. "There's no need. I have my own papers."

"That's right. You were planning to travel. Let me hold them, then. It took some doing, these last two weeks, but with Holt's help I've gathered every piece of paperwork the Veriboldans demand foreigners submit. Fortunately for us, everything for the Irantzen Festival isn't made out in an attendee's name until the border crossing."

"The Veriboldans can be fickle. You're sure you have everything?"

"Very sure. The international travelers' office in Ravensholm is thorough. And faster than the embassy in Aurilien."

Fiona, remembering her dealings with Veriboldan government officials on her previous journeys, said nothing. If Sebastian was wrong, they'd find out soon enough.

---

6

*A*round mid-morning, the rain let up, leaving behind not the fresh scent of wet grass, but a cooler, darker smell of old earth and mud. Fiona shook the rain off her cape and pushed her hood back. In the distance, she could see buildings, some dark, some pale. The twin cities of Westholm and Mai-nien, facing each other across the Veriboldan border like a couple of wrestlers waiting for the other to flinch.

Westholm looked dark and sullen, its buildings made mostly of local brick, dark brown and flaking. Fiona was grateful for the rain that swept away the stink of its gutters. It was an old city, with poor sewer systems, and although a few newfangled sanitation Devices roamed the streets, they weren't enough for the task of keeping Westholm clean.

A few passersby glanced at the riders incuriously, just three more strangers passing through. Fiona judged that about a quarter of the people she saw were travelers, based on their dress and the way their horses and wagons were laden. That seemed like a lot, given the weather, and she wished Sebastian would move faster so they could outrun all of them to the customs office and be on their way.

After half an hour, they left Westholm, which came to an abrupt stop as if someone had drawn a furrow in the brown earth and all Westholm's little brown buildings had been forced to stop and line up along it. Just past this invisible line was the Tremontanan customs office. It was squat and square, with a pyramidal roof of brown shingles, and lights burned behind its windows. It looked warm, for all it was ugly, and Fiona wished for a moment they were going there.

Beyond the customs office was a strip of bare land no more than twenty-five feet wide, marking another invisible line. The border. It always struck Fiona as slightly ludicrous that two countries could decide on a place where one ended and the other began, and then cling to that illusion to the point of going to war over a violation of the invisible line. There ought to be something more tangible to indicate something so important.

She remembered, years ago, crossing the Veriboldan border for the first time with Roderick. That had been a clear, sunny day, but she'd been nervous, having heard so many rumors about the complex Veriboldan bureaucracy and its draconian punishments for foreigners caught breaking its laws. Roderick had laughed at her nervousness and told her there was nothing to fear, teasing her that she was unlikely to meet anyone who might want her imprisoned.

"Veriboldans are more interested in their own politics than the doings of other lands," he'd said.

"I heard they choose their King or Queen by lottery," Fiona had replied. "How stable can that possibly be, politically?"

"The Veriboldan landholders choose their ruler by a series of incredibly complex contests," Roderick had said, "and they rule for seven years, after which time they award themselves a government job they'll hold for life. It works for them. Might be stronger, in the long run, than having a hereditary monarch who's weak or venal and can't be gotten rid of short of assassination. Don't worry. It's not like *you'll* ever have contact with royalty, of whatever country."

Looking back on that memory, she realized that even then Roderick had been disdainful of her, of her ignorance of things he knew well, as if she were somehow inherently flawed just because she didn't have his education. She discovered her jaw was clenched in anger and made herself relax. Roderick wasn't in a position to disdain her, not anymore, and she'd defied him by becoming more knowledgeable about Veriboldan laws than he was. She hadn't realized until that moment what an act of defiance it had been.

Just past the border lay a delicate, pearly-gray two-story structure that gleamed with the rain still slicking its surface. It had an elegant tiered roof tiled in blue with the same pearly sheen as its walls, and small windows piercing its side winked at them as figures within the building passed between the windows and the lights illuminating them. A sheltered porch with a long rail extended out to the left, and a few horses were tied there. Sebastian led the way to the porch, dismounted, and tied his horse to the rail. "Time to see what my money's bought me," he murmured.

The front door opened on a small entry whose floor was filthy with muddy footprints and traces of rain. Fiona wiped her feet pointlessly on a square of sodden carpet just inside the door and took a few more steps, out of the way of Holt coming in behind her. The white walls of the entry made the room feel even colder than it was, though there were warm drafts coming from behind a few of the doors lining the walls. Each door was labeled with a sign written in Tremontanese and Veriboldan. Sebastian made for one that said ENTRANCE—HAVE PAPERS READY. He carried a large leather portfolio under one arm. Fiona and Holt followed him.

The second room was warm, too warm, from all the bodies crowded into it. A man wearing a silver-white bodysuit and a cloud of purple gauze robe, the universal uniform of Veriboldan officials, approached them. He held a box in one hand that he dipped into with the other. "Your number will be called," he said, handing Sebastian a flat oval token with a number burned into it. It read 41. Just then, another man virtually the twin of the first called out, "16," and a woman carrying a crying baby crossed the room and exited by a second door.

Fiona and Sebastian exchanged glances. *I wish I'd brought a book,* Fiona thought, and settled in to wait.

They waited for nearly an hour, long enough for Fiona to become truly bored and begin inventing histories for the men and women waiting in the room with them. The woman with the narrow face like a well-bred pony was secretly the heir to a Veriboldan fortune, returning to Veribold in disguise. The man and boy, probably father and son, dressed in overalls and farmer's boots, were taking the boy to an apprenticeship in Veribold where he'd learn to make watches using mechanics rather than Devisery. The woman with half a dozen crying children intended to find the father of her brood and force him to pay for their upkeep, currently in arrears. She wondered what stories the others made up for her.

When the Veriboldan called their number, they exited the room into a much chillier one. This one had a tall desk with a trapezoidal top and a tall stool with a seat like a basin, in which sat a woman, cross-legged, in bodysuit and gauzy blue over-robe. "Papers," she said in Tremontanese with a strong Veriboldan accent.

Sebastian opened his portfolio and began taking out papers, sorting them into three piles. The Veriboldan scrutinized the contents of each stack of paper, reading the contents of each page slowly. Fiona stilled her left leg, which wanted to fidget. Government officials could get testy if you implied you resented them delaying you.

The woman glanced up from a paper and stared at Fiona as if trying to see beneath her skin. If the woman decided they were lying to her, what would she do? Kick them out, probably, but would she want them arrested? It had been too long since Fiona had had dealings with Veribold over border violations. She mentally went over what she did remember, hoping she wouldn't need it.

The woman dropped the page back onto its pile and squared the stack neatly. "You are missing the *aperte*," she said. "You will need that to be allowed to enter the Irantzen Temple."

"What?" Sebastian said. "But I was told I have everything in order. The papers—"

"The *aperte* is approval from the Proxy of Veribold," the woman said. "All foreigners must have it who attend the festival."

"The Proxy's in Aurilien. We'll miss the festival if we have to go all the way back."

"Then you should be better prepared." The Veriboldan woman uncrossed her legs and stood.

Fiona's heart was beating too rapidly. *When did this start to matter to me?* There had to be something—she remembered, vaguely, some part of treaty law...damn, it had been most of seven years, but there was something about the number fifteen...

"Article Fifteen of the Selkirk-Axante Treaty," she said.

Everyone turned to look at her, even Holt, whose face remained impassive. "What treaty?" the Veriboldan said.

"The Selkirk-Axante Treaty governs international relations between Veribold and Tremontane," Fiona said. "Article Fifteen, clause 17-b. Citizens wishing to enter either country who lack one of the documents on a given list may post a bond redeemable when they return with said document, duly signed and witnessed by a representative of the host government."

Sebastian's mouth hung open. The Veriboldan looked like Fiona had stood up and barked instead of speaking. "It's mutually binding," Fiona continued. "You can look it up. In fact, you probably should, because the amount of the bond is listed for each document. I'm sure the *aperte* is on it."

The woman nodded, slowly. "I...will see," she said, and left the room.

Fiona nodded at her companions. "It's probably going to be a stiff fee," she said. "I'm afraid I don't know the exact amount. I've never heard of the *aperte*."

Sebastian shut his mouth. "Sweet heaven," he said. "Miss Cooper, if you just made all that up, we should probably run now."

"It's all true."

"Sweet heaven," he repeated, running a hand over his face. "How did you know that? The customs official didn't even know that!"

"My husband and I used to travel to Veribold twice a year," Fiona said. "Trading journeys. I—" She didn't want to say *I resented him treating me like a useless hanger-on*, it sounded so bitter. "I became

47

familiar with the laws governing trade interactions between Tremontane and Veribold." And then Veriboldan law in general. It had been too fascinating to ignore.

"That's far more than familiarity," Sebastian said. "You sounded like a native just then." He let out a long breath. "Miss Cooper—"

The door opened. The Veriboldan woman returned with another woman and a man. The man held a tattered leather-bound book open to a page about a third of the way from the front. "It is so," he said. "The bond is five hundred fifty *naxhit*, or seven hundred Tremontanan guilders. Each."

Fiona thought Sebastian went a little pale, but he opened his money belt and brought out a handful of notes, which he gave to the first woman.

The second woman said, in Veriboldan, *"She is no Veriboldan."* Fiona kept her face very still. No sense letting them know she spoke the language, and causing them to become more circumspect. *"Is she a Tremontanan government official?"*

"Her name on her papers is Fiona Cooper, and she lists her occupation as 'trader'," the man said in the same language. *"Should we detain her?"*

"On what grounds? That she knows obscure parts of the law too well?" the first woman said. *"Send a message ahead that she should be watched. It's probably nothing, but I'd rather pass this problem on to someone else."*

Fiona made herself relax. So they'd be watching her? That was probably all to the good, if it kept their attention off Sebastian and Holt. Even so, the idea irritated her.

The second woman removed some stamps and a shallow dish of ink from inside the desk and stamped a couple of the sheets of paper. "These are your receipts for the bond. Show these other papers to the officials at the Jaixante and they will allow you entry," she said. "Welcome to Veribold."

"Thank you," Sebastian said. He gathered up their papers, and the three were escorted back to their horses. Once there, Sebastian stood with his face pressed against the bay's neck, heedless of how damp it still was. "Miss Cooper," he said. "I think you may have saved this quest. I'm sure Lucille wouldn't have had your secret knowledge."

"Well, I want to protect my investment," Fiona said lightly, mounting Mittens and giving her a pat. She ignored the part of her that whispered *It's your quest now, too.*

"Yes, about that," Sebastian said, lifting his head. "I'm afraid paying the bonds has made it impossible for me to pay you when we reach the Jaixante. Will you wait until we return?"

"I suppose I have to."

"That's a relief. Though I admit I'm not unhappy to have to share your company on the road a while longer." He grinned at her, and mounted. "Two more days, and the real work begins."

"We should move on, sir, if we wish to reach Poe-nien before dark," Holt said.

"Wise words. Miss Cooper, if you'll ride with me, we can talk about the Irantzen Festival and what will be expected of you. I don't know much, but it's better than nothing."

Fiona nodded. "I'd like that," she said.

———————

7

*F*iona had forgotten how *green* the Kepa Valley was. Once they were past the high wastes and near-desert of the flatlands, the road to Haizea wound between low hills, verdant with winter's crops—if you could call it winter when the air was so balmy and snow and rain were a thing of Tremontane's uplands. In six months, the rains would come, and then the river would swell and the entire country would take to its boats, but for now, the weather was perfect. Mittens liked the way food grew at every turn, and Fiona had to strongly encourage her to keep moving when what she wanted was to stop every few yards to tear up another mouthful of rich, tender grass.

She smelled the tanginess coming from one of the little roadside stands, out of sight at the moment, that sold food to travelers, pan-fried vegetables coated lightly with a dark sauce that tasted of garlic, ginger, and fish. They'd had it for their dinner that day, and the day before, and Fiona wasn't tired of it yet. It brought back so many memories of the good times, before everything had fallen apart, that she was having trouble remembering why they were there now. The previous night, Sebastian had bid her good night with, "We have to reach Haizea before sunset tomorrow, so we'll make an early start," and the reminder that they had a deadline had been startling.

"Not worried, are you, Miss Cooper?" Sebastian said, coming up beside her.

"I wish I knew more of what they expect. But I can't be the only woman whose first time at the Irantzen Festival this is."

They rounded a curve in the road and the roadside stand Fiona had smelled became visible. It was little more than three wooden walls holding up a shingled roof that sloped to the rear. A woman dressed in Veriboldan laborer's clothes, wide-legged trousers of a coarse weave and a wraparound shirt, came forward to watch them approach. Sebastian waved at her politely but dismissively, and she took a few steps back.

"You said they'd be watching you," he said. "It's safer if you look confident. Not too confident, but not needing too much attention."

"I think if they're watching me, they won't be watching you."

"The priestesses at the Irantzen Temple won't be watching me at all. They don't care about the attendants. To my knowledge."

"Then we don't have anything to worry about."

They left the woman behind and began ascending a gentle slope. Mittens veered toward the long grass of the verge, and Fiona pulled her up sharply. Sebastian said, "I wouldn't say that. We don't know exactly where the blackmail evidence is kept. And attempting to steal from the Jaixante is dangerous. Veriboldans aren't gentle with foreigners caught committing crimes against Veriboldans."

"That almost sounds like nerves. Isn't it a little late for you to be worried?"

He laughed. "Miss Cooper, it's hard for me to feel nervous when you're around to needle me. I'm not nervous. But I am feeling cautious, which I think is a safe feeling. And I think it's reasonable to consider possible disasters and plan a response to them."

"And what disasters are those?"

"Being unable to move freely within the Jaixante. The evidence being held somewhere inaccessible, or worse, not in Haizea at all. Being identified as a—member of my family. Those are the ones that would keep me up at night if I were at all nervous, which we've established I'm not."

"How—" Fiona stopped herself from saying *How can I help?* just in time. She'd gotten them all past the border, she would get them into the Jaixante; Sebastian didn't need any more help than that. "How would being identified as a member of the family whose name you won't give me be a problem?" she asked instead.

Sebastian grinned at her. "The blackmailer, Gizane, would definitely be suspicious if someone with that surname, which you don't need to know, showed up in Haizea."

"Is she here?"

"I don't know. She was in Aurilien—isn't that right, Holt?"

"She met directly with men and women in positions of power in Aurilien, several times," Holt said. "But it is certainly possible she might have returned to the Jaixante. She is the trade liaison between Tremontane and the royal city."

"What if she recognizes *Holt?*"

"I did not make myself known to her," Holt said, "and I believe she is the sort of woman to whom servants are furniture."

"At any rate, if she is here, I'm not worried about her recognizing me," Sebastian said, "and I'll keep my name to myself."

"It's not as if I care who your parents are, Sebastian."

"You might if you knew who they were."

"Meaning they're well-known enough that even someone like me would recognize the name. Are you noble?"

"Miss Nosy, you are in fine form today. I can't wait for us to reach Haizea." He smiled, though, and looked amused rather than offended.

At that moment, they reached the top of the rise, and looked down into a valley that spread in ripples of terraced hills all the way to the river. And there, laid out like glimmering patchwork, lay Haizea. Delicate fairy spires, white or silver, rose here and there over the indistinct masses of colored roofs that were the smaller buildings, purple or blue or green or gray. The Kepa River cut through the city like a murky green ribbon lazily unfurling across the patchwork, with tiny barges zigzagging upstream, leaving trails like broken threads behind. On the near side of the river, a spongy-looking mass marked Haizea's Dusktown, poor and dangerous to intruders. It had been too long for Fiona to judge if it was bigger or smaller than when she'd seen it last.

In the center of the Kepa, breasting its waters like the world's biggest dolphin, lay an island linked to the shores by five broad, white bridges. White and gold buildings, with tapering towers and flying buttresses and aqueducts from which thin, lacy waterfalls fell, covered the island all the way to the blindingly white wall that surrounded it. The Jaixante. By night, Fiona remembered, it would glow with Devices the way Aurilien did, but Veriboldans preferred colors to white lights, and the Jaixante by night looked like a dowager Countess's jewelry box. Even by day, it was stunning.

Fiona looked at the highest spire, a tower surmounting the royal residence near the top of the Jaixante's artificial hill, and thought of Willow North's crumbling black tower, symbol of Tremontane's power, with a sense of guilty disloyalty.

A flight of birds swept low over the river, then rose into the sky, and the dim noise of their chatter reached Fiona's ears, breaking her out of her daze. "We should go," she said.

"Oh. Yes," Sebastian said. He sounded as dazed as she felt. Was it a bad omen for their journey, that they were so overwhelmed by this foreign city? Fiona once again focused on Mittens' ears and vowed not to let it get to her. She was Tremontanan, no matter how beautiful the Veriboldan capital was, and Aurilien had a beauty of its own.

Traffic on the road increased as they wound through the terraced hills into the valley of Haizea, but most of it was leaving the great city. Most of the men and women they passed were ordinary Veriboldans who glanced at them with a lack of interest, which surprised Fiona. Veriboldan commoners weren't as xenophobic and bigoted as Veriboldan landholders—the equivalent of Tremontanan nobles—but usually they were at least curious about strangers dressed in Tremontanan clothing. Holt was dark enough to pass for Veriboldan, and there were Veriboldans with skin as light as hers and Sebastian's, but they were still clearly Tremontanans, and therefore suspect. Or so she'd expected.

"I hope your plan doesn't call for you to pretend to be Veriboldan," she murmured to Sebastian after they'd passed a small group of travelers who in different clothes might have been Tremontanan natives.

"Only as a last resort," Sebastian said. "I don't speak Veriboldan."

"I do," Fiona said, "and I wouldn't want to try it either." She wouldn't have wanted to impersonate a Veriboldan even if she'd been perfectly confident about it. It was too difficult to mimic all the subtleties of culture and behavior outsiders hardly even perceived.

It took nearly an hour for them to reach the outskirts of Haizea, and another half-hour to cross the city to the Kepa and the first of the white bridges leading to the Jaixante. They had to push their way through the crowds filling the streets, people laughing and talking and bargaining at top volume. Canvas booths, their striped sides pressed closely against their neighbors', lined both sides of the street, their wares as varied as their customers. Fiona observed two women haggling over a pottery vase next to a man selling roast tubers on skewers, whose neighbor on the other side sold diaphanous scarves threaded with gold and silver. Maybe they could come back this way when it was all over. Assuming they didn't leave the Jaixante at a run, pursued by the blackmailer Gizane's guards.

The long market ended fifty feet from a boulevard that followed the curve of the Kepa's banks. Beyond the boulevard, a gate of lacy white ironwork framed the entrance to the first of the bridges crossing to the Jaixante. It had no doors and no one stood guard there, but there was a sign posted. Fiona dismounted and led Mittens closer. "It says no horses or wheeled vehicles," she said. "I gather the guards are on the far side."

"We need to *hurry*," Sebastian said. "It's only an hour to sunset."

It took almost all of that time to find someone who would stable their horses for the week of the festival, and Sebastian was almost jogging with impatience by the time he slapped hands with the stable master in agreement and shouldered his bag. They ran through the streets to the bridge, then across, Fiona breathing heavily with the unaccustomed exertion. She'd forgotten how it felt to run.

It was a shame they had to run so fast, she thought, because the Kepa from the bridge was an incredible sight she'd like to have time to admire. Green-glass water flowed unhurriedly downstream, passing beneath the arches holding the bridges up. Fiona saw a barge pass beneath one of those arches; its captain waved, and she did her best to wave back.

Overhead, birds squawked and dove at the water, then came to rest on the white iron pillars lining the bridge. More lacy ironwork spanned the gaps between them. *Do people ever jump from here?* she wondered, and felt disgusted with herself for having that thought when the place was so beautiful. *Still, you have to wonder,* her inner voice said, and she gritted her teeth and focused on running.

There was a gate at the far end, and two guards who came to attention as the three came charging toward them. "*Stop!*" one said in Veriboldan. "*State your purpose.*"

"We're here...for the Irantzen...Festival," Sebastian panted, as if he'd understood their words. "Please...let us pass."

"You will not reach it in time," the first guard said, switching to Tremontanese. "It is almost sunset."

"Please," Fiona said, "help us."

The second guard appraised her, and Fiona was surprised to see a definite light of admiration in his eyes. She wasn't used to being looked at that way. "Papers," he said.

Sebastian already had the portfolio out and the papers spread in his hand. The first guard took them and examined them closely. "Fiona Cooper?" he said. He pronounced her surname with the emphasis on the second syllable.

"Yes," Fiona said. "I'm Fiona Cooper."

The guard scrawled something on one of the pages with the stub of a pencil, then handed the papers back to Sebastian. "Take the second right, then follow the ramp to the top," he said. "If you run, you may not be late."

"Thank you," Sebastian said, and the three of them ran faster than before. Fiona glanced once back over her shoulder; the two men were staring after them—no, after her. It sounded like they had recognized her name. Maybe the customs officials had sent word about her, after all. She hadn't seen what he had written on the paper. Some warning to the priestesses at the Irantzen Temple? *Let's just hope it's not a warrant for our execution.*

The ramp was steep, and curved as if following the contours of the island. Fiona's legs and chest ached, and her shoulder hurt from where her bag balanced on it. She made herself keep running. The sun was nearly below the horizon, outlining it with yellow gold like metal in a forge. What if they were too late? Well, Sebastian would think of a different plan, and she'd go on to Umberan. It might not be too late to join that group going to Dineh-Karit. *Or you might go on helping Sebastian*, she thought. The idea surprised her.

They stumbled off the ramp and kept running down a long colonnade, its pillars bulging near the bottom as if they were wax that had melted in the summer sun. Ahead was one of those fairy structures, towering a hundred feet above them with spires that doubled that height. A flight of shallow steps led up to its base, and two white doors, arched at the top, stood at the top of the steps. They were closing.

"Wait!" Fiona shouted, pushing herself harder, and then all three of them were shouting and waving their free arms. The doors' movement paused, then resumed. Fiona pelted up the stairs with Sebastian and slid between the doors, forcing them to stop again. It was black inside, and Fiona came to a halt only to be shoved forward by Sebastian, entering behind her. Holt followed close after.

"The Irantzen is closed," said a female voice in Tremontanese. "You are too late."

"No," Fiona gasped, "it's just barely sunset. We're not too late. Besides, the guard wrote something—it's on that paper—" She waved desperately at Sebastian, who dug through the portfolio, squinting at its contents. Finally, he handed a sheet to the now dimly visible woman, who seemed to have no trouble reading it. The woman glanced up at the three of them, then settled on Fiona.

"I think you are Fiona Cooper, yes?" she said.

"I am."

The woman read the paper again. "These are your bodyguards?"

Fiona hadn't seen the contents of the papers. "My attendants, yes."

The woman handed the paper back to Sebastian. "Come with me."

The doors slammed shut. Fiona blinked, waiting for her eyes to adjust to the darkness, but then she heard the scratch of a match striking stone, and light flared. The woman took an extremely old-fashioned torch off the wall. It stank of creosote and sulfur and left afterimages of itself when Fiona incautiously looked at it. The woman walked away without glancing back. Fiona looked around quickly. She saw another woman standing nearby, her hand resting on the door, who widened her eyes at Fiona as if urging her on. Fiona didn't need a second reminder.

---

8

*T*he yellow light of the torch made a puddle of light Fiona tried to stay within. Behind her, Sebastian and Holt shuffled along, Sebastian bumping into Fiona once and apologizing under his breath. There were no windows in the white walls, turned gold by the torch's fire, and the floor was of a rough stone that matched the walls in color. It was like being inside a man-made cave, angular and cool and dry, with a ceiling that rose beyond the extent of the light and walls close enough to touch at the same time. Fiona tried not to hunch in on herself. She wasn't afraid of small spaces; she just didn't like not being able to see where she was going. That was it.

The corridor turned frequently at odd angles, and after a few turns Fiona lost track of what direction she was facing. Not that it mattered much, here in this narrow, twisting space…she made herself breathe calmly. It wasn't all that narrow, and it had to open up somewhere.

The woman never turned to see if they were following her. She wore her hair cut short enough to brush her chin, and it bobbed as she walked, making interesting shadows on the walls. She was, strangely, dressed in the clothes of a Veriboldan commoner, the wide-legged trousers and wraparound shirt they'd seen so often in the last two days. Both looked ivory in the torchlight. Fiona had expected more formal garb on someone belonging to the most important temple in Veribold. It was probably a bad idea to make assumptions when she knew practically nothing.

Just as Fiona was about to break the silence by asking where they were going, the narrow corridor opened up into a room shaped like the inside of a pyramid, lit by a dozen more torches. Two more women were in the process of sorting papers into a portfolio like Sebastian's own and looked up when Fiona entered. Their guide carried her torch to a wrought iron stand in the far corner and wedged it securely into the top. Then she went to join the women, who'd stopped sorting, and said in Veriboldan, *"This is the last one for the festival."*

"It's too late. Past sunset," one of the women said. Both women were dressed like the torch bearer, down to the short haircut, though one's clothing was pale green rather than ivory.

"The border sent word about this one. She's to be watched," said the torch bearer.

All three women looked at Fiona. She did her best impression of someone who had no idea what was being said. *"Did they say why?"*

"Government officials never say why," the torch bearer said sourly. *"Just that she was suspicious. I'm sure there's nothing to worry about."*

"She looks clever."

"Cleverness isn't a crime."

The woman in the green clothing came forward with her hand outstretched. "Papers," she said, and Sebastian pulled them out of the portfolio. She examined them, nodded, and handed them to her partner. "We will take you to your lodgings," she said. "You will of course be housed separately, so as to preserve the purity of the festival."

"Of course," Fiona said. "We understand." That had been part of Sebastian's instructions; she was to have her own "cell," a term which unsettled her somewhat but was, Sebastian assured her, temple terminology for a private room. "What if we need to communicate?" she'd asked the night before.

"You'll have to come to us," Sebastian had said. "Men aren't

ALLY OF THE CROWN

allowed within the temple proper. I *think* you're allowed to visit but not stay, but I'm sure you'll be able to figure something out if you have to, Miss Cooper."

The woman in green made a complicated salute which, thank heaven, she didn't seem to expect Fiona to answer. Taking another of the smelly torches, she indicated that they should follow her.

A second doorway opened off the pyramidal room onto a corridor much wider than the first, and Fiona felt tension drain out of her shoulders. Even so, with Sebastian and Holt at her back Fiona felt like someone being escorted to prison, an illusion not helped by the mysterious shadows the torch cast on the walls and the slightly limping gait of the woman in green. Fiona gritted her teeth. She was letting her imagination rule her, and that was unacceptable.

Soon, they came to an even wider passage, a long one lined with doors on both sides that Fiona sternly told herself did not look like a prison corridor. The woman went to a door about halfway down the hall and opened it. "For your attendants," she said. "They will care for your belongings while you are in meditation and prayer. Leave your bag and follow me."

Fiona and Sebastian exchanged glances. She hadn't anticipated being separated so abruptly. She sent up a silent prayer for his success—maybe being in one of the oldest temples in the world might make heaven inclined to hear her plea—and handed her bag to Holt. To her surprise, Sebastian clasped her hand briefly before she could turn away. His skin was warm and dry and his grip strong, and she squeezed his hand in return. Then she followed the woman back the way they'd come.

A few minutes later, they came to a steep, narrow staircase going up, blue-tinged with moonlight, and Fiona had just enough time to realize what that meant when she reached the first of the windows and could look out over Haizea. The windows were tall and thin, barely as wide as her two palms outstretched, but there were dozens of them, spaced closely together. It was like looking at the city through a grille.

And Haizea was as beautiful as she remembered. Veribold had

61

little source, and what Devices they had were imported—they dealt more extensively in what they called mechanics—but one thing Veriboldans had enthusiastically embraced were the light Devices that kept most Tremontanan cities aglow all night long.

The stairway curved, following the rounded shape of the Irantzen Temple, and as she ascended Fiona saw the Jaixante laid out below her, and beyond that, the city proper. One of the bridges between the two was a streak of silver light that glimmered on the river running beneath it. The stairwell grew darker, and Fiona realized she'd stopped to gape and had to hurry to catch up to her guide.

They climbed, and climbed, not fast enough to exhaust Fiona or leave her short of breath, but steadily, until they must surely have reached the top spire and gone beyond. Finally, the stairs ended at a smoothly paved passage whose ceiling arched to a sharp crease. Plain white doors lined it on one side. The woman in green went to one about halfway down the corridor and opened it.

"Your cell, while you are with us," she said. "Change your clothes into the garments provided for you, set your own clothes outside your door, and someone will take them to your attendants. All you will need is within. You will be called at dawn."

"Thank you," Fiona said. "What's your name?"

The woman blinked at her. Fiona had the feeling she hadn't expected Fiona to speak. "Sela," she said.

"Thank you, Sela."

Sela nodded. "Restful sleep to you." She walked away in the direction of the stairs.

The first thing Fiona did was establish that the door of her cell couldn't be locked from the outside. It couldn't be locked at all, which annoyed her. She shut the door and examined her cell. It was much nicer than the name implied, with its white stone walls gleaming blue in the moonlight from the single window. There was a pallet on the floor, which she remembered was typical of Veriboldan bedroom furniture. This one was a couple of inches thick, with no pillow, also typically Veriboldan, and was made up neatly with a linen sheet and thin cotton blanket. Against the wall, beneath the window, stood a flat-topped wooden chest bound in leather and brass, also without a lock.

Next to her, on a squat round table near the door, was a brass lamp that reminded her of a ship's lantern, with a matchlighter that looked like mechanics rather than Devisery next to it. She lit the lamp with a touch of her finger and turned it up until its glow filled the whole small room.

She opened the chest and peered inside. A pile of dark fabric turned out to be a pair of those wide-legged trousers, woven expertly of black linen, and a black wraparound shirt of the same material. She laid them on the pallet. Linen, good for warm climates, but it wrinkled if you so much as breathed on it. Well, it was either sleep naked or look rumpled.

Beneath those were a loose cotton robe in a rich gold that looked even more golden by lamplight and three pairs of undershorts. So they wanted *all* her normal clothes gone. That would be interesting.

There was a wooden hairbrush with bristles of some natural material Fiona couldn't identify, a bag that rustled when she picked it up and proved to be full of thumbnail-sized white crackers, and a heavy pendant the size of her palm. It hung from a woven, knotted silk cord, creamy green jade carved with raised patterns Fiona recognized as meditation rituals.

Finally, there was an unnaturally thick copy of the Book of Haran. Fiona leafed through it; it was actually three copies bound in one volume, in Eskandelic, Veriboldan, and Tremontanese. Fiona had never been particularly religious, but Roderick had owned a copy he referred to sometimes. It contained the revelations Haran had received about ungoverned heaven, as well as commentaries by later clerics, and Fiona hadn't read it in years. Apparently she'd now have the opportunity.

She shucked off all her clothes, put on the undershorts and the linen, folded her own clothes neatly with her undergarments in the center—oh, lovely, they were going to take her things to Sebastian and he'd see her underwear. The thought was unexpectedly embarrassing. It wasn't as if he was seeing her *in* her underwear, and she couldn't imagine why the notion of him handling her clothes unsettled her so. She set the pile outside her door and pinched out the lamp, then settled in to sleep.

The pallet was thick by Veriboldan standards, but uncomfortable by her own, and she turned restlessly, trying to find a good position for sleeping. Sebastian's face again came to mind, lit by that amused, sardonic grin. It occurred to her that he might not be allowed to roam outside the Irantzen Temple, if he was intended to be her attendant. She hoped his plan had provisions for that. It was unthinkable that he'd come all this way only to be denied the chance at saving his family.

Fiona rolled over again. He'd think of something. He was smart, and clever, and stubborn, and he wouldn't let any setbacks stop him accomplishing his goal. And she liked him. How strange, that a friendship could begin under such odd circumstances. *He's handsome, too*, her inner voice chuckled, and she rolled her eyes at its persistence on that subject. True, but irrelevant, because they'd be friends no matter what he looked like. And yet...

She groaned and rolled onto her side. There was no "and yet." It was an idiotic notion that probably came from her empty stomach. She'd only been single for a few months and she was still getting used to the idea that she didn't have to worry about anyone but herself. She didn't need another romantic relationship, not now, possibly not ever. Certainly not one with a man she barely knew.

It was only hunger, and the hardness of the pallet, that kept her from sleeping soundly all night. Of course it was.

---

9

*F*iona came awake instantly at a knock on her door, momentarily disoriented by how close the walls and ceiling were. What inn had they stopped at the previous night? Then she remembered. This was the Irantzen Temple. Pale rosy light illuminated the room without warming it. Fiona ran her fingers over the cold stone of the floor and shivered. Thank heaven the pallet was thick.

She stood, stretching out her aches, and went to the door. A tiny tray bearing a steaming teapot and a porcelain cup without a handle, no bigger than her own cupped hand, lay there. A woman wearing a teal robe over white clothes pushed a trolley whose wheels rolled silently across the stone hall. She bent to set another tray at the next door before knocking.

Fiona picked up the tray and retreated to her pallet. The faint light of dawn shone through the window, four panes of well-polished glass that weren't made to open. She looked out to see the Kepa River flowing out to the distant sea, glimmering silver in the early morning light. More spires of the Jaixante's many buildings rose below her, dull copper or flat pale blue without the sun to turn them brilliant gold and white. A flock of birds winged past on their way to the river, close enough almost to touch. Fiona laid her hand flat against the glass, which felt cold and damp. Were those Tremontanan birds, or Veriboldan?

She sat on the pallet to drink her tea, which smelled of roses and honeysuckle. Its hot astringency soothed her empty stomach. When was breakfast? She'd never felt so hungry in her life. Hopefully it was just an oversight that had sent her to bed with no supper the previous night.

Her clothes weren't as wrinkled as she'd feared, and when she finished her cup of tea, she did some more stretching to get the rest of the kinks out and found that despite her restless night, she felt well-rested and ready to begin this first day. Whatever that day might bring. All Sebastian had known about the festival was that it lasted seven days, that there were times of meditation and times of instruction, and that there was a grand feast at the end to celebrate Haran's return to the world. Well, if she didn't ask, she'd never find out.

She drained the teapot, wishing it were a more substantial meal, and left her room. There were no windows in the hall, so the place was dark and silent, lit only by secondhand sunlight filtering up from the stairwell. Maybe bringing the lamp would be a good idea. Fiona had turned around to return to her room when someone said, in Veriboldan, *"What are you doing? It's unsafe to walk the halls now."*

Fiona made the lightning-fast decision to pretend ignorance of the language and turned to face the speaker, an innocent expression solidly in place. "What?"

"You should be in your room," said the woman, who wore trousers and shirt in ivory white like the women from the previous night. Her Tremontanese was only faintly accented. "It is the day of the fast. You should be cautious."

Fiona's stomach rumbled at this unwelcome news. "I was looking for the facilities," she said quickly. "That is permitted, yes?"

"Here," said the woman, touching a spot on the facing wall that sprang open, revealing a hidden door behind which was an old-fashioned chamber pot. "You were not shown?"

"I arrived late. Thank you for your help. Is there anything else I should know?"

The woman peered at her. "What is your name?"

"Fiona Cooper."

"The very latecomer." The woman nodded slowly, as if something had begun to make sense. "You do not know about the festival, but you come anyway?"

"I've been feeling the need to reconnect with my religious roots," Fiona said. "I know the Irantzen Temple is one of the holiest places, and I took the opportunity to come here when it was presented to me. I'm not as prepared as I could be, true, but I'd like to think I'm welcome anyway."

"Being prepared is part of the experience."

"But each moment is preparation for the next," Fiona said, paraphrasing one of Haran's revelations that Roderick had been fond of quoting. "Fasting today will prepare me for tomorrow's activities, will it not?"

The woman frowned. "Indeed." Then she eyed Fiona more closely. "Always wear your robe when you are outside your cell," she said. "It is respectful. I suggest you speak to someone for more information, so your experience is as...prepared...as you can make it."

Fiona nodded and ducked quickly into the tiny room, where she sat on the chamber pot and took a few shallow breaths; it didn't stink, but there was still the faintest aroma of human waste she didn't feel like inhaling. Then she realized she actually did need the facilities, so she used them and returned to her cell, where she put on the gold robe and sat cross-legged on the pallet. Was she supposed to stay in the cell all day, not eating anything? Fiona couldn't think of anything more boring. She hoped Sebastian's movements weren't as strictly confined.

She lay back and stared at the ceiling, not very high above her. It was smooth stone rather than the plaster she was accustomed to, with its many cracks and swirls that made pictures. No, there were pictures in the stone, too, patterns of light and dark where the stone's imperfections caught the sun. That looked like a man smoking a pipe, and there was a dog's front end complete with lolling tongue, and there was a flock of birds...

...that swooped lazily across the ceiling, circled once, and disappeared.

Fiona shot upright and had to catch herself as her head spun, sickening her. Her vision tunneled, then opened wide again, tilting slightly. Drugs. The tea had been drugged. She got to her hands and knees, then sagged again as the birds once more swept across her vision. Someone had drugged her, but why? Terror gripped her heart. If she lost control—

She crawled to the wall and pulled herself upright so she could look out the window, leaning her face against the cool, damp glass. The spires of the Jaixante shivered, rainbow light clinging to them like dewdrops. Below, the Kepa glittered in broken crystal fragments that hurt her eyes and made her fall, head swimming, back to the pallet.

She lay, sweating, with one arm flung over her eyes to block the dizzying images. Whatever this drug was, it wasn't intended to kill, because what would be the point of that? This was meant to disorient her, confuse her, but for what purpose? They must want her out of the way temporarily, so they could investigate her, but that made no sense, because all her things were with Sebastian—

Her heart lurched. What might they have done to Sebastian and Holt? She needed to find them. She tried to rise and found herself lying crosswise on the pallet instead. She wasn't going anywhere until this drug worked its way through her system. If it wasn't meant to kill her.

Fiona pulled herself around until she lay straight on the pallet, then closed her eyes. *Relax*, she told herself, *this isn't the same as being drunk, you won't lose control.* She held her hand above her head and kindled a tiny flame, then closed her hand around it, extinguishing it. The bite of the dying flame steadied her. She repeated the ritual, spark, flame, out, breathing slowly. She was the master of her magic, not the other way around.

The birds swooped in delicate patterns, like lace, trailing lines of pale smoke as imaginary as they were. When she recovered, she was going to find Sebastian and warn him, or rescue him, or whatever needed doing. Her head was starting to ache. Damn whoever had done this! And how ironic, that she was the one they thought needed watching when it was Sebastian who was a danger to them. Not a danger, really, but certainly a threat to the inviolability of the Jaix-ante. She giggled, and stopped herself. The drug was making her confused as well as light-headed. Well, if it hadn't killed her outright, it was just a matter of waiting its effects out.

She lay on her pallet for what felt like hours, watching the birds fly around her head, kindling fire, until the birds went misty and disappeared. Then she sat up and breathed in deeply, let it out slowly, and stood. When she didn't fall over, she took a few steps to the window and looked out. The sun on the river no longer hurt her eyes, and judging by the angle of the light, it was well past noon.

She brushed her hair, then tossed the hairbrush onto the pallet and went to the door. Time for some exploring. No one was in the hall, and she heard no noises, so she went quietly to the stairs. She had no idea what she might find, but it was probably a good idea to look for Sebastian and Holt and tell them what had happened. She hoped they hadn't been attacked. Did Sebastian have anything incriminating on him? At least whatever identity papers he was carrying didn't have his real name on them. She assumed. Who knew what the priestesses of the Irantzen Temple might make of that if they did?

A low moan startled her as she passed the last door before the stairs. It sounded like someone in pain. Another moan, louder, brought her to that door, listening. Silence. She was about to retreat when she heard a third moan, then indistinct words. Fiona put her hand to the knob and turned it, noting that this door, like hers, had no lock.

The furnishings were exactly like her own, pallet, trunk, low table. A large, dark-skinned Veriboldan woman sat on the pallet with her knees hugged to her chest, staring at the wall. "Are you well?" Fiona asked. The woman didn't answer, just moved her lips slowly as if shaping silent words. Fiona knelt beside her and waved a hand in front of her eyes. No response. "I can help you," Fiona said, though she had no idea how. The woman moaned again.

Fiona put her hands on the woman's shoulders and tried to get her to lie down. The woman twitched away from her. "*The tree is the temple,*" she said in Veriboldan, "*but the temple is not the tree. It's all so simple when you stop thinking about it.*"

"You've been drugged," Fiona said, then sat back on her heels. They'd both been drugged, both been given the same tea—the tray lay a short distance from the head of the pallet—and there had been many more of those trays on the trolley that morning. Suppose this was part of the festival experience? The woman seemed caught in the grip of some vision, and Fiona's perceptions had definitely been altered, in which case it might have nothing to do with Sebastian at all.

Fiona left the room and stood at the head of the stairs. What were they up to, that they didn't want the women wandering around on this day? She probably ought to return to her room, pretend the drug still worked on her, but curiosity was a drug far stronger than any hallucinogen, and she wanted to find Sebastian and hear what he'd learned. She moved off silently down the stairs.

The stairwell was warm and sunny, and a breeze carried the scent of the Kepa to her, a rich, loamy scent. The river ran slowly at this time of year, carrying with it the heavy sediments that made the river country such fertile ground. It would also be cold, probably, not ideal for swimming in no matter how beautiful it was. Fiona peered out through the window slits at the river and the nearest bridge. Pedestrians were crossing it in both directions, and she could see a crowd at the island end of the bridge where the guards were deciding who was allowed to pass. Suppose a crowd like that had been present when they needed to cross? They'd been incredibly lucky in every respect.

She came to a landing with a single white-painted wooden door, hesitated, then continued down. Finding Sebastian was her first priority. Exploring the Irantzen Temple came second.

At the base of the stairs, she stopped to listen, but everything remained silent. The narrow, high-ceilinged hallway was no better lit than it had been the night before. Fiona tried not to think about how close the walls were. She looked up at the ceiling, which was tall and curved like a tunnel, which made her imagine herself a mouse tunneling through the stones. There was plenty of room for her, no reason at all to be unsettled by the walls close around her—she found herself breathing heavily and made herself relax, slow down—

She turned a corner, then had to fling herself backward and press hard against the wall, because there were two women dressed in white wraparound shirts and trousers coming toward her. They spoke quietly, too quietly for Fiona to make out more than that they were speaking Veriboldan. When they were safely past, Fiona crept forward and ran down the corridor in the opposite direction.

The new corridor was wider than the other, and soon Fiona found herself back in the door-lined corridor where they'd left Sebastian and Holt the night before. Fiona counted doors, then remembered she'd come in from the other side and counted again. Steeling herself, she opened what she thought was Sebastian's door and stepped inside into total darkness. Cursing under her breath, she went back into the corridor and took a torch off the wall. It was heavy, its wooden surface almost slick, and it warmed the back of her hand as she held it high above her. The smell of heat and char wasn't as unpleasant as before, though it wasn't a smell she wanted to get used to.

She opened the door again. To her relief, she saw Holt and Sebastian's bags set neatly at the feet of a couple of pallets not as thick as her own. Her bag lay against the wall to one side. She went through it one-handed and saw no one had touched it except to put the pile of clothes she'd removed the night before into it. So at least no one had been prying into their things. She shut the door behind her and returned the torch.

Now to find Sebastian. It seemed unlikely she'd be able to locate him in this place, but if she didn't look, she'd never know. She put the torch back, went up the stairs to the landing, and listened at the door.

She heard nothing. Hoping that meant the room beyond was empty and not that the door was just too thick, she pushed it open.

Beyond the door lay an enormous round room with a sunken floor reached by short flights of steps at intervals around it. A walkway about six feet wide circled it, giving access to a couple of doors on the far side. Great trestle tables like slabs of stone filled the sunken floor, and a handful of women moved among them, setting out utensils. Before Fiona could retreat, one of the women called out, *"What are you doing here?"*

"I..." Quickly Fiona went through possible responses. "I felt strange and came looking for help."

The woman came forward, and Fiona saw it was Sela. "You should not leave your cell," she said. "It is dangerous while the visions are on you."

"The visions," Fiona began.

Sela looked at her narrowly. "The tea does not affect you," she said. "Why is that?"

"It did," Fiona said. "I had a vision. Now it's gone."

"That is not possible. You must not have drunk all the tea." Sela frowned. "Do you not know *anything* about the festival?"

"I drank all the tea. It must not have worked."

"The tea always works." Sela took Fiona by the arm. "Come with me."

Fiona almost jerked away, but realized in time that she didn't want to draw any more attention to herself than she already had. She let Sela lead her out the door and back down the stairs, through the narrow, uncomfortable passages and into a room with several ordinary-looking kitchen chairs and a Veriboldan desk. A woman dressed like Sela, but in pastel blue instead of pale green, sat in one of the strange tall Veriboldan basin-chairs, writing something at the desk. She glanced up when they entered, but said nothing.

"Hien, this...woman has failed to obey the festival guides," Sela said.

Now Fiona jerked away. "I did not," she said. "It's not my fault the tea didn't work the way you want it to. I did have a vision." Maybe flying birds weren't the kind of vision they had in mind, maybe she should have said she hadn't seen anything, but it was too late to go changing her story now.

Hien laid down her pen. "And yet you are alert and conscious now," she said. Her voice was low and sweet, the sound of a river running through darkness. "How is that? Did you not drink all of it?"

"I did." She couldn't tell them she'd been resistant to the effects of drugs since she was thirteen, something she believed was a side effect of her inherent magic.

"Hmmm." Hien leaned forward on her desk, her chin in her hand. "What vision?"

"Birds flying. And a tree." She borrowed the tree from the other drugged woman, thinking to bolster her story of the effects the tea had had on her, and immediately wondered if it was a good idea. She just didn't *know* anything, and she cursed Sebastian for putting her in this position even as she knew that was irrational.

Hien looked at Sela, who shrugged. "You saw those things, but you don't know what they mean," Hien said.

"I don't."

"She should be removed from the festival," Sela said. "Tirin says she knows nothing of what is expected of her. She dishonors Haran's memory."

"Haran didn't know anything when she went to the Eidestal, either," Fiona shot back. "It took her ten days of fasting and prayer before she saw her vision. Now, I don't claim to be as worthy as Haran, but I think I should at least get some credit for trying." *Thank you, Roderick, for telling me the stories.*

"I agree," Hien said. "But you will not be able to fully participate unless you have a vision you understand. That is reality."

"Then help me understand. I don't want to go home." Where was Sebastian right now? Investigating some place he wasn't allowed to be? She needed to keep their attention on her.

"Tell me what the tree means."

Fiona blinked. "I told you, I don't know what the vision means."

"But you know of the tree."

"I...know it was Haran's first vision, the one that led her to the Eidestal. It was a fir tree that grew all alone on the plains. She camped there and continued to fast and pray until ungoverned heaven opened up before her."

"And the birds?"

"I don't know."

"Birds are symbolic of souls," Sela said. It was a reprimand, delivered in a prim voice. Fiona ignored her.

"So...the fir tree, and souls? What does that mean?" she asked.

"You will have to meditate and discover the truth," Hien said. "Symbols speak to our inner minds the way words speak to our conscious thoughts. Sela, bring a stronger tea. We will find a private room where you can be observed. Perhaps you just need a different perspective."

Fiona lowered her head so they couldn't see her irritation. A stronger tea and observation? All that meant was she would be watched while she had her "vision" and she'd have to be drugged for all that time. Well, if it kept their eyes off Sebastian...even so, four thousand guilders and the chance to help a friend was looking like poor payment.

1 0

Sela and Hien escorted her to a small, windowless room whose sole furnishings were fat cushions strewn upon the floor. Then Sela left, and Hien sat smiling at Fiona, not speaking, until Sela returned with a teapot and a sizeable mug. She poured for Fiona, also not speaking, and watched with Hien until Fiona drained her cup. Then she poured another. Fiona said, "I need to use the facilities."

"Better not to until the vision is over," Hien said.

Fiona examined her face closely. Was this all a ruse to toy with the ignorant foreigner? But Hien's eyes were wide and guileless, so Fiona drank down the second cup. Her head began to swim, and Hien became blurry, her outline edged with rainbows in shades of black. Fiona set down the cup and closed her eyes against the dizziness. "I feel strange."

"Do not be afraid," Hien said, and Fiona felt her take her hand briefly. "You follow in Haran's footsteps."

She smelled lilacs, and swallowed; her throat was dry despite the two cups of tea. Distantly, she heard Sela say, *"This is a waste of time. She's not here for the right reasons. We should send her and her companions away."*

"*She deserves a chance, Sela, just as the others do,*" Hien replied. "*It's not our place to judge.*"

"*Of course it's our place to judge. We do it all the time.*"

"*You know what I mean. And I think there's no reason to be suspicious of her. What could she hope to gain by pretending to be interested in the festival?*"

"*I don't know. Does anyone know where her companions are?*"

Fiona quickly let out a moan, which shut the two women up. There was silence for a moment. "*I think—*" Sela began, and Fiona moaned again.

"The tree is the temple, but the temple is not the tree," she said in a low voice. "It all makes sense—"

Silence, and then the sound of wind rushing across miles of tall grass. Fiona opened her eyes and saw, not the tiny room, but the endless grassy plains of the Eidestal. Hien and Sela were gone. Fiona tried to stand, but her legs wouldn't obey her. She smelled the distant dry tickling odor of a grass fire, but when she turned her head, she saw nothing but blue summer sky. Moving her head made the scene sway, so she held still and said, "Am I here, or there?" Which made no more sense than any of this did.

In the distance, something tall and thin appeared, and as Fiona fought to bring her eyes to focus on it, it sped toward her so rapidly she cried out and threw her arms up to protect her face. Nothing struck her, and after a moment she lowered her hands and saw, two feet away, a skinny fir tree. Its needles were scant, but so dark a green as to be almost black against the sky, and there were stumps where branches had broken off halfway up the trunk. It seemed to be looking at her, and Fiona threw back her head and glared at it. "This is a vision, it's not real, and you can't frighten me."

The tree continued to look at her with an impassivity that made her struggle to rise again, to attack the tree and tear off a few more of its branches. She still couldn't stand. She shouted in fury and pushed off the ground—

"You were better at patience than this," said a familiar voice, and Fiona gasped. The tree's trunk wasn't wide enough to conceal a person, but the woman stepped out from behind it anyway. Her red ringlets shone in the sunlight, her eyes were warm and loving, and she came forward until she was only a few paces from Fiona.

"*Mother*," Fiona said. "Sweet heaven, is it really you?"

Mother shook her head. She looked so much younger than she had when Fiona had seen her last, wasted and ill. "It's a vision," she said, "and it's all in your mind. But sometimes your mind can tell you truths the waking world can't manage."

"You can't see heaven from earth," said another voice, and Fiona sucked in a breath, because her father had just emerged from the non-space behind the tree, looking just as young as her mother. "And we can't see you. Heaven only knows how Haran managed it."

"But you…" Fiona tasted tears and wiped them harshly away. She never cried. "Why am I seeing you? After what I didn't do?"

"Longing," said Mother. "Sorrow. Regret. It's not your time yet. Fiona, don't let yourself be alone."

"I don't have much choice, do I?" Her bitterness surprised her. "Do I?"

"You always have a choice," Father said. "You stayed too long with Roderick, but it hasn't destroyed your life, has it? And now you have an opportunity to start over. It's time for a change."

"What change?"

"You don't know, so we don't know either," Mother said. "But change is coming, and you can either make it your own or go on hiding from it. And we'll love you no matter what you decide."

"We're waiting for you, Fiona," Father said. He took Mother's hand. "For as long as it takes."

"Promise," Mother said.

The smell of grass fire was stronger suddenly, and dizziness struck Fiona hard, making the world swing like a pendulum. She closed her eyes and the dizziness lessened. Dimly, she realized her hands were clenched tightly in her lap, and she made herself relax, smoothing the robe over her knees. "It will be too long," she said, opening her eyes. The Eidestal, the tree, and Mother and Father were gone. Hien sat cross-legged a few paces from her, watching her intently.

It was like losing them all over again.

Grief, and fury, struck her hard in the chest, and she lurched at Hien, catching herself mid-lunge on her hands. She panted, feeling as if she'd run a mile without stopping. "What did you do to me?"

"You had another vision," Hien said, sounding pleased. "What did it mean?"

"I *don't know*," Fiona ground out. "I saw the Eidestal. I saw my dead. You tell me what it means."

Hien looked past her, toward Sela. "Do not," Sela said.

"I will not," Hien said. "But I can say that when you see the dead in vision, you should follow their instructions. That is the meaning."

Fiona thought back over what Mother and Father had said. "Change," she said. "Change, and a decision."

"Then seek change," Hien said. "Why are you not now in vision?"

"I don't know."

"*She's not being honest with us,*" Sela said. "*We should confine her. She won't know it's not part of the festival.*"

"*Be more compassionate,*" Hien said. "Rest here until suppertime," she said, "and meditate on your vision, so it becomes more clear to you." She stood and walked past Fiona. The door opened, then closed. Fiona settled herself on the cushion again. Sela's presence was a dark, ominous cloud filling the room. She silently cursed. No more exploring for her. Now she really did need to find Sebastian and warn him that at least a few people were suspicious of her and, by extension, him.

She closed her eyes and relived her vision. Was she really so lonely that her unconscious mind had conjured up the two people dearest to her? She didn't have time to be lonely. She was too busy worrying about Sebastian and the success of this mad adventure she'd fallen into. True, her longing for family was always at the back of her mind, but she never dwelt on it; that was a fool's errand, and Fiona Cooper was no fool. It was just all this talk of Haran and ungoverned heaven that had made her remember her lost loved ones and wonder what heaven was like for them.

She sat, letting her mind roam free, until Sela said, "Supper." Then she followed the woman back through the corridors and up the stairs to the landing, where they met dozens of women coming down, all clad in rose or teal or gold robes like Fiona's own. Sela gestured at the round room with an expression that said she didn't care if Fiona starved to death. Fiona gave her a cold, cutting stare and was pleased to see the woman recoil. She turned her back on Sela and followed the women into the room.

Robed women settled themselves at the trestle tables like butterflies coming to rest. Fiona found a seat off to one side, grateful not to be sitting on a cushion on the floor anymore. Her neighbors, a couple of Tremontanan women wearing teal, nodded and smiled at Fiona but didn't speak. Shy, or was this another expectation of the festival Fiona was once again not privy to?

Men and women clad in dull brown shirts and trousers moved through the room, carrying steaming bowls. The sound of their feet striking the floorboards, and the rustling of their clothes, were the only sounds in the room. Fiona leaned back as an elderly woman set a bowl in front of her. It was black kiln-fired ceramic, hot to the touch and filled with a thick soup that smelled of garlic and tomatoes. The smell woke Fiona's drug-dulled appetite, and she picked up her spoon and ate as rapidly as good manners would allow. Another server set down a chunk of heavy black bread Fiona used to mop up every drop of broth, washing it down with water that was warm and tasted strongly of minerals. It wasn't enough to satisfy the demands of her stomach, but there didn't seem to be any more forthcoming.

She looked around at the other women. Most of them were probably Veriboldan, though there were a handful of Eskandelics and several who were too pale not to be from northern Tremontane. They ate with little attention to their surroundings, and Fiona wondered what visions they'd had. No one sat very close together, but between the women and the servers, the room was full of bodies, and it was growing warm enough that Fiona felt herself relaxing. She hadn't realized she was tense. Sleep would be nice.

A hand took her bowl, and Fiona looked up to find Sebastian standing there, clad in brown like the other servitors. He was looking at her intently, as if he wished he could send a silent message into her brain. His other hand rested palm-down on the table, his fingers tapping urgently, and on a whim Fiona laid her hand atop his. Instantly his hand slid away, and Fiona felt the corners of a folded piece of paper. She swept it across the tabletop and into her lap. Sebastian nodded, the barest motion of his head, and walked away with her bowl and cup.

Fiona glanced at her neighbors. Neither of them were watching her; they were still intent on their food. Without looking down, she tucked the folded note tightly into the sleeve of her linen shirt. Her sleepiness was gone. She wanted to get to the privacy of her cell to find out what Sebastian had to communicate. Nothing good, she feared.

When all the tables were cleared, Hien stood on the walkway where everyone could easily see her. "*Haran fasted and prayed, and a vision was given to her,*" she said in Veriboldan. "*The vision of the tree became the reality of the tree. Tomorrow you will meditate on the reality of your vision. The doors of the Jaixante are open to you, but take care—not all visions are true. Use cunning and wisdom to know the difference.*"

Two more women repeated her words, one in Tremontanese, one in Eskandelic, then Hien clapped her hands three times and everyone around Fiona rose. Fiona hurried to her cell and, with the door shut safely behind her, unfolded Sebastian's note.

meet in this room when everyone's asleep. must talk. unexpected development.

She folded the note, then after a moment's thought set it on fire and let it burn to nothing. She rubbed the residue off on her inner sleeve. Unexpected development? That could be anything. At least Sebastian hadn't been caught doing anything he shouldn't, though she did wonder why he'd been pressed into serving duty. She sat on her pallet and waited.

The room was so still she could hear nothing but her own breathing and the distant thrumming of her pulse. How long should she wait before meeting Sebastian? Tired aches spread throughout her body, the remnants of the drug, probably. The other festival attendees would likely feel as tired as she did, so they'd be asleep quickly, but there was no way to know how long it would take the priestesses to settle in for the night.

She stood and went to the window. It was full dark, and the lights of Haizea made its walls and roofs glow. The one bridge visible from her window stretched in a silver line across the dark waters of the Kepa River. Fiona leaned her forehead against the cool glass, wishing she were in a position to better see the Jaixante, with its masses of colored jewel-like lights. *Change is coming*, Mother had said—no, that hadn't been Mother, it had been her mind trying to communicate with her. What change did she anticipate without knowing it consciously? This adventure had already turned out to be more than she expected. If something else was coming, Fiona wasn't sure she welcomed it.

11

When the moon finally rose, Fiona removed her bright robe and turned off the lamp. She crept down the hall in the darkness, feeling her way to the stairwell. Moonlight illuminated it faintly, enough to keep her from tripping and rolling all the way to the bottom, which would hurt and leave her in an embarrassing position if she broke something. She heard nothing, sensed nothing but the smell of cold stone and, as she descended, the tang of garlic and tomatoes from supper.

The door to the eating hall was ajar. Fiona pushed it open slowly and slipped inside. A bluish glow from near the ceiling revealed tiny windows she hadn't noticed before. Moonlight barely illuminated the tables, which looked even more like funeral biers in the gloom.

A shadow detached itself from the wall and came toward her. "Miss Cooper?"

"Sebastian," Fiona said, feeling unexpectedly relieved at the sound of his voice. "Were you waiting long?"

"Not very." Sebastian still wasn't more than a shadow, even right next to her, a shadow with gleaming teeth and eyes. "They shut everything down a few hours after sunset, and the priestesses go into the temple for prayers. This is as safe a room as any to meet, but we probably shouldn't take too long. How was your day? The other attendants, the ones who've been here before, say everyone has visions, but I couldn't tell if that was true or metaphor."

"They give you a drug that induces visions, yes. But I don't know what it means."

"Does it have to mean something? It can't be real if it's drug-induced."

Sometimes your mind can tell you truths the waking world can't manage. "I'm not sure it matters. What about you?"

"Complete waste of the day. They put us to work cleaning and doing laundry and preparing food because all their regular servants are busy preparing for the Election, which happens a couple of weeks after the festival. We never got a chance to go into the Jaixante."

"What did you intend to do?"

"The foreign trade ministry has offices in the Jaixante. I'd planned to say you needed something Tremontanan, something they might reasonably have imported, and go there to collect it. That probably wouldn't gain me access to Gizane's private rooms, but it would tell me where to look when Holt and I make the actual snatch later. But it doesn't look like I'm going to get the chance."

"So you need a different plan."

"I do."

The doors of the Jaixante are open to you. "Maybe I can go," Fiona said.

"I doubt it. You're watched even more closely than we are. No, Holt and I will have to sneak out later tonight and hope we aren't caught and hung up by our ears, or whatever it is Veriboldans do to sneak thieves."

"It's too dangerous. And I have a better idea." It was coming to her slowly, like the rising tide. "Tomorrow we're meant to meditate on our visions. We each have these jade pendants to use in our meditations. Suppose I tell them my vision specifically showed me something different I need to focus on? Something Tremontanan? I can ask them to send you to find it, and you can go to Gizane's offices to get it."

"Like what?" Sebastian sounded skeptical.

"A watch. A Tremontanan Device. Veribold doesn't make their own Devices, and their watches are all mechanical. The only place in the Jaixante likely to have watch Devices is the foreign trade office. That should get you in the door, at least."

"What if one of these priestesses has one?"

"Then we'll have to make a different plan. I know it's a stretch, but it's no more foolish than you and Holt sneaking in with no idea of where you're going."

"It's a measure of how desperate I am that I'm willing to try it." Sebastian sighed. "This was always a fool's errand. I'm sorry I dragged you into it."

"Hardly that. I volunteered, remember?"

"You did." He favored her with his sardonic smile. "So I'm not the only fool."

"I don't know that it's foolishness to want to protect your family, even if you don't like your brother much."

"Sometimes I wonder if he's worth protecting. But I suppose it's really the rest of the family I'm doing this for. Typical of D—of my brother, that he'd get himself into trouble that will spill over onto the rest of us."

He was smiling, but his hazel eyes were dark and serious. Fiona said, "Was it that bad, what he did?"

He shrugged. "I don't actually know what hold the blackmailer has on him. Just that she's slowly bankrupting my parents on his behalf, and at some point, when the money's gone, she'll reveal all."

"Then why don't they call her bluff now? At least then they'd still have something."

"I'm told that's impossible. My older brother pretends none of it is happening, my younger brother acts like he's done nothing wrong... they're both stupid in their own special way."

"So how did you end up the way you are?"

Sebastian chuckled. "Stubborn, secretive, and independent?"

"The kind of man who'd risk his freedom for the sake of people who don't respect him."

"Meaning the Veriboldans are likely to lock me up if I'm caught pilfering their most important city? You have a knack for turning a reprimand into a compliment, Miss Cooper."

"Fiona," Fiona said. "I think you should call me Fiona. Since we're likely to be locked up together."

He smiled. "I certainly hope so. I'll want your perspective on the proceedings when we're hauled up in front of whatever Veriboldans have for courts. I suppose you know what that is."

"I do, but it won't cheer you up if I tell you."

"Of course not." Sebastian sighed. "I don't know what made the difference between me and my brothers. Possibly being sent away to school during my formative years. The influence of my Great-Uncle Sebastian, who's as good a man as you can be without actually entering heaven. I'd like to think I'm inherently prone to see things from the other fellow's side. School gave me a different perspective."

"I can imagine." Her inherent magic certainly made her see the world differently. "Your brothers are lucky you're not like them. I'm guessing if you were the one in trouble, they wouldn't be so ready to put themselves out."

"Oh, they might, if they thought it would protect the family name." Sebastian paused, then added, "Which I still can't tell you."

"You know I'll eventually guess, if they're politically prominent enough to be worth blackmailing."

"It's a risk I'm willing to take." He sighed. "I suppose I should be grateful this hasn't happened to my family before, but my stores of gratitude are running low. Mostly I'm imagining going back to Tremontane when this is all over. What do you plan to do?"

The question, so abrupt, startled her. "I...suppose I'll continue on to Dineh-Karit."

"As you'd planned, I remember. You never said whether there was something waiting there for you."

"It was supposed to be an adventure. Somewhere entirely new."

"That certainly qualifies. I've never been that far south. Went to Umberan, a few times, for the holidays." He leaned against the wall. "I hear Dineh-Karit's nearly as rich in lines of power as Tremontane."

"Maybe you should visit, and find out."

"Maybe I should." He smiled. "Maybe our paths will cross again, after this."

We should travel together almost escaped Fiona's lips; she managed to smile and nod. Had she nearly invited him to go south with her? What was she *thinking*? He was a friend, true, but that had felt... almost intimate. "You're not so bad, for a filthy kidnapper," she said with a friendly wink, and he laughed, then covered his mouth as if he could hold back the sound.

"I have to say I'm really glad I failed to kidnap Lucille," he said. "She was a chatterbox and not nearly so interesting as you."

"Well, for my part, I'm almost glad to have been kidnapped," Fiona said.

"You are a strange woman, Fiona Cooper. When this is all over—"

"What?"

"Nothing. I promised I wouldn't pry, much as I'd love to know your secrets." He took a step closer, bringing him near enough that she could feel his breath on her cheeks. "Tell me something. One thing you haven't told anyone else."

He was close enough to touch. "Why should I do that?" she asked, feeling unexpectedly breathless.

"Because I want to know you better. Just one thing."

There was only one thing she was hiding from him, and it was the one thing she dared never tell anyone. "If you'll tell me your family name," she said, stalling.

"That's not my secret to tell."

"Neither is mine." It made no sense, and she regretted her words. What was it about the darkness, and his nearness, that had lowered her reserve? She waited, holding her breath, for whatever he might say next. But he was silent.

Finally, he said, "You're easily the most interesting person I've ever met, Fiona. I don't want to intrude on your privacy."

"Thank you." Her heart was beating a little too rapidly. "I'm making myself seem more mysterious than I am."

"That seems unlikely. And now that we're both profoundly uncomfortable, shall we call it a night? I'll wait for your summons tomorrow, and if we're lucky, they'll let me into the foreign trade office."

It felt like a release. "Of course," Fiona said. "And it will work. Trust me."

"After what I've seen, I'd believe you could talk birds out of the trees. Veriboldan birds, who are so snooty they only whistle in three-quarter time." Sebastian grinned at her. "Good night, Fiona, and good luck."

"To both of us," Fiona said.

She hurried back up the stairs, conscious of how exposed she was —there was nowhere to hide on the long flight, not even a window casing—but met no one. Probably Sebastian was right, and the priestesses were all within the temple, praying.

Back in her room, she went to press her face against the cold window. She felt uncomfortably warm. It was the exertion of hurrying up the steps that did it. That, and the warmth of her clothes. Nothing more.

Oh, you great liar, she told herself. Even now, remembering the conversation with Sebastian left her warm and muddled inside. All those years of anger and resentment of her husband had left her vulnerable to the first man who came along—the first friendly, clever, attractive man, because she wasn't this forthcoming with Holt. She *could not* tell Sebastian the truth about her inherent magic, and yet she'd come right up to the edge of what she dared say just minutes before. She was a fool.

She lay down on her pallet and closed her eyes. They would retrieve Gizane's information, Sebastian would pay her, and she would bid him goodbye and head south. End of story, end of relation-ship. Anything else was chimerical, a delusion born of, she could admit to herself, loneliness. She wished to be back in that vision, to have just five minutes' conversation with her mother, who had always been good at seeing to the heart of a problem. Five minutes' conversation with *herself* would be almost as good.

Despite her mental turmoil, her body began to relax. Sleep would at least give her some respite from the confusion she couldn't seem to shake. Sebastian could be a friend without her spilling all her best-kept secrets to him. She had plenty of experience with that kind of friendship. *I don't need any other kind*, she thought, and drifted off to sleep.

Snow sifted down from the sky, covering the cobbles with white, slick flakes. Fiona's steps left no trace in the drifting snow. Houses rose above her on both sides of the street, tall enough to extend into the sky past the limits of her vision. She was alone on the street, and the houses were dark, without the gleam of candle or lantern that might indicate inhabitants.

Something was wrong. She didn't know what, but a sense of urgency crept over her, a need to stop something from happening. Her feet moved faster, and then she was running, slipping on the cobbles and catching herself before she could fall.

Ahead, a short, ramshackle house crouched at the end of the street, its windows dark and blank and its door ajar. She pelted toward it, threw the door open fully, and stumbled into the dark hall beyond. It was her childhood home now, with a small entry chamber off which three doors opened. Her father stood opposite her, his left hand holding a shovel, his right hand holding a bucket. Fiona didn't stop to puzzle this out. She lurched forward, and just as fire blossomed on her father's wrist, she closed her hand over it, extinguished it—

and she pulled herself out of the dream, gasping and sweaty. That had been close. She curled in on herself, shaking with the intensity of the dream. She'd stopped the fire. He hadn't burned. She hadn't woken to find her bed in flames. How careless she'd been, letting her daydreams about Sebastian distract her from performing her nightly ritual. Tears spilled over her cheeks that she didn't wipe away, feeling obscurely that they were a penance of sorts, a reminder that she had to be constantly on guard if she didn't want to give herself away.

She couldn't change the past by saving her father in dreams, she knew, but the dreams indicated that some part of her believed otherwise. If only life were that simple. She closed her fists as if daring the fire to return, and eventually fell asleep.

here was breakfast the next morning, thank heaven, not drugged tea but bowls of unsweetened porridge Fiona tried to feel grateful for. She sat in the same seat in the eating hall next to two silent women, one of whom smiled at her when a brown-clad servant took their empty bowls. The only light came from the tiny windows high above, and the room was mostly in shadow. Fiona covertly examined the other women, wondering what had brought each of them to the Irantzen Temple. Some sat with their eyes closed, their lips moving slightly, probably in prayer. Others looked around as curiously as Fiona did, though more openly. It would be interesting to speak with them, possibly during the great feast at the end of the festival—no, they might not even be there for that. She'd never asked Sebastian whether his plan involved sneaking away in the dead of night or walking out openly.

"*This is a day of purification and meditation,*" Hien said, and a rustle of fabric went up as every woman in the room moved to face her. "*You will be washed clean, and then you will meditate on the vision you received yesterday. Remember Haran, how she came to an understanding of her vision after many days. You may not receive a full understanding in this day, but as Haran taught, the act of meditating is itself a blessing. Return to your cells, and someone will call for you."*

The words were repeated in Tremontanese and Eskandelic, but Fiona was off her seat the moment the third speaker finished. She pushed past brightly-robed women to where Hien stood on the circling platform. "I have a request," she said.

Hien looked down at her. "Yes?"

"My vision," Fiona lied. "In it, I'm holding a watch Device and I can see source—magical power—spiraling into it. I feel strongly that I need that watch as a focus for my meditation."

"You have the *toan* jade," Hien said. "We cannot make exceptions."

"I'm not asking for an exception for me, but for my vision. And it's such a small thing. It's just..." Fiona cast her eyes down as if embarrassed. "It was so hard for me to see a vision yesterday, I don't want to disregard any of its instructions. Please."

Hien glanced at Sela, who'd drifted toward their conversation. Fiona kept her expression calm and respectful. Sela was starting to annoy her. "I'm sure my attendants can find a Device somewhere in the Jaixante," she added.

"You should go to your cell and wait," Sela said. "You do not need a Device."

"We have many watches here in the temple," Hien said.

"No, it has to be a Tremontanan watch Device," Fiona said. "Though Veriboldan mechanical watches are superior in many ways." Too much? She watched Sela out of the corner of her eye and saw her lips thin.

"You're not seriously considering this," Sela said to Hien. *"We don't need to coddle the foreigner. She can meditate like the rest."*

"She made a great effort to come here, and to stay here," Hien said. *"It's a small thing.* We'll send someone to find a Device for you," she told Fiona. "Go to your cell and wait."

"You shouldn't inconvenience your people," Fiona said. "My attendants can go. Besides, they'll know to pick the best one. I feel strongly that it should be a well-crafted Device."

"No Veriboldan will treat with a foreigner," Sela said.

"Don't you have an office of foreign trade?" Fiona said, going for cheery helpfulness. "They must be used to dealing with foreigners. Please, I really don't want to inconvenience any of the temple attendants. They must be busy. Isn't the Election coming up soon?"

Hien regarded her with a long, cool look, and Fiona felt she might have overplayed her hand. Then she said, "We will send one of your attendants. But if he is turned away, you will meditate like the others."

"That's fair. Thank you."

"*You're too soft,*" Sela muttered as Fiona turned away.

"*She has something more in mind than meditation,*" Hien replied, and Fiona slowed her steps, trying to listen. "*Why insist on her own man running the errand? We should...*" and then Fiona was too far away to hear any more. She ran up the stairs to her cell and dropped to her knees on the pallet. She might have just exposed them all to greater scrutiny. Well, it wasn't as if she'd had much choice. Everything depended on Sebastian or Holt entering the foreign trade office instead of a Temple servant. She'd just have to be a model of decorum from this time forward, allay their suspicions, and hope Sebastian figured out a way to retrieve the documents quickly.

It felt like about half an hour before someone knocked at her door. A Tremontanan woman in white shirt and trousers beckoned to her to come. "Underclothing and hairbrush," she whispered when Fiona stood. Fiona tucked the objects into one of the wide sleeves of her golden robe and followed the woman down the stairs, past the eating hall and the ground floor to another flight of stairs descending into the smoky dimness of a torch-lit hall.

Fiona kept one hand on the wall to steady herself. The stairs curved sharply on themselves, their dark stone cool and slick underfoot, and she slowed, afraid of falling and knocking herself and the woman all the way down the spiral to the bottom. She could hear echoes, not just of their footsteps but of voices, just at the edge of her perception. She strained to hear them, but heard nothing but mad laughter coming from ahead and behind and both sides. She stopped, and said, "Wait."

"It's nothing," the woman said. "The way the water echoes sounds like laughter. You don't have to be afraid."

"I'm not afraid," Fiona lied. "Just...curious."

"Then come with me, and you'll have your curiosity satisfied." The woman proceeded down the stairs. Fiona took a deep breath and followed her.

They came out in a tunnel, cool and damp and smelling of old stone, and Fiona took in a deep, slow breath and released it. She refused to cringe away from the walls; the tunnel was just stone, and would not close in on her, even though the ceiling was short enough she could touch it with an outstretched arm. Holt would have to crouch to walk through it. It curved like a switchback mountain pass, following some contour invisible to Fiona, who kept her gaze fixed on the priestess's back. The stone pressed down on her, weighing her down. If the ceiling collapsed, how long would she lie there, unable to see or move or breathe?

She felt the open space, heard running water, before she and her guide stepped out of the tunnel. She took a few too-hasty steps, almost running into the woman before controlling herself. The cavern was blessedly large, too large for the torches to fully light, and she could imagine it opening to a starless night sky except that it still smelled of stone and, now, of water. The rough floor felt comfortable against her bare feet, though part of her wearily wondered if these people had ever heard of rugs.

She couldn't see the source of the running water, but it sounded like it was flowing over the stone like a waterfall. At the center of the room lay a square pool, surrounded on all sides by a black marble ledge that glimmered in the torchlight. The water was dark and slopped the edges as if something were stirring it. Four women dressed in white, unadorned gowns stood near the pool, all of them watching her. It was like facing four statues, they were that unmoving.

Fiona's guide put out a hand to stop her. "Haran, having accepted her vision, wishes to purify herself to gain greater understanding," she said.

One of the white-robed women stepped forward. "Wash, and be clean," she said in thickly accented Tremontanese, and gestured into the darkness. Fiona's guide took a torch from a stand near the pool and walked away. Fiona hurried to follow her.

The wall of the chamber wasn't as far away as Fiona had thought, only a few dozen paces into the darkness. It bulged as if straining against the weight of the stone pressing down on it, and Fiona's heart beat faster for a few seconds before she controlled herself. Water sheeted down the face of the stone and disappeared into an iron grate set into the floor, some of it slicking the wall, the rest pouring out like a waterfall from a few feet above Fiona's head.

Her guide gestured with her free hand at a table that looked as if it had come from someone's sitting room. A bar of soap lay atop it, and below that were a couple of empty shelves. Fiona glanced at the white-clad women, but none of them were watching her, and her guide just stood patiently holding the torch. Fiona disrobed. She wasn't self-conscious about her body, but it had been a while since she'd been naked in front of anyone but Roderick. She shivered as she laid her folded clothing on the table; the spray from the waterfall spattered her, chilling her. She picked up the bar of soap and stepped under the water.

Sweet merciful heaven, it was *cold*. Fiona bit back a shriek and soaped herself as rapidly as she could. Cold, cold, *cold*. She rinsed quickly and stepped away from the spray. "Hair, too," the guide whispered, and Fiona groaned and ducked her head under the water. She was numb enough it had started to feel almost warm. She scrubbed, rinsed, and darted away from the frigid water, dashing water from her skin and rubbing feeling back into her arms.

Her guide handed her the torch. "Haran approaches the well," she announced, and made a little shooing gesture. Fiona walked back toward the women at the pool, holding the torch as close as she dared so its heat would warm her face. She shivered again and tried to control herself.

The women didn't look at her when she arrived, shuddering and wishing she had a bathrobe, or a towel, or even a handkerchief. Fiona set the torch back in its holder and waited. The moment stretched out. One of the women made a tiny gesture in the direction of the pool, and Fiona abruptly realized they were waiting for her. Squatting, with both hands on the marble ledge, she swung one foot over and into the pool, feeling for the bottom.

The pool was as warm as the waterfall had been cold, not quite enough to steam but more than enough to relax her shivering muscles. Her questing foot found the bottom of the pool almost immediately; the water was just more than waist high on her, and she sank into it happily, bending her knees to let it cover her to her collarbone. She saw the same woman frown and shake her head. Quickly she stood and crossed her arms over her breasts. Heaven forbid anyone should have a little pleasure around here.

"Haran enters the well," one of the women said. "She is made clean and washed free of impurities. She is prepared to look on heaven's wisdom."

There was silence again, broken only by the sound of water rushing over stone. "You can get out now," said the frowning woman after a long moment.

Fiona scrambled out of the pool. The frowning woman handed her a towel. "Dry, and we will dress you," she said. Fiona could hear the words she wasn't saying: *heaven save me from ignorant foreigners.*

Fiona rubbed herself vigorously, as much for warmth as for dryness. Then she stood and let the women manipulate her like a life-sized doll into clean underclothes and new linen shirt and trousers, white this time, with the gold robe over it all. She managed not to cry out as one of the women dragged her brush through her hair, catching on every tangle. Maybe it was time to cut it again.

Then they returned the hairbrush to her, and Fiona followed her guide back up the steps, all the way to her cell. Fiona tingled with cleanness and the remembered shock of the cold water. Everything felt sharper, more alive—the feel of the stone under her feet, the air brushing her cheeks, the chilly dampness of her wet hair hanging halfway down her back. It was unlikely Haran had undergone that ritual—where was she going to find a waterfall in the Eidestal?—but as a symbol, it was potent.

She saw it immediately she pushed open the door to her cell: a palm-sized Tremontanan pocket watch Device, lying in the middle of her pallet. She snatched it up and opened it; it was empty. She closed it again and held it in her two cupped hands, close to her heart. This didn't mean Sebastian had succeeded, just that someone had found her a watch. It didn't even have to have come from the foreign trade office. And yet...no, Sebastian likely wouldn't have left her a note, if he'd been the one to bring it, because it would be too easy for someone else to open the watch and discover it. So that was no evidence.

Fiona sat on her pallet and closed her eyes, letting her hands clasping the watch fall into her lap. There was nothing for it but to wait until supper, when she might see Sebastian again. And hope he'd accomplished his goal.

She sat cross-legged on her pallet until dinner arrived, a wedge of thick yellow cheese and a slab of bread and more of the mineral-tasting water. It was filling but boring. Her mind drifted toward food, hot steak cooked rare in the middle, bowls of thick creamy broccoli soup, masses of sautéed onions on bread hot with melted cheese, rich dark chocolate cake served with cream... She made herself trace the outline of the watch, wishing she hadn't had to lie. If she were going to pretend to meditate, it would be nicer to use the pendant they'd given her. How did one meditate, anyway?

The surface of the watch wasn't perfectly smooth, but had a raised pattern of interlocking spirals molded into it. She could just barely feel the edges. She traced their outline and thought about her vision. Change was coming. More change than she'd already had, with divorcing her husband, leaving her family, and setting out on this new life? *Don't let yourself be alone*, Mother had said. That was pure foolishness. She'd settle down somewhere, make new friends. She never had to be alone.

But that wasn't what Mother had meant. She'd been talking about true friendship, the kind that didn't have to hide anything. And that was a different kind of foolishness. Wanting someone she could be totally honest with, someone she could share her inherent magic with, was stupid. Sharing that knowledge with anyone else was dangerous, and she didn't know anyone she trusted that much.

Not Sebastian, she told herself. She barely knew the man, and he had his own problems. But she couldn't help remembering the night before, and how close she'd come to telling him...what? Something far too private for their fledgling friendship, that's what. Maybe that's what the vision meant—a warning that she was becoming careless. *Don't let yourself be alone* might mean something more like *Don't let your loneliness get to you.* She wasn't lonely; she had a whole new life to begin.

A quiet rap sounded at the door. "It is supper," Hien said. "Did you meditate well?"

"I think so." Fiona set the watch Device on the little chest. "How will I know?"

"We will discuss tomorrow, and see." Hien withdrew, shutting the door behind her.

Fiona left the watch in her cell and went to supper with the rest of the women. The room smelled deliciously of beef, but the portion they were served, diced small and pan-fried with vegetables in that uniquely Veriboldan fishy-tasting sauce, was far too small. Fiona was sure Haran hadn't gone this hungry on her own journey, though as she'd had to carry all her supplies with her, maybe that was false.

She pushed shreds of meat around in her bowl while she searched the room for Sebastian. Instead, she saw Holt approaching at a saunter, casually collecting bowls on the tray he held. She pretended not to notice him and rose, dish in hand, as if looking for someone to give it to. In a handful of quick strides he was at her side, taking the bowl from her.

"This room, after dark," he murmured, took empty dishes from her neighbors, and was gone again. Fiona sat down and thrummed her fingers on the table. She saw Hien watching her and let her gaze continue to travel the room as if she hadn't noticed. Standing like that might have been a mistake, but better than letting her neighbors overhear what sounded like an assignation. Did other women leave their rooms at night for trysts with their attendants, or someone else's attendants? If they did, she hadn't seen them, but how careless of her not to have thought of the possibility before.

Sela stepped up to where everyone could see her and cleared her throat, an indelicate sound like a rasp on metal. "*Tomorrow we will meet for discussion and instruction,*" she said. "*We will discuss the nature of your visions and how they relate to Haran's experience. This will prepare you to enter heaven on the following day. Sleep well, and may heaven guide your dreams.*"

Fiona stilled her hands and sat patiently as the words were repeated, then waited to let her table companions leave before rising and following them out the door. There was no need for her to hurry. It would be a few hours before full dark, and there was nothing she could do but wait. She caught Hien's eye again and smiled. The priestess nodded, but didn't smile back. Suspicious, or just tired? Also something Fiona could do nothing about.

She lay on her pallet, playing with the watch, until the moon rose, then silently left her room and crept down the hall toward the stairs. Her cold, bare feet made almost no noise on the steps, and her new white linen clothes made her less conspicuous against the white stone of the stairwell than the black had. Despite her caution, she grinned. This must be what being a thief felt like.

Then she heard it—steps, louder than hers, farther down the stairs. Growing louder. Fiona turned around fast, lost her balance, and fell, a few steps only, but enough that by the time she scrambled to her feet, Hien was there. She looked at Fiona with a neutral expression, the face of someone considering her options.

Fiona said nothing. In situations like this, it was smart to let the other person speak first, reveal what *she* thought was going on.

"There is a curfew," Hien finally said. "Or is this another thing you do not know?"

"I hoped it would be all right if no one saw me," Fiona said.

"Thanks to watchful heaven, there is never a time when no one sees you." Hien had her arms crossed and her hands tucked into her sleeves. "There are also rules about..." She bit her lip, looking for the right word. "About sex."

"I know. It wasn't for sex. I forgot to return this to my attendant." Fiona displayed the watch. "It's probably valuable, and I'm sure he only borrowed it. I didn't know if I'd see him tomorrow morning, so I thought I'd hurry down and give it to him to return to wherever he got it."

Hien pursed her lips. "That is a good story that I do not believe," she said. "I came now to see if you were in your room. If you break the rules, we can send you away."

"No, please don't!" Fiona closed her hand tightly on the watch. "I meant well. I wasn't trying to break the rules. My attendants are just that—not romantic partners at all."

"Then tell me the truth." Hien held out her hand. "Why the watch? Why your attendant?"

Fiona breathed out slowly. "My attendant has always wanted to see the Jaixante," she said. "He came with me in the hope of being allowed inside. But, of course, we stay within the Irantzen Temple while we're here. When I had the vision of the watch, it gave me the idea to send him out looking for one. I thought it would help him fulfil his dream. Tonight I...just wanted to hear how it went. I was impatient. I could have waited until the festival was over, but I was curious. I'm sorry."

Hien continued to hold out her hand. Fiona gave her the watch. She examined it closely, running her fingers over the ridges of the design. "That is a better story," she said, "and one that should see you expelled from the festival. You should not lie about your visions."

"I didn't lie. I saw the watch," Fiona lied. "It gave me the idea. And it helped my meditation, so that wasn't a lie, either."

Hien made a "hmph" sound. "Return to your room, and do not leave it again tonight," she said. "I have given you much leeway, Fiona Cooper, and I do not trust you, but I believe you will benefit from this festival and I do not want to send you away if that is the case. I will see that this watch is returned."

It took Fiona a moment to realize she'd been dismissed. "Thank you," she said, and went back up the stairs. Hien followed her like an uncomfortable shadow.

Back in her room, Fiona went to the window and looked out over Haizea and the Jaixante, and cursed. If Sebastian's information was important, she couldn't afford to be stuck here all night. On the other hand, if she was caught wandering the halls of the Irantzen Temple again, they'd all be kicked out and Sebastian's plan, whatever it now was, would fail. She cursed again and went to sit on the pallet. She didn't have much choice.

She sat there, listening to the sound of her breathing, until she couldn't stand it any longer. When she opened her door, Hien sat across the hall, her legs folded into what looked like an uncomfortable position, her eyes closed. Fiona took a step out of the room, and Hien's eyes opened and focused on her. Fiona indicated by gestures that she needed to relieve herself, and stepped into the little room, cursing some more. Hien really didn't trust her, which showed how smart Hien was.

She returned to her cell and lay down on the pallet to sleep. They'd just have to think of something else.

13

Fiona saw Sebastian immediately on entering the eating hall the next morning. He bore a tray filled with steaming bowls of porridge, like the other servants, but despite that and his brown clothing he moved confidently, like a lord playing dress-up. Fiona took her seat and watched him draw nearer. She had no idea how to approach him without drawing Hien's attention; Hien was looking elsewhere at the moment, but that could quickly change. Fiona folded her hands on the table in front of her and waited.

Sebastian placed the last of his bowls long before he reached her, but continued in her direction. Fiona pretended not to notice him, keeping her eyes on Hien. Then, as Sebastian reached the end of Fiona's table, he stumbled and went to one knee. The tray skidded across the floor and ended up at Fiona's feet. She bent to pick it up and found herself facing Sebastian, also reaching for the tray. With his other hand he clasped hers swiftly, and she felt smooth paper glide across her palm. Then he'd retrieved the tray and was moving on. The whole thing had taken no more than three seconds.

Fiona tucked the note into her sleeve and began eating the gluey, unappetizing mess. What she wouldn't give for poached eggs on toast, or crisp bacon, or even a dish of stewed peaches. When this was over, she was going to buy the biggest, most delicious meal she could find, and she was going to savor it. No, she'd make Sebastian buy it. She doubted he and the other servants had to suffer such dietary restrictions.

"Today you will be instructed on the nature of heaven and your visions," Sela said. Fiona grimaced. The idea of being lectured all day when she didn't know what Sebastian had learned wearied her. She took another bite of porridge. It was going to sit like lead in her stomach, she was sure of it. Her next bite was too large, and she gagged on it before forcing it down. That made her pause, laying her spoon down in her half-finished porridge. It was a stupid idea, but it would get her some privacy, if only for a short while.

She picked up her spoon and fiddled with it. "Oh, I don't feel very well," she murmured. One of her neighbors, a Veriboldan woman, looked at her curiously, but by her expression she didn't speak Tremontanese. Fiona laid her spoon down again and rubbed her stomach. "I really don't feel well," she repeated, then picked up the spoon and took another incautiously large bite. She closed her lips, took a quick breath, and jabbed the back of her throat with the spoon.

She must have hated the porridge more than she knew, because her stomach immediately convulsed, and she yanked the spoon out of the way as she vomited the porridge back onto the table. Both her neighbors cried out and shied away from her as she gagged, vomited again, and clutched the table to keep herself steady. More noise arose as nearby women exclaimed and stood to see what was happening. Panting, Fiona pushed her hair back from her face and tried not to react to the stench of bile and oats puddling on the table in front of her.

"What is happening?" Hien was beside her, crouching to look into her face.

"I just...didn't feel well...I'm so sorry," Fiona said.

"Excuse me," Sebastian said, "let me just take—"

"Back to your duties," Sela said.

"I'm a doctor," Sebastian said, and Fiona had to hide a laugh at how scornful he sounded. "And she's my responsibility."

He took Fiona's hand in his warm, dry one and placed his other hand on her forehead. She closed her eyes and tried to breathe normally, ignoring the stench. "She has no fever," Sebastian finally said, and Fiona opened her eyes to discover him addressing Hien. "She ate too quickly. She needs only to rest somewhere for a few minutes, to make sure she won't vomit again."

"No one else will be ill?" Hien said. She looked alarmed.

"Unlikely. This is not uncommon for her. I'll sit with her and monitor her condition."

"We do not have time," Sela said. "The day's activities will begin soon."

"Better this not happen again," Hien said. "But you are not allowed into the temple. Sela, take Fiona to one of the small rooms where she can change her clothes and be treated. Then, doctor, you will return to your duties. This should not interfere with Fiona's instruction."

"I'm sorry," Fiona said.

"It is illness, and no one's fault," Hien said. "The rest of us will wait here."

Fiona felt Sebastian's hand on her elbow, supporting her, and she leaned heavily on him as they followed Sela's rigid back out of the eating hall. They went down the stairs and through the passages to a windowless room with a couple of Veriboldan basin-chairs and a vase filled with long, wide blades of striped grass that smelled spicy. All the walls were lined with cupboards that went to the ceiling. Sela went to one of them and pulled out a stack of white linen, then a teal robe. She handed the pile to Fiona. "Your man will wait outside," she said, holding the door open and glaring at Sebastian. He smiled his crooked smile, shook his head, and left, followed by Sela.

Fiona immediately stripped out of her spattered clothes and dressed. She wondered, as she put it on, why she hadn't been given another gold robe, then decided she didn't care. Probably the colors didn't mean anything. She bundled the stained, smelly clothes into a ball and set it in the corner, then cracked open the door. A few seconds later, Sebastian entered. "We don't need an audience," he told Sela, who reddened. She snatched up the ball of stinking clothes and slammed the door behind her.

"Sweet heaven," Sebastian said. "I can't believe you did that. No, actually I can believe you did that, but—"

"We don't have much time," Fiona said. "Hien suspects me of…I'm not sure what. Of having some sinister purpose in being here, I think, and of course she's totally right. She watched my door all night and I couldn't get away. What did you learn?"

Sebastian tried to sit in one of the basin chairs, then gave up. "I was able to enter the foreign trade office. It's not too far from here and isn't a very big building. So that's two things in our favor. But those are the only two. There are a dozen smaller offices, all of them crammed with paperwork, and they're all labeled in Veriboldan so I couldn't even identify which office belongs to Gizane. It's also a very busy office, and I was watched carefully the whole time I was there. If I hadn't been wearing the brown of a temple servant, there's no way I'd have gotten inside."

"So you'll have to go at night, when everyone's gone home."

"No, *we'll* have to go at night. I need someone who can read Veriboldan to narrow down the search. You'll have to sneak out of the temple with us tonight. Holt to break us in, you to find the right office, me to identify the papers."

"I told you, Hien's suspicious. I don't think I can get away."

"You'll have to, or that's the end of it."

Fiona deftly hopped into a chair and pulled her legs up. "Where do I meet you?"

"There's a small door around the corner from the main doors. The main doors only open for ceremonies, so they use the small door for normal traffic. It's locked at night, but that's not a problem for Holt."

"Holt's proving remarkably versatile for a manservant."

Sebastian grinned. "He wasn't always a manservant. Anyway, we'll meet there at full dark, raid the office, and be back in our beds before anyone notices we're gone."

"You are far too optimistic. I can think of half a dozen ways this can go wrong."

"Really? I came up with seventeen. The trouble is, there's not much we can do to minimize the risk short of giving up, so we'll just have to see what happens and adapt accordingly. I realize I'm asking a lot—"

"I'm already involved, aren't I?"

"Yes, but until now you haven't done anything except fake a vision. What I'm asking you to do now could get you thrown in prison."

The chair felt like a throne, tall and commanding the room. "I'm confident it won't come to that."

Sebastian shrugged. "You can't say I didn't offer you an out. Thank you, Fiona. I'd say my family thanks you, but they'd probably hate that you know their weakness."

"I'm not doing this for them. I'm doing it to help a friend," Fiona said.

"You—" Sebastian stepped closer to the chair and took her hand. "I am *very* glad," he said, "you're not Lucille."

His grip was firm, and Fiona squeezed his hand lightly before removing hers. She hopped off the chair. "I'll meet you tonight."

Hien was waiting outside the room when they emerged. "You are well?" she said. Her hands were clasped tightly in front of her, twisting slowly.

"I'm so sorry to be a burden," Fiona said.

"You will come with me," Hien said. She took Fiona's elbow and marched her rapidly away, her grip tight and insistent. Fiona flung a quick look backward over her shoulder at Sebastian, but he could only shrug and shake his head.

They ended up in the pyramidal room, which was now empty of furniture. Its white walls gleamed yellow in the torchlight, disorienting Fiona. She knew it was still morning, but it might have been any time of the day or night in that angular, uncomfortable room. "You are not here to worship," Hien said. "Tell me the truth."

"Why would you say that? Of course I'm here to worship," Fiona said.

Hien made a snorting noise of dismissal. "You know nothing of the festival. You know nothing of the rites. You try to sneak about in the night and you ask for exceptions that set you apart from the others. You want something from this festival that is not what we offer, and I demand you tell me what that is. I should make you leave."

"Then why don't you?"

"I have instincts that tell me you need to be here. Tell me those instincts are not wrong."

Guilt struck Fiona hard enough that she forgot to breathe for a moment. She'd gone this whole time thinking of the Irantzen Festival as a means to an end and only now did it occur to her that for everyone else, this was a religious experience. She was lucky heaven didn't strike her down where she stood. This was a good woman who didn't deserve to be used, who didn't deserve to have her faith mocked, even indirectly. And the lie Fiona was about to tell on behalf of people who didn't deserve it would probably damn her further. *Sebastian's family,* she thought, *you had better be worth this.*

She cast her eyes down. "I'm...very ill," she said. "Not with a simple sickness, but something much worse. My doctor controls my symptoms, but he can't cure what's wrong with me. When I heard about the Irantzen Festival, I wanted to come, but that was only a few weeks ago and...no one's sure if I'll be around for next year's festival, so it was this year or..." She shrugged, hoping to convey calm resignation. "That's why I travel with my own doctor. I was feeling ill last night when you found me on the stairs."

"You could have said this."

"I don't want anyone feeling sorry for me! And it wasn't much. It's just that the doctor worries if I'm not honest with him. And it was true what I said about the watch. I just didn't mention that the doctor wanted to find an apothecary to see if they had any remedies he hasn't tried."

Hien put her hand on Fiona's shoulder. "There is no shame in this," she said. "No shame, and no fear. I think you were moved to come here for a reason, Fiona Cooper. You have seen a vision of change. Today we will talk further, and discover what change is in your future. Maybe it is death. Maybe it is life where you now expect only death. But you deserve answers."

Fiona couldn't bear to look anywhere but at Hien's bare feet. They were plump, and a little dirty, and the nails were cut very short. "Thank you," she said. "I want to understand my vision." *And maybe then I won't feel like an utter heel.*

FIONA LAY ON HER PALLET, WISHING SHE HAD THE WATCH. EVERYTHING in this place felt so timeless, if she hadn't had a window she'd never have known if it were day or night. She waited, as she had before, for moonrise. One more moonrise, and they'd do what they came here for, and then Fiona might be able to salvage some of the tattered shreds of her honor.

She'd spent most of the day talking to the priestesses—*not* Sela, thank heaven—and some of the other women, discussing visions and symbols and what it all meant, and it had been *interesting*. Not least the moment when a woman had said, "Fiona, you don't understand it because you don't want to," and that had left Fiona speechless, because of course she wanted to. Didn't she?

At the end, it had just been her and Hien, and Hien had pointed out that change is always frightening even when it gives you something you want. "You might simply be anticipating reuniting with your loved ones in heaven," she said, so casually certain Fiona had forgotten for a moment that she wasn't a dying woman. "But tell me —if you were cured today, how would you feel?"

"Afraid," Fiona had said, "because it would mean having to live again." It wasn't until later that she realized how easily that answer had come to her, and now, lying on her pallet, she turned the matter over again in her mind. It had come easily because in a sense, she *was* ill—her fire was a condition no one could cure, that had come to define her, and if it were gone...the thought terrified her. Yes, she could have a normal life, but it would be that of a stranger, someone who didn't have to fear sleeping too deeply or losing her temper or even picking up a hot pan the wrong way in public. All things that didn't touch Fiona Cooper.

She closed her eyes and remembered her vision. Mother, looking at her with those so-familiar brown eyes, saying *Change is coming, and you can either make it your own or go on hiding from it.* Go on hiding from it? She wasn't hiding—well, yes, she was, but it was for her own protection and that of her family, because where one Cooper had inherent magic, others might too, and people like those hunters might not stop at killing just her. But what if things were different? Suppose she could live openly with her inherent magic? Even if no one feared her as a potential Ascendant, her magic was something terrifying, destructive and deadly. It wasn't as if she could control the fires she started. Put in those terms, she almost feared herself.

She opened her eyes and saw pale blue moonlight filling the room. Time to go. Introspection could wait.

No one lurked in the hallway outside her door, and Fiona felt again the pangs of guilt that filled her whenever she remembered lying to Hien. She'd have to find a way to make it up to her. Somehow. Without telling the truth.

The temple's silence hung over her like a shroud, making her quiet footsteps seem to echo in the stairwell. She passed the eating hall, whose door hung slightly ajar, and heard the distant sounds of washing up. She hoped to heaven Holt and Sebastian hadn't been pulled into that chore.

There were no torches lit in the entry chamber, but Fiona fumbled along the wall and around the corner until she found the outline of a small door, and then hinges and a knob. She leaned against it and waited, reminding herself that the entry was large, and tall, and if she walked away from the door she would not immediately run face-first into another wall. The darkness smelled of old torches, and damp stone, and when she breathed out, she smelled supper, spicy chicken and peppers. It had been unexpectedly delicious, and when Fiona caught Hien watching her, she felt guilty again.

Footsteps, approaching in the darkness—boots on stone. Fiona pressed herself against the door and tried to breathe slowly. The boots came closer; there were two sets, scuffing along quietly.

"The door's here," Sebastian said, and Fiona squeaked as Sebastian's reaching fingers found her shoulder. "Fiona?"

"Yes."

"Thank heaven. Shall we go? We made a clean escape, but I don't want to waste any time."

Fiona stepped to the side and felt a large body move past her. "Can you...are you picking the lock, Holt?"

"I am, Miss Cooper, and if you don't mind I would prefer not to carry on a conversation while doing so."

"Sorry."

She heard tiny scraping sounds, like mice with metal claws, thought about asking if light would help, then decided Holt knew what he was doing and she shouldn't interfere. Sebastian came up close behind her and said in her ear, "The priestess Hien asked me what foods were healthiest for you. Do I want to know what you told her?"

"Probably not. Do you suppose you're damned more thoroughly for lying to a priestess than to an ordinary person?"

Sebastian chuckled. "When we return to Tremontane, you can ask absolution at the first bethel we reach."

She didn't much feel like laughing. "I may do that."

His laughter ceased. "That sounded serious," he said. "Fiona, what—"

The lock clicked. "Master N—Sebastian, Miss Cooper," Holt said, "shall we proceed?"

1 4

Fresh, chilly air brushed Fiona's cheeks, reminding her that she hadn't been outside in three days. Sebastian and Holt were already heading down the shallow steps toward the colonnade, and she followed them, wishing she'd thought to have them bring her shoes. The stone was like sandpaper on her bare feet, rough and cold.

The pillars of the colonnade towered over her as she passed through their moonlight shadows, pale in the dim light and stippled with color from the tiny lights outlining their bases. It was hard to imagine them being made by human artisans, they were so big and bulged so oddly. She glanced back at the temple, which was dark and still. The fairy spires she'd barely had time to notice in their mad sprint for the doors looked more like spikes in a giant crown now, as if some creature had put his head down for a nap and might wake at any moment. She trotted a few steps to catch up with Sebastian. This was not the time for fanciful thoughts.

The steep ramp at the end of the colonnade was brightly lit by lamps on wrought iron posts twice as tall as Fiona, their blue glass turning the light ghostlike. Fiona wondered how they reached the Devices to repair or replace them. Her white linen clothes glowed in the lamplight, and Sebastian and Holt's brown garb had a purplish tinge to it. Sebastian gestured, and they set off down the ramp.

Now that they weren't racing against time, Fiona could appreciate the view of Haizea visible from the ramp, which followed the curve of the island's shore. The city glittered like broken glass, colored shards strewn across the landscape, with the Kepa a silvery ribbon barely visible below. Movement still threaded along the wide streets across the river despite the hour, men and women carrying out their nocturnal business. How many of them intended crime, like they did? Probably anyone who did was skulking in the shadowed places and not strolling along the well-lit streets.

Where they were, streets opened off the ramp at intervals, and Sebastian took the third one, staying close to the side of the road. The buildings all looked the same, tall white structures rising to spires outlined by hundreds, thousands of light Devices. Blank façades rose a hundred feet in the air, windowless and unmarked except for the faint outlines of doors set flush into the walls. Fiona crept along after Sebastian, listening for the sound of anyone who might accost them. Their own footsteps—or, rather, Sebastian and Holt's boots—echoed faintly off the white buildings.

Sebastian stopped abruptly, holding up a hand, and Fiona nearly piled into Holt's lean back. They'd stopped at the corner of one of the buildings, and Fiona rested her hand on its smooth marble surface that gleamed blue in the light from the lamps. Faint streaks ran like cracks across it, though she couldn't imagine anything more solid. Then she heard it—the distant sound of footsteps, quiet but unmistakable. Sebastian peered around the corner. He made a gesture; two guards. Fiona realized she was holding her breath and let it out slowly. The sound died away. Sebastian gestured again, and they moved forward, more slowly this time, around the corner and onto a new street.

"We have to be careful," he whispered, unnecessarily as far as Fiona was concerned. "Heaven only knows how many of those guards are around. There's nowhere to hide on these streets, have you noticed?"

"Nowhere to hide, no porticos, no public parks. And no one about except for us and the guards. It can't be *that* late."

"I suggest we leave the speculation for later," Holt said. Sebastian nodded.

They had to dodge two more pairs of guards, one of which they only avoided by crouching low in a shadow barely big enough to fit all three of them. Fiona felt horribly exposed in her white clothes. Even in the shadows, she felt she stood out by a mile. But there were no shouts of "stop!" or cries of alarm. It was dreamlike, the kind of dream where you can will things to happen or not, and Fiona felt irrationally as if she were keeping the guards at bay simply through force of will. She made herself focus on the present. What was keeping them safe was sheer luck and, possibly, the guards' belief that no one would dare breach the grounds of the Jaixante.

A few minutes later, Sebastian stopped at a building that looked the same as all the others. Its door was barely visible as a crack in the marble façade. "Holt?" Sebastian said.

Holt stepped up and laid his enormous hand flat against the door's surface. Fiona turned around and scanned the street. Now would be the worst possible time for someone to appear, wanting to know what they were doing. She heard something scrape across the stone with a *skree* that set her teeth on edge and her nerves jangling. "Sorry," Holt said, and there was another scrape, less shrill.

"So what is it they do to criminals in Veribold?" Sebastian said.

"Is that really something you want to know right now?"

"Surprisingly, it's at the top of my mind."

"Well, I'd rather not think about it, if you don't mind."

"So it's not pleasant."

"I can't imagine criminal sentences ever are. But no, it's not pleasant."

Another scrape, a click, and then the sound of stone grinding against stone. "We're in, sir," Holt said.

The smell of woody incense filled the air. The interior of the foreign trade office was completely lightless except for what little came in through the door, and when Holt shut the door, even that was gone. "Wait," Sebastian said, and a few seconds later there was a *click* and soft white light emerged from a small cubical Device in his left hand. He handed one to Fiona and another to Holt. "Stay by the door, just in case," Sebastian told Holt.

Fiona turned her Device on and looked around. They were in some kind of reception area, its tall ceiling vanishing out of the range of the light. Large square cushions, purple and green, lay on the floor instead of chairs. Beautiful woven fabric depicting men and women dancing covered the walls, interrupted by a couple of doors and a hallway leading off into darkness. A five-foot-tall counter made an arc across one corner of the room. Fiona went to the tall counter, behind which were a basin-chair and a cabinet with three deep drawers. The cabinet was filled with blank printed forms and, in the bottom drawer, a box of colored ink in jars and a tray full of stamps in backwards Veriboldan script.

"This is as far as I got," Sebastian said. He pointed off down the dark hallway. "The person who gave me the watch came out of the third door on the right, but I don't know if that means anything. We need to find which of these offices belongs to Gizane."

Fiona waded through the cushions and went down the hall. "No names, just titles," she said. "What is Gizane?"

"I don't know her title. She's responsible for overseeing trade between Tremontane and Veribold."

Fiona ran her fingers over the first name plaque she came to. The curly Veriboldan script was only lightly incised on the brass plate, making it even harder for her to read. *CHIEF COMPTROLLER*, she read, shook her head, and moved on. Her slowness was driving even her crazy, but this was still faster than searching every office one by one.

It was the last office on the left. *MINISTER OF FOREIGN TRADE*. "This one," she told Sebastian, who'd been hovering over her shoulder. Sebastian tested the knob, then pushed the door open.

"Already open," he said.

Sebastian and Fiona looked at each other. "That's ominous," Fiona said.

"No one knows we're here," Sebastian said. "No one knows what we're after. She just doesn't lock her door."

"Gizane's not in Haizea. Why would she leave her door open while she's out of the country?"

"Let's just see what we can find, all right? And worry about the rest later."

Gizane's office was surprisingly small—or maybe it wasn't so surprising, if she spent most of her time elsewhere. Fiona had no doubt her personal quarters were far more luxurious. There was a mahogany desk, Tremontanan, not Veriboldan, and a padded rolling chair to match. Five cabinets stacked with books, scroll cases, and loose sheets of paper lined the wall opposite the desk. Framed artwork, mostly oils of Eskandelic landscapes, hung on every wall, like little windows on a distant world. The smell of incense was stronger here, and Fiona traced it to an ornate burner on the corner of the desk. She flipped it open and prodded the stick of incense. Cold. So no one had been in here for a while.

Sebastian eyed the cabinets with dismay. "We're never going to find it," he said.

"I doubt she keeps her blackmail materials in with her other paperwork," Fiona said. "Didn't you say she probably has a plan to expose your family if she turns up suspiciously dead? In order for that to work, she'd have to keep it separate from the rest of her files— she has five cabinets, for heaven's sake, who's going to work through all of those for the sake of carrying out a dead woman's vengeance?"

"That's true." Sebastian removed one of the paintings from the wall. "Help me check these. It's cliché, I know, but a safe in the wall...I prefer to think of it as 'traditional.'"

Gizane, however, wasn't traditional; there was nothing but wall behind all the paintings. "Now what?" Sebastian said.

"See if those cabinets are made to move. I'll check the desk." Fiona removed every drawer, carefully examining their undersides and tapping the bottoms for false panels. Nothing. "It might not be here," she said.

"She told my parents she'd sent it to Veribold and not to bother trying to find it," Sebastian said, sounding short of breath. He had both hands on one of the cabinets and was trying to shift it, with no results. "She might have been lying."

"Let's not give up yet. I meant, look for a button or lever or something that makes them move."

"I did. There's no sign that they've shifted position in the last twenty years."

Fiona sat in the chair and regarded the desk. It stared back at her, smirking. The secret had to be there. Somewhere. There was a carved border all around the edge of the desk's top, tiny apples and pears. Suppose one of them was a button? Too obvious, and too easy to accidentally press. But if there were a secret panel or button or something, it would be convenient to anyone sitting in the desk.

Fiona stretched her arms underneath again and closed her eyes, feeling for the anomaly. "You think you're smarter than the rest of the world," she murmured, "but you're just a petty—blackmailer." The fingers of her right hand brushed a rough spot. She pushed on it, heard a *click*, and the top of the desk popped open half an inch.

"Sweet heaven," Sebastian breathed, and then he pulled the top open further. It only opened three inches, but it was enough for Fiona to reach inside. She pulled out a round, tightly fastened scroll case, its waxy leather clearly waterproof, then a flat portfolio like Sebastian's.

"There's more. A lot more," she said, bringing out two more scroll cases and a folder tied with black ribbon.

"Let me look," Sebastian said, holding out his hand. Fiona began handing things to him. There were five scroll cases in all, two portfolios, the ribbon-tied folder, and a fist-sized velvet sack that rattled when she lifted it.

"What should we do with the rest?" Fiona said.

"I hate leaving them," said Sebastian, prying the tight cap off the first scroll case, "but I don't feel obligated to find their owners and return them."

"We could keep Gizane from blackmailing them further."

"I don't think her losing the material would matter. As far as her victims are concerned, she'd still have it. She could lie to them forever." Sebastian shook the contents of the first scroll case into his hand, a sheaf of tightly rolled paper, and spread it out. "It's not this one."

Fiona opened the bag and shook some of its contents into her hand. They were round chips of white ceramic roughly twice the size of her thumbnail that made a sound like raindrops striking metal when they struck each other. Each tile had a strange symbol incised on one side in which ink or paint had pooled, purple or orange or red or green, colors that were dim in the low light. "I wonder what these are for," she mused. She poured them back into the bag.

A loud thump came from the reception area, then the sounds of a scuffle. "Holt?" Sebastian called. There was a wordless grunt, then silence. Sebastian rushed out of the room. Fiona followed him, her hands full of scroll cases.

Holt had just lowered a still bundle to the ground. The man was dressed in black and his face except for the eyes was covered. His clothes were loose and tattered, though the tattering was unusually regular. Fiona thought they were made that way on purpose. A Jaix-ante guard.

"He did not anticipate my presence at the door," Holt said. He didn't sound the least bit winded. "What concerns me is that his partner was not with him. I cannot guess where the man might be."

"Take everything," Sebastian said, handing off a few of his burdens to Holt. "We'll look at it later. We need to find a back way out of this place."

Fiona stowed a scroll case and the rattling sack inside her shirt. One of the doors off the reception area turned out to be a hallway, headed away from the front door, and she followed Sebastian and Holt down the passage. It was gray and utilitarian, uncarpeted, smelled faintly of mildew, and its low ceiling sagged in places from water damage. It was hard to reconcile this stinking, depressing hall with the beauty of the Jaixante, though it did make the Veriboldans seem more human.

The hall dead-ended in a blank wall, or at least it looked like a blank wall to Fiona. Holt, however, went down on one knee and brought out his lock picks. When she looked closer, she could again see the outline of a door, and hinges painted gray to match the surrounding walls. Sebastian put a hand on hers and clicked off her light Device, then turned off his own. "No light when the door opens. Damn, but I wish there were windows. What is wrong with these people, that they don't have windows?"

"They have windows, just not at ground level," Fiona said, thinking of her cell.

"Even so. Veriboldans are strange. All right, maybe just the noble Veriboldans. I can't wait to be home again."

Fiona said nothing. Planning too far ahead when there might be guards waiting to snatch you seemed like asking for trouble. Or was it just that she no longer had a home to return to? She closed her eyes in the dimness made by Holt's light, focused on the keyhole. Wrong time for those kinds of thoughts. Possibly there was never a right time.

The lock clicked. Holt turned off his light and Fiona shivered at the darkness that surrounded them. She could feel Sebastian standing near her, the body heat he gave off, and she knew where all the walls were; there was no need for nervousness. Then a slim line of pale light appeared, stretching to outline the door. "Careful," Holt said, and pulled the door open all the way.

They stepped into an alley between buildings, featureless and blank like white canyons surrounding a dry riverbed of concrete. The half-moon rode higher in the sky, casting more faint shadows that were overcome by the blue light of the lanterns. "Do we leave now?" Fiona said.

"We go back to the Irantzen Temple and pretend we never left," Sebastian said. "And then—"

A shrill whistle split the silent air, echoing off the walls until it sounded like a dozen screams. Down at the far end of the alley, a man in dark clothes that fluttered around him like malevolent moths ran at them, alternating blows on his whistle with shouts of "*Intruders!*"

"Run," Sebastian said, and they sped away down the alley.

15

Fiona caught her toe on the concrete and bit her lip to keep from crying out, though the guards already knew she was there. The hard surface tore at the soles of her feet. She felt dampness and was sure she was leaving a blood trail. She risked a glance backward. They'd left the man behind, but that wouldn't last long. And he'd no doubt have friends.

"What now?" she said as they ran.

"Have to get...back to the Irantzen Temple," Sebastian panted.

"That's the first place they'll search for foreigners. We have to get out of the city."

"We left all our money...if we don't have our things, we'll never make it out of Veribold."

"Then we have to split up."

Sebastian stopped running and leaned, panting, against one of the white fairy buildings. "We'll never find each other again."

"Meeting place," Holt said. "The stables where we left the horses. Those are in Sebastian's name, but we are registered at the temple under Miss Cooper's name. It is unlikely they will make the connection, and there are many foreigners in Haizea."

The whistling grew louder. "Holt, you return and collect our things," Sebastian said. "Fiona, come with me. We'll draw them away from Holt."

"It will be better if we separate." Fiona rubbed her foot. "Give them more targets to chase."

Sebastian looked torn. "But—" He scowled. "All right. Just don't get caught."

"You too," Fiona said.

"Then *go*," Sebastian said, and took off running. Holt headed back toward the ramp. Fiona turned and ran.

She had no idea where she was going, other than that she needed to draw attention to herself so the guards, or whatever they were called in the Jaixante, wouldn't follow Holt back to the temple. So she retraced her steps. Almost immediately she saw them: dark, indistinct figures milling around the front door to the foreign trade office. She slowed, thought about hailing them, decided that would be ridiculous, and settled for jogging past in her white linen clothing that practically glowed under the blue lights. Someone shouted, figures began moving toward her, and she ran.

Her feet felt raw, burning against the rough road. What she wouldn't give for a pair of shoes. She rounded a corner and dashed across the street. More whistles told her they were still following. Good. She put on a burst of speed as she crossed an intersection, skidded, and turned another corner. Even more whistles, these coming from ahead of her. Not good.

She nearly ran into the second group and managed to stop her headlong flight in time to stay out of sight around a corner. Breathing heavily, she waited, listening to their running feet and the shrill whistles until the sounds faded. Drawing attention was one thing; being captured was unacceptable. She rubbed her foot and her hand came away bloody. She couldn't be leaving much of a trail, or they'd have caught her already. She set out again, this time heading downhill.

The white, faceless buildings, the pale moonlight, the blue lamps all left Fiona feeling disoriented, as if this were no city, but a nightmare realm populated by ghosts. More whistling echoed through the canyons—no, they were streets, this was a real city, if a strange one, and she needed to get out of it. Surely Holt had had enough time to make his escape.

Fiona pressed her hand to her side and felt the bag shift. Why was she still carrying it? At least it weighed hardly anything. The scroll case jabbed her hip, and she moved it to a more secure position. Past time to leave.

She rounded a corner, took a few strides, then skidded to a halt, tearing the soles of her feet further. Two of the dark, indistinct figures were staring right at her. Beyond them, she saw one of the bridges, its guard station unmanned. One of the figures raised a pistol and pointed it at her. *"Stop there,"* he said. His voice was muffled by a scarf drawn closely around the lower half of his face, and he and his partner were dressed in dark robes that fluttered around them like tattered wings.

Fiona screamed, making them both jerk, turned and ran. She heard a loud clap of an explosion behind her, and a ball whined past her ear, then another bang and whine as the second man's shot went wide. She turned a corner and reviewed her path, madly looking for a way out. If she could get them sidetracked, double back, she could reach the bridge and disappear into Haizea. With her luck, the bridge led to the wrong side of the river, but she could make that work. She just needed not to get shot.

She turned a corner, wishing there was shelter—even a shallow porch would do—and heard running footsteps coming after her. Her feet were screaming pain, her side and chest ached, and it wouldn't be long before she couldn't run anymore.

More whistles, from ahead. They'd driven her into a trap. Desperate, she turned and ran back the way she'd come and saw a narrow street she hadn't noticed before. It wasn't narrow enough to hide her, but it had to lead back toward the bridge. She tossed a quick prayer heavenward, then a second prayer apologizing for her impiety, and ran.

The pavement of the narrow street was cracked, not nearly as well-kept as the main streets, and Fiona stumbled over a chunk of concrete and went to her hands and knees, her eyes watering from the pain. She pushed herself up and limped on. Giving up was not going to happen. They'd have to take her by force.

When she came out onto the main street, it was empty. And there was a clear, unobstructed path to the bridge. She forced herself to run, but could only manage a rapid hobble. It was good enough. She passed the empty guard post and headed out onto the bridge, hearing the whistles grow louder again. She grinned. Too late. They'd lost their prey.

But...no. Her grin faded. More whistles, these coming from the far side of the bridge. She stopped with both hands on the railing, panting, and stared into the distance. Something was moving on the shore, indistinct, fluttering movement. More guards. She couldn't believe they'd gotten ahead of her.

She looked back over her shoulder. There were the other guards, their gun Devices held aloft as they ran. Or were they Devices? She laughed. They could kill her just as well if they were mechanical. And kill her they very likely would.

She looked down at the dark water rushing past, then at the approaching guards. She had exactly one option left, and it was a terrifying one. Quickly she swung her leg over the rail and heard the shouts grow louder, more urgent. *That's right, you can't afford to let me escape, even if it's to death by drowning,* she thought. She brought her other leg over and stood with her bare, bloody feet pressed against the bridge and both hands gripping the rail. The water was moving more rapidly than she remembered. She shivered once, took a deep breath, and dove into the murky waters below.

Hitting the water felt like diving face-first into the cold, hard concrete of the Jaixante streets. Stunned, she let the river buffet her along for a few moments, tumbling her until she couldn't remember which way was up. Water rushed into her nostrils, and she gagged, coming to her senses. She struggled, thrashed her way to what she hoped was the surface, and burst into the air, gasping for breath.

The wild current swept her along, dragging her down. She flailed her arms and legs, hoping she remembered how to swim. She'd never swum more than a paddle at the seashore and a couple of swims in one of the rivers near Kingsport. This was like trying to make headway against a windstorm powerful enough to carry her off her feet. The best she could do was keep her head above water and hope the current would slacken soon.

She couldn't see anything of Haizea from where she was, none of its lights, just the gleam of the half-moon riding high above. Something large and dark loomed ahead of her, and she had just recognized it as the piling of a bridge when the river slammed her into it, knocking the breath out of her. Instinctively she clung to the rough stone, sucking in sodden air and wanting to weep with pain and terror. The river tugged at her, trying to pull her back into its embrace. Her fingers and toes were numb with cold, she could barely feel the stone of the piling, and her muscles cramped and ached enough that it was only a matter of time before she lost the battle with the river.

Faintly, she heard the shrill sound of whistles cutting across the roar of the water. Surely they couldn't see her from the bridge? Her grip loosened further. She pressed her face into the piling and prayed for strength. Slowly, her fingers and feet scraped across the stone, pulled inexorably away until her tortured muscles let go all at once and she was flung into the river once more. Probably this was heaven's punishment for all the lies she'd told Hien.

The river dragged her along past two more bridges that she saw in time to scrabble away from the pilings and avoid being slammed into the stone. No more whistles sounded. They might have been her imagination. She was so tired. Her kicking and paddling grew weaker until she could barely keep her head above water. *I'm sorry*, she thought, though she wasn't sure what of all the sins she'd committed she was sorry for, and fell beneath the waves a final time.

FIONA CAME TO CONSCIOUSNESS SLOWLY, FEELING LIKE SHE WAS floating. Water pooled around her hips and shoulders, and her entire body ached and shook with cold. She blinked river water out of her eyes and stared up at the sky, which was the charcoal gray of a pre-dawn overcast. Rain was coming later that day.

She tried to sit up, but failed to make her muscles obey her. To her right, the river rushed past, its song not the loud roar it had been when it tried to swallow her but still loud enough to obscure any other sounds. She managed to turn her head to look at it. She was lying in a natural backwater along its bank, with chilly water lapping at her body. The realization of how cold it was made her shiver, and then she couldn't stop shaking. The heavy linen of her clothes soaked up the water and chilled her further. Nearly convulsing with shivers, she finally managed to push herself up and then roll out of the river onto the bank, where she collapsed on her face.

The damp earth beside the river wasn't much warmer, at this hour of the morning, than the water. Fiona had never been so desperate to see the sun. She tried to control her breathing, tried to master herself, but she hurt everywhere and she had no idea where she was, and fear made her shivering worse. Inside her shirt, the scroll case and the bag rattled as she shivered, reminding her of why she was in this position. She needed to get back to Haizea, find Sebastian and Holt, and get out of Veribold as quickly as possible.

Finally, breathing heavily, she got to her hands and knees and crouched, her head hanging down. She had to get up. She had to figure out what to do next. And she had to get dry. She squatted back on her heels and looked around. Haizea was nowhere in sight. In fact, she saw no signs of civilization anywhere, just clumps of trees she couldn't identify here and there some distance from the riverbank. The gray sky was lightening, and a line of pale gold along the eastern hills heralded the appearance of the sun.

Fiona stood shakily and tottered in the direction of the nearest copse. Her gait grew steadier as she walked, though she still shivered and had to wrap her arms around herself to still the shivering. Shelter, and if she dared, a fire, would take care of that.

The trees were slender, narrow enough that she could encircle even the thickest of them with her arms, leafless at this time of year, with lots of skinny branches fallen beneath them. Fiona began gathering them, relieved that heaven's displeasure didn't extend to having her die of exposure. With her arms full of sticks, she found a sheltered area within the copse where she could lay out a fire. She was expert at doing so after all these years. When it was built up to her satisfaction, she set her hand in the center of the pile and let it burn.

The sticks were dry, and caught fire almost immediately. She pushed her sleeve back with her free hand and let the flames lick over her skin, relishing the warmth. If only her clothes were fireproof as her body, she might lie down in the center of the blaze and bask like a reptile in its warmth. She was definitely going south after this. Someplace warm.

She pushed her hair out of her face and saw Sebastian standing no more than twenty feet away, staring at her.

16

Shock rooted her to the spot. She didn't even think to snatch her hand out of the fire. Sebastian's expression was completely blank, as if he were a statue carved by an inexperienced craftsman who didn't know how to render human emotion in stone. They stared at each other for a long, long moment while Fiona scrambled desperately for some way to rewind time, or strike Sebastian blind, anything to reverse his discovery.

Finally, Sebastian took a short step backward. Fiona snatched a thick branch from the fire and brandished it at him, making him stop. "Don't," she said.

"What do you think I'll do?" he asked, but he stopped moving.

"I won't let you—" She didn't know how to end that sentence. She had to force him to keep her secret, and the only way she could see to do that meant his death. She quailed at the thought.

Sebastian took another step, this time toward her. "Fiona—"

"I said *don't*," Fiona said. She realized she was holding the branch flame end first and switched it to her other hand, where it burned like a torch. "I don't want to kill you."

"Then don't. Are you afraid I'll tell someone? I wouldn't do that."

Fiona laughed. His still face was so at odds with the intensity of his voice, it was either laugh or run screaming. "As if I believe that."

"You have inherent magic. That's not a crime."

"You're a fool if you believe that makes me safe. Makes you safe from me. Lie on the ground. Face first."

"Why?" He didn't move.

"Because I want a head start on you. Down. Now."

"Fiona, you don't have to run. I'm not going to betray you." He still made no move to lie down or to walk toward her.

"Do you think I won't turn this power on you?"

"That's exactly what I think. You're not evil, and I don't believe you've ever hurt anyone intentionally in your life. Put the branch down and let me come closer. I'm freezing."

Fiona realized Sebastian was as sopping wet as she was, and he trembled occasionally. His brown hair was dark with river water. "Did you jump in the river, too?"

"I was on the next bridge north from you. I saw you jump. It seemed like—" He shivered convulsively. "Like a good idea at the time. Now I'm damned cold and your fire looks like salvation. Please, Fiona. I just want to warm up. We can worry about the rest later."

If he came closer, close enough for her to lay hands on him, she could burn him, stop him telling anyone about her permanently. The idea made her want to vomit. The smell of cooked human flesh—it was a memory she wished she didn't have. She lowered the branch. "You stay on your side, and I'll stay on mine," she said. "Don't come near me, or you'll find out how easily flesh burns."

Sebastian nodded and walked swiftly to the fire, crouching next to it and holding his hands up to savor its warmth. He closed his eyes as if experiencing profound bliss. "Thank you," he said. "I thought I might die out here. It's not that cold, I suppose, but between the river and the overcast...thank you."

Fiona tossed the branch back into the fire and knelt beside it, breathing in the delicious smell of burning wood. Whatever the trees were, their wood or bark had a sweetish, spicy scent that reminded her of cinnamon and cloves mixed together. She didn't feel much like talking, and meeting Sebastian's eyes felt wrong, since killing him was still a possibility. *You won't do it,* she admitted to herself. She likely couldn't even have killed him if he were a stranger, chance-met in the wilds outside Haizea, but a friend? No. Tears slid down her cheek. He knew her secret, and that was the end for her.

"How long have you had this magic?" Sebastian asked.

There was no point in concealing anything, not anymore. "Since I was thirteen."

"And you've kept it secret all that time? That's...I can't imagine how hard that would be."

Fiona said nothing.

"How does it work? Do you have to be touching something to burn it?" Sebastian asked.

"Why do you care? Are you looking for evidence to use at my trial?" she shot back.

His brows drew up in surprise. "I told you, I'm not going to tell anyone."

"Like I believe that."

"What kind of friend betrays a trust like that? Fiona—"

"Fear breaks all manner of bonds, even friendship."

"I'm not afraid of you."

"Maybe you should be."

"Why? It's not as if you burn things against your will. I assume. We've traveled together long enough, I think I'd have noticed if people went up in greasy pillars of fire wherever you passed."

It startled a laugh out of her. "It's still frightening."

"Not to me. Though I can imagine *you* might be frightened of it. That's an incredible power to have. And so much like an Ascendant's..." His voice trailed off. "I probably shouldn't have said that."

"You see why I can't afford to let anyone know."

"You're not going to kill me."

She sighed. "No."

"So, you can set things on fire with a touch, you can't be burned—is it only your own fire that doesn't burn you, or all fires?"

This was the strangest conversation she'd ever had. "All fires."

"That's amazing." He sounded genuinely impressed, and it startled her into looking at him. He had his hazel eyes fixed on her, did not look at all terrified or disgusted, and a pang of some unfamiliar emotion struck her. It wasn't fear, or sorrow—it was loneliness. As if revealing her secret had put a distance between them she didn't know how to bridge.

Sebastian stood and turned his back on her, and the pang redoubled. She blinked away tears. Even if he wasn't going to tell anyone, even if he wouldn't bring the hunters down on her, they could never go back to what they'd been before.

"I'm not ignoring you," Sebastian called out, "I'm just getting dry. Sweet heaven, I don't think I've ever loved anything more than I love this fire right now. Can you build it up a bit?"

His matter of fact tone confused her. "What do you mean?"

He gestured aimlessly with one hand. "Stir it up higher, or something? Can you control it without touching it?"

"No." She reached into its heart and moved a few branches, making it blaze hotter.

"That's unfortunate. What a tremendous power that would be, being able to extinguish a house fire, for example."

Her mouth fell open. "Why doesn't this bother you?"

Sebastian shrugged. "I suppose it's because fearing you is impossible, no matter what you're capable of. And...I know someone else who has inherent magic. He always knows where his family is, wherever they are in the world. It just doesn't seem like anything to get worked up about, not if you're not an Ascendant and tyrannizing others. It's all in what you do with it, I think."

Fiona stared at him until the heat of the fire dried her eyeballs. "Who is he?"

"I can't tell you. It's not my secret to tell. You wouldn't want me to tell anyone about you, right?"

"No, I wouldn't." Slowly, Fiona turned her back on him, trying to ignore the warning that screamed through her, telling her not to lower her defenses. The heat of the fire warmed and dried her back and her thick red hair, spilling loose past her shoulder blades. He couldn't possibly be this well-adjusted about her secret, not even if he knew someone else with inherent magic. She needed to run as fast as she could away from this place, away from him. She contemplated her sore feet, scraped and raw from running through the Jaixante. She was in no condition to run anywhere unless she was desperate. And, she realized, she wasn't desperate.

She heard Sebastian shift position again, then his feet rustled the winter-dry grass that grew around the copse. "I swear you don't have anything to fear from me," he said, squatting beside her. "And..."

"What?" She glanced at him, but he was looking past her toward the river.

"Doesn't it feel good to share that burden?"

"I...don't know. You're the only person who knows about it."

She looked off into the distance, feeling uncomfortable about meeting Sebastian's eyes, and saw movement. "Someone's coming," she said. Dark figures, their clothes fluttering in the breeze... A cold hand gripped her heart. "Those are Jaixante guards."

Sebastian grabbed her hand and began pulling her eastward, away from the fire that might as well have become a screaming beacon. "There's nowhere to hide here," he said. "We have to reach the hills."

"There's nowhere to hide there, either," she pointed out, but ran with him.

She didn't look over her shoulder to see if the guards had seen them, were chasing them, just concentrated on running and ignoring the pain in her feet as she lit on stones concealed by the tall grass. Her lungs and legs ached with exertion. Ahead, the terraced hills looked like stairways to nowhere, growing ever larger as she and Sebastian fled. They would provide no exit, but there was nowhere else to run.

They came out of the grassy field onto a dirt road, stretching out in the direction of the nearest farm. "We can't risk it," Sebastian panted. "Veriboldans...will give us up...to their own."

"Need to find...a place to hide," Fiona said. Sebastian's feet were as bare and filthy as her own. "Off this road."

Shouting drifted toward them on the breeze. It was unintelligible at this distance, but Fiona could guess what it meant. She ran faster, dragging Sebastian along with her, until the road began to rise into the hills. Then she veered sharply left, toward a farmhouse sited halfway up the nearest hill. "We can't hide there," Sebastian said, "they'll search it."

"We just...want them to think...we're there," Fiona said.

She turned to follow the curve of one of the terrace steps and plunged headlong into the barley field. The waving heads of grain were only chest-high on her, not tall enough to conceal them. They'd have to keep running.

They reached the farmhouse, where a startled woman paused in hanging laundry on a line to stare at them, and pelted up its short front steps and into cool darkness. The woman screamed and shouted something in Veriboldan, but Fiona was too far away to understand it.

The house was built with a single long hallway running from the front of the house to its back, with doors opening off it on both sides. Fiona slowed her pace, grabbing Sebastian and signaling him to be silent. They trotted down the hall, moving almost noiselessly on their bare feet, and let themselves out the back, Sebastian holding the door carefully so it wouldn't slam. The woman was still screaming, and there was the distant shouting again. Fiona nodded, and they took off running again, around the back yard where chickens browsed placidly.

The farmhouse was halfway up the hill, which grew steeper from that point up—but the terraces, and the barley fields, stopped there too. Fiona let go Sebastian's hand and went ahead until she was climbing, hand and foot, up to the flat top of the hill where a sort of ledge protruded over the eastern face. She stood at the top and looked out over the hills stretching all the way north to Haizea. "We've still got a long way to run, and more of those guards could be watching for us."

"We need to keep moving," Sebastian said, pulling himself up to join her. "They won't be fooled for long. If they're fooled at all. I doubt the Jaixante employs stupid men in their guard."

"We'll have to stay low. The best outcome would be to stall them until nightfall, when we can move more freely under cover of dark."

"That's at least seven hours away. You think we can stay ahead of them that long?"

"I think—"

To the north, farther down the hill, a dark-clad figure came into view, then another. Fiona dropped to lie flat on the sheltering ledge and cursed. "They went both ways."

"Definitely not stupid men," Sebastian said, going to his knees beside her. "Let's hope they don't know where we really are."

They lay, listening to the guards' approach. Fiona's heart pounded painfully fast. She and Sebastian had gotten high enough, fast enough, that the second set of guards hadn't seen them, or they'd be moving more rapidly. Instead, the men were moving through the barley fields at a comfortable speed, crushing the tender plants underfoot and sending up a fresh green scent. They were like a couple of housecats, certain of their prey and choosing their ground. If the wind shifted, if the guards were truly alert, she and Sebastian might be betrayed by the smell of the river Fiona was sure still lingered on both of them.

She couldn't see the guards, only hear them, but Sebastian, who was closer to the edge, tensed, then grabbed her hand and squeezed. The crashing grew louder until it felt as if the men were right below them, close enough for Fiona to leap out and tackle them, if she'd been idiot enough to do that. Then it began to fade. Sebastian's grip grew tighter. Fiona heard one of the guards say something in Veriboldan that was carried away by the growing wind. Then the crashing vanished, and Sebastian released Fiona's hand. "Sorry," he said.

Fiona shrugged it off. "Can you see the farmhouse?"

"Yes. There's quite a lot of activity. The guards—the ones who just passed us—are out of the fields and running now. We need to move."

They went over the summit and down the back side of the hill, moving as quickly as they could over the steep terrain. There was no terracing on that side, and Fiona sometimes found herself slipping, sliding downward for several feet before catching herself. It would have been fun if she hadn't been so tense. It wasn't a large farmhouse, and as soon as the guards finished searching it, they'd spread out over the hills. She and Sebastian had to stay ahead of them.

They reached the valley between the hills and began running down another of those dirt roads that led between farmhouses. It was wide open, offering nothing like concealment, but they didn't have time for that, or for winding their way over the hills. Fiona's feet ached, there was a stitch in her side, and her lungs had started reminding her that they'd been nearly drowned scant hours before. She kept moving, trailing Sebastian by a little. There was a trace of blood on the sole of his foot, and he was limping.

"Are you all right?" she said. "Should you bind that up?"

"No time. We need to put as much distance between them and us as possible."

"Yes, but you'll move faster if it's tended."

Sebastian jogged to a halt and stood bent over, with his hands on his knees. "I hope we won't regret this," he said. He lifted his injured foot, rubbed it clean of dirt as best he could, then tore a strip from the hem of his brown shirt and wrapped his foot.

Fiona watched the road behind them. It was reassuringly empty of Jaixante guards, though there were a few people dressed in Veriboldan commoners' clothing. No doubt traffic would pick up the closer they got to Haizea. That could be a problem. Fiona had no idea how distinctive their clothing was, whether it would be identified as Irantzen Temple garb, but they definitely looked like they'd been for a swim. Maybe they could pass for beggars—though, Tremontanan beggars in the capital of Veribold? That wouldn't be much of a disguise. On the other hand, it didn't need to be; it only had to get them to the stable, and then they could change into their own clothes and hurry out of Haizea as fast as Mittens and the others could run.

In the distance, dark, fluttering figures appeared.

"We have to move," she told Sebastian, who dropped his foot and looked past her at the approaching guards. Without a word, he broke into a run.

17

Fiona didn't dare look behind her to see how quickly the guards were approaching. She just ran. Sebastian stumbled, then resumed his pace. They passed a man and a woman wearing packs who looked at them in astonishment. *Wait until they meet those guards, and learn what real astonishment feels like.* It was probably too much to hope for the guards to stop to interrogate those two, but it was a nice fantasy that gave Fiona a boost of much-needed energy.

The closer they drew to Haizea, the more crowded the road became, until Fiona and Sebastian had to leave the road and run beside it, which slowed them further. They could no longer see the guards, just the masses of people entering the city. "I think we did it," Sebastian said.

"Let's not celebrate just yet," said Fiona.

Sharp pain lanced through her foot, and she cried out, stumbling and falling to one knee. Sebastian was beside her in an instant. "Show me," he said, and Fiona lifted a foot dripping with blood.

"Glass, I think. A broken bottle," she said, gritting her teeth against the throbbing pain. "It's just a cut."

"*Good heaven, that looks terrible,*" said a voice, and a woman

MELISSA MCSHANE

stopped and knelt beside Sebastian. She was young, barely out of her teens, and she unslung a backpack and rummaged in it. *"Damned fools, tossing their garbage anywhere—though going barefoot around here probably isn't the best idea."*

"I'll be fine," Fiona managed, then had to bite back a cry as the woman prodded her foot.

"What's she doing? What are you doing?" Sebastian said.

"Really, I don't need help," Fiona said.

The woman came out with a thick scarf and used the end of it to wipe blood away. *"You need to bind this up,"* she said, *"and then you shouldn't walk on it. Maybe we can get someone to help carry you. Where were you going?"*

"Thanks, but I'm fine," Fiona said. "Sebastian, help me up."

"How bad is that?" Sebastian said.

"Not bad," Fiona lied. "Just bloody."

The woman bound Fiona's foot with the scarf and tied it in a neat bow. *"You're Tremontanan, aren't you,"* she said. *"I've never met a Tremontanan before. My sister trades with your people all the time, but always across the border. Let's find help, all right?"*

"No, my friend can help me. You've already done more than—"

The woman had already turned away. Fiona cursed. "Help me up, Sebastian."

"How can you run on that?"

"I don't know, exactly, but we—"

"Sir, can you help this woman? She's going to the city. Sir?"

Fiona flung her arm over Sebastian's shoulders. "Let's go."

"But you—here, I'll help." The woman shouldered her pack, then grabbed Fiona's arm and slung it around her neck. Fiona tried to remove it, but the woman had tight hold of her wrist. *"Just hop along and we'll support you."*

Fiona closed her eyes and cursed inwardly. There was no way the guards wouldn't catch them now, and this innocently helpful woman was going to get herself arrested with them. *"My friend is enough support,"* she tried one last time.

"Well, if you're sure," the woman said, releasing Fiona. She turned

and walked away down the road away from Haizea. The abruptness of it left Fiona taken aback. So solicitous, and then she just walked away? It was downright suspicious…

Then she realized what had just happened, and patted herself down. The bag of mystery tokens was missing. Fiona cursed again, this time aloud.

"Does it hurt badly? Damn, I wish there were something I could do."

"She stole the bag. I should have known no one would be that helpful to a stranger."

Sebastian helped her limp along the road. Pain shot through her foot with every step. She ought to be sitting down. "It's not like we were using them," Sebastian said. "We don't even know what they were for."

"It's the principle. I let down my guard and she took advantage of that."

"You can hardly expect to get the better of *every* thief that crosses your path, Fiona." Sebastian sounded amused.

Someone grabbed Fiona's shoulder and pulled her around. The young woman said, *"Don't kill me. I didn't know. I swear I'll never steal again. Just—take them, and leave me alone."* She shoved the little sack of tokens into Fiona's hand, then disappeared into the crowd.

Fiona and Sebastian exchanged looks. "'Don't kill me,' she said," Fiona told Sebastian. "She was terrified. Now I'm concerned that these things could get us into trouble."

"They're not money. They don't look like anything important."

"And yet they were stowed with all the rest of the blackmail material." Fiona tucked the pouch into her waistband again. "Let's go. We need to move faster."

They couldn't move faster. It was getting on toward late afternoon, and horses and wagons vied for space on the road with the many pedestrians. The gray overcast grew darker, promising rain, and it looked like everyone was trying to outrace it. Between the crowding and the need to lean on Sebastian, Fiona felt she was crawling, her one foot scraping across the paving stones that had replaced dirt about a mile back, her other foot throbbing and soaking the thief's scarf with her blood. The air was rich with the smell of bodies scented with a profusion of odors, jasmine and musk and patchouli, that forced their way into her nose and mouth and made her want to gag. She made herself keep moving, though she was exhausted and almost ready to give herself up to the guards. They might let her sit down for a while.

Haizea had no city wall. Instead, its buildings of yellow brick or brightly-hued ceramic started appearing more frequently and closer together until Fiona and Sebastian found themselves in the city rather than the country. Most of those houses and shops were three or four stories tall, with wide arched windows and doorways and flat roofs. Fiona remembered those storms and cast her eye on the clouds. It wouldn't be a downpour, but they would very likely get wet.

She shifted her grip on Sebastian's shoulders. "Do you know where we're going?"

"No. My plan was to head north and west toward the river, then find my way backward from there. If we can get to the main roads, I'm sure I can find the stable."

Someone shoved past them, jarring Fiona's foot and sending a twinge of pain up her leg. A twinge, not a throb, thank heaven, which meant it wasn't as bad a wound as she'd thought. She tried putting her full weight on it, but had to pull back immediately. Maybe she was wrong.

They passed through an outdoor fruit and vegetable market that was being dismantled for the evening, with stall holders packing up what remained of their wares. The golden smell of oranges reached Fiona's nose, awakening her hunger. She hadn't eaten since supper the previous day and now she was starving. "Do you have money?" she asked.

"I don't think we have time for shopping."

"I was thinking more of what we'd do if we can't find Holt right away. If he got stuck on the island."

"Ah. No, I left everything in my bags in the Irantzen Temple.

Though right now I'm wishing I'd been more foresighted. I'm hungry."

A shout behind them of *"Stop there!"* in Veriboldan made Fiona jerk. "What?" Sebastian said.

"Keep going. They probably don't mean us."

"You! Fugitives from the Jaixante! Stop!"

Fiona cursed. "They mean us. We have to find a place to hide."

"Can you run?"

Fiona put her weight on her foot again. It still hurt, but not as much. "Yes."

Sebastian grabbed her hand. "Then let's go."

Fiona limped rapidly in Sebastian's wake as he tugged her between stalls, ducking and turning at random while the shouts followed them, terrifyingly near. Men and women cursed them as they pushed past, knocking one man off balance so he fell on his capacious rear end. Fiona hopped around a corner and down a short alley filled with smelly refuse and a dark trickle down its center she tried to avoid. Brick walls gleamed a sickly yellow in the uncanny light of the oncoming storm, which would certainly wash away the trickle. Well, it wasn't as if she hadn't been soaked once already.

Sebastian dragged her around a corner into a dead-end nook and pressed her up against the wall, breathing heavily. "Do you hear them? I think we outran them."

"I can't hear—no."

Running footsteps were approaching down the alley, at least three men, and someone said, *"Be careful. They may be armed."*

She looked up at Sebastian, who was looking away toward the alley as if he could see through the walls. He glanced down at her, his lips tight with frustration. They were *so close*, if they'd known Haizea at all they probably would have made it. She wasn't sure what the punishment was for stealing from the Jaixante, but she knew what Veriboldans did to thieves in general and it wasn't pretty. It could only be worse for them.

She gripped Sebastian's arm, afraid to speak—there might still be a chance, mightn't there?—but no, they were caught, there was nowhere else to go. Not that she intended to go out there and make a present of herself to the guards. They were going to have to take her by force.

Sebastian's expression had gone neutral, and his eyes were asking a question of her, though she had no idea what. Then he slid one hand behind her neck and kissed her, firmly, his lips hard and passionate on hers.

She let out a startled sound. Sebastian kissed her again, then released her, his expression still perfectly neutral, as if his kiss had come from some well-buried need that didn't show on his face. Then hands grabbed them both, dragged them out of their nook, and shoved them against the rough brick wall. Fiona's cheek felt raw, scraped by the brick, and she threw up her hands to catch herself. She felt the bag shift in her waistband, threatening to slide down her trouser leg, and instinctively she reached down to grab it. Another hand grasped her wrist and pulled it behind her, bringing the bag with it.

"*What's this?*" said the same voice she'd heard before, and her captor took the bag from her. She stood with her face mashed against the wall and listened to the sound of the bag opening, its contents rustling like chips of tile. Then the man sucked in a breath. The bag fell to the ground, spilling at her feet.

"*What are you doing with that?*" The man sounded terrified and outraged at the same time. Fiona turned around. All she could see of his face were his eyes, but they were wide and panicked. His three companions had backed away down the alley, and as she watched, one of them turned and bolted, his dark robes fluttering like tattered flags in the rising wind.

Fiona fixed him with a sharp-eyed gaze. "*I don't think that's any of your business,*" she said, bending to gather the contents of the bag. They clinked when she swished them together. "*Why do you think we have them?*"

"No one should," the man said, switching languages. "You should not know of them."

Fiona shook the bag in his face, making another of the guards turn and run and the remaining two take a few steps back. "Why did you pursue us?"

"Because you were in the Jaixante illegally. No outsiders are allowed."

"Are you sure?" She shook the bag again. "No Tremontanan should have this, either. Maybe you should think about why you might be sent to pursue the holder of this bag." *No fear. Never back down. Play your hand as if it's a royal flush and not a pair of twos, which this might well be.*

The man looked confused, what little she could see of him. Then his eyes widened. He glanced over his shoulder at his remaining companion, then back at Fiona. "No. Let it be on your head. I refuse to be..." His voice trailed off. He backed away, slowly, keeping his eyes focused on the bag. When he and his companion reached the mouth of the alley, they turned and ran.

Fiona heard Sebastian push off from the wall and approach her, but she couldn't stop staring at the place where the guards had been. She'd never done anything that risky in her life. That wasn't a low pair; it was a handful of cards she'd never seen. She shoved the bag back into her waistband. Whatever it was, Gizane had been right to keep it concealed.

"That...was incredible," Sebastian said.

"It was lucky," Fiona said. "Let's go before we run out of luck."

They watched carefully as they emerged from the alley, but no fluttering guards hovered to snatch them. Sebastian led the way through the growing crowds of the evening, eventually taking Fiona's hand so they wouldn't be separated. Fiona watched his profile as they went, how intent he was, and that reminded her of something else.

"You kissed me," she said.

He smiled. "I hoped you hadn't forgotten that."

"Why did you kiss me?"

"Well, the guards were closing in to take us to prison, and I didn't think I'd get another chance."

"Yes, but...why kiss me at all?"

They'd come to an intersection heavily trafficked by ox carts moving ponderously along the street, and Sebastian stopped to wait for them to go pass. "Because you're amazing, and beautiful," he said, "and I've felt like doing that ever since our first night in the temple. I think that's more than enough reason."

Fiona opened her mouth, but nothing came out. Sebastian put his free hand on her shoulder. "Look. I know it's only been a week, and this...heist...has consumed most of that time, but I'm not going to tell you I don't look forward to seeing you and talking to you, no matter what it's about. That I'm not constantly thankful you switched rooms with Lucille, and not just because of your knowledge. I should have asked first, and I'm sorry I startled you, but I'm never going to be sorry for kissing you."

She gaped again, closed her mouth, then blurted out, "But I hardly know you! And—you're wealthy, and I'm practically home-less!" A woman wearing a heavy rain cape over a gaudy multicolored robe gave her a startled look as she passed. In a lower voice, Fiona added, "You can't possibly not care about that."

"You've got four thousand guilders coming to you," Sebastian said with a grin, and tugged on her hand to make her cross the street with him. "And whatever you might be now, you won't let that stop you becoming whoever it is you're meant to be."

"But—"

He brought her to a stop again, this time to avoid a passing caravan whose brightly painted wagons proclaimed that it was one of Veribold's most famous circuses. "Fiona, I'm not proposing marriage. I just want to get to know you better. To kiss you again, if you're will-ing. And I think it might be what you want, too."

"What makes you think I'm at all interested in you?" She'd wanted to sound defiant, but it came out sounding more like a plea.

"Maybe you're not. But I'm willing to take the chance that you are." He raised her hand and kissed the back of it, his lips lingering on her knuckles, and Fiona shivered at the depth of emotion in his eyes. "Come on, I think we're close," he said, and pulled Fiona along without giving her a chance to respond.

She wasn't sure what she'd say if she had the chance. *You know you find him attractive,* her inner voice told her, *and that was some kiss, even if you were too startled to appreciate it fully. He's interesting, and funny, and he knows your secret and isn't repulsed by it.* His hand was warm and firm in hers, and she found herself acutely aware of the way his fingers curled around hers, how he gripped her hand securely without squeezing too tightly. She wished she dared pull away from him, but the press of the crowd was great enough she'd likely never find him again if she did. But the truth was she liked having his hand in hers, liked the thought of him touching her cheek, her neck...

She blew out a long breath. She was being ridiculous. Yes, he knew her secret, but she'd been a fool already, ten years ago, and she wasn't going to be a fool twice. Her judgment when it came to men was clearly suspect—she'd chosen Roderick, after all—and Sebastian was still keeping secrets from her. And what would happen when their quest was over? She didn't need a romantic entanglement in her life, no matter what her foolish heart was telling her.

Rain began falling, a patient drizzle that seeped into the heavy linen and dampened Fiona's hair. The crowd thinned as men and women found shelter in doorways or inside houses. Fiona limped along, wishing she dared remove the thief's scarf from her foot, but that would only start the wound bleeding again. She wiped rain from her eyes. Was that the Jaixante, up ahead? The white walls and fairy spires looked dull in the rainy overcast, but it was definitely growing nearer.

Sebastian made another turn, and she recognized the street just moments before he led them into the stable yard. In a stall across the yard, Mittens raised her head and whickered a greeting at her. It was so unexpected Fiona dropped Sebastian's hand and crossed the yard to say hello to the horse while he went into the inn. She hadn't realized she could be so sentimental. Mittens slobbered on her hand, and Fiona patted her nose and thought about joining her in the stall, which at least had a roof.

"Bad news," Sebastian said, appearing beside her. "Holt hasn't been here."

145

That killed Fiona's good mood dead. "You don't suppose he was caught?"

"I don't know what to suppose. It's certainly possible." Sebastian petted Mittens absently. "More to the point, we're both hungry and filthy and we have no money."

"We could try the tokens again."

"I'm afraid that might be like trying to swat a fly with a burning brand. I was thinking we could offer to work for room and board. If Holt…" He shook his head. "At worst, we sell Holt's horse and make our way back to Tremontane."

"He's probably just hiding somewhere. He had a longer way to go than we did, and he was hauling three people's bags." She didn't think she sounded as confident as her words proclaimed.

"I'm grateful the inn's owner remembered me. I was afraid she'd kick us out as vagrants. Let's see if she'll let us wash her dishes."

It didn't look as if the inn's kitchen had been cleaned in a year. Fiona almost refused to eat anything that had been cooked in it, but when the cook brought out bowls of thin soup and hunks of black bread, her stomach growled so loudly even Sebastian heard it. They ate sitting in one corner on the filthy floor, Fiona reasoning that they could hardly get dirtier. The soup tasted faintly of chicken and more strongly of soap, but the bread was rich and the cook let them have second helpings of it.

Full, Fiona took a turn at the mountain of dishes in the porcelain double sink, while Sebastian began mopping. Water sloshed around her bare feet, cool and soothing despite how filthy it was. She hoped the cut wouldn't become infected. There was a little mop on a stick for scrubbing the dishes, and the tap ran with both hot and cold water, so aside from how tedious it was, it wasn't such an awful chore.

Fiona fell into a reverie, soothed by the sound of the rain falling more heavily on the tiled roof and pattering on the window panes. They needed to get out of Haizea, but that didn't mean she had to return to Tremontane; she could go directly to Umberan from here. *Or you could stay with Sebastian,* her inner voice said gleefully. She remembered his kiss and flushed. It had been awkward, she hadn't been expecting it, and yet the memory made her tingle all over. She hadn't been kissed like that in a long time. Roderick's embrace had failed to excite her for several years before the marriage was over.

The back door opened, startling her out of her fugue and making her fumble the dish mop. "Thank heaven," Holt said. He looked worse than they did, bent under the weight of their bags, his dark face ashy with exhaustion. "We have to leave immediately. The guards will be here in minutes."

18

Fiona flung the little mop into the sink, where it sank with a splash. "How close?"

"Very," Holt said. "We have no time to talk."

Sebastian took his bag from Holt. "No time to change?"

Holt was already through the door. "Time enough to saddle the horses and ride," he said over his shoulder.

Fiona wiped her pruny hands on her wrecked trousers and followed him. "How do they know who we are?"

Holt dumped his bag and hers on the wet ground outside the stable and began saddling Mittens. "The whole story will have to wait," he said. "I know only that they are inquiring after Fiona Cooper by name, and they have your description. They have spread out through the city and are being extremely thorough in their examination of every foreign woman in Haizea. It seems disruption of the Jaixante is taken quite seriously."

"Let me do that," Fiona said, fumbling with the horse's tack, but Holt took the leather straps from her firmly and gave her a little push out of his way.

"You still don't know what you're doing," Sebastian said to her, saddling his own horse. "This is faster. Put your boots on. Holt, are you sure we can't just hide?"

"They have already arrested two women with Miss Cooper's coloring, one far too young to be their quarry. My impression is that her capture is of such great importance that they are unwilling to take chances on letting her slip away. We need to put Haizea behind us, as quickly as possible." Holt handed Mittens' reins to Fiona and turned his attention to his own horse.

Fiona secured her bag and mounted, then had to turn awkwardly and dig for her rain cape. Riding had started to come more easily to her, but Sebastian was right, she couldn't do this on her own.

She turned Mittens in a circle, fidgeting. Sebastian and Holt worked in grim silence, and Fiona waited, one eye on the street, watching for those fluttering robes. Finally, the men mounted, and without a word the three rode out of the stable yard and down the street at a fast trot.

The sun was setting, somewhere past the lowering black clouds, and street lights were flickering into life all along the street. Their orange-tinged light turned the raindrops gold as they hissed past the lamp glass and made white-and-black Mittens look a ghastly yellow. Fiona hunched into her rain cape and tried not to imagine Jaixante guards coming up behind them. The ones she'd scared off with the mysterious tokens hadn't known her name, so there had been two groups, one sent off down the banks of the river on a fool's quest that had turned out not to be so foolish, at least in terms of finding them. But the other group...the only way they could have known her name was if someone had put Fiona Cooper's absence from the Irantzen Temple that morning with the mysterious intruders of the previous night.

She hunched further, this time trying to avoid her feelings of guilt. What must Hien have thought when she turned up missing? Had she been the one to conclude that Fiona Cooper was involved in the break-in? Fiona had become an excellent liar over the years, concealing her secret, but she'd never felt this guilty about any of her lies. And there was no way to make amends or explain.

"We can't travel through the night," she said to Holt, who rode just behind her.

"No, but we cannot risk finding a place to stay within the city," Holt said. "Our only hope is that we outpace our pursuers. A farm, with outbuildings, is what we need."

A man holding his coat over his head rushed past Fiona going the other direction. She glanced back after him, but the street was still; no sign of pursuit. The inn was already out of sight. "I think the rain is helping."

"It had better be, because I won't risk going faster on these slick stones," Sebastian said.

It felt like they were crawling at that pace, creeping along an inch at a time. The darkness was complete. The sun had set, the storm clouds filled the sky, and the orange lamps made puddles of light on the cobbled streets that shone wetly below the horses' feet. Soon they had the street to themselves. The darkened storefronts were hollow, gaping eyes and mouths, not the brightly lit plate glass windows of a Tremontanan city, but smaller spaces, some of them shuttered against the night, none of them revealing what could be bought inside. Fiona remembered the lively activity they'd seen when entering Haizea and was struck by the stark difference. The rain was letting up, but she couldn't hear anything beyond the sound of rain-drops hitting the ground. Like the Jaixante, it reminded her of a city of the dead.

Ahead, dark shapes emerged from a side street and ran toward them, shouting commands in Veriboldan. "What—" Sebastian said, but Fiona didn't need to understand to know what they wanted.

"We have to run," she said.

Holt turned his horse and kicked it into a faster gait. "This way."

They bolted down a side street, skidding on the paving stones, Holt now leading the way. Fiona clung to Mittens' reins and prayed she wouldn't fall off, that Mittens wouldn't trip and break a leg, that they would lose their pursuit in the winding, narrow streets. They crossed another wide thoroughfare, this one crowded with people despite the weather, and Holt turned to parallel it, but was forced to turn again, and again. Fiona was utterly lost. All she knew was that they were gradually moving east, away from the Kepa River and the city center. Did Holt know where they were going? He couldn't possibly.

She wiped rainwater out of her face and followed Holt around another turn, then gasped as a dark-clothed Jaixante guard stepped out practically under Holt's hooves. The horse reared up, startled, and Holt flung himself forward to keep his seat. The guard held a pistol on Holt. "Down," he said.

Holt's horse jigged nervously. "Down," the guard repeated. "All down."

Fiona looked at Sebastian, whose face was set and tense in the orange light. "Do as he says, Fiona."

The guard's attention flicked to her as she dismounted, then to the street behind him as he realized his partner hadn't followed him. In that moment, Sebastian lunged forward, the pistol came around to point at him, and Holt leaped from his horse to bear the man to the ground.

The pistol went off with a loud bang, and then Sebastian had joined Holt in the scuffle. Someone kicked the pistol away; it skittered across the paving stones toward Fiona, and she picked it up carefully. She knew nothing of gun Devices and even less of their Veriboldan counterparts, which was what the weapon was, but she held it with her finger carefully away from the trigger and said, "Let him up."

Holt had the man pinioned, and he looked up in surprise at Fiona. More movement in the darkness turned into another guard running into the street, pistol at the ready. Quickly Fiona brought her pistol to bear on the man and rested her finger lightly on the trigger. "*Drop it*," she said in Veriboldan. The man, his pistol swinging wildly from target to target, finally dropped his weapon. "*Kick it to me.*" He kicked it so it rattled across the stones toward her.

Sebastian came to her side and picked it up. "What now?" she murmured to Sebastian. "We don't have any way to tie them."

Someone screamed behind them. Fiona jerked in surprise, but

kept her attention on the guard. "Someone's noticed us," Sebastian said. "We have to move."

"*Lie down on the street with your hands where I can see them,*" Fiona said. "Holt, let that one go." She kept the pistol pointed at the prone guard while Holt released his captive and kicked his knee so he fell heavily to the ground. The screaming continued, joined by several voices shouting. Fiona cursed and mounted her horse, thrusting the pistol into her waistband. Holt kicked his horse again, and the three of them took off down the street. Behind them, the guards' whistles joined the din.

They rode far too fast down the narrow street. The street lamps were further apart now, and some of their lights were broken. The street narrowed again. The ceramic-tiled houses were gone, replaced by haphazardly constructed shanties of wood and concrete blocks. Light leaked from behind doors that didn't fit properly, falling on heaps of refuse, some of which moved. The air felt oppressively heavy, like a wet woolen blanket weighing Fiona down. Dusktown. The guards might not be their biggest problem anymore.

Silent figures watched them from every corner, but made no move to approach them. Fiona carefully didn't meet anyone's eyes. She hoped they didn't look like targets. Holt was a big, sinister figure, and Sebastian wasn't small, and she...well, Holt and Sebastian didn't look like targets, and she was armed, if it came to a fight.

Ahead, someone moved into the street and stopped, facing them. Holt drew his horse up. "*Stand aside,*" Fiona said.

"*Just want a coin or two for a hungry man and his family.*" The man didn't have his hand out.

Fiona sensed other figures moving in on both sides. She drew the pistol and pointed it at him, startling him into taking a few steps backward. "*Back away,*" she said.

The man glanced to his right, then put two fingers to his lips and whistled. The other figures melted away into the shadows. Fiona realized her hand was shaking and stilled it. The man nodded at her as if they'd just been having a polite conversation and stepped back to one side.

"The pistols are only going to take us so far." Sebastian's low voice carried clearly through the rain.

"We should move faster," Fiona said, and Holt picked up the pace.

She rode with one hand on the reins and the other holding the pistol, her shoulders stiff with tension every time something moved in the shadows. Distantly, she heard the guards' whistles, calling to their friends, probably capturing some poor Tremontanan woman with red hair who'd spend an uncomfortable night in a cell, not the kind the Irantzen Temple offered.

Something scuttled across the street in front of them, and she jerked the pistol around to point at Holt's back, then swiftly brought it away, cursing silently. This was no worse than the slums of a Tremontanan city, but the strange buildings, and the smells, and the dim lighting, made it feel alien, worse than the Jaixante and its windowless fairy spires.

Then there were fewer buildings, and no lamp posts, and they'd left the city behind them. The cobbled streets had turned into a dirt road that was almost indistinguishable from the long grass that grew on either side of it. Sebastian and Holt were barely visible in the gloom, and even Mittens looked pale, a patchy ghost. "We have to keep moving," Fiona said.

"Carefully," Sebastian said, and headed off along the road, this time at a walk.

After a few minutes, the rain stopped, but dark clouds still covered the sky, blocking out the moon and stars. Fiona pushed back the hood of her rain cape to breathe in the wet, chilly air. Her foot no longer hurt as badly, her various aches from running were subsiding, but she was wet despite the cape and her filthy clothes chafed her. She held her tongue. Complaining about minor inconveniences seemed stupid, given that they were still running for their lives. If you could call it running when they were groping along the road, trying not to stumble.

They rode for what felt like hours, Fiona all the time straining to hear the sounds of pursuit. But it really did seem they'd left the guards behind. She refused to feel relief. Time enough for that when they were safely back in Tremontane. Her head jerked, and she realized she'd nearly fallen asleep on Mittens' back. "Should we look for shelter?" she said.

"I think I've found something," Sebastian said. She saw a dark shape that might be his arm pointing off to the right. In that direction, a handful of hunched buildings huddled for mutual protection, and a few lanterns gleamed like earthbound stars. "That's a farm."

"We cannot ask them for shelter," said Holt, "without risking exposure later. We should not assume those guards will give up their pursuit entirely."

"I was thinking we'd just borrow one of their storage buildings." Sebastian turned his horse in the direction of the farm. "Change clothes, sleep a few hours, and move on."

Holt made them stop some fifty yards from the closest building. Sebastian and Fiona waited while he crept up to it and slinked around its weathered sides, dark with rain. "So if he wasn't always a manservant, why did your parents hire him as one?" Fiona whispered. They weren't anywhere close to where anyone could hear them, but the chill in the air and the darkness in the sky made her feel inclined to quiet.

"He did a service for my father," Sebastian said in the same low voice. "Something not entirely legal, I gather. On a whim, my father hired him as a footman—heaven only knows why he thought that was a good idea. My mother likes them to be a matched set. So when she complained about him ruining her aesthetic, he assigned Holt to me. Something about taking on whatever my exclusive, expensive school might throw my way, as if assassins and thieves might infiltrate it. It was a good choice, but probably not for the reasons my father believed."

Holt had disappeared beyond the building, which was windowless and had the same steeply-sloped roof every other farm building Fiona had seen possessed. "What, you never had his help sneaking out at night?"

"No, but I honed my own skills sneaking out past him, or trying to. Though he did teach me to pick locks. I'm not very good. He never showed me how to pick pockets, which I thought would have been much more useful—there, he's coming back."

Holt was remarkably silent for such a tall man, and made almost no silhouette against the darkness. "It is a storage shed," he said, "and there is room, barely, for all six of us."

"Thank heaven. I'm about dead on my feet," Sebastian said.

They led the horses around to the front of the shed, which had a single large door that creaked open to reveal a warm, cavernous interior. Shed was probably the wrong word for it, though "barn" didn't quite fit either; it was a single large room with no loft, packed with pallets on which rested burlap sacks stacked twenty high. It smelled dusty, and floury, and Holt patted one of the sacks and said, "Wheat."

Sebastian found an empty burlap sack and began rubbing his horse down. "I wish we had food for them," he said. "Or food for us. All this wheat, and it does none of us any good."

Mittens nuzzled Fiona's arm as she followed Sebastian's example. "I know," she murmured to the horse, "in the morning we'll find you something. I want to change into something less filthy," she announced to the room.

"There's space beyond the pallets where you can have some privacy," Sebastian said, "and I think we can sleep on the sacks."

Never had any bed looked so welcoming. Fiona took her bag into a corner and rapidly put on her own clothes, kicking the dirty temple clothes into a corner. Then she changed her mind and folded them neatly into her bag. They might come in handy, though she couldn't imagine how.

She tossed the little sack in one hand, feeling the ceramic tokens shift, then put it and the scroll case into her bag. Speaking of things she didn't know what they were for. It worried her somewhat, carrying around this thing that had been hidden so carefully away and had such an effect on people. Even the young thief had been afraid of it. And the guard had drawn some kind of conclusion about her before running away—

She cursed, loudly, then kicked her bag in frustration. "What? What's wrong?" Sebastian exclaimed.

"That guard is going to tell them we have these tokens."

"So?"

"So they're never going to stop chasing us."

Sebastian came around the corner, buttoning his shirt. "Or they'll leave us alone because they're afraid of what it might mean that we have them."

Fiona let out a short laugh. "They're going to be mightily confused, in any case. They know only that we were in the foreign trade office and that we have the tokens. But Gizane had them hidden in her desk, which, by the way, I don't remember closing. What do you think the odds are that the tokens were supposed to be there? I bet Gizane stole them first. So they're going to start asking a lot of questions."

"None of which have anything to do with us."

"If we're lucky, they'll turn their attention on Gizane."

"Probably. But I think you're right that they won't stop chasing us, just in case." He gestured to the sacks. "Sit there."

"Why?"

"I want to look at your foot. It should be washed and bound up properly."

Fiona sat and extended her foot to him. He took it gently in one hand and used his little light Device to examine it. "It's not a deep cut, but I'm sure it's painful. Holt, do we have water?"

"I drew some from the well in the farmyard," Holt said. He had a bucket in one hand and a length of cloth in the other. "If you'll allow me, sir?"

Sebastian gave way to Holt, who swabbed her foot gently enough that she didn't do more than wince at his touch. He dried her foot and wrapped it tightly in the clean cloth, tying it off around her ankle. "That should do for now," he said. "We can thank heaven you did not require stitches."

"Thank you, Holt."

"It was my pleasure, Miss Cooper. Now, I suggest we all try to sleep. We will have to leave here before first light." He disappeared with the bucket. Fiona stood and put her weight on the injured foot. It throbbed, but felt less painful.

Sebastian leaned against one of the tall pallets of wheat sacks. "Still glad you came along?"

He was a dim shape in the darkness, but she could see him smile. "Surprisingly, yes," she said, and his smile broadened.

"Dare I hope it's the company you enjoy?" he went on.

"Sebastian—"

"Don't say anything else." She felt the touch of his hand where it gripped hers briefly, then released her. "We're friends first, Fiona. Remember that. Just—I'm not going to stop hoping for more." Lightly, he caressed her cheek, and then he was gone, leaving her gaping and her heart racing.

She closed her eyes and leaned against the stack. The musty, dry smell of wheat filled her nostrils, and she rested her forehead against the rough burlap and sighed. Roderick had been like this at the beginning—persistent, gentle, inexorable. And every bit as wrong as Sebastian was, though for different reasons.

She tossed her bag atop some of the lower piles of sacks and climbed up after it. The piles were solid and heavy and made for a good, if lumpy, bed. She heard Sebastian and Holt settling themselves nearby and thought about suggesting they set a watch, but the moment she lay down she felt all her muscles relaxing despite the hardness of the makeshift bed and realized she was too tired to worry overmuch about the slim possibility that someone might come out there during the night.

Wearily, she went through her evening routine, terrifyingly conscious of how flammable wheat dust was. She hoped she wasn't tired enough to sleep too deeply, or Sebastian would find out first-hand how frightening her magic was.

She tucked her bag under her head, then had to shift it because something inside was digging into the base of her neck. Her journal. She hadn't had access to it since they reached the temple, and now was a completely inappropriate time to use it, but she found herself wishing she could write down some of what troubled her now.

Dear Diary, she thought, *we're being chased by men who believe we've stolen something terrifying, this pallet of wheat sacks is hard and lumpy, and someone's romantically interested in me for the first time in nearly ten years. I realize I wanted a change, but I didn't know this was it. And to be honest, I'm not sure I'd ask for something different if I had the chance.*

She fell asleep mid-thought, wishing she'd kissed Sebastian back.

A hand shook her gently awake. "Miss Cooper," Holt said, "we should be on our way."

Fiona sat up quickly, shaking wheat dust off her clothes. "What time is it?"

"Not sure," Sebastian said. "My watch was ruined by the river. But it's well before dawn. I don't know how early these farmers wake, but I don't want to take any chances."

They saddled the horses, who didn't seem bothered by the early morning, and led them one by one out of the shed. The sky had cleared, and the setting moon cast a dim glow over the farmyard. Smaller buildings of weathered board and tiled roofs lay scattered here and there, most of them windowless, a few with the same wide doors as their ersatz inn. There was a stable to the right of the main house, both of which were dark and silent. To the left was a chicken coop. Fiona heard the mutterings of the hens as they drowsed in their nests. The sound made her hungry. "I wish we could cook eggs," she said as she prepared to mount Mittens.

"Or hens," Sebastian said.

"I'd settle for eggs."

"Leave it to me," Holt said, handing his horse's reins to Sebastian.

"Holt, I wasn't serious."

"There are other foods on this farm we can eat. Go ahead, and I will catch up to you in due time." Holt nodded at Fiona and slunk away in the direction of the farmhouse.

Sebastian looked at Fiona. "He's going to get caught," Fiona said.

"Possibly, but I'm more worried about slowing down. Still, there's nothing I can do to change his mind once he's made it up. Let's just do as he says. Sweet heaven, I wish the world would run as I want for once."

They picked up the road almost immediately. It was muddy, and the horses slogged through it with none of their usual cheerfulness. Fiona patted Mittens' neck and wished she had some way to reassure the animal that things would improve. She didn't urge her on when Mittens stopped to graze in the tall grass by the road. The poor horse must be as hungry as she was, maybe hungrier.

"He's coming," Sebastian said, and Fiona looked back to see Holt loping along the verge, his arms full of something. When he came near, she saw it was a large burlap sack, bulging and lumpy.

"Enough for now," he said, and dug into it. He held out a red, ripe tomato the size of Fiona's fist. "To sustain us until we are across the border. Though if we are to stay with the road, I think it is no more unsafe to buy from the roadside stands than it is simply to pass them by."

Sebastian took a handful of carrots and saluted Holt with them. "I've never seen anything more delicious," he said, and bit down hard, ignoring the dirt that lingered on the vegetable.

Fiona took a bite of tomato as if it were an apple, then swiped away the rosy juice that spilled out of it. "Agreed," she said.

They rode on, eating tomatoes and carrots and handfuls of shelled almonds from a couple of smaller sacks. The sun rose, turning the world golden, and brought with it the songs of a hundred tiny black birds that swooped past overhead, their wings making a rushing sound like wind through treetops. The road wound through the verdant hills, and from somewhere in the distance came the smell of burning wood, a warm, bitter smell that enhanced the bright greenness of the hills. Fiona wiped her mouth with her sleeve. It was easy to forget, on a day like this, that they were being chased.

The reminder stung Fiona out of her relaxed state. She'd been so tired the night before. "Holt!" she said. "Do you have the blackmail?"

Sebastian cursed. "I can't believe I forgot," he said. "Everything I was carrying got washed away by the river. Please say you've got it."

Holt pulled up his horse and turned around to rummage in his bag. "I have what I was given," he said. "Whether that is what we seek, I do not know."

He withdrew two scroll cases, a flat leather portfolio, and a stack of folders tied with black ribbon, and handed them to Sebastian. "Do we have time for this?" Fiona said, removing the scroll case from inside her bag.

"It won't take long." Sebastian handed her the folders. "Untie that, would you?" He worked his fingernails into the cap of the first scroll case and wiggled it. Fiona picked at the knot until it loosened, then handed the folders back to Holt.

The scroll case she'd carried with her until she'd forgotten it was there was waterproofed leather, sealed at both ends with blobs of red wax unmarked by sign and shield, or whatever Veriboldans used to signify their noble ranks. She chipped away at one blob with her fingernails until it cracked and fell apart into a dozen shards. Beneath it, the cap was plugged into the case as firmly as a cork in a wine bottle. Fiona worked at it until finally she coaxed it out and shook free the last clinging remnants of the seal, wiping her hand on her trousers.

She tipped the contents into her hand. There were three sheets of expensive paper with a thick texture rolled up inside, two of them faintly blue-tinged, the other creamy white. All of them were barely water-spotted despite their submersion in the Kepa River. Fiona unrolled all three into a thin sheaf. Beside her, Sebastian cursed again and thrust a page back into his scroll case. "Not that one," he said.

The paper on top, the white one, was covered in a scrawling handwriting, difficult to read, but Fiona had no trouble identifying it as a hunter's affidavit. Hunters were supposed to procure proof that the people they captured had inherent magic and had used it against others, though this almost never stopped them from enacting vigilante justice against anyone even suspected of it. This one was signed and countersigned, but not stamped, meaning the hunter had identified a target but not yet brought that person in for trial.

She skipped back to the top of the page and began puzzling out its contents. The hunter's credentials, his evidence, the name of the accused... It brought her to a stop, unable to read further. She'd found what Sebastian was looking for. It couldn't be anything else.

She read the name again, her stunned brain insisting it was impossible. She gripped the paper in suddenly nerveless fingers. Oh, how Sebastian had deceived her. *You might care if you knew who my parents were.* He was so right.

"The documents in these folders are in Veriboldan," Holt said. "Miss Cooper?"

Sebastian looked up. "That's probably not it, but maybe you shouldn't read those. I don't want you to...is something wrong, Fiona?"

Fiona swallowed to moisten her dry throat. "This is a hunter's affidavit swearing to the existence of a man whose inherent magic is to manipulate the minds of others to make them do his bidding. To make them believe it's what they want. The hunter lists times and places this man has used his magic on people. I don't know how he can prove something like that, but it doesn't matter, he has all the right signatures." She looked at Sebastian. Surely it just her imagination that he seemed to be a thousand feet away. "The man he accuses is Douglas North."

Sebastian's eyes widened. Then his expression changed to one of wary uncertainty. "Fiona, I can explain."

"You don't have to," Fiona said. "This is what you were looking for, isn't it? You're Prince Sebastian North. Douglas North is your scandal-ridden younger brother. And this is one hell of a scandal."

Holt gently took the documents from her. Fiona thought about fighting him for them, then realized she didn't care. The memory of

Sebastian kissing her flashed past her inner eye, and she wished she could lash Mittens into a gallop and ride for the border, leaving the men behind forever.

"These other pages are worse," Holt said, turning over the blue-tinged sheets, which were written on front and back. "A copy of a death certificate, and a testimony by a doctor whose name I do not recognize. Taken together, they paint a picture that sickens me. The death certificate is that of one Melanie Tippets, named in the affidavit as one of Prince Douglas's victims, and the testimony avows that Miss Tippets was, despite appearances, murdered. The implication is that Prince Douglas used his inherent magic on the young woman, for what purpose it does not say, then either murdered her himself or caused her to be killed to prevent her revealing his actions."

Sebastian looked sick. "He can't have. Doug is an idiot, true, but he's not evil."

"I fear it does not matter whether it is true or not," Holt said, letting the pages roll back together. "This is evidence strong enough to convict him. Even without Miss Tippets' death, the knowledge that the North family is tainted by inherent magic will lose Queen Genevieve the Crown."

"No wonder Mother didn't want me to know what Doug had done," Sebastian said faintly. "She must have known...he can't be allowed to get away with murder, no matter what his reasons."

"But it will destroy your family if he's publicly tried," Fiona said. There, she'd sounded calm and rational. He couldn't hear the tiny voice shrieking inside her head to run, forget the four thousand guilders and leave him in her dust.

"There has to be something Mother can do." Sebastian looked at Fiona more closely, appeared about to say something, then shook his head. "Let's move on," he said. "We have to return to Aurilien as quickly as possible."

"Can't you just destroy the evidence?" Fiona said.

"Mother insisted I return with it. I don't know why. She might want the reassurance of destroying it herself." Sebastian gathered the rest of Gizane's documents and shoved them roughly into the saddlebags. He glanced at Holt, hesitated, and said, "Would you ride ahead and...I don't know. Just...give us some privacy, please?"

Holt nodded and spurred his horse onward. "Fiona, let me explain," Sebastian said.

"Explain what?" Fiona said. Her voice shook with anger. "I already knew you were above my station. I just didn't know how far. And you were so careful not to let me know."

"That's not how it went. I couldn't tell you at first because you were a total stranger and it wasn't my secret to reveal."

"So when were you going to tell me? When you paid me off? And I'd almost forgotten this was a business transaction."

Sebastian swore explosively. "Look, I know you're angry, and you deserve to be—"

"Thank you for your permission, your Highness."

"I didn't have a choice! I swore I'd keep the family name out of it. By the time I knew I could trust you, it was too late to simply blurt it out. I've been trying to figure out how to tell you the truth for the last three days. I'm sorry you learned about it this way."

Fiona unclenched her jaw, which was painfully rigid. "And what about the rest? Am I supposed to be grateful that a prince deigned to give me his attention? How far were you going to take this, Sebastian? Did you want me to fall into your bed, or were you going to be satisfied with a few stolen kisses?"

Sebastian closed his eyes briefly and visibly controlled himself. "Fiona," he said, looking at her, "I never lied to you about that. You're the most amazing woman I've ever met and it thrills me to be near you. I was serious when I told you I wanted the chance to see if that feeling could grow into something more. As far as I'm concerned, we're just a man and a woman learning to fall in love. My being a prince has nothing to do with that."

Fiona's hands trembled, and she clamped down on Mittens' reins more tightly, as if she might bleed off her anger and confusion into the leather. "Maybe to you it doesn't matter," she said tightly. "It's not exactly fair to me."

"If I don't care, why should you?"

His intent expression, his utter surety that he was right, struck her an almost palpable blow. "I'm not part of your world, your Highness," she said. "I'm a divorced tradeswoman who's never been closer to high society than watching the Queen open the Midsummer festivities at the Zedechen Bethel, and that was from so great a distance she was the size of an ant. I wouldn't have the first idea how to act at a palace reception, I don't know how to dance, and I'd probably insult any Count or Baron I was introduced to because I have no idea how to behave to nobility. You and I have no future. We never have. The only difference between us is you seem not to believe this."

Sebastian's hands closed tightly on his reins. "You can be anyone you want to be, Fiona. It's part of what I love about you. Are you telling me you'd let such petty concerns as your birth and upbringing stand between what we might have together?"

"Petty?"

He winced. "That was the wrong word."

"It certainly was." Fiona flicked the reins, and Mittens stepped out after Holt, who'd gone just far enough ahead to be out of earshot and stood waiting for them to finish. "We need to keep moving. I don't want to be caught by the Veriboldans."

"Fiona—"

"I don't think there's any point in arguing more. Let's just ride."

She prodded Mittens gently into a faster gait, the fastest she could manage without falling off. Sebastian didn't come up even with her. At least he had the decency to obey her wishes. Her heart was too angry for tears. She should have followed her instincts and spurned him. Her judgment when it came to men was truly abysmal.

They rode on eastward into dawn, the sun pinking the horizon, then flooding the hills with golden light. The skies had cleared, and it was going to be a pleasant day, warmer and drier than the day before. Fiona remembered being soaked to the bone and shivered. They were heading back to the uplands and a Tremontanan winter. Too bad they were wanted fugitives, because staying in Veribold's warm climate had some appeal.

Holt fell back to the rear of their procession around noon,

watching behind them for pursuers, but the road remained clear of all but a few travelers, heading west. They passed Fiona and Sebastian without so much as a nod of acknowledgement. Fiona superstitiously kept her eyes on Mittens' ears, as if anyone might read her guilt on her face. What did Hien think of her now? The truth, probably, that she'd been at the Irantzen Festival solely for the purpose of stealing from the Jaixante. If the guard had told Hien about the mystery tokens, she no doubt believed Fiona had succeeded.

Put in such bald terms, it made her look like a criminal. Which she was—and for the sake of a murderer and...was it rape if Douglas North was capable of gaining consent by making women believe they wanted what he did? Of course it was, if a roundabout sort of rape. It was still evil.

As the hours lengthened toward evening, she became more incensed with herself. She'd deceived an honorable woman, and for what? She glanced ahead to where Sebastian rode, hunched in on himself as if the cool breeze were an arctic wind, and her heart softened. How much worse it must be for him, tricked by his mother the Queen into helping his brother escape justice. Fiona might be angry with him, but she couldn't help feeling sorry on his behalf. *He lied to you*, a tiny voice inside her head told her, but she ignored it. She'd seen how he looked when the blackmail was revealed, and he'd been devastated.

Hooves pounding the hard road heralded Holt's return. "There is movement on the road to the west at the limits of my vision," he said. "Many travelers moving rapidly."

"You think they're pursuing us?" Sebastian said.

"I think we cannot take the chance that they are not." Holt looked at Fiona. "Can you ride faster?"

"Maybe a little," Fiona said, gripping Mittens' reins more tightly.

"Even a little helps," Sebastian said. He urged his horse onward, and the other two followed.

Fiona started glancing over her shoulder every half hour or so, straining to see signs of pursuit. Holt's eyes must be better than hers. All she could see was Holt, still riding at the rear, backlit by the setting sun. Sebastian rode even more hunched over than before. They came to a town straddling the road and passed through it; nobody suggested stopping for the night. Exhaustion settled over Fiona like an iron blanket, her legs and bottom were sore, and she couldn't remember a time when Mittens' ears weren't her whole world. "I can't go on much longer," she called out. "I'm sorry, but I'm going to fall off."

"We cannot ride through the night," Holt said. "But we also cannot stay near the road."

"We'll have to cut across country," Sebastian said. "There's another border crossing south of here, nearer where the Snow River crosses the Eskandelic border. It will add half a day's travel to our journey, but if it keeps us from being captured…anyway, we'll be sleeping rough for a couple of nights." He carefully didn't look at Fiona.

"I don't mind," Fiona said. "But let's hurry. We need to get away from the road before they're close enough to see where we've gone."

Sebastian immediately turned off the road into the short, rough grass of the verge. Fiona and Holt followed. They had left the hills behind just after noon and had traveled steadily upward since then, into the desert plains so unlike the green richness of the Kepa Valley. The uneven terrain jolted Fiona back and forth in the saddle, making it even more difficult for her to hold on. On the other hand, it kept her awake, so there was something good to come of it. She prayed none of the horses would fall lame, and prayed even more fervently that whoever was following them wouldn't see they'd left the road.

The sun set, and the moon rose like heaven's half-lidded eye watching over them. Fiona's body ached, and despite the rough terrain she found herself nodding off and jerking back awake, over and over again. She didn't realize at first that Sebastian had stopped, and rode a few paces past him before he jogged ahead of her horse and grabbed hold of her reins. "We're stopping here," he said quietly, as if afraid someone might overhear, though there was no one but the three of them for miles around.

Fiona nodded, blinked tiredness from her eyes, and slid off

Mittens awkwardly. When her feet touched ground, her legs wouldn't support her, and she landed in a graceless heap beside Mittens' feet. Sebastian cursed and dropped to the ground beside her. "You're exhausted," he said, putting his arms around her and helping her stand. "You should have said something."

She clung to him for support, not caring what message that might send. "I didn't realize," she said, her voice coming out as a croak. She cleared her throat and went on, "We probably shouldn't light a fire."

"No, that would be as good as a beacon to draw attention to us," Holt said. He offered Fiona her heavy cloak, which he'd removed from her saddlebag. "This is the only bedding I can offer you."

"It's fine. Thanks." Fiona let go of Sebastian, who removed his arms from around her a moment later. She tried not to think about how comforting it had been to be held by him. Wrapping her cloak around her, she dug through her other saddlebag for something to rub Mittens down with and came up with her ruined temple clothes.

A hand reached over her shoulder. "Let me do that," Sebastian said. "You need to sit before you fall over."

She thought about pressing the issue and realized he was weaving in her vision. A moment's reflection told her she was the one moving, swaying with weariness. "All right," she said, and retreated a few paces to sit where Holt had unloaded his horse's burden and was rubbing him with a spare shirt.

"There's a river—more of a stream, I suppose—somewhere around here," Sebastian told Holt. "We'll come across it if we keep going southeast. Until then, we'll have to go thirsty, unless you have waterskins tucked away somewhere?"

"I do, but the water should go to the horses," Holt said. He finished his task and rooted around in the food sack, coming up with a handful of crooked carrots, and handed some to Fiona. "Eat, then try to sleep."

Fiona took his offering and began gnawing on a carrot. It was dry and hard, but better than nothing. She watched Sebastian care for Mittens, then for his own horse, before settling on the ground some distance from her. She was grateful that he didn't seem inclined to renew his attempts to reason with her. She still didn't know how she felt.

She lay back with her head pillowed on the hood of her cloak. The night air was cold, and she pulled her cloak more tightly around herself and stared up at the stars, brilliantly white against the black sky. Roderick had claimed to be able to find his direction by the stars, but she'd never believed him. Now she wished she'd paid more attention to all his talk of constellations, because it would give her something to think about now that wasn't dwelling on Sebastian and his lies of omission.

She was just drifting off to sleep despite her aches when she heard Holt say, "This is an impossible situation."

"I know," Sebastian said, his voice pitched low, and Fiona realized he thought she was asleep. "Mother had to know what information Gizane had on Doug. She knows what he's done. Sweet heaven, Holt, what have we lent ourselves to?"

"We could hardly have done otherwise," Holt said. "There are too many innocents who would suffer if this were to be made public knowledge. Think of Princess Emily."

"I am. And my Great-Uncle Sebastian. Damn it, Holt, I still feel used."

"The Queen is intelligent enough to know you would not have agreed to this had you known the truth."

"And we dragged Fiona into this. I can't forgive myself for that."

There was a pause. Holt said, "Is that all you cannot forgive?"

Sebastian laughed once, a low, bitter *hah*. "I couldn't have screwed that up worse if that had been my plan to begin with."

"You think she will not forgive you?"

"I don't think it matters. She's convinced we could never have a future together. I don't know what to say, Holt. I finally..." He let out a long, pained sigh. "Willow North was a common thief before becoming Queen. It's not like there's no precedent."

"I do not believe anyone could call Queen Willow a common anything. But I understand your point."

There was a pause. "I think I'm in love with her, Holt. How big a fool does that make me?"

"She is worthy of being loved. I do not believe that makes you a fool, to recognize that."

Fiona realized she was holding her breath and let it out in a long, thin stream that steamed in the cold night air.

"But I think pursuing her aggressively, trying to change her mind, would be a mistake," Holt went on. "A mistake, and an insult to her free will."

"I know," Sebastian said. "I just don't want to give up entirely."

"Give it time, and perhaps things will look different."

"They could hardly be worse." Sebastian sighed. "It's another day and a half to the border. Anything could happen."

Holt grunted in reply, and both men fell silent. The stars above were blurry, and Fiona blinked away the beginnings of tears. It didn't matter what Sebastian felt. What they both felt, she had to admit to herself. They were too different to make a life together. How would Sebastian feel about giving up his world of wealth and privilege to be a commoner like her? He wouldn't be so cavalier about their different worlds then. She would be a fool to let her heart override her head. She would travel with him long enough to get her four thousand guilders, and then she never had to see him again.

20

Filthy slush filled Aurilien's gutters, making the golden city dingy and tarnished. Winter in Aurilien was something Fiona hadn't missed, though her years with Roderick in Kingsport had never acclimated her to the wild storms that blew in off the ocean between Wintersmeet and the spring equinox. Still, the relief of finally having reached their destination made Aurilien beautiful in her eyes.

The familiar buildings of Lower Town, their dark beams criss-crossing white and pale blue plaster, gave way to the stone of the great mansions casting smaller buildings into shadow. Men and women bundled up against the chill in the air didn't even look up at them as they rode past. So familiar, and so heart-wrenchingly forbidding. This hadn't been her home in more than a decade.

Nobody paid much attention to them, just another party of anonymous travelers visiting the great city. Beside her, Sebastian rode with his hood up. She wasn't sure if he was cold, or if he just wanted to avoid being recognized. Probably here in the capital, the latter was more likely. She certainly hadn't recognized him. How different things would have been if she had.

She caught the eye of a beautiful young woman with shining black hair who gaped at her from a street corner. The girl was waif-thin and looked hungry. On an impulse, Fiona nudged Mittens to the side and handed her a coin. "Get something to eat," she said. The girl clutched the coin, her mouth hanging slack with astonishment, but said nothing.

"You don't know that girl was a beggar," Sebastian said when she returned to his side.

"She looked starving. I couldn't not help." But she half-turned in the saddle. The girl was gone. "And she didn't turn it down."

"Even so, suppose she was just an ordinary person? You might have embarrassed both of you."

"I know. It just...felt right."

It was the longest conversation they'd had all day. They hadn't spoken much on the week-long journey back to Aurilien. Sebastian had treated her with quiet if distant courtesy, nothing of the easy familiarity she'd grown accustomed to in his manner, and Holt was his usual taciturn self. They had crossed the border with no incident —getting out of Veribold was far easier than entering it—and no one had challenged them on the Tremontanan side. Fiona had recalled their first crossing and it made her heart ache. It had been the first time Sebastian had looked at her not as a curiosity or an eccentric stranger, but as a woman who intrigued him. If she'd known then what would happen, would she have continued? It disturbed her that she didn't know the answer.

Even when they were safely back in Tremontane, and had confirmed no one had followed them, they had stayed away from the big cities and taken shelter in tiny roadside inns. Sebastian and Fiona had continued to take meals together, but their evenings had been strained. Fiona found herself constantly aware of little things about him, of the way he held his knife and fork, of how he never met her eyes if he could help it. At night she lay wakeful in whatever narrow bed the inn had provided and cursed her weakness. He was a prince, she was a commoner and possessor of illicit magic. She was such a fool to even consider falling in love with him.

Now she said, "What happens next?"

"We'll go to the palace and turn this mess over to my mother," Sebastian said, his voice muffled by the folds of his hood. "I sent a message ahead so she knows we're coming. Then we'll go to the Bank of Aurilien and I'll get your money. I suppose you'll want cash, and not a banker's draft?"

"That would be more convenient."

"Where will you go after this? Dineh-Karit, still?"

"I suppose."

They fell back into silence. "Fiona," Sebastian said after a moment. She hadn't heard her name from him in a week. "If I'd told you immediately who I was, if you hadn't found out that way...would it have made a difference?"

She turned to look at him. He had his attention fixed on the road. "I understand why you couldn't tell me. I'm not angry about that anymore."

"Thank you. But that's not what I meant."

"I know what you meant. Sebastian, we—"

"State your business," a harsh voice demanded. Fiona brought Mittens to a halt before a pair of guards liveried in Tremontanan brown and green. The one who'd spoken brought his pike, clearly not ceremonial, into a guard position in front of the ornamental iron gates that would bar the way to the palace grounds when they were closed. She hadn't even noticed they'd reached the end of the road.

Sebastian pushed back his hood. "Prince Sebastian North," he said coldly. "Or have you forgotten my face?"

The guard took a step back. "Your Highness," he said, fear touching his voice. "I beg your pardon, I didn't realize—of course you may pass."

"Thank you," Sebastian said, edging past Mittens and proceeding up the long, curving drive, its cobbles clear of snow and shining dully in the mid-morning sunlight. Fiona followed him, Holt bringing up the rear.

Patches of snow still lay here and there on the sweep of lawn covering the slopes of the hill the palace was built on. The shrubberies lining the drive, however, looked as green as they would at Midsummer, their thumbnail-sized dark green leaves impervious to such outside impositions as weather. Beyond them, oak and maple trees stretched bare branches to the blue sky as if imploring it to hold back the next storm. A gray squirrel darted past and spiraled up a fat trunk, scampering along a branch nearly parallel to the ground and leaping to the tree's neighbor. Fiona thought about where it might be going, whether it had a family or was alone in the world. She resisted feeling sorry for herself.

The road ended at a vast paved area with more paths—they were almost as wide as roads—curving off to the left and right of the palace steps. Fiona eyed the steps with trepidation. They were dark marble, shallow but wide, and they rose nearly twenty feet in the air to the great black double doors of the palace entrance. They would be a nightmare to keep clear of ice.

Soldiers in green and brown stood sentinel at the base of the stairs and flanking the doors. They made no move to either bar the way or welcome the travelers. More men and women, these dressed in North blue and silver livery, ran toward them from the right-hand path. "Why am I here?" she murmured to Sebastian. "Surely you don't need me to report to the Queen."

Sebastian dismounted and handed his reins to one of the liveried servants, hesitated, then held out his hand to help Fiona dismount. "I didn't think about it. It didn't make sense to leave you kicking your heels in some tavern somewhere, waiting for me to return, and I wanted—" He closed his mouth in a hard line, stifling further words. "I'm sorry. Do you want to wait in the antechamber? This shouldn't take long."

Fiona eyed the monstrous edifice before her. The palace had the look of a patchwork building, half a dozen architectural styles vying for precedence, all of them opulent and overwhelming. "I'd...rather wait," she said, quashing the feeling that she was being a coward.

She followed Sebastian up the steps and through the doors into one of the largest rooms she'd ever seen. It was floored with white marble, its walls were painted flat white, and the iron railings of the staircase that spiraled up and out of sight were also painted white. A white arched opening wide enough for four people to walk abreast led to an equally wide hallway that led deeper into the palace.

The overall effect was that of a wintry fairy palace, complete with a chandelier that hung suspended by a white chain over the center of the room, dripping with light Devices. The spires of the Jaixante had had the same effect, but warm instead of chilly. Maybe wealth looked the same whatever country you were in. Fiona realized she was gawking and closed her mouth.

Sebastian indicated a couple of chairs to the right of the doors. Two ordinary-sized doors, both closed, flanked the chairs. "Holt, will you wait with Fiona? I'll return as soon as I can."

The door to the left opened. An older woman in North blue and silver emerged, a stack of heavy books cradled in the crook of her arm. "Prince Sebastian," she said. Her voice was rough, as if she coughed frequently. "The Queen wishes to see you immediately."

"I assumed as much, Master Thornton," Sebastian said. "Where is she?"

"You may join her in the gold receiving room," Master Thornton said. She cast her eye on Fiona, who'd taken a seat in one of the white-upholstered chairs, and Holt, who'd remained standing. "All of you."

"I'd prefer to see Mother alone."

"Her Majesty's instructions were quite clear. You and your companions are to wait upon her when you arrive."

Sebastian caught Holt's eye and a wordless exchange Fiona couldn't read passed between them. "All right," Sebastian said. "Thank you."

"I gather it is we who should thank you," Master Thornton said. She bowed, as deeply as her burden would permit, and stalked off down the wide hallway.

"I have misgivings," Holt said.

"So do I, but it's too late to do anything about it now," Sebastian said. "I'm sorry, Fiona."

"It's all right," Fiona said, though inwardly she quailed at the news that she was about to meet her Queen, particularly in her travel-disheveled state. She had never imagined being presented to royalty. Was she supposed to curtsey, even though she wasn't wearing a dress? Or was bowing appropriate? And not just the Queen, but Sebastian's mother, though why that mattered, she didn't know.

They passed through hallways as varied as the patchwork of the palace's exterior, lined with portraits or landscapes in oils, filled with random statuary Fiona was sure cost a fortune. It was too bad most of it wasn't out where ordinary people could see it, because the artwork was beautiful, even if she wasn't a connoisseur to truly appreciate it. Climbing a staircase from one floor to the next, Fiona caught sight of a small statue, no more than two feet tall, tucked away in a nook. It was of a half-naked girl caught mid-step, apparently fleeing from someone or something, and Fiona was seized with a desire to look at it more closely. But they rounded a curve, and the statue vanished from her sight.

Sebastian strode confidently through the halls—well, that made sense, he'd grown up here and no doubt knew it as well as she knew her childhood home, though the palace was large enough she doubted anyone could really know all of it well. He came to a stop before a door that looked like all the others and blew out his breath. "Don't be intimidated by her," he said, and opened the door.

The room beyond smelled strongly of a sweet incense Fiona couldn't identify, a blend of flowers and berry scents that forced its way into her brain by way of her nostrils. Holt sneezed, the most uncontrolled sound she'd ever heard out of him. Master Thornton had called it the gold receiving room, and it took no imagination to see why: the carpet, the floor-length drapes, even the paint on the walls was a deep goldenrod color. Gilding decorated the moldings framing the high ceiling, which sported a mural covering the entire surface. Fiona didn't dare stare at it to discover what its subject was, because her attention was caught by the woman seated in a golden chair just two steps from being a throne, her back to the tall windows that let in very little of the early afternoon sun.

The Queen sat ramrod-straight in her almost-a-throne, her hands loosely clasping the arms of the chair. Her black hair, streaked with silver, was pulled back from her face tightly enough to stretch the skin taut over her cheekbones, which were prominent in her gaunt face. Sharp blue eyes regarded the three of them, lingering longest on Fiona. Fiona straightened her spine and returned her gaze, trying not to shrink. She knew Queen Genevieve was in her early sixties, but as thin as she was, she looked older. Her pale green gown seemed chosen for how well it coordinated with the deep gold of the room.

Sebastian took a few extra steps to put himself well ahead of Fiona and Holt. "Mother," he said.

The Queen regarded him with narrowed eyes. "You have what I sent you for." It was not a question, but then Sebastian had no doubt told her the details in the message he'd sent when they crossed the border.

"I have it," Sebastian said.

"I take it you read the documents." She held out her hand, and Sebastian put the scroll case into it. She didn't bother opening it.

Sebastian squared his shoulders. "You must have known I would, in order to confirm they were the ones you wanted."

"You have a criticism? In front of these people?" Her dismissive hand gesture indicated that Gizane wasn't the only one who saw servants as furniture.

"'These people,' as you put it, risked their lives to retrieve information you *knew* I would be appalled by." Sebastian didn't raise his voice, but there was an intensity to it that unnerved Fiona.

"I will not justify myself to you," Queen Genevieve said. She did speak more loudly, leaning forward in her chair for emphasis. "It's my duty to protect this family, by any means necessary."

"Then it's true Doug has that inherent magic, the one that lets him manipulate other people's minds. Mother, that is *exactly* the sort of thing that people fear most about magic! If he's hurting others, he has to be stopped."

"He's no Ascendant," Queen Genevieve said with another wave of her hand. "His magic is limited to persuading already susceptible young women to sleep with him. He can't force people to do his bidding."

Fiona couldn't see Sebastian's face, but his back was rigid. "And the murder?"

"Circumstantial evidence. Douglas would never kill anyone."

"That documentation says otherwise."

"It's not your concern, Sebastian. You've done your part. Let me do mine." The Queen leaned forward again. "Unless you think you're qualified for the role of King?"

"You know damned well that's not what I want."

"Language, Sebastian. What *do* you want? Think carefully before you answer."

Sebastian let out a long breath. "There's nothing I want that you can give me," he said, "except your word that you won't let Doug go unpunished. You can stop him."

"Don't worry about Douglas." A smile touched the corners of the Queen's mouth. "I have everything well in hand. And speaking of parts to play, who is this young woman?"

"This is Fiona Cooper. She made it possible for us to retrieve the blackmail from Gizane's office."

"Really? Step forward, Fiona Cooper."

Fiona had no choice but to do as the Queen bade. She took a few steps toward the chair, hesitated, then bowed. "Your Majesty."

"What do you think of all this?" This close, Fiona realized the fruity sweet smell came from the Queen. It made her feel sick. Queen Genevieve's sharp blue eyes, surrounded by wrinkles like a topographical map of the Kepa Valley, transfixed her.

"I...don't have an opinion, your Majesty," she lied. "I did the job I was paid for."

"I see." The Queen sat back in her chair and tapped her fingertip against her lips. "No fear of the North family being tainted by inherent magic?"

She could hardly admit to her own 'taint'. "It's not my place to criticize, your Majesty. I won't tell anyone, if that's what you're asking."

"Of course. I trust anyone Sebastian enlisted in this cause would be...discreet. You will have to allow me to recompense you."

"Seb—Prince Sebastian has already arranged for that, your Majesty."

"Nevertheless. You have our thanks."

"I—you're welcome, your Majesty." The sick feeling was growing. The Queen's regard felt like spiders crawling through her scalp and across her cheeks, a tangible threat, but of what?

"And where will you go after this?"

"She's not going anywhere, Mother," Sebastian said. He put his arm around Fiona's waist. "Fiona and I are married."

Fiona whipped around, slack-jawed, to stare at Sebastian. He had his eyes fixed on his mother. "I'm sorry, darling, I know you wanted to tell your parents first, but I see no reason to keep it a secret," he said.

Confusion made her head whirl, so powerful she at first wondered if this was a discussion they'd had that she'd simply forgotten. Married? No, it was impossible, and Sebastian knew that. He also knew her parents were dead, so what game was he playing? She closed her mouth on a denial and waited.

The Queen's eyes widened. "Sebastian, you can't be serious," she exclaimed. "Who is this woman? Who is her family? Why was I not informed?"

"I'm well of age, Mother, and I don't need to tell you everything I do." Sebastian's arm tightened around Fiona. "Fiona is intelligent and well-bred, an acceptable bride for a North. And you can hardly criticize my choice when you've already given tacit approval to Doug's many illicit affairs."

"Even so—" Queen Genevieve went suddenly silent. The corners of her lips curved up in a smile that didn't quite reach her eyes. "On your own head be it. I hope Miss Cooper is prepared for her elevation in status."

"That's our business," Sebastian said. "Now, if there's nothing else?"

The smile broadened. "I'm sure I'll think of something. Have Mrs. Moreton prepare your rooms, unless you want a larger suite now you're a married man? Supper is at seven. Welcome to the family, Miss—that is, Lady North."

Fiona bowed again, dazedly, and allowed Sebastian to lead her out of the room. She was stunned enough she couldn't see straight and depended on his strong arm to guide her in a straight line. "Sebastian, why—"

"Not a word until we have some privacy," Sebastian murmured.

She wasn't conscious of the many rooms he steered her past, down long hallways and up narrow stairs until they came to a final hallway, this one bare of decoration. At the far end was a double door guarded by two men in North livery, armed and armored. They saluted Sebastian and stepped aside for him, the guard on the left opening the door so they could pass.

Another hall greeted them, at the end of which was a comfortable sitting area with a large fireplace made of river stones. A cheery fire flickered a welcome at them, and Fiona, in her stunned state, nearly reached out to touch the flames. The room was unoccupied, but Sebastian hurried her through it as if hoping to avoid conversation. Three other halls branched off it, and Sebastian went down one of them to a door about midway down and opened it. "My rooms," he said.

The room beyond was a sitting room, much smaller than the one they'd passed, that would have been cheerier had a fire been lit in the small fireplace. Sebastian released Fiona and headed for the long sofa, sinking onto it with a sigh and burying his face in his hands. "I'm sorry," he said without looking up. "I'm afraid I panicked."

"You made the right decision," Holt said. He walked to the fireplace and knelt beside it, busying himself with building a fire.

"Are you out of your mind?" Fiona shouted. "What possessed you to—"

"These walls aren't that thick," Sebastian said, overriding her. "Yell at me all you like, but do it quietly."

"How can I do that?" But she subsided and took a seat in an overstuffed chair near Sebastian. "Explain yourself."

Sebastian lowered his hands. His eyes looked haunted. "I didn't like the way Mother was talking about having everything in hand. She's ruthless and utterly committed to maintaining her power, whether as Queen or as head of the North family. It occurred to me that just having the documents might not be enough, as far as she was concerned—that she might have taken steps to silence the witnesses permanently. And she might see you as another witness to silence."

Fiona gaped. "But I'm not going to tell anyone!"

"She doesn't know that. She's the kind of woman who sees everything in terms of conflict and political maneuvering. It wouldn't occur to her that anyone might possess that kind of information and not use it against her."

"I believe Master Sebastian is correct," Holt said. He'd succeeded in getting a fire going and was dusting off his hands. "The only way to keep you safe was to convince her Majesty you had a vested interest in keeping the secret, and the only way to do that was to make you a North by marriage."

Fiona couldn't speak for a moment. "I can't spend the rest of my life pretending to be married to you!"

Sebastian's lips twisted in a mirthless smile. "It will only be for a short time. We'll get your money and see you on the ship to Dineh-Karit, which should take you well out of my mother's reach. I apologize for dragging you into this."

Fiona let out a deep breath. "I chose this path. And I'm not sorry."

Sebastian's smile became briefly real. "We'll spend the night here, then leave for Umberan in the morning. I'll tell Mother it's a wedding trip. By the time she learns we were never married, you'll be safely aboard ship."

"You don't have to put yourself out for me. I can travel alone."

"Not if you want the deception to survive," Holt said. "It would be unlikely for Master Sebastian to allow his new bride to travel south alone."

"But—"

"It's the least I can do," Sebastian said.

Fiona gave in. "All right. Why not leave now?"

"That would look suspicious too," Sebastian said. "I'm sorry you'll have to endure a family dinner. But I'd like to introduce you to my Great-Uncle Sebastian. He's the last surviving son of Willow North and has some remarkable stories."

"I'd like that," Fiona said, finding to her surprise it was true.

21

The gown Mrs. Moreton, the housekeeper—it seemed such an unlikely title for someone with responsibility for a palace—had found for Fiona felt both awkward and comfortable at the same time. It fit her perfectly, the full skirt with its many petti-coats swishing pleasantly around her ankles, the bodice fitted but not tight, the deep green color contrasting beautifully with her red hair that fell loose over her shoulders. She'd never worn anything like it before, and maybe that was the problem: she knew, if no one else did, that she was an imposter. She felt as if the Queen might at any moment denounce her to the rest of the family, strip the gown off her and thrust her out into the winter night.

She'd used Sebastian's dressing room to change, thanking heaven that high fashion for women was, unlike the styles of thirty years previous, easy for one to don unassisted. She didn't think she could keep a straight face if she had to have a lady's maid dress her.

When she emerged, Sebastian was there in the bedroom, straight-ening his formal tunic and knee breeches. His eyes widened. "You look beautiful," he said.

"Thank you. So do you." He looked unbearably handsome,

making her wish she really were the lady her gown proclaimed her to be.

"You don't have anything to worry about," he went on. "Just watch me to see which fork to use. It's not hard."

She wasn't worried about which fork to use. Well, that was a lie. She wasn't worried *much* about which fork to use. She was more worried about encountering Sebastian's family. Reminding herself that they put their trousers on one leg at a time just like everyone else was small comfort when she considered they probably had servants to dress them. "I'll be fine," she said.

"Of course you will. Fiona—"

"Don't say it." His eyes were dark and intense and she wished she could hide from them. "This is all make-believe. It doesn't change anything."

His lips compressed in a tight line, and he turned away from her. "It's just a small family party," he said. "But I think Doug will be there."

"How many of your family members know the truth?"

"I doubt anyone but Mother knows, aside from us. Landon might, but he's so painfully forthright I could see Mother thinking he'd be a liability. She'd never tell Great-Uncle Sebastian or Emily. We should behave as if we know nothing, either."

"I can do that." She hesitated, then said, "Tell me about your family. What should I expect?"

Sebastian took a seat on the long sofa and leaned forward, his elbows on his knees. "Landon only cares about two things, food and hunting," he said. "He'll talk about those for hours if you let him. His wife Veronica is so reserved it's hard to get her to talk about anything, but she won't seek you out. It's not an insult—she's just like that. My sister Emily, though, will want to befriend you."

"That makes me uncomfortable."

"You won't be. Emily was born understanding social graces. She'll make you feel welcome."

"But I'll be lying to her. We're lying to all of them."

"Does it matter, if you're not staying?" He raised his head and fixed her with that dark, intense gaze again.

"I...suppose not." It did matter, but she couldn't explain why. "So Landon is boring, Veronica is reserved, and Emily is friendly. Who else?"

"Great-Uncle Sebastian. He's my favorite relative. He doesn't get out much anymore, being in his eighties, but he's still sharper than anyone I know. He and Mother don't get along, and he despises Doug and Landon, but he has always been kind to me. I don't think it's just because we share a name. I think you'll like him. I know he'll like you."

"What about the Consort? What's your father like?"

Sebastian went still. "You know he's not well."

"I'd heard that, yes." It was common knowledge that the Consort, James North, had a debilitating illness neither doctors nor healers could cure.

"He can't sit for long periods of time, so he won't be joining us for the meal. I was thinking we should visit him after supper. It will look strange if I don't bring my new bride to meet my father."

"I don't mind. We need to keep up the pretense, after all."

"And if Doug's there..." Sebastian blew out his breath. "Let's just hope Doug's not there. I'm not sure I could maintain my composure."

"Would he really come to supper, just like nothing's wrong?" She secretly wanted to meet this prince who'd caused them so much grief, but Sebastian was right, it would be hard to act as if she didn't know anything about his inherent magic or his crimes.

"Knowing Doug, yes. I don't know if he's in Aurilien. It would make sense for Mother to keep him close, but just as much sense to send him away while she's cleaning up his mess. I don't know." He stood and offered Fiona his arm. "Shall we?"

The enormous sitting room with the fireplace big enough to sleep in was occupied when they reached it. A young woman sat on one of the sofas, staring pensively into the fire. She looked up when they entered, and a smile spread across her face. "Seb, how could you?" she exclaimed, rising from her seat. "You got married and you didn't tell anyone!" She was short and plump, with fine brown hair a few shades lighter than Sebastian's, and her blue eyes twinkled with merriment that said she was amused rather than angry.

"It was a whirlwind romance. I wanted to capture her before she met the family and came to her senses," Sebastian said. "Fiona, this is my sister Emily. Emily, Fiona, my wife."

He said it so casually Fiona shivered, as if the deception had not been real until his words made it so. Then it was a little too real for comfort. "How do you do?" she said politely.

"Oh, you don't need to be formal with *me*," Emily said, and to Fiona's complete surprise she ignored Fiona's offered hand and swept her up in a hug. Startled, Fiona returned it. "I'm so glad to meet you. Don't let the family overwhelm you. We can be a little loud, but it's just how we communicate. Seb, did you take her to meet Father yet?"

"After supper," Sebastian said. "Is he having a good day?"

"As good as it ever is," Emily said, her good humor evaporating. "The new treatment seems to be working, even if all it does is ease his pain. So he's less irritable."

"Sebastian!" someone boomed, and Fiona turned to see a tall, handsome man enter the room with an equally tall woman on his arm. He looked so much like the Queen, with his black hair and bright blue eyes, Fiona knew he had to be Landon North, Crown Prince of Tremontane.

"Good to see you," Landon said, clasping Sebastian's hand firmly and clapping him on the shoulder. "And this is the woman you married. About time you settled down. Welcome to the family, Lady North—what's your name?"

"This is Fiona, Landon," Sebastian said. "Fiona, may I introduce my brother Landon and his wife Veronica."

"Charmed," Veronica North said. Though she was as tall as her husband, she was thinner, and gave Fiona the impression of a stick insect, though she was attractive enough. It was just the way she moved, as if she had to think about every step required to extend a hand for Fiona to clasp, as she did now. "Do I know your family?"

"Unlikely," Fiona said, and was saved from elaborating by the entrance of a short, stout man with thick white hair and a short white beard to match. His blue-eyed gaze scanned the room and lit on her, and she felt unexpectedly flustered, as if he could see through her skin to the heart of her. He smiled at Sebastian and strode across the room.

"Good to have you home again, boy," he said, his voice a deep bass rumble. "Why don't you introduce me to my...new niece." He gave Sebastian a strange, unreadable look.

"Of...course," Sebastian murmured. "Great-Uncle Sebastian, this is Fiona North."

Again that frisson of discomfort passed through Fiona. Great-Uncle Sebastian fixed his blue-eyed North gaze upon her again. "Of course she is," he said, taking her hand and raising it to his lips. "Welcome to the family."

"Thank you," Fiona said. He had the oddest expression, like he knew a secret and was waiting for the right moment to reveal it. She glanced at Landon and Veronica, who'd lost interest in her and were moving away to greet Queen Genevieve, who entered the room at that moment trailed by Master Thornton, still in North blue and silver. The Queen was dressed more formally than she had been that afternoon, but her forbidding expression was the same.

"I want to talk to you privately later," Sebastian whispered to his great-uncle.

"I'm sure you do," Great-Uncle Sebastian said, "you and your...wife."

That chilled Fiona further. Sebastian had spoken so highly of his great-uncle, but the man seemed terribly unwelcoming despite his pleasant words. If he disapproved of the supposed match, how would that affect his relationship with his favorite nephew? Fiona felt even more guilty at their deception. She didn't want their pretend marriage to hurt Sebastian's family standing.

Across the room, the Queen turned to look at Fiona and Sebastian. Her eyes narrowed, though Fiona couldn't tell what she was thinking—that Fiona's dress was wrong? She should have worn her hair up? Or, more likely, that Sebastian had made a fool of himself marrying someone unknown to the family or high society in general. Fiona smiled politely at the Queen, who regarded her for another long moment before turning away and saying, "Please join me for supper, everyone."

Fiona took Sebastian's offered arm once more and allowed him to lead her down one of the halls to a door on the left. The royal family's residence had her confused with all its identical doors and hallways. She wouldn't be able to find Sebastian's room without help. Well, it was only for one night. It wasn't as if she needed to get used to the place.

The dining room was as enormous as the sitting room had been. The table, which seated twelve, was far too small for it, though Fiona suspected it was modular and could be expanded as needed. Or perhaps there were more tables hidden behind the wainscoting. Sebastian held a chair for her just as if she were a noble lady —tonight, that's what she was, and she needed to remember that.

He seated himself beside her and gave her a reassuring smile. She needed it. There were no fewer than five forks, three spoons, and two knives at her place, along with two wine glasses and a snowy white napkin folded in the shape of a fan. She followed Sebastian's example and draped it across her lap. And this was just a family dinner. Imagine a full state affair with fifteen courses.

Emily sat on her other side and put her own napkin in her lap. She smiled pleasantly at Fiona, but said nothing until servitors had brought out huge tureens of clear soup and filled their bowls. "So, Fiona, tell us about yourself," she said. "I don't think I know your family."

"You probably don't," Fiona said, flashing a glance at Sebastian. He'd applied himself to his soup bowl and didn't give her any hints by expression or word. They hadn't discussed what she would say to them, whether she should lie to make herself seem more acceptable. The thought irritated Fiona. None of this was real. She wasn't Sebastian's wife, wasn't going to be his wife, and she was who she was.

"My family has lived in Aurilien for generations," she said, "tradesmen and –women, mostly. My parents passed away years ago, and I went to live with my aunt and uncle after my divorce."

Veronica made a sputtering sound around a mouthful of soup, but recovered quickly. Landon, his brows rising, said, "Divorce?"

"Yes. My ex-husband and I parted ways about four months ago. It was best for everyone." *Take that, your Highness.* She wasn't going to let him make her feel ashamed of her choices. That was her business.

"But—" Landon cast a quick glance at his mother, seated at the head of the table. She was placidly eating soup and showed no reaction to this revelation. Landon clearly wanted someone to back him on his appalled reaction, but when no one stepped forward, he subsided.

"So how long have you and Sebastian known each other?" Great-Uncle Sebastian asked. He was seated directly opposite Fiona, and his sharp blue eyes bored into her with a steady pressure she wished she could duck away from.

"A few weeks," Sebastian said. "We've only been married a week, but it's been an exciting one, don't you agree, love?"

She wanted to kick him under the table, but refrained. "It has," she agreed.

"She quite swept me off my feet," Sebastian continued. Fiona sipped her soup and hoped her annoyance wasn't obvious. Between that and the divorce, she sounded like a gold-digging social climber. Not that it mattered what these people thought.

"Oh, you did all the sweeping, *love*," she responded. "You were irresistible." Too much? No, Emily looked as if this were the most romantic thing she'd ever heard, though Great-Uncle Sebastian still had that look as if he were ferreting out her secrets.

"I'm so happy for both of you," Emily said. "Seb's had far too many relationships that went nowhere. It's past time he settled down."

ALLY OF THE CROWN

"Don't embarrass me in front of Fiona," Sebastian said with a smile that said he wasn't the least embarrassed. "She doesn't need to be reminded of all my failed relationships."

"Sounds like she's had at least one failed relationship of her own," Landon rumbled.

Fiona's face went hot with embarrassment. "Excuse me?" Sebastian said, sounding dangerously calm.

Landon looked startled. "I mean, you both have pasts, right? Not that—I apologize, that came out wrong."

"It's all right, I understand what you meant," Fiona said, willing her face to return to its usual shade. Sebastian had his hand curled tightly around a fork and looked ready to use it on his brother. "Sebastian tells me you're a great hunter. Is this the season for it? I'm afraid I don't know anything about hunting."

"Never rode to the hunt? Pity," Landon said, sounding relieved that she wasn't going to challenge him on his faux pas. "There's nothing like it. True, this is the wrong time of year for a real hunt. I much prefer the autumn, the smell of falling leaves, the excitement of running a fox or a stag to ground—"

"I'm sure Fiona isn't interested," Queen Genevieve said. It was Landon's turn to flush. "Fiona, you said your people are tradesmen. Is that what you've done all your life?"

"My former husband and I were traders for many years, then importers centered in Kingsport." Fiona wished she'd allowed Landon to keep talking. She had no desire to carry on a conversation with the Queen, whose sharp blue eyes were as piercing as Great-Uncle Sebastian's. "It's how Sebastian and I met, traveling to Veribold together."

The Queen's eyes narrowed. "A trip to Veribold? How...romantic."

She clearly expected Fiona to spill Douglas's secret. Fiona's dislike of the woman deepened. "It was," she said, not elaborating further.

The servitors returned, removing the soup plates and serving some kind of mutton in gravy that disguised its contours. Fiona took a bite. It was both bland and over-salted. So much for how the rich and powerful ate. Her aunt was a better cook than this.

"We intend to leave for Umberan in the morning," Sebastian said. "A real wedding trip. Veribold is pretty, but it's full of Veriboldans and not nearly so nice as the seashore."

"But you only just got here!" Emily protested. "I want a chance to get to know Fiona."

"There will be plenty of time for that." Sebastian was taking very small bites, Fiona noticed, and concluded he was as unimpressed with the food as she was. Even the Irantzen Temple had had better cuisine, if less of it. "We should only be gone for four weeks."

"Then we'll have a grand reception and dance when you return," Emily said. "Fiona, you'll let me plan it, won't you? I can take care of all the details while you're gone, and you need only wear a beautiful gown and enjoy yourself."

Fiona wished she could kick *herself* under the table. Emily was so innocently pleased at the thought of having her for a sister Fiona felt like an utter heel for deceiving her. She stole a glance at Queen Genevieve. If Sebastian was right, and the Queen had arranged the elimination of the witnesses to Douglas North's crimes, Fiona's life was in danger if they didn't keep up this charade. The necessity burned within her. Under other circumstances, Emily was someone she might have wanted to befriend, princess or no. She remembered Hien and felt even sicker. When had she turned into someone who could lie so readily to honorable women?

"That would be nice, but you really don't have to go to all that trouble," she said.

"It's no trouble. I love planning parties. It's one of my favorite activities." Emily put a gentle hand on Fiona's arm. "I hope we will be friends."

"I...hope so too." Fiona scraped away some of the salty gravy and choked down another bite of mutton. She tried not to look at Great-Uncle Sebastian, who wouldn't stop staring at her. Would she be too rude if she challenged him on it? Of course she would. That would be rude even by the standards of her own class.

The door flew open. "Sorry I'm late," a man said, strolling in and taking a seat at the end of the table opposite the Queen. He was

194

absurdly handsome, even more so than Landon, with black hair that waved back from his forehead, a dimple in his chin, and blue eyes exactly like the Queen's. Beside her, Sebastian stiffened. Now he held his knife like a weapon as well as his fork.

"Douglas," Queen Genevieve said. "When did you arrive?"

"About an hour ago."

"And what were you doing for an entire hour that you could not appear on time for supper?"

"Come, Mother, you wouldn't expect me to appear at table dressed in my travel clothes?" Douglas North smiled, a lazy, confident expression that made Fiona feel like stabbing him herself. His eyes swept the length of the table and stopped at Fiona. "Well, well," he drawled. "And who is this?"

A peculiar feeling began behind Fiona's eyes, a pressure like a headache, only pleasant instead of painful. She blinked, and the feeling spread like warm butter through her veins, settling in the pit of her stomach and starting a little fire there. Douglas was certainly attractive, and she found herself wondering what it would be like to kiss him—

"The lady is Fiona North," Sebastian said. "My wife."

The feeling vanished, leaving Fiona cold and sick from more than the horrible mutton. Douglas's eyebrows quirked upward with astonishment. "Your *wife*?" he exclaimed. "Don't tell me you've gotten yourself leg-shackled finally! I thought you had an arrangement with Lady Louise Peppard."

"That was years ago," Sebastian said, his voice frosty. "Though I don't expect you to remember the details of my relationships. I'm astonished you can remember the details of yours, as many as you've had."

"That's enough, Sebastian," the Queen said. "Douglas, sit up straight and for heaven's sake use a napkin. Will you be staying long?"

"Until winter's over," Douglas said. "Kingsport is so dull this time of year."

"Fiona is from Kingsport," Emily said, with the eagerness of someone who wanted to head off a fight. "At least, recently from Kingsport, isn't that right?"

"Really? I'm surprised we've never met," Douglas said. He leaned back in his chair as the servitors set out the second course, a kind of fish Fiona had never seen before. It was dressed with lemon slices and looked dry and unappetizing. Surely the Queen could afford to hire a better cook? She took a bite and had her guess confirmed; it flaked readily and, she suspected, wasn't intended to. She watched Sebastian closely and mimicked his choice of utensils, keeping her mouth too full to answer Douglas. Being drawn into conversation by this man...had he really just tried to use his magic on her? She could imagine no other reason why she'd feel compelled to kiss him, here in the middle of the dining room with Sebastian sitting beside her.

"Were you at the Abernathys' ball at Wintersmeet?" Douglas went on, forking up fish with every evidence of enjoyment. "It was the event of the season."

"I don't move in those circles," Fiona said. "And I was back in Aurilien at Wintersmeet, with my family."

"Who is your family, then?"

"No one you know. We're not wealthy or noble." Her sick feeling at having been the target of his magic sharpened her tongue.

"I see. And Seb married you?" He put the faintest emphasis on "married." Sebastian shoved his chair back and stood, anger distorting his features.

"*Douglas*," his mother said sharply. "Sebastian, sit down. I won't have fighting at this table."

"Then you should tell him to mind his manners," Sebastian snapped. Fiona wished she dared flee. She ducked her head and picked at her fish, which flaked further.

"Oh, I didn't mean any insult," Douglas drawled. "I was just surprised that you didn't choose someone of your own station. Not that I blame you. If I'd seen you first, Fiona, I might have snapped you up before Seb had a chance. How unfortunate."

"I call it fortunate," Sebastian said, slowly resuming his seat. His thigh pressed against Fiona's briefly. She had no idea what it meant—

was it a warning? And if so, against what? She already knew Douglas was potentially dangerous. "But I don't think Fiona is your type."

"If she fell in love with *you*, that's probably true."

"Douglas," his mother warned him. Douglas shrugged again and went back to eating.

"Have you been to Veribold often?" Great-Uncle Sebastian asked.

"I used to go frequently, with...on trading journeys," Fiona replied. The fish, and Douglas's regard, were making her mouth dry, and she took a drink of wine without thinking. The alcohol, so unfamiliar after all these years, burned her throat. No more for her. "But this was the first time in several years."

"I spent many years in Veribold when I was young," Great-Uncle Sebastian said. "I was my mother's ambassador to the Jaixante, and later, my sister's. They're a fascinating people, if a tad standoffish. *Do you speak Veriboldan?*" he said in that language.

"*I do*," Fiona replied in the same tongue. "Though I'm rusty." His mother. Queen Willow North. It suddenly struck her as ludicrous that she was sitting at table with a man who'd known the first North Queen—of course he'd known her, he was her son. She, Fiona Cooper, rubbing elbows with royalty. It was too ridiculous for words.

"You'll have to tell me how you found Haizea," Great-Uncle Sebastian said. "I understand they've embraced light Devisery to the same degree we have. In my day, Devices were still a new thing, though my father must have singlehandedly lit Aurilien by the time I was five."

"In your day, the earth's crust hadn't yet cooled," Landon said, and laughed at his joke. Fiona winced inwardly. She had expected better from the Crown Prince, but it seemed he was the sort of man who lived with his foot in his mouth.

"I'm glad you find my age so amusing," Great-Uncle Sebastian said coolly. "Coming from someone with the mental age of a five-year-old, that fills me with great hope for the rising generation."

Landon blinked, looking for all the world like the cousin of Fiona's fish. "What?"

"Our great-grandfather Kerish North was the most talented

Deviser of his generation," Emily said hastily. "Have you been to the Zedechen Bethel? He invented the Devices that make the statues glow at the solstices."

"I have. I grew up in Aurilien, remember?" In a neighborhood none of these people would ever have visited. She wished the interminable meal was over, that she was free of them and their tense familial relationships and headed south. Emily was nice enough, but it was clear none of the others knew what to make of her, and felt free to express that confusion as rudeness. Even if some of it was unintentional.

"Oh." Emily turned away, and Fiona wished she hadn't sounded so abrupt. Sebastian pressed his thigh against hers once again, but she had no idea what he meant to convey. Gratefully, she leaned back in her chair to allow the servitor to remove her plate, but was taken aback when he set a third plate in front of her, this one with a steaming slice of roast beef and a pile of limp asparagus decorating it. She couldn't think of anything more expensive than asparagus in winter, and the cook had ruined it by boiling it until it was stringy. So much food...she was already full, and heaven only knew how many more courses were on the way.

She picked at the roast beef, which was unexpectedly tender and delicious, and wished she hadn't eaten so much of the earlier courses. Sebastian left his asparagus, too. If she were the Queen, she'd fire the cook. But Queen Genevieve seemed perfectly content with her meal, and Landon, who Sebastian had said enjoyed his food, had cleaned every plate put in front of him despite the low quality. This meal couldn't possibly go on much longer.

Master Thornton, who sat at the Queen's left hand, had been silent throughout the meal, but now said, "Perhaps we should arrange for a second wedding ceremony. We would not like the people to believe there is anything shady about your union."

"Fiona and I are satisfied, and it's nobody else's business," Sebastian said.

"You are a prince, and therefore your life is everyone's business,"

Master Thornton said. "Or do you have so little respect for your lady wife that you wish to expose her to gossip?"

"We can discuss it when we return," Fiona said, quickly over-riding whatever Sebastian had been about to say. There was no point arguing over a marriage that didn't exist. "I think it's a good idea."

"If it's what you want," Sebastian said. "I still don't think it's necessary."

"Oh, but a big ceremony, and a reception afterward—" Emily said, regaining her spirits. "It will be such fun, Seb!"

"You don't know that," Douglas said. "Fiona might not know how to dance. She's probably not used to high society. You'll just embar-rass her."

His tone of voice, verging on mocking, made the sick feeling return. Sebastian dropped his napkin on his plate and rose. "I'm going to take Fiona to meet Father now," he said. "I think we're finished here."

"The meal isn't over, Sebastian," his mother pointed out.

"I've lost my appetite," Sebastian said. "Fiona?"

She'd never been more grateful to anyone in her life. She laid her napkin across her plate in imitation of Sebastian and accepted his arm. He didn't exactly drag her out of the room, but he did set a brisk pace that had her stretching to keep up.

They left the dining room and turned left. Sebastian strode down the hall in silence. His face was grim, his jaw clenched. "Sebastian, slow down," Fiona protested. "I can't run in this dress."

"Sorry," Sebastian said, slowing to a walk. "I hope you were finished eating. You looked as if you were just poking at your food, there at the end."

"I was. I didn't have the stomach for most of it."

"Mother's taste buds have atrophied over the years. She can't tell the difference between good and bad food anymore. Her cook is lazy, but Mother won't fire her because she's been with the family for so long." He sighed. "That was a disaster."

"It wasn't so bad."

"I had no idea my family could behave so rudely. I apologize for them."

Fiona refrained from pointing out that it was exactly what she'd warned him about. "I don't hold it against you." It wasn't his fault he believed the impossible. She was an outsider, and that would never change.

23

Sebastian stopped at one of the identical doors. "Father might be...tetchy...tonight," he said. "Please don't take offense. He tries to be polite, but he's in pain much of the time, and he hates being weak."

"I understand."

Sebastian opened the door. The room beyond was warmer than the hallway and smelled distantly of stewed peaches. It was a sitting room much like Sebastian's, but where his had a homey feel to it, as homey as a room in a palace might be, this felt unused, the furniture arranged at severe right angles without the small adjustments that said people sat in the chairs or wrote at the tables. The curtains were drawn back, revealing the darkened sky and a glimpse of another ell of the palace. Light Devices made to look like candles flickered on the black marble mantel, making Fiona think not of wealth, but of a tomb.

Two other doors flanked the cold fireplace. Sebastian made for the right-hand one and knocked softly, then opened it without waiting for a reply. Fiona followed him, hesitating before stepping across the threshold. The smell of peaches struck her in the face, an almost tangible wave of sweetness followed by damp, muggy heat. Fiona suppressed a choked gag of disgust and breathed shallowly.

The only light in the room came from the fire in the white marble fireplace the inverse of the one in the sitting room. Where the sitting room fireplace had been empty, the fire here blazed bright and hot, making her wish she dared take it in hand. An enormous pot filled with water boiled happily over the flames, filling the room with hot steam. The steam clung to her face and bare arms like a second skin, making her even more uncomfortable.

A four-poster bed big enough to fit five people was pulled up into the center of the room, next to the fire. A man lay there, propped on half a dozen pillows, regarding Sebastian with steady dark eyes that crinkled at the corners. His hair was as white as Great-Uncle Sebastian's, but thinning and receding from his forehead. He looked hale enough, but lines dragged down the corners of his mouth, giving him the appearance of a puppet whose strings had been cut. "Sebastian," he said, his voice gravelly. "Who is this young lady?" Fiona had a feeling he already knew—well, the Queen would surely have told him of his second son's unexpected marriage.

She thought Sebastian might have come to the same conclusion, but he said politely, "Father, may I introduce Fiona North, my wife."

"Come closer. My eyes aren't what they used to be," James North said. Fiona complied, coming right up to the edge of the bed to stand by Sebastian. "She's pretty enough. What's your family, young lady?"

"Cooper, sir. You won't have heard of them."

"You're right. But I don't care, so long as you make my son happy." James coughed, a barking sound that turned into a hacking, wet noise that shook his whole body. Sebastian helped him sit up more fully and supported him until he regained his composure. "Genevieve tells me she's a nobody. Said it like I should be shocked."

Sebastian said nothing. James went on, "She's not pregnant, is she?"

Fiona gasped. "Of course not!" Sebastian said. "You think that's the only reason I'd marry a woman not of the nobility?"

"Stop bristling at me, boy, it's a natural question." James turned his dark-eyed gaze on Fiona. "No, I think I see very well why you'd marry her."

"Because of my looks?" Fiona said, irritated by his casual appraisal. "You must have a low opinion of Sebastian if you think he's that shallow."

"Hah!" said James. "So you can speak. And speak up for yourself, more to the point. Good." He coughed again, not as violently, wiped his mouth, and added, "I've long wondered whether Sebastian would ever find a woman who meets his appallingly high standards. What made your first marriage fail?"

Fiona gaped, caught without words. "Father, that's irrelevant," Sebastian said.

"Where one marriage can fail, another might too," James said. "Well, girl?"

"We didn't love each other," Fiona said. "Worse, we didn't respect each other, and that came out as fighting and recrimination. He was dismissive of me, and I wasn't open with him. It was a bad match that only became worse as time went on. I don't intend to repeat those mistakes." She remembered in time it was all a ruse before saying *Sebastian and I won't fall into that trap.*

"Good," James said. Pain briefly creased his features, and Sebastian took a step toward the bed, but his father waved him off impatiently. "Good. You own your failings as well as your former husband's. I despise people who can't admit to weakness."

"I don't think we can learn from our mistakes unless we admit we've made them," Fiona said.

"Very wise." James closed his eyes and breathed deeply as if exhausted. "Go now. You have my blessing, though I notice you didn't ask for it. I suppose that tells me how I rate in my own home."

"You know how much I respect you, Father," Sebastian said, taking James's hand and gripping it tightly.

"Yes, yes. Leave me. I need to rest. And ring the bell, would you? I think I could eat something."

Sebastian pulled a rope dangling near his father's head. James could have reached it himself, Fiona judged, but she wondered how much strength he had. He didn't look as if he could support himself, let alone raise his arms. "It was nice to meet you," she said, and meant it.

"Come back again soon," James said, his eyes still closed. "And give me grandchildren before I'm too sick to appreciate them."

Sebastian guided Fiona out of the suite, then stood in the hallway, fists clenched. "What is it?" Fiona asked.

"He's been sick for three years," Sebastian said in a low voice. "I can remember when he was strong and...he used to play with us, all these roughhousing games, and now..."

"I'm sorry."

Sebastian nodded. "Are you tired? It's early yet, but I don't feel like socializing. You can have the bed."

"Where will you sleep?"

"I'll figure something out."

That didn't seem to invite her to comment further, so she held her tongue.

Fiona watched the halls closely on their return and observed that the wallpaper in each hall was subtly different. It put her that much closer to being able to find her way back to her—to *Sebastian's* room. Too bad the doors were identical. Maybe she needed to count.

Sebastian opened the door to his suite for her, and she took two steps across the threshold and stopped. Great-Uncle Sebastian sat on the long sofa, his legs crossed at the ankles. "How's your father?" he asked.

"Better than usual. I think the new treatment is working." Sebastian shut the door and took a seat near his great-uncle. Fiona took the chair opposite him. "But you didn't come here to chat about Father."

Great-Uncle Sebastian shook his head. "I would like to know," he said, "why you're pretending to be married."

Fiona's eyes widened. She looked to Sebastian for her cue, but he didn't seem at all surprised by his great-uncle's question. "I can't tell you," he said. "All I can say is that it's to protect Fiona."

"Can't tell me. Does the Queen have anything to do with this?"

Sebastian said nothing. "Never mind," Great-Uncle Sebastian

said. "Of course Genny has something to do with it. She's gotten conniving in her old age. Her mother would not have been proud of her, more's the pity."

"How did you know?" Fiona asked.

"That's not—" Sebastian began.

"I have inherent magic," Great-Uncle Sebastian said. "I always know where the members of my family are, anywhere in the world. That means I know *who* they are. And since I didn't suddenly gain one recently, I know you're not sworn and sealed to the North family. Nor is Sebastian sworn and sealed to yours."

Fiona shot Sebastian a startled look. So this was who he'd meant when he said he knew someone with inherent magic! No wonder he wasn't afraid of it; it was hard to imagine being afraid of Great-Uncle Sebastian, though not because he was ineffectual and powerless. It was the eyes, Fiona realized, calm and direct and capable of seeing through you to your core, and yet she was certain he had never hurt another person, physically or emotionally, in his life.

"That's quite a secret to entrust to a total stranger," she said. "For all you know, I might spread the news around, especially since I'm not really a North."

"If you're lying to Genny about being married, you must be afraid of something, and that's a secret I might use against you in turn," Great-Uncle Sebastian said. "We're both in each other's power now. But in truth, you strike me as someone who knows how to keep a secret."

You have no idea. "Thank you. I think."

The elderly man smiled, making his blue eyes crinkle at the corners. "So, you met on the way to Veribold," he said. "How was your trip?"

"Well enough," Sebastian said. "I can't tell you the details."

"More secrets. Sebastian, are you in trouble?"

"No more than usual."

"So you're protecting someone else."

"I think we should discuss other topics. I told Fiona you have some amazing stories."

The blue eyes crinkled more. "Very well. I'll stop badgering you. But I won't promise not to lean on Genny until she tells all."

Fiona thought that was unlikely, but said, "When was the last time you were in Veribold, sir?"

"Oh, it must be twenty years now. No, twenty-one almost exactly. I was there for the Election, and that's coming up in a week or so."

"They were preparing for the next Election when we were in Haizea," Sebastian said. "Were you there officially?"

"As an envoy, a neutral observer. The priestesses of the Irantzen Temple, who oversee the ceremonies, invite representatives from the neighboring countries to watch the proceedings. They say it's to showcase their superior form of government, but I've always thought it was to keep the candidates honest. They wouldn't want to make their country look bad in front of foreigners." Great-Uncle Sebastian leaned back on the sofa and clasped his hands in his lap. "Veriboldans are very big on not losing face."

His mention of the Irantzen Temple sparked a line of thought. "Maybe you can help us, sir," she began.

"You might as well call me Great-Uncle, even if you're not really my niece," he said. "So long as we're keeping up appearances."

"All right...Great-Uncle...we came across something neither of us understand. With your knowledge of Veribold, possibly you can identify it."

Sebastian stood. "That's a good idea," he said, and went into the bedroom.

"Something you picked up on your mysterious trip, but not a secret you need to keep from me?" Great-Uncle said.

"It's this," Sebastian said, returning with the bag of tokens. "Everyone we encountered had the most extreme reaction to it. Do you have any idea why?"

Great-Uncle took the bag curiously and opened it. His eyes widened. "Sweet merciful heaven," he whispered. "Where did you get this?"

"Then you recognize it," Fiona said.

"It's—" He closed the bag and held it clutched tight in one hand. "Tell me where you got it."

Fiona and Sebastian exchanged glances. "This is no time for being coy," Great-Uncle said. Looking at him, Fiona couldn't remember why she'd ever thought him harmless; his blue eyes bored through her like icy spears. "*Tell me.*"

"We found it among the possessions of the minister of foreign trade, Gizane," Sebastian said.

"She shouldn't have it either," Great-Uncle said, in a low voice as if talking to himself. "She must have stolen it, but how?"

"What is it?" Sebastian asked.

Great-Uncle transferred his freezing stare to his grandnephew. "This," he said, "is one of Veribold's oldest and most sacred relics. The Jaoine Stones are a key part of the ritual surrounding the Election. Without this, Veribold cannot elect a ruler."

"That can't be possible," Sebastian said. "How do you know it's not a fake?"

"No Veriboldan would dare make a copy of these. And no Tremontanan or Eskandelic would know how."

"Gizane might do it. She's ruthless and opportunistic, as far as we can tell."

"She'd have to enlist help to craft them, and it's unlikely she could find five people with the requisite skills who are equally ruthless and opportunistic. You said you'd seen extreme reactions to the Stones— few Veriboldans will have actually seen them, but everyone knows what they look like. It would be like trying to fake the statues in the Zedechen Bethel."

Fiona stared at him. "But...why would Gizane have it?"

"She must have thought to influence the Election somehow," Sebastian said. "When you consider where we found it—"

"Then you haven't heard," Great-Uncle said, rising to pace in front of the fireplace. "Gizane left for Veribold a week ago. She's a candidate for Election."

Fiona choked back a laugh. "I wish I could see her face when she realizes these are missing," she said.

"This isn't anything to laugh about," Great-Uncle said. "You have to return the Jaoine Stones to the Irantzen Temple immediately. The Election is only ten days from now. If Veribold can't elect a ruler, it would be disastrous."

"For them," Fiona said.

"For all of us. Tensions are high between Veribold and Tremontane. It wouldn't take much to turn that into outright war. And without a ruler, Veribold will be at the mercy of whatever factions its government fractures into. But..."

"But what?" Sebastian said.

Great-Uncle looked horribly conflicted. "Possession of the Jaoine Stones by anyone but an Irantzen priestess is punishable by death. Even if you were restoring what a thief took, you would be the ones executed. And it's unlikely they'd believe you *weren't* the thieves. But they must be returned."

"I'll tell Mother. Let her find a diplomatic solution."

"Genny can't know about this. She'll use it as leverage to attack Veribold, either physically or politically. The balance of power would swing so far it wouldn't be visible anymore." Great-Uncle's hand closed tight on the bag again. "Damn. You would bring trouble home with you, wouldn't you?"

"It's not our fault," Fiona protested. "We—" She closed her mouth on the truth about Douglas North.

"I know. You can't tell me." Great-Uncle blew out his breath. "I suppose you could leave it secretly on the doorstep of the Veriboldan embassy, but you'd be condemning someone else to death."

"We can't go back to Haizea," Sebastian said. "We left just steps ahead of the Jaixante guards. And forget about getting into the Irantzen now the festival is over. There's just no way."

"Don't we have to try?" Fiona said.

Sebastian raised his eyebrows at her. "I don't see why."

"Because it's our fault the Jaoine Stones left Veribold. If we hadn't taken them—"

"If we hadn't taken them, Gizane would have done heaven knows what with them. We might have spared Veribold a worse fate."

"Even so." Fiona stood to face him. The weight of her guilt over her lies bore down on her, but she felt as if the burden had begun to lift. "We seem to be the only ones who can do this."

"Fiona," Sebastian said, "this is madness."

A knock sounded on the door, startling Fiona. She'd almost forgotten there was anyone else in the palace but the three of them. "Enter," Sebastian said.

A servant in North livery opened the door. "Her Majesty would like a word with you, your Highness, Lady North," she said.

"With regard to what?" Sebastian said.

"Her Majesty did not confide in me. She asks that you come immediately."

Sebastian glanced at his great-uncle, who still held the bag of tokens. Great-Uncle casually set them on the mantel. Well, that was as safe a place as any, though Fiona cringed inside at the idea of leaving them lying around. Taking them along when they went to see the Queen seemed like a really bad idea, though. "I'll speak with you more later," Great-Uncle said, just as casually, and left.

Sebastian offered Fiona his arm. "Mother doesn't like to be kept waiting," he said.

It might do her good once in a while, Fiona thought, but she took Sebastian's arm and left the room.

The servant led them to the far end of one of the halls and opened the door on a tiny sitting room, dimly lit by actual candles rather than Devices. No fire was laid in the fireplace, and the room was freezing. Gooseflesh rose up on Fiona's bare arms, and she drew closer to Sebastian for what warmth he might provide. The room was filled to bursting with little porcelain statues of shepherdesses, glass balls containing models of Aurilien landmarks, jeweled eggs on stands, and other knickknacks. Fiona caught the eye of a particularly sappy shepherd dressed in knee breeches and carrying a beribboned crook and controlled a shudder. She couldn't imagine anyone being comfortable in this room.

The Queen sat on a sofa covered with petit point designs that were indistinct in the low light. She still wore the gown she'd worn at supper, a sky blue satin confection similar to Fiona's, but layered in white lace that must have taken a dozen women a dozen days to tat. "Have a seat," she said, gesturing at a sofa facing hers. Fiona sat, and discovered the cushion was rock-hard and bumpy as if it had molded itself to some long-ago sitter's bottom. She shifted, but found no comfortable spot. Beside her, Sebastian fidgeted as if having the same problem. Fiona gave up and folded her hands in her lap. She wasn't about to be the first to speak.

The Queen waited for them to stop wiggling. Her expression was bland, giving nothing away, though Fiona thought, from the way her hands were clenched into fists in her lap, that she was impatient. "So, you intend to travel south tomorrow," she said.

"Yes. I want us both as far from this mess as possible," Sebastian said.

"Don't try to ride your high horse over me, Sebastian. You're as much involved as anyone."

"Only because you deceived me, Mother."

The Queen smiled, a cynical expression that chilled Fiona more than the room. "I gave you the information you needed to know, when you needed to know it. Unless you think you'd somehow be exempt from the storm that would come if Douglas's secret was revealed?"

Now Sebastian's fists were clenched. "Did you call us here to gloat, or did you have something else in mind?"

The Queen's smile fell away. "The documentation you brought has been destroyed," she said. "The witnesses have been...taken care of. One loose end remains."

"Gizane," Sebastian said. "She's out of your reach. You can hardly send your assassins into Veribold after her."

The Queen didn't rise to this bait. "No," she said. "But I can send you."

24

"*What?*" Fiona exclaimed, forgetting she was talking to her Queen.

"You're out of your mind," Sebastian said. "I'm no assassin. You can't force me to do this."

"You are the one who keeps using that word," Queen Genevieve said. "I have said nothing about killing anyone."

"But that's what you mean," Sebastian said. "There's only one way to ensure witnesses won't talk. Were you the one who killed Miss Tippetts? How much blood do you have on your hands?"

"I refuse to justify myself to you," the Queen said. "The North family has ruled Tremontane for eighty years. I am not going to allow a freak magical talent to destroy Willow North's legacy. That means doing whatever it takes to protect this family."

"Willow North's legacy? Do you really think she'd approve of what you've done?"

"She killed the pretender Terence Valant herself. She knew all about the greater good."

Sebastian took Fiona's hand and squeezed. "It's irrelevant. I won't do it."

"As it happens, Sebastian, assassination was not what I had in mind." The Queen smoothed her skirt over her knees. "Gizane can't reveal what she knows about Douglas without implicating herself, and now that she has no evidence, she is no longer a threat. Or, I should say, no longer a personal threat. She is very much a threat to Tremontane."

"You mean because she wants to be Veribold's Queen?" Sebastian's grip on Fiona's hand tightened, not painfully, but enough that she wished she dared remove it.

"I have had my agents investigating her for months. Our friend Gizane is a very busy woman. It turns out we are not the only ones she has blackmailed. She has manipulated her way into a number of noble houses, compelling them to do her bidding. I had no idea Tremontane was so full of corrupt, venal people." She smiled, a thin, humorless smile. "She has also manipulated the Election to ensure her victory, or to give her a strong edge, at any rate. And once she has won, she will bring Veriboldan troops against Tremontane."

"How is that possible?" Fiona asked, and immediately regretted drawing the Queen's attention. Queen Genevieve focused on her sharply, as if she'd forgotten Fiona was in the room.

"She has suborned the Countess of Harroden," she said. "I am still gathering information, but it seems she has convinced Clarissa Barrington to allow Veribold's troops free passage into Harroden in exchange for land and titles in Veribold. I am certain seeing me humiliated influenced Clarissa's decision, but Gizane's promises have been extensive. Gizane's goal is to extend Veriboldan territory to the Snow River. If she succeeds in taking half of County Harroden, she will certainly attack Eskandel next."

"Then build up Harroden's defenses," Sebastian said. "Oust the Countess. Even if Gizane becomes Queen, she won't be able to attack Tremontane."

"I have my reasons for allowing Clarissa to believe her treachery is still a secret. If I act against her, Gizane will change her plans, and now that she's out of Tremontane, my resources for learning those plans are limited. I have no reason to believe Gizane will give up her dream of conquest just because one avenue is closed to her."

Sebastian shook his head. "It doesn't matter. I'm certainly not in a position to stop her."

"You are if you're my envoy to the Election," the Queen said.

Sebastian laughed. "Mother, we left Veribold two steps ahead of the Jaixante guards. You want me to walk back in there, pretending nothing is wrong? That's insanity."

"A diplomatic envoy has protections even the Jaixante must acknowledge. No one will challenge Prince Sebastian North, or be so crass as to accuse him of theft."

"So you say. I think the Irantzen priestesses are exempt from following those rules."

"They will be too busy with the Election to take action against you."

Sebastian's grip on Fiona's hand tightened further. "And what exactly do you propose I do?"

The Queen smiled that crooked, humorless smile again. "Use your initiative. You brought that documentation out of Veribold—I have faith in your abilities."

"You can't force me to do this."

The smile widened. "Shouldn't it be your patriotic duty?"

"There have to be alternatives."

"There is no alternative. I have gone over this problem for weeks, Sebastian. Preventing Gizane from being elected Queen of Veribold is the only way to prevent war. And, incidentally, save this family. Think of your sister."

"That's a low blow, Mother."

"But a telling one."

Sebastian sighed. "Send someone else."

"Who?"

"I don't know. You said you have agents. Send one of them."

"Only the diplomatic envoy can get close enough to the Election to reach Gizane, and I would insult the Veriboldan government if I sent someone of low rank, which my agents are. Stop whining and accept this."

"I'm not whining. I genuinely—"

"Do it, or I annul your marriage."

Fiona sucked in a startled breath. Sebastian said, "What?"

"You heard me. You should never have married without my permission. If I judge your union to be against the best interests of the North family, I can have it annulled. And I guarantee your continued refusal will qualify as against our best interests."

Sebastian's grip was painful now. For a moment, Fiona's heart beat more rapidly. Then she remembered they weren't married. The Queen's threat had no force. She wished she could remind Sebastian of that.

"You wouldn't," Sebastian said, but he didn't sound certain.

"Try me," the Queen said. She sounded utterly certain.

Don't give in, Fiona thought.

Sebastian let go of Fiona's hand. "I suppose I have no choice."

"You really don't," the Queen agreed. "Be prepared to leave in two days. The Election starts soon, and you'll need to be there when it begins."

"This doesn't change anything," Sebastian said, rising. Fiona followed him, struggling a little to rise from the uncomfortable sofa. "I do this, and you leave us alone."

"You're still a North, Sebastian."

"Right now I wish I wasn't," Sebastian said. He left the room without further argument.

Fiona followed him, once again having to run to keep up with his long strides. He walked like he was trying to conquer the ground he trod on, like a man pushed to his limit. She couldn't tell if he had genuinely forgotten they weren't married, or was just angry at being manipulated. She wished she dared speak to him, but even though the halls were empty, they were still public, and Fiona didn't think this was the kind of conversation they should have where anyone could hear.

Sebastian slammed open the door to his suite and flung himself on the sofa, making it scoot back a few inches. Fiona closed the door quietly behind her. "You realize that's a threat with no meaning, right?" she said.

"To annul our marriage that doesn't exist? Yes, I realize that. But how depraved do you have to be to make a threat like that?"

"Or desperate."

"Or both." He ran his hands through his hair, disordering it. "I guess I won't be coming to Umberan with you, after all."

His casual words, so lightly said, left her feeling bereft. "No."

"I'll send Holt with you. You shouldn't travel alone."

"I'm perfectly capable of doing so. I traveled alone for months before I met you."

Sebastian raised his head to look her in the eye. "Nevertheless."

It irritated her that he could so casually dispose of her future. An idea glimmered into life. "I don't want to go to Umberan."

"Well, you can't stay here. Mother might think to make you a hostage against my good behavior."

The idea was growing, taking hold of her and filling her with confidence to replace the bereft feeling. "Then I'll go to Veribold with you."

"Fiona, that's absurd!" Sebastian shot to his feet and took a few steps toward her, taking her by the shoulders in a tight grip. "This isn't your fight."

"I owe a debt I need to repay. It sounds as if you can get me close enough to do so." The thought of being able to make something up to Hien, whatever that might be, bolstered her confident feeling.

"This isn't going to be simple. Whatever Mother thinks about diplomatic immunity, if we're caught interfering in the Election, they're not going to let us off. You know better than I do what kind of punishment that would entail. I can't let you do this."

"Well, I'm not staying here. And it will look strange if you go to Veribold without your new wife. I'm sorry, your Highness, but this is how it has to be."

Sebastian released her and turned away. "This isn't your fight," he repeated, but less certainly.

"We've come all this way together. I don't see how it's not."

He shook his head ruefully. "I should have returned you to Ravensholm the instant we knew you weren't Lucille."

It was like a punch to the jaw. Fiona drew a few calming breaths, then said lightly, "Really?"

"No. I wouldn't give up the past two weeks with you for anything. I don't care if that makes me selfish."

He spoke with such conviction it sent a shiver through her. "Sebastian—"

"It's all right. I know what you're going to say." He half-turned toward her, leaving his face in shadow. "I just wish I knew what to do about Gizane."

"We'll think of something." Fiona's eye fell on the little sack resting on the mantel. She picked it up and shook it, listening to the *clack* of ceramic tiles striking each other. How strange that she'd carried such a valuable relic for so many miles without knowing its importance. She'd have thought something like that would be more obviously important. Well, it was to the Veriboldans. She was just the wrong nationality to notice.

"And then there's that," Sebastian said, pointing at the bag. "What the hell are we supposed to do with it?"

"We have to return it if we don't want to see Veribold fall into chaos. As snooty as Veriboldan landholders can be, there are so many ordinary people who will suffer even more if that happens."

"Return it without getting ourselves executed. It seems impossible."

"We have most of a week to figure out how to do it." Return the Stones, see Gizane neutralized, all without implicating themselves— it did seem impossible. Fiona's hand closed over the bag more tightly. If she could return the Stones, surely that would make things right between her and the Temple. She set the bag back on the mantel. It was as safe a place as any. "I'm...ready to sleep, if that's all right."

"Of course." Sebastian crossed the room to open the bedroom door. "I'll sleep on the sofa. We'll have to lock the door so no servant comes in and finds me there. That would spread the kind of gossip we want to avoid."

The thought left her feeling empty again. She dismissed it and said, "I'm sorry to evict you from your bed."

"I don't mind. It's just for the one night, after all." Sebastian smiled. "I'm sorry I involved you in my family's politics."

She couldn't think of anything to say to that. *I don't mind* was a lie; she minded very much the Queen's high-handed co-opting of them. *I don't want to leave you* would send entirely the wrong message. *I want to serve my country* was facile and stupid, especially since she wasn't sure she was that committed to her country. So she smiled, then wished she hadn't, because his cheerful expression turned more serious, his smile reflective. "Why can't we leave in the morning? I'd have thought the Queen would want us out of here at the crack of dawn."

His smile faded, and she felt as if she'd kicked him. "I doubt we can get started so quickly," he said. "We'll travel in somewhat more grandeur than we did the last time, and that takes time to get moving. And you'll need a wardrobe. But we shouldn't oversleep. Tomorrow will be a busy day, even if we don't travel."

"I see," Fiona said. "Well...good night, then."

"Good night."

She went through the bedroom into the dressing room and wearily stripped off her gown, then looked around for a place to put it. Both wardrobes were packed full of Sebastian's clothes, and she took a moment to examine them. She'd never seen clothing this elegant and varied. Everything was of the highest quality, even the tunics and hose in the bottom drawer of one of the dressers. There were court costumes and riding gear and everyday clothing, enough that Sebastian could wear a different outfit every day for a month and never run out of options. She fingered the fine velvet of a cloak and sighed. This wasn't her world. She would never belong, no matter what Sebastian thought. The reactions of his family certainly proved that.

25

She put on her nightdress and returned to the bedroom. Sebastian had shut the door on her, and it was only her imagination that it glowed with her awareness of his presence beyond it. They had slept near each other the whole trip, had even shared a room at one of the tiny inns, and yet being in his own bedroom felt intimate as none of that had.

She turned down the coverlet and climbed into the bed. It had two soft mattresses into which she immediately sank. It felt like drowning. She struggled upright and arranged the pillows to support her, then lay back and closed her eyes. Sebastian's bed. She drifted off to sleep trying not to wish he was in it with her.

Snow sifted down from the sky, covering the cobbles with white, slick flakes. Fiona's steps left no trace in the drifting snow. Houses rose above her on both sides of the street, tall enough to extend into the sky past the limits of her vision. She was alone on the street, and the houses were dark, without the gleam of candle or lantern that might indicate inhabitants.

At the end of the street, a much shorter house squatted, its windows blank and its door hanging ajar. It drew Fiona toward it as if she were a fish on a line, reeled in by an invisible fisherman. Urgency struck her, and she ran, faster than she'd believed she could. She had to reach the door before something bad happened. She had no idea what the bad thing might be, but her heart ached with the need to stop it.

She slammed open the door. It was the farmhouse she and Sebastian had pretended to hide in, with its single hall running the length of the house and doors opening off it. At the far end of the hall stood a man, his face in shadow. Fiona ran, desperately reaching for him. He held out a hand, fingers outstretched, and just before the tips of her fingers brushed his, fire blossomed along his hand, running up his arm like a burning stream flowing backward.

She cried out, but could hear nothing, not her voice, not the sound of the flames. Fire spread across the man's body, up his chest toward his face. The stranger's visage blurred, became her father's. His eyes met hers, and his mouth moved, once more without sound. She screamed, grabbed his burning wrist, and tried to turn her power outward on him as she had done a hundred times before—

She hit the hard floor, cracking her elbow painfully against the floorboards, waking out of her dream to a stunned incomprehension. She inhaled sharply and smelled smoke. Scrambling to her feet, she flung herself at the bed and whipped the coverlet off to smother the incipient blaze. Not too late. She pounded the smoldering sheets with the coverlet bunched in her fists, willing the fire to go out, though it wasn't within her magical power to make it do so. The memory of her dream clung to her like cobwebs, insubstantial but persistent. It wasn't real. None of it was real. She flung the ruined coverlet aside and ran her fingers across the sheets. Her fire had scorched a hole the size of her outstretched palm into the fine satin. That would take some explaining in the morning.

Her legs suddenly nerveless, she sank to the floor and pressed her face into the side of the mattresses. The dull ache at the sight of her father's face blossomed into a sharp, terrible pain, and she sobbed, howled out her grief and misery into the uncaring mattresses. She'd been so *careful*, hadn't drunk or let herself become exhausted or any of the dozen other things that might trigger an...accident, but she'd forgotten her ritual and it had happened anyway. She was a danger to everyone around her, though not, curse heaven, a danger to herself.

Someone knocked on the door. "Fiona? Are you all right?"

Sebastian. How much noise had she made? "I'm fine," she managed, but it sounded weak and tearful, not at all the voice of someone who was fine.

After a moment, the door eased open. "I heard you fall," Sebastian said, "and...this room smells of smoke. Did something catch fire?"

She looked up at him. The fire in the fireplace had burned low, casting his features into shadow. "It was an accident," she said. It was so inadequate an explanation that she began to cry again and had to once more muffle her sobs in the mattress.

Footsteps sounded on the bare floorboards, and then arms went around her as Sebastian drew her close to him. "I didn't understand," he said. "Are you all right?"

She let him hold her as she cried, unable to speak, not caring that it was everything she'd told herself was impossible. He smelled good, like the pine forests surrounding Kingsport, he was warm and solid and held her without speaking, without demanding anything of her, and that made her cry harder. For a moment, she indulged herself in the fantasy that they really were married, that she had a right to take comfort in his arms. Suppose—but that was a fool's game, and she was through being a fool.

When her sobs died down to shuddering breaths, she shifted her weight, but Sebastian didn't take the hint to release her. "What happened?" he said, his whisper almost inaudible. The room was so quiet it felt wrong to disturb that with speech.

Fiona shuddered once more. "There's a dream I have," she said quietly. "If I don't wake myself before...anyway, I use my magic in my sleep. It doesn't happen often. It's been over a year since the last time."

"I'm not afraid of you, Fiona."

It wasn't what she'd expected from him. "Maybe you should be. I'm dangerous."

"Not consciously. I don't believe you've hurt anyone in your life."

She said nothing, but even she could tell it was the kind of silence that was filled with words she didn't dare say. Sebastian's breath stirred the hair over her forehead. "You did hurt someone," he said.

"No. I never have. But I couldn't save him."

"Who?"

The darkness was lowering her reserve again, as it had when they stood in the dining hall of the Irantzen Temple and he'd asked her to share her secrets. "There was a house fire. I didn't start it, I wasn't even in the house when it happened, but my father...he was trapped, and they pulled him out, but it was too late. It took him three days to die." She drew in another shuddering breath. "I know I couldn't have extinguished the fire because my magic doesn't work that way. But I could have walked into the fire and rescued him before he was so badly hurt, and I didn't because I was terrified of what people would do if they saw me walk out unscathed. Things would have been so different if I'd had the courage to act."

Sebastian shifted, sitting with his back to the bed. "How old were you?"

"Fourteen."

"So not even an adult. Fiona, you can't blame yourself for being afraid. They would likely have killed you even if you'd saved the lives of a dozen orphan children and their puppies. Would your father have blamed you?"

"He never did." She remembered her vision, how her father hadn't spoken words of recrimination. "I suppose even unconsciously I don't believe he would. But—"

"It was a horrible tragedy for which you are not to blame."

"You don't know that." It sounded stupid, but she resented him for being so certain, as if that dismissed her pain and all her fears.

"Of course I do. You just told me as much." He stroked her hair, and reflexively she leaned into his touch. "I can't begin to imagine how hard your magic makes your life, but I am in awe of how you face the world so fearlessly. Don't let yourself be burdened by this guilt. You don't deserve that."

She'd been looking at her hands, clenched in her lap, but now she turned to meet his eyes. In the dimness, they were dark smudges, unreadable. He smiled at her, the faintest curve of his lips, and it made her heart turn over in her chest. She searched for something to say, anything that might tell him what it meant to her to have his good opinion, but came up blank.

Sebastian's smile faded. Slowly, giving her plenty of time to turn away, he lowered his head and kissed her.

She hadn't expected the first kiss back in Haizea, which had been hard and desperate and over almost before it began. This time, his lips on hers were gentle, questioning, promising more if it was what she wanted. Without hesitating, she put her arms around his neck and returned his kiss, not caring about what message it might send. He put his arm around her waist and pulled her closer to him, kissing her with a fierce joy that made her heart ache with longing. They explored each other's lips in the near-darkness, touching each other tentatively, fingers caressing skin until Fiona thought his hands might start her body burning and not the other way around.

The thought of fire, the smell of char that lingered in the air, brought her to her senses. Carefully she withdrew from him, resting her head on his shoulder so he wouldn't feel rejected. What had she been thinking? She hadn't been thinking at all, that was the problem. She had no right to encourage that level of intimacy when she couldn't make a life with him. She was a fool, and she needed to control herself.

Sebastian shifted position to draw her closer into his embrace. "I didn't plan that," he said, "but I'm not sorry."

Fiona couldn't think of anything to say. She couldn't let him believe their love—and she did love him—was that simple, but rejecting him outright would hurt them both terribly. They sat together in the quiet darkness, Fiona staring at the fire and wishing she didn't need to lay hands on it to make it blaze brighter. Despite

Sebastian's arms around her, she felt a chill that came from deep within her. She shivered. Sebastian's arms tightened around her. "Are you cold?" he said.

"I need to stir the fire," she said, gratefully seizing on an opportunity to move away from the forbidden comfort of his embrace. She knelt by the fireplace, shifting the logs and poking at the embers to make them glow. Heat bathed her face and arms, and she closed her eyes and sighed with pleasure.

She returned to Sebastian's side and knelt next to him. He raised his hand as if to put his arm around her again, but lowered it without touching her. "You regret it," he said. His face lit by the growing flames was still and expressionless, and it made her want to cry again.

"It's not that simple," she said.

"It *is* that simple. I love you, Fiona. And I think you're not entirely indifferent to me."

He said it with such straightforward certainty she shivered again. "Does it matter?" she said.

"Of course it matters. When a man tells a woman he loves her, he likes to know he's not the only one feeling that way."

She could lie to him, tell him she was carried away by her emotions and the terror of her nightmare, but she was so tired of lying to people who deserved better. "I mean," she said, struggling to keep more tears out of her voice, "what we feel doesn't matter if there's no way for us to be together."

Sebastian swore and went to his knees, clasping her hand in both of his. "You'd let fear come between us? Fiona, I keep telling you, I don't care that you're not wealthy or noble. Look—the Norths were commoners, worse than commoners, only four generations ago. You can be anything you want to be. If it doesn't matter to me, what do you care what other people think?"

She removed her hand from his and drew a deep breath. "You were at supper," she said. "You saw how your family behaved. It's not going to be any different with the rest of the court and all your social circle. I don't want a life in which I'm constantly ridiculed or patronized or snubbed. Maybe it doesn't matter to you, but you're not the one who'd face that."

"No one would dare behave that way to you."

"Of course they would. Not in your presence. But you can't fight all my battles for me."

Sebastian sat back on his heels, fists clenched on his thighs. "And my love's not enough to overcome that."

It was a low blow, and Fiona didn't know how to respond. She sat silently wishing he would leave and let her return to her stinking bed and cry herself to sleep.

Finally, Sebastian rose. "You're right that we come from different worlds," he said. "Maybe you're also right that it's impossible we could ever overcome that. But I never dreamed I'd meet someone I'd love the way I love you. Every day we're together fills me with joy. There's no way I'm letting that go just because it seems impossible. And I'm not giving up on proving you wrong."

Fiona stared up at him, her mouth hanging open in astonishment. Sebastian turned and left the room, shutting the door quietly behind him. She blinked away the dryness in her eyes and realized she had the ruined coverlet clutched in her hand. She let it go and flexed her hand to return feeling to it. For a moment, she'd felt the rightness of his position. So what if she knew nothing about being noble? She could learn their society's rules. And should she really throw away love just because she was afraid?

She almost went to him. She was at the door, had her hand on the knob, before common sense asserted itself. If she went to him now, their next conversation would almost certainly end with the two of them naked in his bed.

She retreated to the bed and lay on it with her face turned away from the charred sheet. All right. So it was possible. But was it what she wanted? She knew very well how hard it was to make a marriage work when you shared a background. If she married Sebastian—neither of them had said the word, but she knew he wanted nothing less than a lifetime's promise—how long would it be before he grew impatient with her lack of social graces, or she got fed up with being treated poorly by her newfound peers?

She squeezed her eyes tight shut against a vision of herself blundering through a ballroom in a gown whose train she kept tripping over. She was jumping to conclusions, maybe not totally unwarranted ones, but who was to say that vision of the future was the only possible one? Sebastian wasn't the type to lose patience with her just because she didn't understand his world. Maybe he was right, and she'd make a place for herself at court. And when she thought about the two of them, just themselves without any of the trappings of their respective societies, it was with a sense of wonder that she'd found love again after so many years of being trapped by her youthful bad decision. Being married to Sebastian would be wonderful. It was being married to Prince Sebastian North that had her worried.

She groaned and punched her pillow a few times, then fell back onto it and squeezed her eyes shut so tightly she saw yellow sparks. How ironic, that Sebastian was the one who'd shown her what she wanted after all those months of aimless drifting. She'd had ten years of marriage to the wrong man, and now what she wanted was someone she didn't have to hide from, someone she could truly share a life with. If Sebastian wasn't a Prince, he would be that man.

But Sebastian wasn't going to adopt out of his family, no matter what he said about wishing he wasn't a North—that was just his anger at his mother speaking. And maybe Fiona could eventually claw her way to a position within the nobility, but even if she could, she didn't think it would make her happy, even if it meant marrying Sebastian. Which meant every moment she spent with him, letting him go on believing there was a chance for them, was a huge mistake. She needed a middle ground, and nothing like that existed.

She opened her eyes and resolutely began her nightly ritual, though she knew from experience it would be several weeks before another accident was possible. It was two weeks until the end of the Election. Two weeks in which she would pretend to be Sebastian's wife and help him find a way to neutralize Gizane and, she hoped, make amends to Hien. If there was a middle ground, however impossible that seemed, maybe she would find it during that time.

Her ritual finished, she closed her eyes and turned away from the charred spot on the sheet. Or maybe nothing would change, and at the end of two weeks she would leave Sebastian forever. The thought made her heart hurt. *It's for the best,* she told that traitorous organ, *that pain won't last forever*, but she fell asleep feeling she'd already betrayed them both.

26

Haizea hadn't changed in the weeks since Fiona had been there last, but it still looked different, more elegant and less welcoming. Some of that was Fiona's residual guilt over lying to the Irantzen Temple priestesses, no doubt, but most of it was the carriage she and Sebastian traveled in, surrounded by their entourage. Where before they had blended in despite being visibly foreign, now they drew every eye. In the carriage painted with North colors, dark blue and silver, with armed guards on horseback fore and aft and followed by a second carriage bearing their personal servants and luggage, they were clearly foreign nobility.

Fiona had asked Sebastian, on their first day of travel, whether so many aggressively armed men and women in their train didn't send the wrong impression. "Veriboldans, the upper class ones, respect shows of power," Sebastian had said. "Tremontane is a greater military power, but within Veribold, the Veriboldans hold the upper hand. Our bringing guards is a way of saying we believe them strong enough that we need a powerful defense. Though of course nobody's going to attack us and start a war Veribold would almost certainly lose."

That sounded complex and political, and Fiona was just as happy she didn't need to worry about it. That was Sebastian's world, not hers.

Sebastian. He hadn't made any more attempts at intimacy, hadn't tried to kiss her or get her alone. He'd even arranged for them to have separate bedrooms on the road, ignoring the speculative glances their servants gave him and each other. He'd assured her back in Aurilien that it was common for noble married couples not to share a bedroom, but Fiona guessed from what the servants didn't say that newlyweds ought not to care about that custom.

But she'd caught him looking at her when he thought she didn't notice, and the depth of emotion in his gaze made her tremble with mingled longing and pain. When he offered her his arm to escort her from the carriage, or to their rooms in whatever inn they were staying at that night, he would sometimes touch her hand where it rested on his sleeve, the briefest touch, but filled with such tenderness it made tears well up. If he was trying to convince her to change her mind, he'd settled on a damned effective way of doing it.

Every night after her ritual, she tried to convince herself that all her objections, all her rational reasons why love wasn't enough, were foolish. And every night she remembered that terrible, awkward dinner with his family and knew that was only the surface of what she would face as an outsider at court. She wanted a life unconstrained by the demands of a social class she didn't care about, not a constant struggle against others and herself. So far, reason was winning.

Now she looked out the carriage window and asked, "Will we stay in the Jaixante?"

"We're outsiders, and therefore we're not holy enough," Sebastian said. "We'll stay in the Tremontanan embassy. Great-Uncle Sebastian said it's very comfortable. It's close to the Jaixante, on the far side of the Kepa."

"It must be elegant." Fiona leaned against the window frame and admired the marketplace they were passing through. Fragments of words drifted through the window, nothing she could string into meaningful sentences, so she let the sounds wash over her like pebbles clattering down a stony hill.

"We'll have plenty to keep us busy," Sebastian went on. "We're nominally respected auditors of the Election, though if we tried to challenge them I'm sure we'd learn just how nominal that respect is. Mostly we're supposed to watch the proceedings and look impressed at how civilized Veribold is."

Fiona turned away from the window. "And how will we stop Gizane? Do we have a plan?"

Sebastian grimaced. "Not yet. I was hoping once we got here, something would happen to suggest a plan. But nothing's coming to mind. Mostly I'm thinking about how I don't even know what she looks like."

"That's a problem." Fiona fingered the bag of ceramic tokens, the Jaoine Stones, where it fit deeply into her pocket. "Another problem is what to do about these."

"That might be easier. Holt could sneak into the Irantzen Temple and leave them somewhere conspicuous."

"I thought we weren't allowed in the Jaixante."

"Not allowed to stay there. All the contests in the Election are held there, and we're allowed to visit." Sebastian sighed and ran a hand through his hair. "It's a possibility, anyway."

"It could work." It didn't satisfy Fiona, though. While it would make things up to Hien, it wouldn't let Fiona apologize or make things right in person. Though maybe that was a stupid desire, given that she couldn't hand over the Jaoine Stones without getting herself killed. Still, she wanted—needed—something to ease her guilt.

The carriage left the market behind and rattled across one of the white bridges. It wasn't the one Fiona had jumped from, but one farther south that didn't connect to the island of the Jaixante. The white paint adorning the lacy ironwork between the bridge's pillars was chipped in places, making Fiona feel like less of an outsider. Veriboldans were as human as anyone if their constructions could be flawed.

She watched the green-glass flow of the Kepa ambling slowly

beneath them until they left the bridge and made a sharp right turn onto the wide boulevard flanking the river. Tall houses with tiered roofs like the customs house, painted light blue or pale green or stark white, lined the inner side of the boulevard, giving their owners a beautiful view of the Kepa, the Jaixante, and the houses clustered on the far side of the river. Fiona had never been on the west side of Haizea, where the wealthy lived, and the view took her breath away.

Soon the carriage took another turn, this one to the left, and proceeded up a wide, curving driveway that reminded Fiona of a scaled-down version of the drive going up to the palace in Aurilien. Rhododendrons in full bloom lined the driveway, filling the air with their scent. Fiona leaned out the window, drew back when it occurred to her that might not be appropriate behavior, then leaned out again. She wasn't noble and she wasn't going to pretend otherwise when it came to perfectly reasonable curiosity.

The mansion the driveway led to was three stories tall, with the strangely curved tiered roofs tiled in dark blue making it seem wider than it was. Small round windows pierced its sides, making the upper stories look like eyelet lace. The whole thing was as delicate as a spun-sugar confection and more fragile than the stone mansions of Aurilien, built to withstand much harsher winters.

The carriage came to a stop at the foot of the shallow steps leading up to the front door, which was, in contrast to the rest of the house, heavy and stained nearly black. Sebastian waited for the footman to hop down and open the carriage door, then stepped down and offered Fiona his hand. She took it, concealing how her heart sped up at his touch. Sebastian didn't release her, but tucked her hand around his arm and led the way to the stairs.

An army of neatly-dressed people, most of them wearing Tremontane colors of forest green and walnut brown, lined the steps. A woman whose short gray hair trembled in the breeze coming off the Kepa stepped forward. "Prince Sebastian," she said. "I'm Marion Emory, ambassador to Veribold. Welcome to the embassy."

"Thank you, Mistress Emory," Sebastian said. "Lady North and I are pleased to be here."

Emory shot Fiona a glance that, to Fiona's surprise, was more curious than critical. "We hope your stay here will be pleasant. My staff has been instructed to provide you with anything you might need during your stay. The Election begins tomorrow evening, and tonight I've arranged for a banquet in your honor and that of your lady wife."

A banquet. Fiona's heart froze over. So much for keeping the respect of these people once they saw Fiona didn't belong.

"That's very generous of you," Sebastian said. "We would like to settle our things and rest from our journey now."

"Right this way," Emory said. "My majordomo, Charles Carris, will see to your needs. Anything you require, just ask him." She indicated a young man, blond and with wire-rimmed spectacles that gave him the look of a snowy owl. Carris stood at attention, making Fiona wonder if he was a soldier out of uniform. Tensions between Tremontane and Veribold were high enough that the government might think a secret fighting force would be reasonable.

"Please allow me to show you to your rooms," Carris said. Fiona kept hold of Sebastian's sleeve as they proceeded through the door into the dimly-lit hall beyond. Spots of light here and there marked where the little round windows let in just enough sunlight to keep the darkness from being total. Fiona remembered the heat of Veriboldan summers and reflected on how comfortable this house would be during the hottest part of the year.

Stairs with treads as dark as the door and risers a brilliant white contrast stood just opposite the entrance. Carris led the way up to a long, wide hall with several doors opening off it. "The embassy's business is conducted on the ground floor," he said. His voice was soft but penetrating, the voice of someone confident in his job. "The second floor is the residence. We have made the guest suite available to you, of course."

"We will require two bedrooms," Sebastian said.

Carris shot him a glance considerably more inquisitive than Emory's had been. "The suite has two bedrooms," he said, his voice suddenly more neutral in tone. Fiona held her head high and dared him to say anything further, but Carris was silent as he opened the door.

The sitting room was nearly perfectly round, a motif echoed in the arrangement of round windows in the far wall. Six small circles of glass surrounded a much larger one, making an abstract flower pattern that made Fiona feel even more alien than she already did. Low couches that would be difficult to rise from surrounded a round table, also low, painted white to match the furniture. A carpet woven in an intricate pattern of blues and reds covered the floor from wall to wall, making Fiona wonder how they had possibly known how large to weave it. Or, for that matter, how they'd woven a perfect circle.

A lamp glowed on the little table next to the sofa, its flame dim against the still-brilliant sky. Soft, gauzy drapes hung from every wall, giving the impression that the room was larger than it was and hushing conversations to a near-whisper. Three doors at irregular intervals around the room, two open, one closed, added to the alien appearance of the room. That it was functionally no different from Sebastian's rooms in the palace didn't ease Fiona's mind at all. It was an entirely Veriboldan room, and could not have been calculated to make Fiona feel more of an outsider.

Carris walked to the nearest open door and bowed. "Lady North," he said. Fiona swept past him into the room, pretending she was the lady he'd named her. To her relief, the room was an ordinary oblong one, with proper corners and right angles, and was filled with Tremontanan furniture rather than a Veriboldan pallet on the floor. There was a single round window above the bed, true, but Tremontanans had round windows sometimes. It surprised Fiona to discover how comforting this taste of home was, given that she'd spent many years staying in Veriboldan inns on Veriboldan beds. Maybe she was more discomfited by her unnatural elevation in status than she'd thought.

Carris had already moved on, so Fiona explored the room further. In addition to the elegantly carved four-poster bed, there were bedside tables with lamp Devices, an armchair upholstered in gold brocade drawn up to a small round table, and a door that proved to lead to a dressing room. She left that door open and returned to the sitting room, where a quick peek confirmed that the single closed door was the water closet. She used it and felt more comfortable.

When she emerged, the sitting room teemed with servants bearing trunks and boxes they carried into the bedrooms. Sebastian sat on one of the low sofas, regarding the furor with amusement. He patted the cushion next to him in invitation. Fiona sat. The sofa was low enough that her knees bent awkwardly high, and she was sure she would need both hands to get up again.

"Sorry about the banquet," Sebastian said in a low voice. "I know you don't like formal affairs."

"I don't mind," Fiona said. It wasn't precisely true, but she'd committed to this ruse, and she wasn't going to pitch a fit. "But I'll need to finish fitting my gowns. There wasn't time before we left."

Sebastian smiled. "The intimidating Georgette laying down the law again?"

"I chose her because she was the only one of the maids who met my eyes when I spoke to her," Fiona said with a matching smile, "but I didn't know how opinionated she was. I understand now how you were never able to get Holt to eat with us."

"It's true, personal servants tend to care more about their masters' status and reputation than we do." Sebastian glanced over his shoulder. "And now Georgette is looking at me as if I'm monopolizing your time, so maybe you should go for those fittings now." He stood with ease and offered his hand to Fiona. She let him pull her up and kept hold of his hand when she teetered a bit upon rising. Laughing at her awkwardness, she turned to face him and was caught off-guard by his still, somber expression.

"What..." she said, and let her words trail into nothingness.

Sebastian shook his head, the tiniest movement. Then he raised her hand to his lips and kissed it lightly. "Until later," he said, releasing her. He walked to his room and shut the door, leaving her standing like a statue, frozen by his kiss, her heartbeat pounding in her ears. She closed her eyes, capturing the way he'd looked in her memory.

He loved her.

It didn't matter.

But what if it did? her inner voice cried. She took two steps toward his door and stopped herself. That was how it had started with Roderick. She'd been in love and hadn't thought any further than that. She wasn't going to make the same mistake twice.

She turned and walked to her bedroom. The intimidating Georgette stood in the doorway, assessing Fiona. Fiona had no idea what she'd made of that interaction and didn't care. "Let's get this over with," Fiona said.

Georgette had already laid out the three gowns that still required fitting on Fiona's bed. "It will not take long, milady," she said in the stern schoolmistress voice Fiona had to work at not bowing to. "Must I remind you of your obligation to the Crown? You are its representative in Veribold and must dress accordingly."

"I know, Georgette." Fiona stripped off her clothes and let Georgette help her into the first gown. It was true, Georgette was bold and hadn't...well, "groveled" was still the best word for how the other maids had behaved around her. They'd made Fiona feel like an utter fraud—which she was, granted, but she didn't like being reminded of that fact. Georgette was proud and tough and knew everything about high society, and Fiona was grateful for her guidance.

The dressing room had a full-length mirror on a stand in the corner, and Fiona stood with her arms held away from her body as Georgette tucked and pinned the fabric. She couldn't look anywhere else but her reflection without earning a reproving hiss from Georgette. "This dress is lovely," she said, wanting to break the silence.

"It suits milady well," Georgette said around a mouthful of pins. "You will outshine all the other women, as is proper."

This was the other thing Fiona wished she had known about Georgette before taking her on. The woman made no secret of her disdain for everything Veriboldan, which she apostrophized as being "foreign," an adjective equivalent to "heathen" in her vocabulary. To her, Tremontane was the pinnacle of civilization. Heaven only knew what she thought of the Ruskalder, who didn't even share their religious faith.

"Isn't it rather...old-fashioned?" The gown was of gold silk the color of evening sunlight, embroidered with creamy pearls around the neckline and in a starburst pattern over her hips.

Georgette sniffed. "I am told," she said in a way that suggested she resented whoever had passed on the information, "for the opening ceremony of the Election, each observer is to dress in their national costume, which in Tremontane's case is interpreted to mean the style of Queen Willow North's court."

"I see." How unfortunate that they hadn't interpreted it to mean the style Willow North had dressed in before becoming Queen, which would have meant trousers and linen shirts, far more comfortable and less likely to be ruined by an accidental spill.

"There we are, milady," Georgette said, sticking unused pins into the pincushion strapped to her left wrist. "Take care stepping out of it."

Fiona eased her way out of the gown and waited for Georgette to bring the next one. This was the sort of boring thing fashionable women did all the time. She was so grateful not to be a fashionable woman. The thought *If you married Sebastian* began to cross her mind, and ruthlessly she snuffed it.

She endured the fitting of the last two gowns in silence and increasing impatience. When Georgette helped her out of the final gown, Fiona breathed a sigh of relief and immediately donned her trousers and shirt. "I'm going for a walk," she declared.

"You should not go unescorted," Georgette declared. "And walking is inappropriate for ladies of high status."

"I've walked all over Haizea in the last ten years," Fiona said, "and I don't think it's inappropriate. Neither does my husband."

Georgette's lips thinned, but she said nothing more, just gathered up the froth of green satin and tulle that was the final gown and left the dressing room. Fiona suppressed an uncomfortable feeling. For one thing, it had been five years since she'd been familiar with Haizea, and that had been with its less upscale neighborhoods. For another, she was pretending to be a high-class lady, and maybe that meant she *shouldn't* go walking by herself. But she felt a sudden need to be alone, away from the trappings of her pretend life and away from all the scrutiny.

She left the suite without a word to Sebastian, in case he might feel the need to invite himself along, and trotted down the stairs to the dimly-lit entrance hall. A couple of green and brown men in attachés' uniforms crossed it, giving her curious glances but not addressing her.

She had her hand on the door latch when she heard someone call her name—her false name, Lady North. Turning, she saw Charles Carris approaching in a hurry. "Lady North," he repeated, "where are you going?"

"Just for a walk," Fiona said.

"Please wait while I call for a carriage," Carris said.

"That won't be necessary. I said I wanted to walk, not ride."

Carris looked confused for a moment, and then his face smoothed back into the affable, alertly helpful mask. "If you wish... I'll summon an escort, then."

"I don't need an escort. I'm familiar with Haizea and it's perfectly safe."

"Lady North..." Carris looked as if he couldn't decide what to say next. He settled on, "No member of the royal house should walk unescorted through a foreign city. There are dangers—if you were harmed—"

"I won't be harmed. And it's not as if I'm recognizable as a North, if you're worried about kidnapping or something."

Carris gave up his pretense at diplomacy. "Lady North, if something were to happen to you, this embassy would be to blame. I don't know how you normally behave in Aurilien, but that's simply not possible here. If you insist on going out, you *will* have an escort. Please wait here."

His tone of voice angered her. "You mean a minder," she said. "Mr. Carris, I'm leaving now. If you want to send someone to make sure I don't trip and stub my toe, that's your affair. But he'd better stay far enough back that he doesn't interfere with my business." She threw open the door and left before he could do anything rash, like lay hands on her. Behind her, she heard him swear and then shout for someone whose name she didn't catch. A minder. As if she weren't a grown woman and capable of taking care of herself.

On the street outside, she breathed in the cool air and relaxed for the first time in weeks. The smell of the Kepa, a rich, silty scent, tugged at her, and she walked at a leisurely pace toward the bridge.

There weren't many pedestrians in the embassy's neighborhood, making Fiona wonder if Georgette's comment about ladies not walking anywhere applied to more than just Tremontanan behavior. She kept walking, ignoring the stares of Veriboldans who rode past in high-sprung carriages with wheels nearly as tall as she was. Even with carriages taking the place of pedestrians, the road wasn't very well trafficked, and silence nearly as complete as that of the Jaixante surrounded her.

The roar of the Kepa grew in volume as she neared the bridge until it filled her ears, a welcome relief from the unaccustomed silence. Fiona walked along the bridge until she was near its center, then leaned on the ironwork railing and looked out at the island of the Jaixante. Her midnight run through its streets seemed forever in the past. By day, it looked so unreal, all those white and gold towers shading to pale blue and bronze where the shadows of early afternoon touched them. Again the feeling of being an alien touched her heart, and she shivered. Time to go somewhere familiar. Mostly familiar, anyway.

The east side of the Kepa, thronged with pedestrians as the west side was not, was loud and chaotic and comforting. Fiona bought a bowl of meat and rice in the delightfully fishy sauce and felt better immediately. She strolled through the streets until she found the market they'd passed through and spent some minutes browsing its wares. She didn't particularly feel like buying anything, but sometimes looking was enough.

She saw no one in green and brown, no one who might be embassy staff, and began to feel uncomfortable at the scene she'd made. Carris's point about the embassy being held to blame if anything happened to her in Haizea made more sense now that she wasn't angry and, yes, embarrassed at being reprimanded. Lady North probably *shouldn't* go walking alone even in Aurilien, let alone in a foreign capital, and she burned with greater embarrassment. Just one more reason she didn't belong with Sebastian, because she didn't want to live her life under such scrutiny. She liked being able to walk unescorted through a market and not buy anything. Or travel to a foreign continent. And if Sebastian weren't a prince, she'd want to do those things with him.

The thought made her heart hurt. If he weren't a prince...but he was the man he was because of his upbringing, and royalty was part of that. She couldn't wish him different with any seriousness, even as she immediately considered what it would be like if he married her and adopted into her family, leaving the Norths behind. But any man who was willing to do what he'd done for the sake of saving his family wasn't likely to adopt out, and he loved his sister and great-uncle enough not to want to lose that family bond. Which put her back where she'd started—in love with a man she couldn't have.

She made her way back to the boulevard flanking this side of the river and once more leaned on the railing. She was near the gate they had entered back when they'd first come to the Jaixante. She could cross the bridge to the island and ask permission to go to the Irantzen Temple...which they would almost certainly deny. If she showed them the tokens...that would mean imprisonment and death, though if she could get past that, they'd probably gain her entrance to the temple. Fiona sighed and ran her fingers over the bag's velvety surface. She'd have to find some other way to restore the tokens, and restore her honor.

She returned across the bridge without stopping to admire the beautiful water and found her way back to the embassy without difficulty. Sebastian met her at the door. "Where the hell have you been?" he exclaimed, grabbing her upper arm tightly.

"I went for a walk."

"You can't just go for a walk in Haizea! Anything might have happened to you!"

In time, Fiona realized he was afraid rather than angry, and controlled a sharp response. "I'm sorry I didn't tell you where I was going. You know Haizea is perfectly safe for someone dressed the way I am. I used to walk all over the east side, and so long as I stayed out of Dusktown, I was never in any danger." She grimaced. "And Mr. Carris probably had me followed, so I wasn't exactly unescorted."

A woman dressed in a green and brown uniform, a guard rather than an attaché, came through the door at that moment. She didn't look at all uncomfortable or upset, just saluted Sebastian and Fiona with a neutral expression. "Your Highness. Lady North," she said, and walked past them into the gloom.

Sebastian loosened his grip on her arm. "Fiona, maybe this didn't occur to you, but you're a member of the royal family now. If you were attacked—yes, I know, that's unlikely, but if you were attacked, it would cause an international incident. It might even disrupt the Election. You can't go on behaving as if you're nobody."

He was right. That hadn't occurred to her. "I...I'm sorry, Sebastian. I didn't think of it that way. I just wanted to get out for a while."

"I didn't realize you felt trapped."

"Not that. Just tired of the carriage after so many days on the road."

He grimaced. "And yet..."

"And yet what?"

"Nothing. Just...nothing." He converted his grip on her arm to an outstretched hand. "Come inside. I want to discuss the opening ceremony tomorrow. Ambassador Emory has been telling me details, and it's more complicated than I thought."

"That sounds dire." She took his arm and was glad to see him smile with pleasure. "Let's talk," she said, "and maybe some solution to our problems may occur."

iona wriggled into the gold silk gown without help and settled its skirts around her legs. The gown's skirt was split up the front to reveal the embroidered satin underskirt, and the bodice fit perfectly, flattering her curves. The color made her hair glow like a corona of fire. Beautiful. She looked like a lady. If only it were as easy as putting on the right gown.

"Hold still," Georgette said. She slid one of the gown's sleeves up Fiona's arm and stitched it into place while Fiona did as instructed. The needle whipping past so close to her skin made her nervous. If this was how noble women had dressed in Willow North's day, she couldn't believe the formidable North Queen hadn't put a stop to the fashion. Or maybe she had, and the Veriboldans had used the fact that it had once been the fashion to torment their guests, make them uncomfortable and thus throw them off balance.

"Shoes," Georgette said, extending a pair of white slippers that matched the pearls. Fiona slipped them onto her feet and took a few tentative steps. Her formerly injured foot flexed easily, painlessly. It still felt odd to her, even more than a week after being healed. She had never received magical healing before, and the palace healer had been gentle, if silent. The healing hadn't been painful—hadn't felt like anything at all, just the warmth of the healer's hand on her cold foot. A faint white scar across her instep was all that remained of the wound. What would it be like to have a magic no one feared? No, it was better to have no magic at all, at least in Tremontane.

"Thank you," Fiona said. "Please don't wait up for me."

"My thanks, milady, but I'll finish hemming this gown first," Georgette said, her arms full of shimmering North blue silk. "Enjoy your evening, if you can," she added darkly.

Sebastian waited in the sitting room, his arms slung across the low back of a Veriboldan sofa. He wore formal knee breeches and a gold satin coat too warm for this climate. He gave her an appreciative look that made her blush. "We make a very attractive couple. Holt must have spoken to Georgette, to coordinate our clothes so perfectly."

He stood with no effort—Fiona had struggled off the sofa when she'd sat there earlier that afternoon—and offered her his arm. "Shall we go?"

"Is it all right if I'm nervous?" she said as they walked down the hall to the stairs.

"I don't think there's any reason to be. We're meant to be uncouth foreigners—it makes the Veriboldans feel superior, which makes them happy."

"That's rather cynical."

"I don't think it's true of all Veriboldans, just the landholders. They have a high opinion of themselves. Not that I'm suggesting you slurp your soup, just that they expect us not to know all the rules."

"I'm never comfortable when I don't know what to expect."

"Neither am I." Sebastian put his hand over hers and squeezed lightly. "I haven't forgiven Mother for putting us in this position."

The staircase was wide enough to let them walk side by side, and they descended in silence to the front door, which a brown and green servant held open for them. "For example," Sebastian said when they'd left the woman behind and were safely in their carriage, "I don't like that we don't know which of the candidates Gizane is. We have to pretend she's nothing to us, and suppose she's introduced and catches us off-guard?"

"I suppose we just have to...not react to everyone," Fiona said. "What if *she* starts a fight?"

"Unlikely. She won't want to give away her crimes. She'll have to behave as politely to us as we do to her."

Fiona shifted and slid on the carriage seat as the golden silk moved unexpectedly. "I know this gown is pretty," she said, "but it's not exactly comfortable."

"This is rather old-fashioned, actually. I think the idea is to dress the envoys from the different countries in their national garb, like dolls."

"That's what Georgette said. That this was the fashion in Willow North's time." Fiona looked out the carriage window. They were traveling along the wide boulevard that flanked the river, and in the distance, the Jaixante drew nearer. Late afternoon sunlight warmed the white stone and made the buildings gleam painfully, blinding Fiona. She looked back at Sebastian, hoping to surprise a look of tenderness, but he was looking the other way, at the mansions facing the river.

The carriage turned and rattled up to the gate of the bridge to the island, where it came to a stop. Of course. No horses or wheeled vehicles allowed in the Jaixante. A footman—no, it was Holt, garbed correctly in livery indicating his service to the North family—held the carriage door for Sebastian, who helped Fiona out, for which she was grateful; the skirt tried to tangle her legs, and she almost tripped over the hem. She emerged without falling on her face and took Sebastian's arm, resting her hand loosely on it instead of taking it in a death grip the way she wanted to.

A man dressed all in black waited for them, his hands clasped so his sleeves covered them completely, and nodded for them to follow him across the bridge. Holt was apparently included in that invitation, because he trailed along behind them.

Fiona was too nervous to appreciate the sight of the Kepa at sunset, though the light hitting the water was almost as blinding as the white buildings. A few minutes more, and they were surrounded by the tall, windowless buildings Fiona remembered from their night flight. After seeing the blank walls of the Jaixante, she wondered whether any of its residents ever got lost. The Irantzen Temple was the only thing she'd seen with any individual character.

She hesitated as they passed between the first buildings, not wanting to draw attention to herself because she superstitiously feared being recognized. It was an irrational fear, not only because no one was likely to have seen her closely enough to remember her face, but also because the Jaixante guards in their fluttering, ragged robes were nowhere to be seen. Nevertheless, she took Sebastian's hand and gripped it tightly, hoping he would understand her fears.

Their guide brought them to a wall so high it looked like a white cliff in which were set a couple of black-stained wooden doors tall enough to look normal-sized in that giant wall. Unlike the fairy spires of the Irantzen Temple, this looked like a fortress, or a gate guarding the treasures of a kingdom.

As they approached the doors, they swung open silently, weight-lessly, with no apparent hand to set them swinging. Fortunately for her peace of mind, Fiona noticed black-clad servitors holding the doors as they passed through. The servants in black had their heads bowed low so they were apparently looking at their feet. Fiona averted her gaze. It wasn't that she felt embarrassed, or worried that looking was wrong; they were so still and so determined not to impose their presence on her she felt noticing them was rude.

The doors opened on a long hall paved in white stones joined so closely the seams were invisible. Wide enough to admit two carriages side by side, the hall was lined with pedestals on which stood statues of black marble. The statues didn't look like anything real, and gave Fiona a funny feeling when she looked at them, as if it said some-thing about her intelligence that she couldn't identify the subjects.

Another set of identical doors stood open at the far end of the hall, and the sound of stringed instruments playing atonal chords emerged from them. Other figures made small by distance passed through the doors, garbed in colors as bright as their own. Sebastian and Fiona followed them. Fiona realized her palm was sweating and wished she dared wipe it on her gown, but it would leave a mark. She waved it surreptitiously at her side, willing the air to dry it.

The room beyond the doors was the largest Fiona had ever seen. She didn't know how it compared to the grand ballroom at the palace in Aurilien, but it had to be more than a hundred feet long in both directions with a ceiling at least forty feet high. Terraces draped in filmy white left it open to the sky, which was orange and peach and gold with the sunset, and a cool breeze scented with a spicy cinnamon odor caressed Fiona's cheeks and dried the sweat from her hand. It kept the room from being over-warm with so many bodies filling even that great space.

"Your Highness, Lady North," a Veriboldan man said, approaching them. He was dressed in a peacock-blue knee-length robe open over black linen trousers and a matching shirt with a deep V-neck that blended with his dark skin. The robe was embroidered with threads of what Fiona suspected were real gold, and tiny emeralds in an abstract pattern winked at her. The man's feet were bare, his toenails lacquered bronze, and he wore his hair cut short to frame his face.

"I am Mitxel," the man said, bowing at the waist low enough that Fiona could see his black hair was thinning on top. "I am honored to be your guide throughout the Election."

"What does that mean?" Fiona said, her curiosity getting the better of her manners.

"It means, milady, that I am to answer your questions, to show you to your place during the ceremonies, and to anticipate your needs. I will also introduce you to your counterparts, if you will follow me?" Mitxel bowed again, not quite as low this time. His Tremontanese was barely accented, like Hien's had been, making him sound more like a northwestern Tremontanan than a Veriboldan.

"Thank you, Mitxel," Sebastian said. There had been no mention of "translator" in that list of Mitxel's duties, Fiona noticed, and she wondered if they knew Sebastian spoke no Veriboldan. If they thought it was a slight, that Tremontane had sent an envoy who didn't speak their language, they didn't show it. Sebastian hadn't been at all uncomfortable at the idea when Fiona had brought it up two days before, saying only, "Then you'll have to translate for me," and Fiona had let it drop. She didn't mind translating, but it was one more reminder that she had no idea what the Veriboldans expected of her.

Fiona examined her surroundings as they followed Mitxel into the vast chamber. If the parquet floor had a pattern, it was invisible from this angle, appearing only to be a variegated mass of browns and golds. The lights that burned high overhead had to be Devices, as they didn't increase the warmth of the room, just glowed with a soft white light that cast faint shadows across the floor. Fiona gripped Sebastian's sleeve more firmly and reminded herself she was here by invitation.

Sebastian seemed to have been right about the Veriboldans' desire for everyone to dress in their national costume. Most of the men and women in the room were Veriboldans dressed much as Mitxel was, in brightly colored and embroidered knee-length robes over linen shirts and trousers in either black or white, and all were barefoot. Fiona was certain the colors meant something—she knew enough of Veriboldan nobility to know their society was highly stratified with complex rules—but the meaning wasn't obvious at a glance.

The little knot of people they approached, however, stood out from the gaudily dressed Veriboldans, though two of them were as brightly garbed as their hosts. Those two wore floor-length divided skirts of jade-green silk, embroidered thickly with gold and silver thread in a rich floral pattern, and matching cropped long-sleeved jackets open at the front over bare skin. The curves of the woman's breasts were barely visible in the gap. Fiona wondered if the jacket chafed her, or if she worried about it flying open and exposing her to the world. Only the scions of an Eskandelic principality would dress that way.

The second couple were clearly Ruskalder, their fair hair and wintry blue eyes pale enough to look bleached. Ruskalder national costume for men apparently consisted of a fur-trimmed suede shirt and trousers dyed a deep blue, tucked into knee-high boots of shiny leather that looked never worn. The woman's shirt was similar to the man's, but she wore a calf-length skirt with at least two petticoats, bright blue to match her companion's trousers, embroidered with tiny white flowers all around the hem. Both their fair complexions were pink, and beads of sweat clustered at the man's temples. Fiona found herself grateful for the thin silk of her gown.

But it was the last person in the little group that kept Fiona's attention. He was tall, easily six and a half feet, with long honey-blond hair pulled back from his face in a braid that fell halfway down his back and blue eyes like a summer sky. Where Holt was gaunt, this man was well-built, his sleeveless leather jerkin displaying the muscles of his arms and his tightly-fitting leather pants showing off a well-rounded posterior. Fiona realized she was staring and quickly turned her attention back to Mitxel.

"*My lords and ladies,*" Mitxel said, switching to Veriboldan, "*may I present the envoy from Tremontane, Prince Sebastian North, and his lady wife, Fiona North. Your Highness, Dekerian Nikani and Dekerian Salena of Eskandel, Morten of the Ruskalder and his wife Venelda, and Stannin of the Kirkellan.*" He accompanied his introductions with delicate hand gestures as if to connect the names to their faces.

"Fiona?" Sebastian said. Fiona flushed. She'd already forgotten herself. Blame it on the gorgeous Kirkellan warrior.

"*My...husband speaks no Veriboldan,*" she said quickly, "*and begs your pardon for the need for a translator.*" To Sebastian, she said, "Did you catch all the names?"

"Dekerian Nikani, Dekerian Salena, Morten, Venelda, and Stannin," Sebastian repeated promptly, bowing to each in turn. Well, he'd probably been trained from birth to remember people. "Do any of you speak Tremontanese?"

"Most children of principalities speak Tremontanese and Veriboldan as well as Eskandelic," Dekerian Nikani said smoothly. His accent was even better than Mitxel's. "You are a child of Willow North."

"She was my great-grandmother."

"Eskandel remembers the Queen fondly. We honor you in her

memory." Nikani made a bow that Sebastian returned without a hint of self-consciousness. Fiona, uncertain whether she'd been included in that bow, stayed still. Dekerian Salena gave her a pleasant smile, which she did return. At least some people at the Election were friendly.

"*Tremontane is disrespectful to send an envoy who doesn't speak the language,*" Morten said in Veriboldan. His voice was somehow gruff and whiny at the same time. "*I have practiced many years to show respect to our hosts.*" Next to him, Venelda closed her eyes briefly as if in pain, an expression Fiona was familiar with. She'd worn it herself many times when Roderick had said or done something embarrassing.

"*Prince Sebastian North is the Queen of Tremontane's own son, and a fitting envoy,*" she said, putting steel into her words. "*And I speak Veriboldan for both of us.*"

Morten scowled and opened his mouth to say something else, but Nikani cut across his words with, "A prince of the royal house of North is certainly worthy of attending the Election, whatever language he speaks."

"*He not speak?*" said the giant Stannin. He clapped Sebastian on the shoulder. Sebastian staggered, but managed to remain upright. "*I not speak well! Is hard, Veriboldan, it tangles tongue.*" He then said something Fiona couldn't understand, a long string of gutturals that made Morten scowl harder and Venelda cover her mouth to hide a smile. Stannin ended his sentence with a booming laugh and a smile for Fiona. She laughed too, though she had no idea at what. Hopefully Stannin hadn't just made a joke about Morten's mother that would earn Fiona Morten's enmity.

"I'm starting to question the wisdom of sending me as envoy," Sebastian murmured.

"Nothing to fear," Nikani said. "We are all of us outsiders in Veribold. Even speaking their language is not enough to make us one of them."

A deep ringing tone echoed through the chamber. Instantly, every Veriboldan turned to face one of the terraces. Fiona looked in that direction, but saw only the fluttering drapes filtering the cool evening air. The sound rang out again. The Veriboldans began walking in the direction of the terrace, silent, the only sounds the hissing of linen rubbing against linen and the faintest noise of bare feet on wood. Fiona hesitated, unsure what the protocol was.

Morten took a step as if to follow them, and Mitxel put a hand on his arm briefly, withdrawing it when Morten turned angrily on him as if he'd punched Morten instead. *"We will wait,"* Mitxel said, then repeated himself in Tremontanese.

They waited, watching the colorful Veriboldans pass through the drapes onto the terrace and disappear from sight. Fiona resisted the urge to scratch under her arm. The room wasn't warm enough to make her sweat, but nerves were doing what the heat couldn't. Morten tapped his foot impatiently. Stannin looked about him as eagerly as a puppy exploring the world outside his basket for the first time. He really was painfully good-looking.

Fiona glanced at Sebastian, who had his attention on the distant terrace, and her anxieties eased slightly. Out of place, unable to speak the language, and he still wore that air of easy competence that made her heart turn over in her chest. Next to him, Stannin looked like a glorious piece of art—beautiful, but nothing you could make a life with.

"It is time," Mitxel said, gesturing for his little flock to follow him. Sebastian quickly followed, putting himself and Fiona directly behind Mitxel as if he had understood the man's words. Fiona could hear the sharp taps of the Eskandelics' shoes on the parquet floor and knew they were immediately behind her, but didn't dare turn to see how the others had ranged themselves. Would the Veriboldans see their order as denoting rank? In any case, it couldn't hurt to be first through the door.

28

*M*itxel stopped at the gauzy drapes and pulled one to the side, leaving a gap. "You will see where you are to go," he whispered to Sebastian. "Walk to your place and stand there. The rest will follow."

Sebastian nodded and drew Fiona with him through the doorway. The gauzy fabric brushed Fiona's head lightly, like butterfly wings, and then they were on the terrace. Though she had seen dozens of Veriboldans pass through the door, she had pictured a tidy little patio, possibly in a garden. She was not prepared for a space paved in white marble, nearly the size of the chamber they'd just left, semi-circular and surrounded by pillars of black stone with capitals and plinths carved to look like seashells.

Beyond the terrace, a lushly overgrown garden formed living walls around it, with ivy circling the pillars and latticed pergolas drip-ping with golden flowers making tunnels leading deeper into the garden. Above, the twilight sky shaded from pink to gold to azure like a silken curtain. It should have been gaudy, but Fiona was awed by its beauty.

All around the perimeter, affixed to the pillars, were round shields painted with stylized animals. The Veriboldans had gathered beneath them in little groups. Fiona stopped, trying to work out what they meant, but Sebastian tugged on her arm. "Keep walking," he said.

"Walk where?"

He didn't answer, just led her off to the left. It took her a moment to realize that the shield he was headed for bore the North sign and shield, a silver panther on a North blue background rearing up as if challenging all comers. Fiona relaxed. Sebastian might not speak the language, but he understood the rules.

A circular depression perhaps half an inch in depth lay directly beneath the North sign and shield, about three feet in diameter. It was large enough for the two of them to stand comfortably next to each other. Fiona turned to put the pillar at her back and watched the other envoys find their places. Nikani and Salena were on their right, beneath a fox head in brilliant green on gold.

Directly across from them, Stannin stood alone, still looking about him with bright-eyed eagerness. The Ruskalder were on his left, Morten still scowling, Venelda looking placid. The shield above them was the only one not painted with an animal; the symbol looked like a seven-fingered hand, painted red as blood. Fiona averted her gaze. Tremontane hadn't been at war with Ruskald in forever, but it was hard to look at Morten's battle emblem and not picture it raised above a host of warriors bent on shedding Tremontanan blood.

Silence fell once the envoys had taken their places. Fiona shifted her weight and hoped it didn't look like fidgeting. Somewhere in the garden, a bird cried, a low, mournful sound some other bird took up and echoed. Snooty Veriboldan birds, singing in three-quarter time, Fiona recalled Sebastian saying, and stifled a grin.

At the far end of the terrace from the doorway, beneath a stylized pattern of dots and curves, stood a gong bigger than Fiona's outstretched arms. A woman clad in the Veriboldan costume, but entirely in gold, trousers and all, swung a mallet whose head was as big as her own to strike the gong. The same deep ringing tone pealed out across the terrace. No one moved. Gradually, the sound faded, leaving Fiona's ears ringing. She realized she was clutching Sebastian's arm rather tightly and relaxed her grip, though not letting go of him entirely.

Movement at the doorway drew her attention. Two more attendants in gold drew the curtains fully aside, and a woman appeared. Her robe, shirt, and trousers were entirely black, but appeared to be of silk rather than linen. Against her dark skin, it made her look like a statue carved of ebony. Her black hair hung loose around her shoulders, and the only color about her was her long nails, lacquered a stunning rose.

Every Veriboldan on the terrace immediately sank to their knees, bowing their heads low to the ground. Fiona looked to Sebastian for guidance. He bowed at the waist, deeply enough to show respect but not deeply enough to be servile, and Fiona saw Salena and Nikani do the same just before she copied him. This had to be Ibarhe, reigning Queen of Veribold.

From that position, she was able to see Ibarhe walk slowly down the center of the terrace and take a position in front of the gong. "*Rise*," she said in Veriboldan, and Fiona straightened as the Veriboldans stood, their hands clasped before them as if in prayer to ungoverned heaven. "*Let them enter*," she added. Her tone of voice, so somber, made Fiona feel as if she were witnessing the return of the lost gods. Now, finally, she and Sebastian would see their enemy.

The gauzy curtains parted again, wider this time, and two men and two women appeared, standing in a row in the doorway. All four wore black shirts and trousers, but their robes were pale yellow and unadorned. Their simplicity reminded Fiona of the Irantzen Temple garb, though none of the newcomers bore the serenity that had characterized the priestesses. They did look as haughty as Sela, though. In fact, the man on the left, with his straight nose and narrow eyes, resembled her strongly.

The four held their position in the doorway for several seconds, as if posing for a portrait. Then they came slowly onto the terrace, pacing each other exactly. Fiona examined them closely. These were the candidates for Election, which meant one of them was Gizane.

All four had the dark skin characteristic of the Veriboldan ruling class, though in different shades of darkness, and all four had black hair cropped short to brush their jawlines. But there, the resemblance ended.

The other man was stocky, like a wrestler, with a powerfully jutting jaw and muscular arms he held somewhat away from his body, as if preparing to grapple the Queen. His face, though, was impassive, and Fiona felt it would be a mistake to underestimate him just because he looked unintelligent.

The woman on the far left was the tallest of the four, not as tall as Stannin, but at least a head taller than any of her companions. She was thin, too, angular the way Sebastian's sister-in-law Veronica was, but where Veronica had moved jerkily, like someone whose body wasn't under her control, this woman moved like a snake, her hips and shoulders describing smooth arcs as her legs and arms moved. Her sharp-featured face looked cunning, and Fiona suspected she was Gizane.

The other woman was, by contrast, the shortest of the lot, and beautiful, her eyes large and bright green, a startling contrast to her skin. She strode confidently, and Fiona could see her reining in her stride to match her companions'. The man next to her, the one who looked like Sela, took a short hopping step to keep up, and Fiona saw the woman smile. It was not a nice smile. Fiona reminded herself that anyone qualified as a candidate to rule Veribold was cunning, clever, and almost certainly not nice, however beautiful they might be.

The four passed Fiona and Sebastian and came to a stop ten feet from where the Queen stood. She surveyed them coldly for a long, painful moment in which Fiona shifted her weight again, then held out a hand. Immediately one of the gold-clad attendants approached, bearing a shallow box. She knelt beside the Queen and held it so it was waist-high to the woman.

"*We are one in the service of My Lady Veribold,*" the Queen said. "*One in knowledge. One in wisdom. One in cunning. One in charisma. One in faith.*"

"*We are one,*" the watching Veriboldans, all but the four candidates, repeated. The effect was unsettling, like hearing stones speak. Fiona suppressed a shudder. She wanted to translate for Sebastian, but she was afraid to break the spell with foreign words.

"You who would be One among Many, step forward," the Queen said. The four candidates simultaneously took a single step forward. It would have been funny if everyone around them hadn't been stone cold serious. Sebastian put his free hand atop hers where it rested on his sleeve and squeezed lightly. He had no idea what they were saying, and *he* was reassuring *her*? Fiona was seized with a desire to kiss him, right there in the middle of the ceremony.

"Bixhor of the Triminon, approach your Queen," the Queen said. The wrestler advanced and dropped to his knees before her. The Queen reached into the box and took out a palm-sized green disk the same color as his robe, attached to a woven brown cord that dangled free. She shook out the cord and looped it around Bixhor's neck. Fiona recognized it as a meditation medallion, a *toan* jade, from the Irantzen Temple just before it was hidden by Bixhor's bulk. Bixhor bowed low, pressing his forehead to the Queen's feet and making the *toan* jade clink against the marble paving stones, then stood somewhat awkwardly and backed away to his original position.

"Gizane of the Araton, approach your Queen," the Queen said. Fiona gripped Sebastian's arm tightly. To her surprise, the small, beautiful woman strode forward, as confidently as before, and received her medallion and made her bow with an air of complete self-assuredness. *That* was Gizane? That tiny thing? Fiona felt her assumptions rearrange themselves in a dizzying manner. She should know better than to let appearances guide her. Well, now they knew the face of their enemy. And although she hadn't looked their way at all, Fiona was sure she knew their faces as well. She moved like someone who always tried to be two steps ahead of her opponent.

The Queen called up the other man, whose name was Luken of the Azergn, and the tall woman, Alazne of the Otsoan, and gave each of them their medallions and received their bows. Then she gestured, and the four turned and walked back through the doorway, once more in lockstep.

Fiona watched the Queen rather than their retreating backs. The Queen's expression was placid, but one of her hands flexed and closed restlessly, suggesting she wasn't as calm as all that. What did the Queen have to worry about? In a week, maybe less, she would lay down her crown and step into the cushy retirement Roderick had once told Fiona was the destiny of all former rulers of Veribold. Her job was almost over. Yet she didn't have the air of someone with her whole life ahead of her.

Behind the Queen, women garbed in white wraparound shirts and white trousers streamed onto the terrace from the garden. They looked like Irantzen Temple priestesses. They fell in behind the Queen as she began walking toward the door. Fiona realized her shoulders hurt from standing stiffly too long and tried to relax them, letting her head sag. Rolling them out was probably frowned on, too informal for this setting and ceremony.

She raised her head, and found herself looking directly at Hien.

29

Fiona's mouth dropped open. "Hien," she said, and couldn't think how to continue. Hien had the same calm, impassive look she always wore, but her eyes blazed with fury. She glanced once over Fiona's body as if assessing her, then turned and walked away, her back stiff and her gait rapid.

"Uh-oh," Sebastian said. "I think we're in trouble."

"I thought she was supposed to be too busy to notice us!" Fiona whispered urgently.

"No one counted on her being part of the ceremony. Maybe we should have." Sebastian tugged on Fiona's arm. The rest of the envoys and the watching Veriboldans were headed inside, customs of precedence apparently no longer important. "Wait until we're alone."

Fiona looked for Mitxel to guide them—was this really the end of the ceremony?—but didn't see him anywhere. Sebastian made for the exit as if he didn't care if it was the end or not, and Fiona, dragged along in his wake, decided if they were supposed to be elsewhere, Mitxel knew where to find them.

Safely across the bridge, into the embassy, and in their sitting room, Fiona let go of Sebastian's arm and sank gracelessly onto the low sofa. She buried her face in her hands and said, "She definitely recognized me. What the hell are we supposed to do now?"

"Brazen it out," Sebastian said, sinking down beside her and gently kneading her shoulders. "I'm the official envoy, and as far as anyone else is concerned, we've never been near the Irantzen Temple. Hien can't prove we were there and she can't prove we stole anything. Does that feel better?"

"Mmm. Yes. How did you know my shoulders hurt?"

"You hold them stiffly when the muscles are tight. Shift over and let me reach the other side."

Fiona gratefully moved closer and closed her eyes as he rubbed. "That feels divine."

"I'm happy to help." His fingers trailed lower, stroking her back gently and leaving tingling trails wherever they touched. "Though we might ask Mitxel about the schedule of events and whether Hien will be attending them. If we can stay out of her way, so much the better."

Her whole body was relaxing under his touch. She wanted to curl up in his lap and fall asleep—no, sleep was the opposite of what she wanted from him right now. She carefully moved away from him, not looking at his face. "I wish I could explain everything to her. I feel awful at having betrayed her trust."

"You didn't have a choice. And...thank you. In case I didn't say it before. Thank you for lying to protect my family, most of whom don't deserve it."

"I did it for you, not them."

"That makes it even better," Sebastian said. He gave her a little half-smile, but his eyes held a different emotion, one that made her catch her breath.

The outer door opened, and Holt entered, his gaunt frame filling the doorway. "I beg your pardon for interrupting," he said, "but I have information I believe you should know."

Sebastian turned away from Fiona. "What is it?"

Holt came into the room and shut the door behind him, then turned the key in the lock. The gesture combined with the somber expression on Holt's face felt sinister, as if his news were some dire portent that might mean their doom. "During the ceremony, I was below stairs, making the acquaintance of the personal servants of the candidates and the other envoys," he said.

"Should you have done that? I mean, won't it look suspicious?" Fiona asked.

"I was told by Prince Sebastian the elder that such interactions are commonplace, if not expected." Holt looked grimmer than usual. "He instructed me to do what I could to cultivate relationships, particularly with the candidates' servants. I did not tell him of our interest in Gizane, so I conclude he is right, and such politicking is a given during the Election."

"I take it you learned something," Sebastian said.

Holt nodded. "What surprised me was that most of the servants are multilingual. Veriboldans are not, as a nationality, inclined to learning the languages of their neighbors, and finding men and women of relatively low social status capable of doing so made me suspicious."

"Do you mean they aren't really servants?" The idea unnerved Fiona. It spoke to a level of deceit she hadn't expected, even from Veriboldans.

"I cannot say. For our purposes, it does not matter. What is important is that those attached to the candidates pretend reticence about telling their masters' business, but they talk with outsiders far more readily than true servants would. My understanding is that the information they share is carefully calculated to incline the envoys in favor of one candidate or another. It is all very proper, and they pretend well to innocence, but we should be careful not to take their information at face value."

"The fourth challenge involves the landholders and the envoys voting on behalf of a cause championed by each candidate," Sebastian said, "and I think you've just seen the opening moves in that challenge."

"Indeed," Holt said. "It is the rest of the information that concerns me. The building where the opening ceremony was held is the central palace, so to speak, and the residence of Veribold's ruler. As such, it is of paramount importance within the Jaixante. Very few of its staff speak Tremontanese, so I was unable to make the acquaintance of key household servants, but those few gave away more, I think, than they intended. There is serious unrest below stairs. The cook, who is Tremontanan, shied away from certain lines of inquiry that were extremely revelatory. All signs point to something being wrong with the Election. Deep uncertainty, and many silences, mark a disturbance that has the servants worried."

"Do you think it has something to do with the missing Stones?" Fiona asked. "They have to be worried about that."

"The Stones will be needed six days from now, for the challenge of faith," Sebastian said. "I'd be beyond worried if I were them."

"Then we only have five days to find a way to return them." Fiona shook her head. "It seems impossible."

"I had a thought about that," Sebastian said. "What if we could plant the Jaoine Stones in Gizane's quarters and arrange for the Irantzen priestesses to find them there? That would neutralize Gizane and return the Stones in one blow."

"That's...brilliant," Fiona said. "But should we...I mean, I know Gizane is a blackmailer, and she's probably hurt more people than just your family, but Great-Uncle Sebastian did say the penalty for being caught with the Stones is death. Should we do that to her?"

Sebastian frowned. "I hadn't thought about it that way. I certainly am not willing to assassinate her, so I don't know how I feel about indirectly causing her death. Damn. That was a good idea."

"It might still be necessary," Holt said. "I suggest you evaluate out situation, sir, and determine which of our many goals is primary. If returning the Jaoine Stones, for example, takes precedence, such drastic measures may be necessary."

"I hate the thought of that, but you're right." Sebastian stood, again without any effort, and paced from the windows to the door and back, his hands clasped behind his back. "Return the Stones. Keep Gizane from becoming Queen. Don't get caught. If it were up to me, I'd say returning the Stones is more important, but Mother's...

assignment...might need to happen first. If we can't do both at the same time..."

Sebastian stopped in front of the windows and looked out over the city, resting one hand flat against the wall next to the glass. "Gizane has to take precedence," he said. "I hate saying it, and I hate even more that Mother is right, but my duty is to Tremontane first. Gizane can't become Veribold's Queen."

"Which means we need more information," Fiona said.

"I will continue speaking to the servants," Holt said. "At the very least, I can learn where Gizane's quarters are and whether they are accessible to any of us."

"And I'm going to think about how to return the Stones," Fiona said. When Sebastian began to protest, she overrode him with, "I know Gizane's more important, but the Stones aren't nothing. We need a way to return them without implicating ourselves. Though Great-Uncle Sebastian did say the Temple was unlikely to pursue us just for having once held the Stones."

"I suppose there's no reason not to work on that, too," Sebastian said. He looked suddenly tired, and Fiona's heart went out to him.

"I will retire now, but I will return in the morning to accompany you to the first challenge," Holt said. He bowed and left the room.

"So," Sebastian said, returning to sit next to Fiona, "tell me what they said. In the ceremony. I can guess some of it was for officially declaring those four candidates for Election."

Fiona quickly summed up what the Queen had said. There wasn't much of it, she realized when she finished. She added, "Gizane isn't what I expected."

"Me either," Sebastian said. "I thought she'd look like a bird of prey, not a debutante. Though I wouldn't underestimate her."

"I think she knows why we're here. I mean, why else would a North show up for the Election?"

"It's a mark of respect to send a member of the royal family." Sebastian yawned and stretched out his long legs. "But I think we should behave as if she does, regardless. She might not have proof we're here to destroy her, but if I were her, I'd be paranoid and suspicious."

"Exactly." Fiona let out a matching yawn. "I don't know why I'm so tired. It's still early, and it's not like we did anything more than stand around. I think I'll turn in."

Sebastian nodded, but made no move to rise when Fiona stood awkwardly, pushing off the sofa with both hands. "Goodnight, Fiona."

His voice sounded strange, almost flat as if he were suppressing a strong emotion. Fiona almost sat beside him again, nearly took his face in her hands to kiss him. Instead, she crossed to her bedroom door without looking back and said "Goodnight" just before opening it. She shut the door behind her and leaned against it. It wasn't fair. Love wasn't enough to build a life on. She'd learned that the hard way.

She tried to take off her gown, forgetting the tightness of the stitched-in sleeves, and wrestled with it for a few moments before ringing for Georgette. She wasn't sure she could bear Georgette's scrutiny and silent judgment of Fiona's nonexistent marriage. But Georgette, when she appeared, didn't say anything, not even to ask about the ceremony. Probably she didn't care what the heathen foreigners got up to. Fiona hung the gown in the dressing room and put on her nightgown, then climbed into the bed and thought about how much she preferred it to a pallet on the floor like she'd had in the Irantzen Temple.

That made her think of Hien again, this time as she'd seen her in the palace. The woman's face, still and emotionless, presented itself for review by her mind's eye. She wished she knew what Hien thought they had been doing at the Irantzen Festival. Scoping out the temple for a theft, probably. Fiona hoped it was true that their envoy status would protect them, because she had to admit it looked bad.

Though Hien also had to know that Gizane's office had been burgled. Would she put it together that the Stones had been in Gizane's desk, or would she assume they'd been stolen from wherever in the Temple they were supposed to be stored? It wouldn't matter that Fiona had no idea where that might be. They'd been mysterious foreigners who behaved strangely and then fled in the middle of the night. That alone suggested guilt.

She rolled over and buried her head under the pillow. If she could get Hien alone, she could explain the truth—no, that was insane, she'd have to reveal they had the Stones and they'd all be executed. She'd just have to suppress her feelings of guilt until Gizane was no longer a threat and the Stones were returned. Maybe Hien would be so relieved she'd be willing to accept Fiona's apology. Fiona wished she knew what she most needed to apologize for.

*G*eorgette, despite her dislike for Veriboldans, proved to have some inside line on the appropriate garb for each day's events. The next morning she laid out ordinary trousers and a bell-sleeved linen shirt in North blue, along with Fiona's favorite pair of ankle boots. "I'm told you aren't to participate in the challenge," she said with a sniff, her only comment on how she felt about her mistress being excluded from any part of the Veriboldan ceremonies. Fiona dressed herself in relief.

She and Sebastian had discussed the Election on the way to Haizea until they were sick of the whole thing, and now she knew more about Veriboldan government than she'd ever wanted, even when she was still married to Roderick and wanted to show him up with her knowledge of their laws. Each of the five challenges tested some aspect of character Veriboldans believed was essential to the perfect human being. While they didn't expect their ruler to be perfect, candidates were expected to come closer to the ideal than ordinary men and women.

Today was the challenge of knowledge. It was the one the envoys had the least part in, a series of tests evaluating the candidates' knowledge of history, mathematics, literature, philosophy, and a handful of other topics Fiona knew nothing about. She had trouble believing that knowing when a famous poet had died made you a better ruler, but it wasn't her government. Maybe it was superior to having rule passed down hereditarily, like some kind of communicable disease. It was nothing she'd ever have to worry about.

Sebastian, dressed much as she was, waited for her in the sitting room. "Mitxel sent a message, informing me that a servant would meet us on the bridge to take us to the place they hold the challenge," he said. "Prepare to be bored."

"I don't see the point of us being present for what's essentially an hours-long test," Fiona said. "Maybe we can talk to the other envoys. Or *I* can talk to the other envoys. Sorry."

"I don't mind not being able to talk to Morten. He looks at me like he's planning a one-man invasion of Tremontane, to rid the country of useless nobles like me." He grinned. "Though that Stannin is certainly a looker. I almost wish I were attracted to men."

"He's too beautiful to be real. I wonder what he thinks of all this. He certainly behaves like it's the best entertainment he's had in his life."

"I'm glad you think he's too beautiful, because I was prepared to be jealous." A knock sounded at the door, giving Fiona an excuse not to look at him and hide her flaming cheeks. "And it's time to go."

Their carriage deposited them at the end of the same bridge they'd crossed on foot the night before. This time, the waiting servant was a woman dressed in ivory linen a few shades paler than her skin. Her light brown hair was cut short in the style of the Irantzen priestesses. Fiona didn't think she was actually a priestess, since the woman didn't seem angry with them...though that might be because she was too low in the hierarchy to be privy to all the Temple's secrets. At any rate, the woman bowed to them politely and led the way across the bridge in silence.

For once, there were other people on the streets of the Jaixante, most of them wearing the gauzy over-robes and body suits of high-ranking functionaries, like the costumes the officials at the customs house wore. Some of them were carried in litters with fluttering drapes borne by muscular men all the same height. None of the Veri-boldans acknowledged Fiona and Sebastian at all, making Fiona feel as if she were invisible. Despite her discomfort at being in the Jaix-ante, it wasn't a nice feeling. It wasn't so much that she was being ignored, she discovered, as that she felt like the Veriboldans had erased her from their awareness.

Their guide led them down the canyonlike streets that felt more open in the daylight, or maybe that was just Fiona's memory of fleeing through them in the darkness, not knowing where she was going or how she would escape the Jaixante guards. Open-feeling or not, the buildings still looked like sheer white identical cliffs with black slabs of oak for doors, or white ones that fitted so closely to the walls they were visible only as hair-fine cracks, geometric and perfect.

Fiona couldn't help comparing the Jaixante to the rest of Haizea, or even to the slums of Dusktown. If this was how the land-holders lived, no wonder they were so different from the average Veriboldan. It also explained some of what she'd learned in studying Veriboldan law, how so much of their legal code had nothing to do with anything ordinary people did or experienced. But she wasn't here to criticize the Veriboldan government, just watch how it dealt with transition. Still, it made her grateful for her own government.

That thought startled her. Was Tremontane's government really that much better? Queen Genevieve had blackmailed her and Sebas-tian into criminal activity not for the sake of the country, but for the sake of her own rule. She'd protected Douglas North from the conse-quences of his careless actions—that was the same as letting a rapist go free. All right, maybe the Norths losing the Crown would cause civil unrest, but that didn't mean the Queen hadn't acted selfishly. And that wasn't so different from the Veriboldans isolating their ruling class on an island and making laws that benefited them more than the common folk.

She realized she'd lagged behind when Sebastian turned and said her name questioningly. She hurried to catch up and accepted his arm, feeling the need for something solid and real that had nothing to do with politics.

Their guide abruptly veered to the left, heading for a cliff face Fiona couldn't remember passing before, and pressed her hand against one of the rectangles outlined by those faint dark lines. Unlike what Fiona now thought of as the palace, whose halls had been comfortingly dim, the door swung open on a hall brightly lit by Devices almost enough to compete with the sunlight. Fiona and Sebastian followed the woman down the hall, which was painted a rich cream that matched their guide's clothing. If Fiona looked at her out of the corner of her eye, the woman blended with the walls and appeared to be nothing but a head and hands bobbing along. It was as unsettling an image as the nearly invisible doors had been.

The hall ended in a pair of wooden doors carved all over with the sort of abstract art Fiona identified as peculiarly Veriboldan. They had no handles, but their guide pushed gently on them and they swung noiselessly inward. "Enter," the guide said, bowing.

They found themselves on a balcony which ran the full circumference of the round chamber. It had no stairs that would allow access to the main floor some twenty feet below, just an ornate wooden rail supported by balusters carved to look like people. The figures were elongated, but still recognizably human. Fiona was sure, based on her knowledge of Veriboldans, that each was unique, though she didn't feel like examining all of them to prove this. Maybe if she were bored enough, she'd change her mind.

The room was comfortably cool, with a draft coming from waving fans mounted in the ceiling. The moving air carried with it the scent of cinnamon, a popular fragrance in Veribold. Fiona liked the smell and hoped she wouldn't get sick of it before they left.

In the center of the ceiling, a clear glass dome let in the early morning light, illuminating the floor below. Fiona let go of Sebastian's arm and walked to the railing. She couldn't see the whole room below, because the balcony jutted out over it, concealing the walls. What she could see were four pedestals with wide, flat tops and a single Veriboldan basin-chair. A woman in the white of an Irantzen priestess sat cross-legged in it, her eyes closed, her hands resting loosely on her thighs as if in meditation. The four candidates stood at the pedestals, all of them writing on sheets of paper piled half an inch thick on the pedestals' wide tops.

Fiona's eye went instantly to Gizane. The woman had just dipped her pen in her inkwell and resumed writing a line of script Fiona was too far away to read. She seemed so *normal*. They all did. They looked like a bunch of overgrown children copying out their lessons in a strange round schoolroom presided over by a silent mistress.

Fiona examined all the other candidates in turn, wondering if they were conscious of being observed. They had to know there were witnesses; it was part of the challenge. The Eskandelic envoys and a handful of Veriboldan landholders were already present. Nikani and Salena, elegant in cool silk robes over white trousers and shirts that were subtly different from their Veriboldan counterparts, drifted over to meet them. "It is dull, isn't it?" Salena said in a low voice.

Sebastian shrugged. "I understand it's more interesting when the oral recitations begin. Not that I'd understand that either."

"They use us as monitors, to prevent cheating," Nikani said. "It is difficult to falsify the exam when one has observers in the rafters, so to speak."

Fiona wasn't sure about that. True, it would be impossible to smuggle in a list of answers without being seen, but nothing said a candidate couldn't somehow get a copy of the exam beforehand and memorize the answers. Queen Genevieve had said Gizane had manipulated the election; that might be one of the things she'd done. Briefly, Fiona wished for an inherent magic that would let her read someone's thoughts, though it wasn't as if she could have done anything with the knowledge if she did.

She heard the slightest creak as the doors swung open again, and turned to see who had entered. To her dismay, it was a group of white-clad priestesses led by Hien. They spread out like a seed pod bursting, drifting silently in all directions. Hien, on the other hand, stood still just inside the door, forcing the other women to step wide around her. She had her eyes fixed on some point directly opposite the doors. Fiona looked in that direction, but saw no one and nothing of interest, at least to her.

When she turned back, Hien was a few steps away and approaching rapidly. Fiona swallowed hard to rid herself of the lump in her throat. Her hand closed tightly on Sebastian's sleeve. "Fiona?" he said. "Is—"

"Prince Sebastian North," Hien said from behind him, making him jump. "Lady Fiona North. Welcome to the Election." Her voice was flat, uninviting. She might as well have cursed their names instead.

"Thank you," Sebastian said, turning to face her and bringing Fiona, her hand still on his sleeve, with him. "It's an honor to be invited."

"Walk with me," Hien said. "I wish to know your opinion of the proceedings."

Fiona didn't dare look at Nikani and Salena to see what they thought of this. Well, it wasn't as if Hien could have them executed in the middle of the challenge of knowledge. Probably.

Hien made a little gesture indicating that they should precede her. Since Fiona had no idea where they should go, this made her nervous, but Sebastian nodded to the Eskandelics and strode off along the curve of the balcony. Fiona was just as happy to let him set the pace, but she wished she could see Hien. Having the woman at her back made her even more nervous.

They made it about a third of the way around the room, passing priestesses who looked at them curiously, before Hien said, "Stop here." Sebastian and Fiona stopped. From where they stood, the priestess overseeing the challenge was visible only as the top of a dark head, and the exam papers of the candidates closest to her, Alazne and Bixhor, were white blotches against the pale blue stone of the pedestals.

"Why are you here?" Hien said after a silence Fiona was afraid to break.

"We're representatives of Tremontane," Sebastian began.

Hien cut him off with, "Then you are who you say you are. This time."

Fiona winced at the sarcasm in her voice. Sebastian said, "I don't know what you mean." *Time to brazen it out.*

"You deny having come to us under false identities before?"

"We have never used false identities. We may not have been forthcoming about our entire identities."

"Then you are a doctor, your Highness?" Hien's voice sharpened. "And Lady North is fatally ill?"

Sebastian didn't flinch. "A ruse to protect our true identities."

"To deceive us."

"For privacy's sake." Sebastian was doing well. He hadn't lied at all yet.

"And to steal from us."

"We never stole from the Irantzen Temple."

"A theft occurred. You fled in the night. We are not supposed to take that as an admission of guilt?"

"You have no proof that we stole anything. Personal circumstances required us to leave the festival early."

Hien let out a hiss of exasperation. "You, Fiona Cooper who is now Fiona North," she said. "Why did you come to the festival?"

Damn. There wasn't a way out of answering that question, was there? "I can't tell you," Fiona said, clinging to the hope that she might yet avoid compounding her guilt.

"Then you are guilty."

"Sebastian told the truth. We did not steal from the Irantzen Temple."

"And from Gizane of the Araton?"

Fiona closed her eyes. She wished Hien weren't standing behind her, armed with who knew what kind of weapons, even if they were only words. "Are you allowed to harass the representatives of a foreign government?" she said. "If you have proof of your allegations, present it. Otherwise, stop trying to put words in our mouths."

Silence, again, for the space of several breaths. Then Hien said, "If you were innocent, you would answer my questions."

"That's an invalid assumption," Sebastian said. "Someone inno-cent of a crime who can't prove that innocence might as well be guilty as far as the law is concerned."

"I have said nothing about the law. I simply want answers."

"Which we've given you." Sebastian turned around, bringing Fiona with him. "What was stolen?"

Hien's lips compressed into a tight line. "You know very well, even if you will not admit it."

"Then you have no proof it was us," Fiona said. "And we're not going to admit to a crime we didn't commit."

Hien's eyes came to rest on Fiona, and Fiona managed not to flinch. "I trusted you," she said. "You deserved to be at the festival. I am ashamed of both of us that you failed to discover why that was."

Fiona opened her mouth to speak, but words failed her. Hien turned on her heel and walked away rapidly, forcing another priestess to step back or be mown down. Sebastian said, "That went better than I'd hoped."

"So she either can't or won't come out and accuse us of theft," Fiona said. "I'm leaning toward 'can't'. I feel awful, Sebastian."

"You know why we're here," Sebastian said. "Achieving that is our primary purpose. Everything else has to wait."

Fiona said nothing. She watched Hien exit through the carved doors, walking stiffly, as if her back pained her. "But it matters to her," she said in a low voice.

"Not to sound callous, but should that be important to us, how Hien feels?"

Fiona shook her head. "Maybe. I don't know. Keeping Veribold from falling into chaos must be at least as important as...the other thing." She didn't know how far sound carried in this room, though their footsteps, at least, were muffled by the thick carpet. Not speaking their secrets even in semi-privacy seemed the best course of action.

She looked down again at Gizane and her heart beat once, painfully hard, when she saw the woman looking up at her. Gizane's eyebrows rose. Then she smiled, amused the way a parent might be at a child's first steps. It chilled Fiona, as if Gizane could read her thoughts and knew Fiona was no threat. Well, let her go on believing that. Fiona turned her back on her enemy. Gizane might know all the rules of this alien society Fiona had been thrust into, but if she thought Fiona was harmless, she was in for a nasty surprise.

iona slept late the following morning, waking sharply the way she did when she was conscious of having missed some important appointment. She rushed out of her bedroom into an empty sitting room. No Sebastian waited impatiently for her to rise. Confused, she knocked timidly on his bedroom door and got no response. Surely he wouldn't have left without her?

She returned to her bedroom and discovered Georgette had laid out clothes for her, this time dark ivory Veriboldan-style shirt and trousers with an over-robe of North blue embroidered with silver cats. That might be a nod to the North sign and shield. The robe made her feel awkward, as if she were accepting an honor not actually due her. It must have taken someone a dozen days to embroider the robe, and whoever it was thought it would be worn by an actual North. *If you married Sebastian*, her terrible inner voice told her, and anger supplanted awkwardness. She donned the clothing anyway. As far as anyone here knew, she was a North, and she needed to behave like one.

The sitting room was still empty when she emerged. Puzzled, she went downstairs in search of anyone who might know what was going on. The interchangeable attachés continued to ignore her, only flicking glances her way that might have been calculating or admiring or even dismissive for all she was able to read them.

"Lady North."

Fiona turned to face Carris, who looked as unruffled as ever. "His Highness asked me to inform you he would meet you at the challenge this afternoon," he said. "He has business in town this morning."

"Oh." Business? She couldn't imagine what business Sebastian might have in Haizea. "Then I haven't missed the challenge."

"No, milady. The carriage will call for you after dinner."

"Oh," Fiona repeated. "Thank you."

"Is there anything else I can do for you?"

The way he said it, so smoothly, as if he practiced in front of his mirror every day, made Fiona uncomfortable. "Thank you, no," she said, and retreated up the stairs to her suite without looking back to see if he was watching her. She had a feeling Carris didn't respect her, probably because of the stunt she'd pulled the day they arrived. Well, she hadn't been very polite to him, and maybe she should apologize... or was that another thing royalty didn't do, apologize to their inferiors? At any rate, it was too late now, because when she reached the top of the stairs, Carris was gone.

It was late enough that even though she was hungry from having missed breakfast, it made more sense to wait for dinner. What didn't make sense was staying in the sitting room for an hour. She decided to explore the embassy. That might also be frowned on as not something a North would do, but Fiona didn't care. She wasn't going to change everything about herself to fit these people's notions of propriety.

A little poking around led her to a library, dimly lit and windowless, stocked with elderly books bound in worn leather. Two chairs matching the books for age and wear flanked an ultra-modern light Device that made the whole room look tawdry, like a set for a historical melodrama. Fiona browsed the shelves until she found something marginally newer, though it was still most of twenty years old, and seated herself in one of the chairs to read.

She'd heard talk of new Devices that would make the production of books easier, but no one ever knew more than that they were possible. Fiona couldn't imagine how making books might be easier, unless it was Devices to carve engraved plates more rapidly than a human could, or to ink the plates more neatly. She turned a few pages. It was a history of Haran's journey to the Eidestal, something that had coincidentally been on Fiona's mind in the past few weeks. Maybe heaven was trying to tell her something, though Fiona didn't think she was important enough for heaven to send her messages.

The library door opened. "Lady North," Emory said. "I'm surprised to see you here. I thought you'd left with his Highness."

"I took advantage of the late morning to sleep in," Fiona said. "Should I not be here?"

"The embassy is open to you. I'm afraid the library isn't much used. My staff and I don't have much time for reading." Emory let the door swing shut and came to take the other chair, easing into it with the air of someone whose joints pained her. Since she wasn't all that old, Fiona found that surprising.

"At any rate," the ambassador continued, "I'm glad to see someone getting some use from all these books." She gestured, a weary expression that suggested the books felt put-upon at not being read.

"I'm not much of a reader, or wasn't for years, but now I feel I have the time." It was true, to Fiona's surprise. Roderick had thought reading a waste of time, and Fiona had always been occupied with business responsibilities, but she'd loved to read as a child.

"I agree. I look forward to leaving this posting behind and taking up a peaceful retirement, sometime soon." Emory leaned forward in her seat and fixed her gaze on Fiona. "You're newly married, am I right?"

"Yes." She hated lying to this woman, but there was nothing for it.

"I understand you were married before and divorced. That must have been a strain."

"Yes and no. It was a relief to divorce my husband. It was a strain to endure all the sidelong looks and even outright criticism." Fiona returned Emory's gaze, steel for steel.

To her surprise, Emory laughed. "You mean as I'm doing now? I mean no criticism. I was divorced myself before marrying my late husband."

"Oh." Fiona felt as if she'd been pushing against a wall that was suddenly removed. "Was it...a good thing?"

"He found someone he preferred to me, but he didn't have the courage to come out and admit it. So we had a couple of years of fighting and anger before I discovered the truth. It was an acrimonious divorce, but yes, it was ultimately a relief. As I'm sure you understand."

"I guess I do."

"And now you've married royalty," Emory went on. "What a strange turn of events that must have been."

Fiona sat back in her chair. "You know I'm a commoner. Was a commoner."

"It was in the information her Majesty sent, yes." Emory's eyes narrowed. "She was subtle, but it was clear she meant me to be appalled by that fact. Forgive my bluntness, but it doesn't seem as if your adopted family is all that happy about your marriage to his Highness."

Fiona thought of Emily and Great-Uncle Sebastian. "Some of them aren't."

"That must be difficult."

Emory sounded like she was inviting confidences. Fiona, to her surprise, wished she could share them. "Love can solve a multitude of problems," she said instead.

"But not all of them," Emory replied. "I won't insult you by giving you advice, but I wish you well. You have a hard road ahead. I know what the Queen's court is like—there's a reason I accepted this posting. Navigating the eccentricities of the Veriboldan nobility is far easier than dealing with the nobles of Tremontane."

"Thank you," Fiona said, not sure what else to say. It felt like vindication, to have someone else confirm her suspicious about how the nobles would treat her. It also felt like a blow to the face. Fiona hadn't realized how much she'd wanted someone to prove her wrong.

Emory stood, grunting softly. "You're welcome to dine with me in half an hour," she said. "I understand you were a trader and a frequent visitor to Veribold. I'd like your perspective, if you don't mind."

"Of course," Fiona said.

When Emory was gone, Fiona opened her book and stared blindly at the pages. That had been unexpected. If all the nobles were like Emory, Fiona's problem would be solved. But it sounded like the opposite was true. She made herself focus on the words. She envied Haran, who had faced danger and misunderstanding and opposition with the rock-hard certainty of faith backing her up. Fiona wasn't nearly so confident.

She closed the book and moved to put it back on the shelf, then hesitated. She'd never thought of herself as particularly religious, but her recent experiences in the Irantzen Temple had changed that. She wished more than ever she'd been able to complete the festival. Well, maybe this book was a step in the right direction. She took it with her back to her bedroom.

3 2

iona's guide, who to her surprise was not Veriboldan, but a stout fair-haired Tremontanan born in Barony Daxtry, led her from the bridge to the palace and then through long, narrow corridors to a door that seemed out of place in its stark plainness. "The Zorion, milady," he'd said in the same reverent whisper with which he'd greeted her. "It is the judgment hall where the most important criminal cases are heard and adjudicated on. Today the challenge of wisdom is held there as a reminder to all that the ruler of Veribold must be a just and wise ruler."

He opened the door and bowed Fiona into a balcony overlooking a high-ceilinged room paneled in expensive mahogany. A row of plain wooden chairs lined the balcony, with a few people seated there. One of them was Sebastian.

He glanced her way when the door opened. A smile lit his face when he realized it was her. It was a look of such happiness it prompted a smile from her in return. She made her way along the row of chairs, passing Morten and Venelda, the latter of whom gave her a pleasant smile. Morten grunted and made no move to get out of Fiona's way. Fiona ignored him and sat beside Sebastian. "They told me you had business in Haizea," she said, feeling shy at how tenderly he smiled at her.

"Nothing serious," Sebastian said. "Though I didn't realize how used I was to seeing you every morning, spending the day with you..." He cleared his throat and glanced away. "Did you have a good morning? Not too bored?"

"No. I talked with Ambassador Emory. I—"

The door opened again, admitting the Dekerians. They and, Fiona realized, Morten and Venelda were all dressed much as Fiona and Sebastian, in robes matching the colors of their houses. Someone had put a lot of effort into either honoring the foreign envoys or making them readily identifiable. Dekerian Salena sat on Fiona's other side. "Yet another incomprehensible challenge, at least for you, your Highness," she told Sebastian with a half-smile.

"I'm used to it," Sebastian said, smiling back. "Fiona is an excellent translator."

"I think this will test your abilities," Nikani said. "I find their legal reasoning difficult to follow."

"Fiona is an expert on Veriboldan law," Sebastian said. "She'll have no trouble."

Nikani raised his eyebrows. "Interesting. You will have to tell me later how you came by such rarefied knowledge."

Fiona was about to respond when Stannin pushed past, apologizing in broken Veriboldan. He took a seat on Sebastian's other side and clapped him on the shoulder, knocking him forward. "*Many talks,*" he boomed, "*many hears. Listens. I think is much—*" He broke off and addressed Morten in that guttural language Fiona assumed was Ruskeldin.

"*Boring,*" Morten said.

Stannin let out a great guffaw. "*Boring! That is boring! I not boring at home, am keep busy with riding.*"

Fiona was about to ask him about his horse, a subject all the Kirkellan could talk on for days, when a hush fell over the room. She leaned on the balcony rail and looked around as she had not when she entered.

Beneath the balcony were rows of pews that looked as hard as the chair she was sitting in. Noble Veriboldans dressed the way the envoys were, though with less elaborately decorated robes, filled every inch of the pews except for the first one. That was abnormal for the Veriboldan upper classes, who normally kept a safe distance of about a foot from any of their peers. It might explain why they looked so uncomfortable, or maybe it was just that they were genuinely crammed together. It didn't explain the empty pew, though Fiona guessed it was reserved for someone else, possibly the candidates.

Facing the pews was an unadorned mahogany desk some ten feet long. No one sat there, but it gave the impression that it was staring at the Veriboldans. If that was where a judge usually sat, anyone defending herself would be at a severe disadvantage, being glared at by more than just human eyes.

Fiona leaned out farther. There were doors at each end of the desk, uncarved slabs of wood Fiona might have expected to see in a kitchen. In fact, the whole room was peculiarly un-Veriboldan in its plainness. If not for the richness of the mahogany, which filled the room with a pleasant resinous scent, she would have thought herself in some provincial Tremontanan justice house, waiting for the judge to roll himself out of whatever bar he'd been drinking in.

She couldn't see any reason for the murmur of voices below to go still, but they had apparently received some silent cue, for in unison they all rose in a whisper of silken robes like a woman's gasp of surprise and stared straight ahead. The doors to the left side opened, and three men and two women carrying stacks of papers and books passed through the door, as perfectly spaced as beads on a string. They wore black shirts and trousers and had no robes, which made Fiona feel embarrassed for them, as if they were naked. How quickly she'd become accustomed to Veriboldan noble apparel.

The black-clad men and women took seats on the front pew, which made them visible as little more than the backs of their heads when Fiona sat back in her chair. From that position, she couldn't see the other Veriboldans, but she heard the hiss of silk as they all resumed their seats.

The door to the right opened, and Gizane walked through and took a seat at the center of the long desk. She wore a crimson robe over stormcloud-gray shirt and trousers. Her large green eyes glinted like glass as she gazed at the onlooking crowd with no sign of discomfort or nervousness.

Abruptly, the man seated at the center of the pew said, "*A man comes before the justice claiming right of reparation against his neighbor. The neighbor's bull sired a calf on the man's cow. The man had intended to breed her elsewhere. Gizane of the Araton, how judge you?*"

Gizane said, "*In such a case, damages may not be assessed, as what might have been is impossible to know. The man cannot say he would have gained more had he bred the cow as he intended. The judgment is that the calf belongs to the man, and no fee for breeding may be collected by the neighbor. So judge I.*"

Fiona whispered the translation into Sebastian's ear, feeling as if her words carried to the far ends of the room. No one shushed her or looked up.

"That's a remarkably rural case," Sebastian whispered back. "I thought they'd all be related to the upper classes."

"Me too," Fiona said, then had to whisper more translations as one of the women addressed Gizane, this time with questions relating to a passage of legal code Fiona was familiar with.

The questioning went on for a while, and Fiona had just begun to think this would be an even more boring day than the challenge of knowledge when the left-hand door opened again. A couple of guards in the fluttering black robes that sent a hiccup of fear through Fiona entered, dragging a woman dressed only in a knee-length linen shift dyed a streaky bright green. The woman's hair was shorn close to her scalp, and she twisted desperately, trying to get away from her captors.

The guards dragged her to a place opposite Gizane, between the black-clad questioners and the desk, and forced her to stand upright. Their complete silence made them even more frightening. The woman also said nothing, but her heavy breathing was loud enough even Fiona in the balcony could hear it.

One of the men on the front pew stood. *"The prisoner is charged with arson,"* he said in a voice that echoed despite the room being full of people. *"Gizane of the Araton, a judgment."*

"Are there witnesses?" Gizane asked.

Another of the men said, *"Witnesses saw her fleeing the burning building. No one saw her light the fire."*

Sebastian gripped Fiona's knee. "What are they saying?"

Fiona had been so caught up in the unexpected twist she'd forgotten her translating duties. She gabbled out a few sentences and missed what Gizane said next. Impatiently, she said, "Wait until it's over," and leaned forward with her arms on the rail.

"She lived in the building and had been fighting with her husband," one of the black-clad women was saying. *"He perished in the fire along with five others."*

"Making this a capital crime," Gizane said. The prisoner gasped. Gizane turned an expressionless gaze on her and added, *"Han La states that in capital cases, the burden of proof lies on the prisoner. What do you say in your defense?"*

"It wasn't me," the woman gasped. She still sounded as out of breath as if she'd run a mile. *"It was Pala Gakoa. He wanted the property cleared out and the owner wouldn't sell. Please. It wasn't me."*

"Why is Pala Gakoa not here?" Gizane said.

The woman at the end of the pew said, *"Pala Gakoa was not present when the arson was committed."*

The woman struggled against her captors and shouted, *"He was there! The woman who accused me was my enemy!"*

"Gizane of the Araton, what of the prisoner's accusation?" the same woman asked.

"Goh Fia says that a prisoner's word carries less weight when it is the only evidence for an allegation," Gizane said. *"Pala Gakoa is not on trial. This prisoner has not given sufficient evidence to corroborate her story."*

Fiona held her breath. Maybe her sympathies were with the prisoner because she hated Gizane, maybe it was her fear of being accused of arson herself, but this all felt very wrong.

Sebastian whispered, "Fiona—"

She waved him off. "Just wait, please?" she said without turning. She felt bound in place, unable to look away from the drama playing out below.

"*Have you any other questions?*" one of the black-clad men was saying.

"*None,*" Gizane said.

Fiona could think of half a dozen questions Gizane hadn't asked. She wasn't sure who she was angrier with, Gizane for her carelessness or the others for not pressing the issue. She was sure those five men and women were judges or law-speakers or something.

"*Then, your judgment?*" the woman on the end said.

"*The prisoner is guilty,*" Gizane said.

The woman gasped again, then burst into tears and tried once more to get away from her captors.

"*And the punishment?*" said the same woman.

Gizane once more cast a cold eye on the weeping prisoner. "*Death by strangulation.*"

Fiona gripped the rail with both hands. Beside her, Salena let out a tiny gasp of surprise. It wasn't an unusual means of execution in Veribold, but Fiona had never heard a sentence pronounced so casually, as if a woman's life weren't in question.

One of the guards passed the woman off to his partner. Then he withdrew a long, slim cord from within his fluttering robes. Stunned, Fiona didn't at first realize what it meant. The man took hold of the wooden handles at each end of the silken cord and snapped the cord taut. The sound cracked loudly, cutting across the woman's desperate cries. The other guard forced the woman to kneel facing Gizane. The man with the cord moved to stand behind her.

Fiona's chest hurt with the pounding of her heart. She shot to her feet. "*Stop!*" she exclaimed in Veriboldan.

Everyone below turned to look at her. Fiona didn't look at Gizane, but at the man in the center of the pew. "*This is unjust,*" Fiona said.

"*You disrespect our legal system by attempting to impose your foreign morality on us?*" the man shouted. "*Do not believe the respect accorded you as envoy entitles you to interfere.*"

"*Veribold's laws are just,*" Fiona countered, "*and I'm not telling you how to punish your criminals. But I challenge the judgment passed down by Gizane of the Araton. It's flawed.*"

The man cocked an eyebrow. Behind him, dozens of Veriboldan landholders muttered among themselves. "*Bold words,*" the man said. "*You claim better knowledge of our laws than a candidate for Election who has studied for years to reach this point?*"

Fiona drew a deep, steadying breath. "*The candidate cited Han La on the burden of proof in a capital case,*" she said. "*But Han La also said that a prisoner in the course of proving her innocence has the right to call witnesses, including those whom the prisoner accuses in her place. Without Pala Gakoa's testimony, the prisoner's case is incomplete.*"

"*Pala Gakoa was elsewhere at the time of the arson,*" the woman on the end said.

"*Quola of the Erbin says that the absence of proof is still proof. You can't prove a negative. All that means is that no one saw Pala Gakoa at the scene of the crime. He has a better motive in wanting the building removed than the prisoner does. He should be questioned.*"

The woman at the end of the bench twitched, her lips quirking in an unreadable expression before her face smoothed once again into impassivity. "*Why do you care?*" she asked.

"*Because injustice is a blot on any nation's character,*" Fiona said, "*and if I'm to be forced to watch a summary execution, I don't want any doubts that the prisoner has been justly found guilty.*"

The woman at the end looked at her associates. The man at the center of the pew nodded. "*Gizane of the Araton,*" he said, "*your competence has been called into question. How do you answer this charge?*"

Now Fiona looked at Gizane. She looked as calm as ever, but her green eyes blazed with fury. "*I do not believe a foreigner has the right to challenge me.*"

"*Your failure to cite proper precedent has already been noted by us. That it was a foreigner who made the challenge is irrelevant. Again, I ask, how do you answer this charge?*"

Gizane shot a poisonous glance at Fiona. Fiona gazed back at her, hoping she looked calmer than she felt. Sebastian's hand gripped hers painfully tight. Finally, Gizane looked at those on the front pew and said, "*My assessment of the crime was...incomplete. I beg the adjudicators' pardon for my inadequacy.*" The words sounded as if they were being dragged out of her.

"*Return the prisoner to her cell in preparation for further investigation,*" the woman on the end said. "*Gizane of the Araton, your challenge of wisdom is complete. You may stand down.*"

Gizane stood and walked through the right-hand door without looking at anyone. Fiona sank into her chair, struck by unexpected trembling. "What the hell was that about?" Sebastian demanded in a low but intense voice.

The five law-speakers, or whatever they were, had come together and were whispering in voices too low for Fiona to make out words. "Gizane made a mistake," Fiona began.

"*Lady North,*" the man at the center of the bench said. Fiona leaned over the railing again. The man had stood and was looking directly at her. "*Please rise.*"

Slowly, Fiona stood. "Fiona," Sebastian said, more loudly.

The woman at the end of the bench rose and left the room. The man said, "*What business do you have interfering in the challenge of wisdom?*"

"*I told you,*" Fiona said, "*I didn't want to see someone murdered because she didn't receive true justice.*"

"*The justice of the ruler of Veribold cannot be contested.*" The man didn't sound angry—didn't sound as if this mattered at all—but Fiona's legs continued to tremble, because the flat, emotionless look on his face scared her. It was the look of someone who'd been willing to allow a woman to die because of a flawed legal prosecution.

"*The candidates aren't rulers yet,*" she said.

"*But one eventually will be. If the ruler of Veribold passes judgment, that is de facto justice. The challenge of wisdom gives each candidate the opportunity to prove their worthiness to hold that responsibility. Your interference mars this proceeding.*"

The gallery door opened. The woman from below stood there,

her face as emotionless as her peer's. Behind her, two Jaixante guards in their fluttering robes stood, bearing polearms taller than the door.

"*Lady North,*" she said. "*You will come with us.*"

33

Fiona grabbed Sebastian's hand. "I think they want to arrest me," she said.

Sebastian shot to his feet. "They can't," he said. "The envoys have diplomatic immunity."

"I'm not sure they care. And even if we protest, there's no way the embassy can protect me right this second."

Sebastian swore under his breath. "Tell them anyway."

To her right, Dekerian Nikani stood. "*What do you intend?*" he asked the law-speaker.

"*Lady North will answer questions about her involvement in the challenges,*" the man replied.

"*Then she is not under arrest?*" Nikani asked.

The law-speaker's gaze flicked from Nikani to Fiona and back again. "*It is a courtesy,*" he said. "*The envoys show respect for Veribold by cooperating in their investigations.*"

"*As Veribold shows respect for its foreign guests by according them diplomatic immunity,*" Dekerian Salena said from her seat next to Nikani. "*If you have questions, you should ask them in public, not as if Lady North were a criminal.*"

"Fiona," Sebastian said through gritted teeth, "tell me what they're saying or I'm going to start shouting."

"That the Veriboldans have no right to treat me like a criminal," Fiona said.

Sebastian leaned on the railing and glared at the law-speaker. "If you're so interested in justice," he said, "you can bring your case before the Tremontanan embassy the way your government is legally obligated to do. But stop trying intimidation and threats to get Lady North to give up her rights."

Fiona translated this for him and was relieved to see the law-speaker's face tighten as if Sebastian had struck a telling blow. "*Lady North's refusal to cooperate suggests guilt,*" he said.

Hah. Big mistake. "*Not according to Veriboldan law,*" Fiona shot back. "*Tuyet Thien, in the Annals of Criminal Law, says it is the right of the accused not to incriminate herself, and that a lack of cooperation cannot be taken as an admission of guilt.*" She couldn't help herself; she glanced at the guards hovering in the doorway, afraid they might not care about the legalities. Nobody in the gallery was armed, and while Stannin might have been able to take on the guards bare-handed, he was following the conversation with the glazed expression of someone who didn't fully understand what was going on and couldn't be counted on to react properly.

Her eye fell on the woman law-speaker standing in front of the guards. To Fiona's surprise, she looked amused by the interchange. Fiona barely had time to register this before the male law-speaker addressed her again. "*So you refuse to confess who paid you to support Gizane of the Araton?*"

"What?" Fiona was so startled she forgot to speak Veriboldan. "*I —nobody paid me off. Is it so strange in your country that someone might speak up against a flawed judgment?*"

The man looked at the assembled Veriboldan audience. "*Who among you knew Gizane of the Araton had judged poorly?*" he asked. Three or four people stood. "*You see?*" he told Fiona. "*You disrespect our laws by thinking to put yourself above a candidate for Election.*"

"*I'm sorry I intervened,*" Fiona lied, "*but I am a stranger to your coun-*

try, and while I am familiar with your laws, I don't know all your customs. I reacted as I would have in my own country. I am not partisan. I want to see the best candidate chosen to rule Veribold because your country's strength benefits mine." The words poured out of her from some source she didn't know. She'd never been much of an elocutionist, and yet her words felt right in a way she hadn't expected.

"I wonder," the woman law-speaker said, startling Fiona. She hadn't expected any of them to speak Tremontanese. "Lady North, you claim to have spoken out to save the prisoner's life, not to benefit the chances of Gizane of the Araton by protecting her from the consequences of her failure. How are you to prove this?"

Fiona's heart sank. It was true, she hadn't thought beyond preventing a death, but the law-speaker had said he'd noticed Gizane's failure to cite proper precedent, and Fiona had hoped that meant Gizane had failed. But if Fiona's interference had saved her instead...

"I don't know Gizane of the Araton," she said, wishing she dared reveal the truth—that would prove beyond doubt that Fiona had no interest in protecting Gizane. "I don't know any of the candidates and don't have any vested interest in promoting one over another. But I can't prove my motives short of repeating what I already said. I didn't want to see someone die because her trial was flawed."

The woman law-speaker took a few steps forward. "*I'm satisfied,*" she said, addressing her male counterpart below. "*The interference does not contaminate our assessment of Gizane of the Araton's wisdom.*"

The man scowled. "*We do not tolerate interference by outsiders.*"

"*We tolerate the envoys' attendance,*" the woman said. "*But I agree we should not be so understanding a second time. Lady North, will you swear to keep silence in future?*"

Fiona drew a deep breath. "No," she said, prompting everyone below to turn to face her. "I can't promise not to speak out if a candidate's lack of knowledge would mean letting injustice win."

The male law-speaker said something under his breath. The woman said, "Thank you for your honesty. You are invited to withdraw."

"Envoys are supposed to observe all the challenges," Sebastian said. "You can't deprive us of that right."

"No," the woman said. She smiled, a little half-twist of the lips that might have been self-mocking. "But we can invite you to respect the traditions of the Election."

"That sounds like you don't trust your candidates," Fiona said.

The woman raised one eyebrow. "Until today I would have sworn there was no need to protect them," she said. "Let us say, rather, that we are not so proud as to believe in their infallibility. Again, I invite you to withdraw."

Fiona glanced at the male law-speaker, whose dark face was set in a scowl of epic proportions. "Thank you, I will," she said. "Sebastian, you should stay."

"I'm not going to leave you alone in this place," Sebastian said in a low voice intended only for her ears.

"If they were going to hurt me, those guards wouldn't have waited for all this conversation to end," Fiona replied. "We have to maintain a presence here. Nikani and Salena will translate for you. I'll wait for you outside."

Sebastian's scowl mirrored the law-speaker's. "You're too trusting," he said. "All right. Don't go anywhere with anyone, understand?"

"I won't. Don't worry about me." She squeezed his hand. Turning, she made her way past the other observers to where the woman law-speaker stood. "Can I wait just outside?"

"We will escort you to a more comfortable place to wait," the woman said.

Fiona eyed the guards, who hadn't relaxed from their alert, prepared-to-attack pose. "I'd rather not," she said. It was an insult, but she was still on edge and didn't care what the woman thought.

The woman gestured to Fiona to precede her. The guards stepped to each side as she exited, just as if they were there to show Fiona honor. "You are in no danger," the woman said as she shut the door behind them.

"I believe my royal husband would prefer I stay close by," Fiona said.

Her voice didn't tremble, but she had to hide her hands in the long sleeves of her North blue robe to conceal how they shook. "And don't you think it's better we avoid even a chance of an international incident?"

The other woman's intent gaze made Fiona feel simultaneously worried and guilty, as if the law-speaker really didn't mean any harm and Fiona was rejecting her generous offer for no reason. Finally, the woman said, "If I were a Veriboldan envoy to Tremontane, and I were in your position, what would you tell me to do?"

Fiona thought a moment, then said, "I'd tell you to trust your instincts."

The woman nodded. "Very well." She gestured to the guards, and they walked away down the corridor. Fiona sagged against the wall and let out a deep breath. She was the wrong person for this job. Knowledge of the law aside, she had no understanding of upper-class Veriboldan traditions, no real appreciation for the customs of the Election, and no sense of how far she could or should push these people. And was it really any of her business how they prosecuted justice? She remembered the desperate prisoner's face and decided the answer to that question was Yes.

She didn't have a watch, so she had no idea how long she waited in the hall. Long enough to regret having refused their hospitality, as her feet and back ached from standing for so long. Pacing the hall only kept her from being bored for so long. When the door finally opened, she stretched surreptitiously and watched the others file out. They all eyed her closely, Morten and Venelda with suspicion, the Dekerians as if they'd half expected her to be gone. Sebastian took her arm and steered her away from the others.

"They didn't hurt you?" he said.

"I'm fine. They didn't even try to force me to go somewhere else. It's all right, Sebastian."

Sebastian shook his head. "They very nearly took you into custody and started a war. I had no idea they would feel so defensive of their Election."

"Started a war?"

Sebastian's grip on her arm tightened. "You think I wouldn't be willing to go to war over you?"

Fiona's face warmed. "Sebastian—"

"Never mind how I feel about you, Fiona. Tremontane can't let Veribold think it can insult us with impunity." He sighed. "It didn't happen, so I suppose worrying about what might have been is pointless. What exactly did you do to make them so angry? You said Gizane made a mistake?"

"She was supposed to try that woman prisoner for arson. She made a lot of mistakes, and made the wrong judgment, and they were going to execute the woman in front of us."

"I saw that part," Sebastian said with a shudder.

They passed through the halls, retracing their steps, until Fiona's Tremontanan guide appeared and bowed to them. Fiona went silent. She didn't want to have this discussion in front of someone who spoke their language. Sebastian seemed to feel the same, because he didn't press her for more details until they were across the bridge and safely in the carriage.

"Anyway," Fiona went on, "I couldn't let that happen. I pointed out the errors in legal interpretation Gizane had made, and they said they had already noted them. That's what horrifies me—that those adjudicators *knew* Gizane was wrong and were going to let her judgment stand. They were willing to kill a potentially innocent woman on her say-so!"

"We're not here to pass judgment on their government," Sebastian said, but he looked as horrified as she felt. "So they wanted to arrest you for interfering?"

"Yes. At least, the man did. I think the woman was on my side. But you heard most of that."

Sebastian's hand clenched into a fist. "That was close. Does it at least mean Gizane failed the challenge?"

"I don't know." Despair threatened to overwhelm Fiona. "I don't know. The fact that they thought I was trying to help Gizane by interfering makes me worried. If she would have failed without my interruption, doesn't that imply that I helped her?"

"We shouldn't borrow trouble," Sebastian said. "In either case, Gizane looks incompetent, and that has to help us."

"I suppose," Fiona said, but she remembered the way Gizane had looked at her and didn't feel all that sanguine about their chances. She'd made a personal enemy that afternoon.

When they returned to the embassy, Fiona headed straight for the safety of her bedroom, managing not to break into a run. Once there, she removed the robe and hung it in the dressing room. Sebastian, watching from the doorway, said, "There's a banquet tonight. Something to do with the challenge of charisma."

"I'm almost afraid to go."

"I understand. I can make your excuses for you, if you want."

Fiona shook her head. "I can't hide in the embassy for the rest of the Election. We still need to—to complete the Queen's task. And return the Stones."

Sebastian came fully into the room and shut the door. "More specifically, we need to keep everyone's attention on us tonight. Holt will search Gizane's quarters and, I hope, will find something we can use to get her disqualified from the Election."

"That sounds dangerous. How much diplomatic immunity does Holt have?"

"Enough to protect him from being executed as a spy. Not enough to keep him from being arrested and tried as a thief if they catch him." Sebastian sat on the bed and ran his hands through his hair. "I shouldn't let him do it, but he feels more loyalty toward the North family than I do."

Fiona sat next to Sebastian. "Why is that?"

Sebastian's lips quirked in a smile. "It's not my story to tell. All I can say is that my father rescued him from a terrible fate, and Holt feels he owes him his life. Which means when my father assigned him to me, he transferred that loyalty to me. He's willing to lay down his life to protect us. I don't know how deserving any of us Norths are of that sacrifice, but I know of no way to stop him."

"Meaning that this was his idea?"

"Yes. He's also the best qualified of the three of us to go sneaking around the Jaixante. But you already knew that."

"So...we have to make ourselves conspicuous at this banquet so no one will wonder where your manservant went?"

"More specifically, we should try to keep Gizane from wandering off early." Sebastian blew out his breath and added, "I don't even know if that's possible. We may have no contact with her this evening, given that you humiliated her thoroughly this afternoon."

"I'm sorry."

"You saved a life. I don't think you have anything to be sorry for."

His smile warmed her down to the bone. She smiled back and saw his expression grow thoughtful. He shifted closer to her and took her hand briefly, running his thumb across her knuckles before releasing her and standing. The gentle touch took her back to that night in his bedroom, and a rush of desire surprised her.

"You know," Sebastian said quietly, "you spoke with authority today. You didn't let them intimidate you."

"Meaning...what? That I behaved like a noblewoman?"

"No." Sebastian's eyes were steady on hers. "You behaved like someone who didn't care what anyone else thought. It's not impossible, Fiona. You just need to believe it."

For a moment, she felt the rightness of his position. If she could feel that confidence within the royal court...but no, there was a difference. She'd been confident today because she had knowledge to back her up, and she'd acted to save a life. "Believing in things isn't good enough," she said. "I'll never be able to fly no matter how hard I flap my arms."

"I'm not asking you to fly. I just want you to see—" Sebastian shut his mouth and turned away. "Never mind. The banquet is in two hours. I'll call for you when it's time to leave." He left the room, shutting the door without slamming it, but it felt like a dismissal anyway.

Tears burned Fiona's eyes. She was right, she knew she was—ten years of the wrong marriage had taught her good sense mattered far more than love—and yet he never failed to make her question her decisions. She wanted more than anything to call him back, give him the answer he wanted...and then spend the next forty years regretting her rash, romantic decision.

She lay back on the bed and let her mind drift, focused on her breathing and heartbeat and the pulse of blood running through her body. She could ask him to marry her. To adopt into her family. She didn't actually know he'd refuse, and suppose he accepted? Then they would only have to finish the Queen's task and they could be together. The idea filled her with hope.

She rolled off the bed and left her room to knock on Sebastian's door. He didn't answer. She knocked again, and the door opened, revealing Holt. "I beg your pardon, Lady North," Holt said, as formally as Charles Carris ever dreamed of being. "Prince Sebastian has gone out. Is there anything I can do for you?"

"Oh," Fiona said, feeling deflated. "No, it's...there's nothing that can't wait. Thanks."

She returned to her bed and stared at the bed's canopy, a delicate confection of netting that would keep out insects if the embassy had had any, until Georgette bustled in some time later.

"Time to dress, milady," she said in her most forbidding tone. Fiona heard it as *time to dress milady*, as if she were a doll Georgette was responsible for. She rolled off the bed and followed Georgette into the dressing room.

3 4

$\mathcal{M}$itxel himself met Fiona and Sebastian at the bridge. "Your Highness, Lady North, good evening," he said with his usual bow. "Please join me."

Fiona took Sebastian's arm and followed Mitxel across the bridge to where a couple of palanquins waited. "This evening's entertainment is at the far north of the Jaixante, and you should not be required to walk so far," Mitxel explained. "Please be seated."

Fiona cast a quick glance at Sebastian. He'd said no more than "It's time" back at the embassy, had been totally silent during the short carriage ride to the bridge, and had barely looked at Fiona the whole time they'd been together. His continuing coldness made her heart ache with sorrow, guilt, and the inevitable hopeless longing for what could never be. In the face of that silence, her intent to propose marriage had frozen and died.

Now he released her arm and climbed into the nearest palanquin. Fiona stepped into the other. It was curtained in red silk and smelled stuffy, as if its last passenger had been a large, sweaty man who bathed in a musky cologne. Fiona twitched the curtains aside and tied them back, not caring if it was a violation of protocol.

The palanquin moved as smoothly as if it were on wheels. The bearers must practice for hours to achieve such an even gait. Fiona watched Sebastian's palanquin with its four matched bearers trotting along before her and wished she'd found a way to break through his anger, or hurt, or whatever fueled his silence. *You could accept his proposal*, she thought, and immediately crushed the impulse. What a disastrous marriage that would be if she gave in to him just to stop him being upset.

The palanquin took them far north, along the route to the Irantzen Temple for a hundred yards before turning left and away from that familiar route. It was later than Fiona was accustomed to arriving anywhere in the Jaixante, and the sun had nearly set, throwing long shadows that made the tall white cliffs and stark black doors even more confusing. Then they turned right, and Fiona gasped.

Ahead, a white pyramid rose sharply against the twilight sky, surrounded by the kind of parkland Fiona had assumed the Jaixante didn't have. It was barely enough to be considered a park; it would be more accurate to call it a grassy strip between the road and the pyramid. But trees grew along the verge, tall cypresses that quivered in the slight breeze like shivering maidens, and the park softened the harsh lines of the pyramid while making it seem even stranger than the rest of the Jaixante architecture.

Two giant brass doors set into the base of the pyramid opened at their approach. The bearers set down Fiona's palanquin, and Mitxel came forward to assist her. Fiona was wearing the silver-embroidered North blue robe again, but instead of ordinary trousers and shirt beneath it, she wore a slim white sheath of a dress that was little more than a tube of fabric ending at her ankles. Georgette had come up with silver sandals to go with it, not footwear Fiona remembered acquiring in Aurilien, but they matched perfectly, so Fiona had worn them without complaint. But the ensemble was difficult to move in, and she was grateful for Mitxel's hand.

Mitxel led her to where Sebastian waited, and Sebastian offered her his arm without looking at her. The gesture made Fiona angry. Maybe Sebastian had some right to be upset, but that didn't entitle him to treat her with such rudeness. Fiona smiled at Mitxel and ignored Sebastian as thoroughly as he was ignoring her.

"This evening is for conversation," Mitxel said, gesturing to them to follow him into the pyramid. "You will be told of the candidate's causes and encouraged to decide which is worthiest. Though you will not need to make a final choice this evening—that is for the challenge of charisma, in two days' time."

"I thought the point of that challenge was for the candidates to convince us themselves," Sebastian said. "Thus proving their skill at leadership."

"There are many ways to demonstrate leadership, Prince Sebastian. Tonight you will encounter those the candidates have already swayed to their side. A leader's true qualities are reflected in the people who follow him, is that not so?"

"I suppose," Sebastian said, "though in Tremontane we don't hold a follower's weaknesses against his leader."

"It would be more accurate to say that in Veribold, attracting the loyalty of a powerful man speaks well of the one who commands that loyalty," Mitxel said. His smile was a little rigid, and Fiona wished she could slap sense into Sebastian. He shouldn't let his anger with Fiona spill over into his interactions with others tonight.

They passed through an antechamber and into a slightly larger room lined with plain wooden benches. Mitxel directed them to sit, which Sebastian did with alacrity, as if touching Fiona burned him. Fiona sat nearby, more slowly. Black-clad men and women emerged from a smaller adjacent room, some of them bearing basins and towels. One woman knelt before Fiona and removed her sandals before Fiona could protest. Another set her basin on the floor and dipped a length of cloth into the water it contained, squeezing out the excess. And a third took Fiona's right foot in her hands and held it off the floor.

Startled, Fiona tried to jerk away, but the woman's grip was tight. The woman with the wet cloth swabbed Fiona's foot, dropped the cloth into the bowl, and dried Fiona's foot with another cloth hanging over her shoulder. They did this in total silence, in the space of a few breaths. When the woman lifted Fiona's left foot, Fiona was prepared and didn't flinch. The water was cool and comfortable, and although Fiona didn't think her feet were all that dirty, she didn't mind being washed.

The women didn't return Fiona's sandals, instead whisking them away into the smaller room. Fiona hoped she would eventually see them again. They didn't offer her new footwear, but one of the women gestured to her to rise. Fiona did so. Sebastian had just finished having his own feet washed, and she caught his eye. He shrugged, a humorous, self-deprecating gesture that made Fiona smile and swept away some of the awkwardness between them. This time, when she took his arm, he didn't tense as if he wished she were elsewhere.

They walked barefoot along a corridor floored in cold black quartz that glittered in the light of dozens of torches, small ones that smelled of creosote and reminded Fiona of the Irantzen Temple. The noise of people talking came to Fiona's ears from ahead, reminding her that she would have to translate tonight. She hoped Sebastian's bad mood really had subsided, because she didn't want to play go-between for someone who resented her.

They emerged into a vast space that felt as if it wanted to swallow Fiona up. The size of the banquet hall, nearly matching the grand chamber of the opening ceremonies, made her wonder what noble Veriboldans felt they had to prove. It wasn't that the room was big enough to seat three hundred people, at a guess; it was the vaulted ceiling, easily as tall as the room was wide, that filled Fiona with mingled awe and curiosity.

Sheets of colorful silk twenty feet long, crimson and emerald and sapphire and violet, hung from the distant ceiling and moved constantly in a breeze not tangible at ground level. It wouldn't have surprised her to learn there were servants in the ceiling, fanning the silk.

She dragged her gaze away from the spectacle and scanned the room. A scattering of robed figures, all Veriboldan, kept the room from being echoingly empty with their quiet murmuring. There were no tables, no furniture of any kind, making her wonder where the food was served. She could smell it, though the aromas were faint: cooked beef and pork, something sweet she couldn't identify, and over it all the scent of spicy fish sauce. From how often they'd eaten it from roadside booths, she'd assumed it was low-brow cuisine. Finding it at a banquet held for the highest nobility was unexpected, and comforting.

Mitxel put his hand on Sebastian's elbow, drawing him and Fiona close enough to suggest what he was about to say should be held in confidence. "You have never been to an event like this before, I assume."

"That's right," Sebastian said, withdrawing from Mitxel's touch, but not in the abrupt way Fiona feared.

"The food is served over the course of hours," Mitxel continued. "Servants will approach you so you may help yourselves. This allows everyone to freely mingle and speak to as many people as possible. It is less limiting than seating you at a table and restricting your conversation to the four people nearest you."

"I see," Sebastian said. Fiona still had questions, like *How do we help ourselves?* and *Where are the dishes and utensils?* But Mitxel had already left, heading toward Venelda and Morten, who had entered behind them. The Ruskalder wore the same style clothing Fiona and Sebastian wore, but in red and black. More color-coding the foreigners for someone's convenience. It occurred to Fiona that the Veriboldans might have as much trouble remembering the strangers' identities as she had in keeping track of who belonged to which Veriboldan noble house.

She drew in a breath. "Sebastian," she said, just as Sebastian said, "Fiona, I—"

It startled Fiona into looking at him. He'd turned his head to face her, his expression unsmiling. "Go ahead," Fiona said.

"I—" Sebastian began.

The hard, resonant sound of an enormous brass gong drowned out the rest of his words. They both glanced around for the source of the sound, but saw nothing but the Veriboldan landholders and the other envoys. Fiona looked up—maybe the gong was hidden in the rafters with the fanning servants—and this time saw ventilation slits in the ceiling, cleverly concealed near where the lengths of silk hung. She reminded herself not to be intimidated by Veriboldan architecture. Tremontane built things differently, but with every bit as much skill.

She turned to point out the slits to Sebastian and was distracted by men and women garbed in dark green wrap-around shirts and loose trousers, filing through a nearby door. They bore trays from which emanated more of the delicious smells. They moved through the scant crowds without pausing or making eye contact with anyone. Between that and the near-total silence of their bare feet on stone, they reminded Fiona of Devices, lifelike ones cleverly designed to fool the viewer into believing them human.

Each servant took up a position that to Fiona seemed randomly chosen, some of them close to a little knot of guests, others standing alone. The smells of beef and fish sauce made Fiona's stomach growl. It had been a long time since dinner at the embassy. All the trays were held high enough that she couldn't see any of the delicious-smelling food, and she thought about edging closer to one of the servants, but Sebastian still had hold of her arm and she didn't think she could gracefully take him with her.

Another door opened, this one opposite the one the servants had used. The murmur of conversation ceased. A double handful of women in white emerged. Irantzen priestesses, with Hien in the lead. Hien led them to the center of the room, passing Fiona closely enough to touch her. But Hien ignored her. Sela, on the other hand, shot Fiona a poisonous glare from her position directly behind Hien. Fiona didn't flinch. She almost smiled politely at Sela, but the woman would likely take it as an insult, and Fiona didn't want to start a war.

Hien came to a halt at the room's center, or at least close to it. Fiona couldn't see any marking that might indicate where Hien should stand, but from what she knew of Hien, she guessed wherever the woman chose to stand defined the center. The other priestesses stood with their backs to her in a loose circle. Hien raised both hands with her palms upward, as if she wanted to hold up the distant ceiling. Her companions mimicked her. Fiona glanced around to see if this was something she was expected to follow, but the rest of the guests simply stood and watched.

"*We are one in the service of My Lady Veribold,*" Hien said in a clear voice that carried throughout the room. "*As we serve Her, so does ungoverned heaven guide our service. May we be ever mindful of our duty, even in the midst of pleasure.*"

"*Ungoverned heaven guide us,*" everyone around Fiona replied, not just the priestesses but the other Veriboldans. Caught off-guard, Fiona hoped this was a cultural thing outsiders weren't expected to participate in.

"It was a prayer," she whispered to Sebastian. "Invoking heaven's guidance."

"I hope heaven doesn't just smile down on Veriboldans," Sebastian murmured back.

Hien and the priestesses lowered their arms. The servants immediately brought their trays down to chest height and turned to the nearest groups of people. Fiona noticed in time that none of the Veriboldans had moved to approach the servants and impatiently waited for one of them to draw near to her and Sebastian.

The servant stopped within arm's reach of her and held the tray forward in offering. It contained a stack of porcelain bowls the size of her cupped palm, a pile of small two-tined forks, and three platters heaped high with a variety of meats and vegetables, all cut into bite-sized pieces. Fiona and Sebastian exchanged glances. It seemed simple enough, which meant it was probably complicated and they were likely to get it wrong.

Sebastian shrugged. "What would you like?" he asked Fiona.

"The beef, I guess," Fiona said, pointing at the platter that smelled most strongly of fish sauce. If she was going to get Veriboldan fine dining wrong, she intended to at least enjoy the food.

Sebastian scooped beef chunks into one of the tiny bowls and handed it to Fiona. She took one of the odd forks and waited for Sebastian to serve himself. The servant gave no sign that he was paying attention to them, not even a show of disdain for the uncouth foreigners, but as soon as Sebastian had his own bowl and fork, he raised the tray and turned away to serve someone else.

Fiona covertly observed the other "diners." The three Veriboldans nearest her held their bowls in one cupped hand, raised close to their chins, and used the little forks to convey morsels to their mouths neatly and rapidly. It didn't look like a dining method that allowed for much conversation, which suited Fiona fine. She mimicked their gestures and chewed and swallowed with satisfaction.

"I think we're meant to have seconds and thirds," Sebastian said between bites. "I wonder if they serve these things like courses, or if it's the same foods served all night long?"

"I'm hungry enough not to care," Fiona said, "but that won't last." She scraped the last bits of sauce awkwardly from the curve of the bowl. That hadn't been enough to satisfy her. "Do you think we can reasonably follow those servants around, begging for more food?"

Sebastian had finished his helping and was looking around. "More to the point, where do we put our used dishes?"

Fiona saw someone set her empty bowl on a passing tray, with the servant not even pausing. "I guess we let them worry about that," she said.

For the next half-hour, she and Sebastian ate without conversing with anyone. It would have worried Fiona more if she hadn't observed most of the Veriboldan landholders doing the same thing. As it was, she couldn't help feeling anxious the way she did when some unknown challenge approached. She reminded herself that they weren't there to make the Veriboldans like them; they were there to keep Gizane occupied, if necessary, so she wouldn't return to her rooms early and possibly catch Holt in the act of rifling through her things.

On that thought, she looked for Gizane. The crowds had grown since Fiona had arrived, though they were still small enough to be swallowed up by the vast chamber, and at first Fiona didn't see anyone she recognized. Eventually, she noticed Alazne of the Otsoan, her tall, angular figure towering over the man she was talking to. The candidate wore an emerald green robe embroidered with dogs—no, wolves—and had her head bent in a stance that suggested she was holding forth passionately on some subject. The man listening to her wore a plain gray robe, unadorned and simple like nothing Fiona had seen on a Veriboldan landholder before.

She surveyed the room more closely and realized that, contrary to her first impressions, the gathering wasn't as brightly garbed as at the opening ceremony, nor were the colors as varied. She saw a lot of gray robes, a handful of green ones, some crimson, some sapphire blue, and some violet. Against this limited palette, the foreign envoys stood out, and the white-robed priestesses even more so.

"What do you think the colors mean?" she asked Sebastian.

Sebastian swallowed a last bite of chicken. "They're the supporters of the candidates," he said. "Green for Otsoan, red for Azergn, blue for Triminon, purple for Araton. Embroidered with, I think, the animals associated with each family. But did you look closely at the purple robes?"

Fiona did. "What...are those *rats* embroidered on those robes?"

Sebastian chuckled. "Araton...rat...it makes sense. I'm guessing rats don't have the same significance in Veribold as they do in Tremontane. Everyone looks so proud to wear them."

Now Fiona spotted Gizane in her purple robe embroidered with, yes, rats climbing up her arms and over her shoulders. The beautiful woman stood at the center of a group of gray-clad Veriboldans, with Stannin of the Kirkellan listening from the outer edges. Fiona fingered her North blue robe, ran her hand over the roughness of an embroidered cat. Cats pursued rats. It was a reassuring symbolism.

"And how does Tremontane find Veribold?" a creaky voice said. It sounded like an old metal hinge. The speaker was an elderly woman dressed in a sapphire-blue robe embroidered with monkeys. Fiona, fascinated by the skill with which the robe had been sewn, didn't think to respond. Sebastian was quicker on the uptake—or maybe that was just his upbringing.

"We have received the warmest welcome," he said, bowing. "Might I have the pleasure of your name?"

"I am Aurkene of the Belatzen," the woman said, returning the bow. "It is good to know my countrymen have good manners. Not all of them respect our neighbor to the east."

"And I suppose Bixhor of the Triminon is not one of those," Sebastian said.

It took Fiona a moment to catch up. Right. Bixhor was the blue robes. And this was one of his supporters.

Aurkene's eyes glinted with appreciative humor. "Bixhor sees the value in a strong diplomatic relationship with Tremontane, yes."

"Queen Genevieve would agree with that." Sebastian handed off his bowl to a passing servant without taking his eyes off Aurkene. "Do the Belatzen support Bixhor of the Triminon, or must he win their support individually?"

"I am matriarch of the Belatzen, and many follow where I lead," Aurkene replied, "but Veribold is only strong when the strong make their own decisions. As I am sure you understand."

"That's how it is in Tremontane as well. Tell me, *yana*, what will Bixhor do for Veribold if he becomes King?"

It didn't surprise Fiona that Sebastian knew the correct term of address for a noble Veriboldan woman; what surprised her was how good his accent was. Aurkene didn't seem surprised either.

"Many things," Aurkene said, "though I assume you mean specifically what cause he has championed." She tilted her head to one side. "You know of *kang-shu* in Tremontane, yes?"

"We do, though I believe our version developed independently of yours. We call it opera."

"*Kang-shu* is one of Veribold's most treasured cultural heritages," Aurkene went on. "It is something all Veriboldans appreciate, regardless of their social status or wealth. Bixhor intends to restore the Sendoha, the place where *kang-shu* is performed in Haizea. It has become sadly dilapidated in recent years."

"That is a noble cause," Sebastian said.

Fiona held her tongue. It struck her as typically Veriboldan that the landholders would think putting money toward a so-called cultural treasure rather than, for example, lighting Dusktown properly was a great use of the nation's treasury. She knew full well that whatever Aurkene said about the unifying nature of *kang-shu*, it was only the wealthy who could afford to attend. Probably all the candidates' causes were similar in nature.

"It is unfortunate that the other candidates are all frivolous," Aurkene was saying. "Refurbishing the King's residence, as Luken of the Azergn intends—so self-centered. Alazne of the Otsoan believes awarding every citizen one day in seven in which they are free from work is a fine idea, but if they are not compensated, how is that anything but taking money from hardworking citizens? And of course Gizane of the Araton's desire to build a sanctuary for the hooded owl is nothing but pandering to the Irantzen Temple."

That got Fiona's attention. "How is that?" she asked.

Aurkene didn't look surprised at Fiona's sudden intrusion into the conversation. "Then you do not know the hooded owl is sacred to the Temple?"

"I know it was the sign given by ungoverned heaven that Haran spoke the truth. I suppose I could have guessed the priestesses would care about it."

"It is true. The hooded owl is dwindling in number, and no one knows why. I suppose a sanctuary for them is a worthy goal, but in the context of the Election, it means only that Gizane thinks to influence the Temple to lean her way."

"I agree, that's not worthy of respect," Sebastian said. "You have given us both much to think about."

Aurkene's eyes twinkled again. "I knew your uncle, the one who shares your name," she said with an impish smile that belonged on someone fifty years younger. "Do give him my regards when you return to Tremontane." She bowed again and walked away.

"That sounded like more than a casual acquaintance," Sebastian said, watching her go. "I wonder...Great-Uncle Sebastian never married, and he's never said why not."

Fiona considered saying something about people from different worlds not being compatible, but decided that would just start an argument. "So now we have some idea of what we're voting on in two days," she said. "Does it matter who we support so long as it's not Gizane?"

"We ought to want the best candidate, which for us means the one most beneficial for Tremontane," Sebastian said. "But I'm afraid I really don't care. All those causes seem good mainly for noble Veriboldans."

"What about giving everyone a weekly holiday? That would help even poor people. Except...Aurkene was right about most people working every day so they can survive. If they have to stop working, they won't eat."

"Thus demonstrating, once again, that Veriboldan landholders don't have any idea what the lives of ordinary people are like." Sebastian shrugged. "We should be looking at who supports each cause, not whether the cause is a good one. But we don't know enough about the nobles to appreciate what it means that they support one candidate over the others."

Fiona was about to say something when she saw Hien approaching them. The priestess moved like a bull who'd just seen a stranger enter his field, implacable and unwavering. The sight drove Fiona's words out of her head. "Um," she said. "Sebastian—"

"Prince Sebastian," Hien said, coming to a stop beside them. "Lady North. You are still here."

"Should we have left?" Sebastian said, making it sound like a joke.

Hien ignored him. "I would speak with Lady North. Privately."

Fiona and Sebastian exchanged glances. "I should...speak with the other candidates and their followers," Sebastian said. His gaze flicked across the room to where Gizane stood, holding forth to a new clot of listeners. Fiona nodded. He bowed to Hien and walked away.

Hien turned and strode off in what to Fiona seemed a random direction. She didn't tell Fiona to follow, but Fiona didn't need direction. She followed Hien like a toy on a string, bobbing along after the priestess.

When they were nearly to the wall, and well away from inadvertent or intentional eavesdroppers, Hien turned on Fiona. "Why are you still here?"

Taken aback by the priestess's abruptness, Fiona stammered, "I—because the Election isn't over."

"You are not here for the Election any more than you were here for the festival," Hien said. "You have another purpose. Why would Tremontane want to destroy Veribold?"

"That's not true. Tremontane wants—"

Hien cut her off with a gesture and a glare that could melt stone. "You have the Stones," she said. "Give them back. Now."

"Y̲ou can't prove that," Fiona said. It was the first thing that came to mind, and even as she said it, she knew it was a mistake. Hien's eyes gleamed, and her lips twisted in a bitter smile.

"I do not need to prove it when we both know the truth," she said. "Tremontane stole the Stones to weaken Veribold so it can invade."

"*What?*" Fiona took a step backward. "That's not true. Tremontane doesn't want to invade Veribold."

"Veribold has everything Tremontane wants. A larger coastline. More mechanics—they do not depend on source the way Tremontanan Devices do. Rich natural resources. What other reason could Tremontane have for interfering with our Election?"

A dozen competing responses welled up inside Fiona. Why couldn't Hien have had this conversation with Sebastian? He knew the politics, he knew what they could or should say. Fiona could only stumble along and cling to what she knew, which was that admitting to possession of the Jaoine Stones meant death.

"Invasion would throw Tremontane into turmoil, too," she said. "Queen Genevieve doesn't want that."

"Because her reign is insecure? Starting a war would give her power within her government."

Fiona had no idea whether or not this was true. "I...am not permitted to speak of internal policy matters," she said. It sounded hopelessly pompous. She hoped it also sounded convincing.

"It is not important. I give you an opportunity to do the right thing. Hand over the Stones, and we will say nothing more." Hien stood as if she expected Fiona to pull the Stones out of her robe right there.

"I don't have the Stones," Fiona said. Only partly a lie, but she didn't have them on her, after all. "And if I did, my life would be forfeit, wouldn't it?"

Hien blew out her breath impatiently. "It would be a private matter."

"But that's not good enough, is it?" Fiona said. "The death penalty is to..." Everything she knew about the Temple and the Stones, which wasn't much, came together. "Taking the Stones—whoever stole them is under heaven's condemnation, right? And anyone not an Irantzen priestess who holds them has to die because otherwise it mocks heaven."

Hien gave a tiny nod, a decisive gesture, but her eyes were uncertain.

Fiona let out a deep breath. "I have a question," she said. "A thought experiment. I think you can tell me the answer. Suppose someone steals the Jaoine Stones from the Temple. It doesn't matter what they want them for."

"It matters if they wish to start a war."

"Okay, true. So let's say the thief wants something else. Maybe she wants the Stones for...for an advantage in whatever the Temple uses the Stones for." Fiona paused, but Hien didn't react. "So this person, like I said, steals the Stones. And suppose someone else comes along and takes them from the thief. Maybe the second person doesn't realize what she took. She doesn't want the Stones, but she has them. And by your laws, that means she's the one who would die for possessing them."

Hien's face continued expressionless. "So who's really at fault?" Fiona asked. "The original thief, or the accidental one? Who would heaven want punished?"

Hien continued to look at her, but her expression went calculating, as if she were considering Fiona's words. "Why would the second person not pass them off to another?"

"Because giving them to someone else just means another innocent person might die."

Hien went silent. Finally, she said, "What do you think of the candidates?"

The sudden change of subject stunned Fiona into silence. "Um...I don't know enough to have an opinion."

"That is a mistake. You are here to judge, Fiona North who was Fiona Cooper." Hien's eyebrows went up. "You have formed no opinions at all? Not of, for example, Gizane of the Araton?"

There was a trap in there somewhere. Fiona had no idea what might set it off. She looked at Hien, whose expression seemed to dare her to lie again. "She is a bad choice for Veribold," she said. "She either doesn't know the law or doesn't care about upholding it, and she sees the Election as a game instead of as a...a sacred rite, or whatever you call it. Doesn't it matter to you that she chose her cause to pander to the Temple?"

A look of disgust crossed Hien's face and was as swiftly smoothed away. "The Temple is unbiased in the Election. We are observers only. Her choice will do her no good."

"Are you sure about that? Because she's not the sort of woman who acts frivolously. I don't know much about the challenges, but I know she wouldn't have chosen that cause if she didn't think it would benefit her."

Hien's eyes narrowed. "Do you suggest we are corrupt, Fiona North?"

Oops. "No, I didn't mean it like that. I meant that Gizane might believe it. I told you, I don't know enough about how the Election works—what the Temple priestesses do—to judge whether she's right. I hope she's wrong."

319

"I did not think it mattered to you what the Temple might want."

It felt like a blow to the stomach, and Fiona wasn't sure why. "I'm sorry," she said, not knowing where the apology came from.

"Sorry for what?" Hien asked.

"For not respecting the festival. For not respecting you." Her need to make things right with this woman filled her, prompting her words.

Hien pursed her lips. "Why did you come to the festival?"

"I...can't tell you."

Hien fell silent. The sound of muffled conversations filled the space between them, punctuated by Stannin's distinctive laugh. Fiona felt she'd been judged and found wanting. But telling Hien the truth was the one thing she absolutely could not do. "It wasn't to steal the Stones," she blurted out. "I swear that's the truth. It had nothing to do with the Election."

"And yet it had something to do with your need," Hien said. "With your desire for change."

Fiona remembered her vision, what her parents had said. "I still don't understand the vision."

"You will," Hien said. She turned her head away briefly, scanning the room, then returned to watching Fiona closely. "Gizane walks close to the sun," she said in a surprisingly placid tone not at all matching her earlier words. "Walks close to the sun, and will be burned."

"Is that a promise?" Fiona said.

"Say, rather, a glimpse of what may be," Hien said. "But you asked a hypothetical question. The answer is that the law is clear: anyone holding the Stones who is not an Irantzen priestess must die so ungoverned heaven will not be mocked. But it is also clear that heaven's blessing touches what it will. If the second person, the one who took the Stones from the thief, has faith in the purity of their intent, heaven will not disregard that."

"I...don't understand."

"It means," Hien said, fixing her eyes on Fiona, "that you should have faith, Fiona North." She turned and walked away without another word.

Fiona felt dizzy and wished she dared use the nearby wall to support herself. Faith? In what? If Hien meant have faith that heaven would intervene to protect her, Fiona didn't think of herself as particularly worthy of that intervention. Maybe that meant she lacked faith, or maybe it just meant she was pragmatic, but in either case, she wasn't inclined to put herself in jeopardy even for a noble cause like returning the Stones.

She cast her gaze across the room, searching for Sebastian. She didn't see him or Gizane anywhere. Stannin was still nearby, laughing at something one of the red-robed women was saying, and beyond him, Venelda was engaged in conversation with a tall crane of a man in a gray robe. No one seemed to notice Fiona at all. After the harrowing encounter she'd had with Hien, she was just as happy to go unnoticed.

She made her way around the edges of the room to where a servant stood bearing tiny glasses shaped like half-opened rosebuds and helped herself. Too late, the sharp scent of alcohol came to her nose. She managed to drink no more than half the liquid, which wasn't anything she recognized, and set the glass back on the tray. She glared at the servant, daring him to make an issue of it, but he paid no more attention to her than any of the servants had.

Wiping her mouth with the back of her hand, she continued along her path, scanning the crowd for Sebastian. She'd lost track of time, but he would know if they'd given Holt enough freedom to search Gizane's quarters. The room that had felt so spacious now seemed to close in around her, the voices echoing the way sounds did when she was ill. She didn't feel sick, just overwhelmed and unsure of herself. Hien had as much as offered to protect her from the Temple if she handed over the Stones, but Fiona wasn't sure that was an offer she could accept. It might only put Hien in more jeopardy than Fiona.

Finally, she caught sight of a dark blue robe with silver embroidery matching hers. In relief, she pushed politely past other guests to

Sebastian's side, too grateful for his solid familiarity to worry about whether he was still angry. He'd seemed to have gotten over it earlier, but that might only have been politeness in public. It wasn't until she'd almost reached him that she saw he was talking to Gizane.

Fiona hesitated, uncertain about interrupting their conversation. Her steps slowed, and she considered waiting far enough away that Gizane wouldn't have to take notice of her. But Gizane looked past Sebastian's shoulder and saw Fiona. She stopped mid-sentence, her lips curving in an unpleasant smile. Sebastian turned to see what Gizane was looking at. The briefest expression of dismay crossed his features, and then he smiled and extended a hand to Fiona.

"I wondered where you were," he said. "I hope you've been enjoying yourself."

"Of course," Fiona managed, taking his arm. "It's so interesting."

"Naturally," Gizane said. Her voice was as lovely as her face, now she wasn't admitting to failure in front of the law-speakers. Then, she'd sounded like the admission had been dragged out of her, and she'd looked at Fiona like she wanted to see her dead. Now she turned a pleasant smile on Fiona and said, "You are...unexpected."

Fiona almost apologized for making her look bad before remembering she didn't care what this woman thought of her. "I certainly didn't expect to be here."

"Such knowledge. Perhaps I should be grateful you are not Veriboldan, and a candidate for Election." Gizane's smile broadened as if she'd made a joke.

"I'm grateful just to be an observer," Fiona said. "Ruling a kingdom is beyond me."

"How fortunate that it will never be an issue for you," Gizane said, this time flicking a glance at Sebastian. It felt like an insult, though a subtle one, and Sebastian's arm tightened.

"We none of us know what the future holds, do we?" he said politely. "What do the candidates who don't win the Election do afterward?"

That was a less subtle insult, though not one Gizane could react to. Her smile disappeared. "They return to their old lives, of course. There is always another Election."

"So you'd be allowed to be a candidate later?"

Gizane's eyes hardened. "I do not intend it to be an issue for me." Unexpectedly, she extended a hand to Sebastian. "I have enjoyed our conversation, your Highness. This is what Tremontanans do to show regard, yes?"

Sebastian took her hand and shook it. "It is. Thank you for your time."

Gizane held out her hand to Fiona. "And you, Lady North, to show I bear you no ill will."

Fiona clasped Gizane's hand and hissed as a sharp pain went through hers. She snatched her hand away and examined it. A thin scratch ran across the outer edge of her pinky, and a tiny bead of blood welled up.

Gizane made a noise of dismay. "I beg your pardon, Lady North. It was my ring. The setting is loose, but I did not think—truly I am sorry to have scratched you." She twisted a ring on her smallest finger, one bearing an emerald-cut amethyst the size of her thumbnail, and indicated one of the tines of the setting. It did look twisted out of true, not much, but enough to have caught on Fiona's flesh.

"It's all right," Fiona said. She wiped her hand on her sleeve, leaving an almost imperceptible smear. "It was an accident."

"Of course." Gizane bowed. "Good evening, Prince Sebastian, Lady North."

When Gizane had walked away, Sebastian said in a low voice, "She is not a good enemy to have. She's smart, and I think she'd like to see us dead."

"I humiliated her in front of her peers. That doesn't surprise me."

Sebastian took his watch out from beneath his robe. "I think we've given Holt enough time. We can leave, if you like."

"We won't seem impolite? I haven't talked to many people."

"I have. Enough to have made up my mind. This place is starting to get to me." He wheeled around and headed for the exit, not quite fast enough to look like they were fleeing. Fiona smiled at the people they passed and hoped no one would stop them.

They waited in the antechamber for their shoes, which they were allowed to don themselves. Fiona fastened her sandals and felt a rush of dizziness as she stood. She'd never been so eager to return to the embassy and her comfortable bed.

She'd hoped the dizziness would fade with the cool night air, but instead it became a feeling of lightheadedness, as if the world swayed past her with every step, every turn of her head. The strange blue lights of the Jaixante had funny halos around them. She leaned back in the palanquin and closed her eyes, and the lightheadedness vanished. She must be more tired than she thought.

The palanquin came to a stop. Fiona sat up and swung her legs around to stand. Something caught her foot, and she found herself on the ground with no memory of falling. Her wrists hurt where she must have caught herself. She heard Sebastian exclaim, and then his arms were around her, helping her rise. "I feel dizzy," she said.

"It's nearly midnight," Sebastian said, surprising her. She'd thought it was much earlier. "You're probably tired. I'm glad we left when we did. Can you walk?"

Fiona nodded, and the world spun, twisting her stomach and making her gorge rise. She managed not to throw up by sheer willpower and said, "I think I...might be coming down with something."

Sebastian's arms went rigid. Then he bent and picked her up, carrying her to the carriage and settling her inside. "Hurry," he told the driver. Fiona lay back on the seat and concentrated on not fainting. The movement of the carriage soothed her stomach, but her head ached and a cold sweat had sprung up at her temples and her hairline.

"I just need to lie down," she said. "I'll be fine."

"Of course you will," Sebastian said. His voice sounded strange, and she opened her eyes to look at him. He was gazing off into the distance, his jaw tight with anger.

"What's wrong?" she asked.

"Don't worry about it. You'll be fine."

His voice echoed with barely contained fury. "Are you…still mad…at me?" she asked. Tears pricked her eyes. She'd thought they were past the argument of that afternoon.

His head whipped around. "What? Of course not!"

"Then why…"

"Fiona, it's not you. Don't worry about it. Just lie still." He took her hand gently and squeezed it. "You'll be fine."

The carriage came to a stop. Fiona's head ached more than before, and her stomach felt queasy. She didn't try to stand when the door opened. This was comfortable enough. When Sebastian eased her off the bench, accidentally jogging her head, the queasiness turned into active revolt. She twisted away from him to vomit all over the drive, crouched on hands and knees and convulsing helplessly. When her stomach was empty, she sagged to lie on the ground, not caring that the puddle of vomit was only inches from her nose.

"Fiona, you have to go inside. Fiona. Stay with me." Sebastian once more picked her up, making her head throb painfully enough that she almost heaved again.

The next moments were a blur: moving from the peaceful darkness of midnight to the brightly lit entrance hall that burned her eyes and sent pain shooting through her head, jogging up the stairs in Sebastian's arms and convulsing with dry heaves halfway up, lying on her bed that was so much more comfortable than the carriage bench she didn't know why she'd ever protested leaving it. Someone removed her sandals and the North blue robe. Her head and stomach were fighting it out for which hurt more, and her body ached as if she had influenza—but it had come on rather suddenly for influenza, so it couldn't be that.

Sebastian was having a low-voiced conversation with someone in the doorway. Fiona couldn't open her eyes to see who the other person was. The twisting ache in her stomach rose, telling her dry heaves were imminent. "Have to…immediately…poison," Sebastian was saying.

Fiona's eyelids twitched. "Poison?" she croaked. She rolled to one side and vomited again, this time bringing up nothing. The convulsions wrung her out, and when they were done, she clung to the edge of her bed, too weak to roll onto her back.

She heard someone approach the bed, and then Sebastian's hands supported her back onto it. "Don't worry about it," he said. "The ambassador has sent for a healer. You'll be fine."

"Gizane," Fiona gasped.

"Yes, with that damned ring," Sebastian said. "I don't know—" He went silent, then said, "You just have to endure a little while longer."

"You don't know if this poison is fatal," Fiona said. Her throat felt scratchy, like she'd had a coughing fit. "Sebastian—"

"It doesn't matter. I won't let you die," he said.

He stood, and Fiona fumbled for his hand and held onto it, squeezing tightly. "Stay. Please."

She heard him kneel next to her, and he put his other hand over their joined ones. "I won't leave you."

Fiona swiped tears away with her free hand as her stomach once more tried to turn itself inside out. If she was dying... She whispered, "Someone turn out the lights. They hurt."

"Georgette," Sebastian said.

A moment later, the lights dimmed and then went out. Fiona tried once more to open her eyes and discovered she could. Sebastian knelt on the floor beside her bed, his head bowed. She reached with her free hand to touch his shoulder, but her arm shook too much, and she had to let it fall. Sebastian shifted, looked up. She could barely make out his features. Her head felt as if it might split open at any moment. She wiped away more tears of pain. She was dying, and Sebastian would never know how she felt about him.

"Sebastian," she whispered, "I..."

Sebastian leaned closer. "I can't hear you." His warm breath stirred the hair hanging over her forehead. "You probably shouldn't try to speak."

Fiona closed her eyes again. "I wanted...to ask...Sebastian, I..."

The lights went on, causing Fiona to cry out weakly in pain. "Excuse me, pardon me, I need you to move, young man," a querulous male voice said. Sebastian released her hand and stood, stepping back from the bed to make way for someone who moved ponderously, like a mountain or a boulder dislodged from a rocky peak.

A dry, rough hand took hers and turned it over, examining the palm. "Clever poison," the man said, his voice slightly less querulous and more dispassionate. "This will take time."

"But she'll live?" Sebastian asked.

"I can't promise that. But I will do everything I can to make it happen. Now, all of you, out. Yes, even the husband. And I'll need food in about two hours—food for me, healing takes it out of you. Shoo."

Fiona wished she could ask for Sebastian to stay, but her lips felt numb and pain shot through her head whenever she moved it even a little. She heard a high, keening sound coming from nearby, and realized she was the one making it just as the healer said, "You won't remember most of this. Sleep, now, and I'll wake you shortly."

Her eyelids felt suddenly leaden, and she knew nothing more.

3 6

Gray mist surrounded her, bulging and roiling like a laundress's pot. Shapes loomed in the distance, drawing near only to dissolve before they were identifiable. Fiona took one step, then another, her feet in their silver sandals making no noise on the floor shrouded in mist. It could be wood, or stone, or tile, but it felt like all of those and none of them.

"Fiona," a soft voice said. Mother. Fiona spun around and saw what might have been her mother's slim form, disappearing into the fog. She ran after her, her feet clinging to the unseen floor as if it were an inch deep in molasses, but it was too late; her mother, if that's who it was, had disappeared.

She heard more voices now, all of them calling her name: her mother, her father, her aunt and uncle, others she barely remembered and some she didn't recognize at all. Roderick's voice rang out, briefly, above the rest: "You're lost, Fiona. You'll never find the way out."

His familiar, mocking words brought her to a halt. "Shut up," she cried. "You don't get to tell me what to do anymore, you bastard!"

Her voice echoed in the sudden silence. The voices were gone. She turned in a slow circle, straining to see anything. There was only the mist, and the clinging floor. When she looked down at herself, she saw the mist drifting around her, obscuring her clothing so she seemed to be wearing nothing but fog. It was cold, and clammy, and she shivered, and then couldn't stop shivering. She wrapped her arms around herself and took a few hesitant steps. She had no idea where to go—no idea whether there *was* a place to go—but she couldn't bear to stand still and do nothing.

Another voice echoed through the gray mists. It was a man's voice, a querulous, elderly-sounding voice, and she couldn't understand his words. She stopped moving and strained to hear, feeling certain the unseen speaker was the key to her salvation. Again the man spoke, and again she couldn't make out what he said. "Please!" she shouted. "Where are you? Where am I?"

Silence.

Fiona shook from cold and fear. Clutching herself for whatever scant warmth that might provide, she once more shouted, "Where am I?"

"The embassy," the old man said.

Fiona was so startled at understanding him that she blinked, opened eyes she hadn't realized were closed, and drew in a deep breath of warm air. She lay in her own bed in the embassy, with the canopy draped high above. The room was dim, the lamps unlit, and wan sunlight came through the drawn curtains.

Beside her, an elderly man stood, his skin dark as ebony and his hair stark white. He looked Veriboldan, but when he spoke, his accent was pure northwestern Tremontanese. "You were hallucinating. It's a side effect of the healing."

"Am I...healed? No more poison?"

"No more poison," the healer agreed. He took her hand in his dry, rough one and felt her pulse. "It was a close thing. If his Highness hadn't realized you weren't just ill, it might have been too late."

Fiona shivered again, though she wasn't cold any longer. "Then I was lucky."

"Extremely. That's not a poison I've seen often. Somebody wanted you painfully dead, Lady North."

Gizane. Fiona tried to sit up and the old man restrained her easily. "You need to rest. Your nervous and digestive systems were severely damaged, and you nearly lost your eyesight. More strain on those systems could cause permanent damage. Just lie still. I'll leave instructions for your care with your lady's maid. Twenty-four hours bed rest in a darkened room, with soft foods, and then limited exertion for a week."

"What day is it?"

"I arrived at nearly midnight, and it's afternoon now. The healing took about sixteen hours." The old man patted her shoulder. "You survived, Lady North, and there's no reason that should change. I'm going to speak to your husband now, and to the ambassador. Make sure you eat. You won't want to for a while, but you need nourishment." He smiled and left the room.

Fiona drew in another deep breath and let it out, slowly. She didn't hurt anymore, didn't feel hungry—didn't feel much of anything except so relaxed the idea of moving felt like too much work. Gizane had tried to kill her. That ought to be enough to get her disqualified as a candidate, maybe tried for attempted murder. Fiona wasn't sure that was worth nearly dying for. She tried to stretch, but again found herself too relaxed to move. It didn't matter. She was alive, and she'd never felt so at peace.

The door opened. "Fiona," Sebastian said. He crossed the room to sit on the bed next to her and take her hand. "Fiona, I thought—I swear I will kill Gizane."

"Can't we let the Veriboldan government do that?" His hand was warm and firm and she clung to it like an anchor. He looked terrible, like he hadn't slept, and he was still wearing his formal robe from the night before.

Sebastian's lips compressed in a tight line. "We have no recourse," he said. "It's our word against hers, and a candidate for Election is practically unassailable, particularly when her accuser is a foreigner. She'll have gotten rid of the ring, and with you healed, there's no evidence of poison. Even the testimony of Mister Keswick—the healer—won't mean anything in a Veriboldan court of law. You probably know better than I do how it would fall out."

Fiona closed her eyes briefly. It was true, Veriboldan law was prejudiced against foreigners. She might not know much about the Election, but she could guess it would be doubly so when it came to protecting their candidates. "Then we have to get her some other way."

"I think it's time for planting the Stones and arranging for her to be found with them."

Fiona shook her head. "I don't think that's a good idea."

"Why not? You can't possibly care anymore if it gets her killed. Fiona, she nearly succeeded in taking your life!"

"It's not that. Think of everything that has to go right to make that successful. If we plant the Stones in her quarters, for example, and she finds them first—we'd be back where we started, with her in possession of them and capable of doing heaven knows what."

Sebastian swore under his breath. "I hadn't considered that."

"What did Holt learn?"

"What did—oh. I'd almost forgotten." He frowned. "Holt was in and out without being seen, no problem. But he didn't find anything we could use against Gizane. If we wanted to put the Stones securely in her quarters, we could do that."

"Except it's a bad idea."

"Except that." Sebastian put his other hand over their joined ones. "Fiona—"

"Yes?" Fiona said when he didn't immediately complete that sentence.

"It's nothing I haven't said before. I love you. I've never felt so helpless as I have these last few hours, waiting to learn if you would live. Please..." He let his words die away, bowing his head as if he was watching them go.

Fiona's heart beat hard enough that she could hear it. Almost she told him yes. She had survived nearly dying, and what were her objections beside that? *But nothing's changed*, she thought.

"Sebastian," she said, and waited for him to look at her. "Sebastian, I love you. If I could, I would spend the rest of my life with you." She couldn't bear the joyful expression that crept over his face, and hurried on. "But you haven't been listening. All of this, us being together—it's all one-sided. You don't lose a thing. You don't have to sacrifice. You're asking me to change who I am and become someone I don't want to be so you can have what you want. And it's not fair to me."

Sebastian's face went very still. She clasped his hand more tightly and said, "What if everything were different? What if you were the one who had to change? Would you be willing to leave your family for my sake?"

His mouth fell open slightly in astonishment. "I," he began, then fell silent. Fiona waited. Sebastian turned his head away. "I can't," he said. "Even with everything that's happened, I'm still a North. I can't give that up."

Fiona blinked away tears. She'd hoped, for the briefest moment, that he might...but no. "You see why it's impossible," she said.

"I guess I do," Sebastian said. "I apologize for trying so hard to change your mind. You're right, I wasn't fair to you. I just—" He shut his mouth again.

"Love is like that," Fiona said. "But it's not enough to build a life on."

"I wish to heaven you were wrong," Sebastian said. He let go of her hand and stood. "Mister Keswick said you needed rest. I'll make your excuses tonight."

The challenge of cunning. Fiona had forgotten about it. "I'll be sorry to miss it. It's supposed to be an exciting game."

"I'll tell you all about it when I get back." Sebastian turned to go, then said, "You won't hold it against me, will you?"

"Hold what against you?"

He had his back to her, his hand on the doorknob. "That I'll never stop loving you," he said.

She couldn't hold the tears back. "Sebastian—"

"Sorry. Try to get some rest. Georgette will bring you food in a little while." He left the room, softly closing the door behind him.

Fiona managed to roll onto her side, clutched her pillow to her face, and wept.

BED REST TURNED OUT TO BE MORE DIFFICULT THAN FIONA HAD imagined. She took the healer's warning seriously, forcing herself to eat the bland gruel Georgette brought her every couple of hours, and didn't leave her bed except to relieve herself. Except for a continued light sensitivity and unexpected occasional tremors, she didn't feel ill. The lassitude passed, leaving her restless and wishing she could be up. She ate, read a few lines before realizing it might hurt her eyes, ate another small meal, and fell asleep before Sebastian returned. When she woke, it was morning, and she was finally hungry.

She finally saw Sebastian mid-morning, when he instead of Georgette brought her the familiar platter. Not so familiar, she discovered; instead of gruel, there were a couple of poached eggs on toast with a light sauce. She sat up eagerly, making him laugh.

"Georgette said you were getting sick of porridge," he said. He settled the tray over her lap and handed her a knife and fork. "I didn't want to wake you last night, especially since the news isn't good."

Suddenly the eggs lost their appeal. "What happened at the challenge of cunning?"

Sebastian grimaced. "Gizane won. Not just won, she trounced her competition. And the awful thing is I'm sure she didn't cheat. She was just that good at the game."

Fiona made herself take a bite of her breakfast. It was delicious, and some of her hunger returned. "But she failed miserably at the challenge of wisdom. That has to matter, right?"

"I have no idea." Sebastian leaned against one of the columns holding up the canopy. "We have to hope she loses the challenge of charisma, because I can't imagine she can succeed if she loses two challenges."

"The voting is tonight, yes?"

"It is. And you're not going."

"But I'm well!"

Sebastian's dark eyes fixed on hers. "We are not taking any chances with your health. Mister Keswick said limited exertion, and I want you well enough to be there for the final challenge. If you overexert yourself tonight...Fiona, what the hell are we supposed to do?"

She didn't ask what he meant. "I don't know. I've been thinking about how to return the Stones and I haven't come up with a solution." That wasn't entirely true. She'd come up with part of a plan that morning. It just wasn't a plan Sebastian would like.

"I think Holt can sneak into the Temple. He can leave the Stones somewhere inside where they'll be found."

"Sebastian, Holt is good, but he's not that good."

Sebastian grimaced. "I know. But I'm grasping at anything now."

"We have until tomorrow morning to figure it out." Fiona finished off her eggs. Her stomach felt content for the first time since she'd been poisoned, not at all as if it wanted to empty itself out. "Maybe... we should look at this from a different angle. Maybe we need to enlist heaven's help."

"You mean pray? I don't know if heaven ever feels obligated to answer prayers from people who got themselves into trouble."

"We didn't mean any harm. And..." She felt uncomfortable telling him what she and Hien had discussed. It felt personal, and private, and while she knew Sebastian wouldn't make light of the conversation, it still felt as if sharing it would make it tawdry.

"And what?"

"I just think we acted in innocence, and maybe heaven cares about that."

Sebastian sighed and stood, taking the tray from her. "Maybe. I guess I don't have that kind of faith."

"I'm not sure I do either. Will you come to me as soon as the challenge tonight is over? Even if you have to wake me?"

Sebastian eased the door open. "I should let you sleep, but I don't think I could bear the news alone. All right. Now, promise me you won't get up no matter how bored you get."

"I promise."

As soon as he'd left, Fiona slipped out of bed and crossed the room on trembling feet. She collected the little velvet bag from where she'd hid it deep inside the armchair and collapsed back into bed. As soon as the shakes passed, she smoothed out the counterpane and emptied the contents of the bag across it. The Jaoine Stones gleamed dully, their colored runes all faded to gray in the low light. Fiona stirred the Stones with her fingertip. They clacked against each other pleasantly.

One by one, she turned them to lie flat on the bedspread so none of them touched. She counted them: forty-nine little round ceramic chips. As far as she could tell, each rune was unique. In the dimness, she couldn't distinguish the colors, but she remembered red, green, orange, and purple when she'd first looked at them. She didn't know how many there were of each color, but it couldn't be an equal number if there were forty-nine stones in total. They looked like game tokens, really, not anything mystical.

She swept them up and poured them back into the bag, then tucked the bag under her pillow. Her half-formed plan came back to her, and she examined it as she lay in her bed, staring at the canopy. It really was only half a plan, which struck her as a flaw, especially considering that the missing half depended on other people's reactions. That wasn't something she could control. But it wouldn't leave her alone.

Finally, she closed her eyes and reviewed Veriboldan land use law until she fell asleep, then dreamed of the Jaoine Stones falling endlessly through Gizane's fingers until they turned into rainfall. She woke to the sound of rain on the windows. To her muddled, sleep-fogged brain, it seemed an omen of triumph over her enemy, and she rolled over and drifted into dreamless slumber.

aking an early nap left her even more restless and unable to sleep when night fell. So she was awake when Sebastian returned from the challenge of charisma. One look at his face told her everything she didn't want to know. "Damn it," she said.

"I don't know how close the voting was," Sebastian said. "They didn't reveal the numbers. Just announced whose cause had won." He sank onto the bed beside her and pinched the bridge of his nose as if his head hurt. "We don't know who won the challenge of knowledge. We know Gizane lost the challenge of wisdom. But she's won the last two challenges. She could very well be the front runner."

"So what do we do now?"

Sebastian didn't look at her. "Sebastian, what's wrong?"

Sebastian's hand lowered, and he gripped the counterpane as if clinging to a cliff's edge. "I think it's time to consider drastic measures," he said. "Holt can't get into the Temple. But he can get into Gizane's quarters."

It took Fiona a moment to realize what he was saying. "*No*," she said. "Holt can't kill her."

"Actually, he can," Sebastian said. "I don't know the details, and I would never ask him, but I know he's taken lives."

"But—what if he's caught? It would mean his death!"

"He won't get caught."

Sebastian still wasn't looking at her. In the dim light of the room, his profile was fuzzy, the profile of an ancient king on a coin too worn to be clear. Fiona examined him closely. "What aren't you telling me?"

Sebastian shifted, making the silk of his robe rustle. He looked down at where his hand twisted the counterpane and relaxed his grip. "Holt...wasn't a good man, before," he said. "I know he's spent the last twenty-odd years atoning for the things he's done. He'll kill Gizane if I ask him to. But I don't know who he'd be afterward."

Fiona let out the breath she'd been holding. "Then you really can't ask it of him. You'd destroy him. Sebastian, he's your *friend*. You can't do this."

"And if the alternative is destruction for Tremontane? What is one man's life compared to that?"

"One man's—" Fiona sat forward and grabbed Sebastian's knee. "Don't think like that. That's how your mother thinks. You're not her."

Sebastian's head came up, and he finally faced her, fury distorting his features. "Am I not? When I think of everything I've done to protect my damned brother, every compromise I've made, all I can see is how much in her image I've made myself. And now Holt—he's like a brother, and here I am proposing to ask him to destroy himself. Fiona, I've never loathed myself more."

Fiona put her arms around him and held him close. "You know what you have to do," she whispered. "Tremontane will survive Gizane's Election. You won't survive sacrificing Holt."

Tentatively, Sebastian returned her embrace. "Thank you," he whispered back. "You see so clearly. I...thank you."

Fiona nodded. He smelled so good, that piney scent she remembered from the near-disaster in his bedroom. She tucked her head into his shoulder and breathed him in, taking comfort in the feel of his strong arms around her. She'd been dying the last time he'd held her, and hadn't been able to appreciate it, but now holding him felt like coming home after a long, terrible absence. She didn't want to let go. But anything else would be cruel.

She released him and scooted back to sit against her pillows. Sebastian watched her go and said nothing, merely stood and straightened his robe.

"The challenge of faith begins at nine o'clock tomorrow morning," he said. "We're meant to arrive an hour before that. Will you be ready?"

"I will," Fiona said.

SHE WOKE EARLY, DISTURBED BY DREAMS SHE COULDN'T REMEMBER, AND then couldn't fall back asleep. So she rose and dressed herself in the clothes Georgette had laid out for her, a white bodysuit and voluminous white over-robe with wide sleeves. The gauzy, billowing robe felt like being at the center of a warm, dry cloud, and Fiona had to practice walking in it, keeping it from dragging on the floor. When she felt comfortable, she sat in the armchair and propped her feet on the low table. Georgette hadn't laid out shoes, making Fiona wonder if barefoot was the order of the day. Since the challenge of faith was held in the Irantzen Temple itself, that might be possible.

She looked at her bed, at the pillows in disarray, and rose from her seat. The little velvet bag containing the Jaoine Stones fit neatly within one of the huge sleeves as if they'd been designed for carrying such things. Fiona returned to her seat and adjusted the robe so the Stones wouldn't fall out. Once they were in the Temple, she might be able to find a place to leave them. Or—she smiled wickedly—find a way to plant them on Gizane, then denounce her spectacularly to the observers. It was unlikely, but the thought warmed her.

She sat, going over fragments of plans, until Georgette arrived with breakfast. She ate rapidly, but not too rapidly, still conscious of the fragility of her stomach. When Sebastian knocked on her door, she was ready to go.

Sebastian wore a bodysuit and robe matching hers. On him, the combination was exquisitely masculine, though some of that might have been how he carried himself like a prince no matter what he wore. She could barely imagine what it would be like to have that kind of confidence.

He didn't offer her his arm, which made her heart ache. Only a few more days, and they would never see each other again. The thought swept away all her worry over the Election. Never again. It was so monstrously unfair she wanted to shout at an uncaring heaven. Even accidentally stealing the Jaoine Stones couldn't possibly be deserving of this punishment. She pushed those thoughts aside. She'd made her choice, and she was done dwelling on what she couldn't have.

It turned out they were, in fact, meant to go barefoot, and Fiona couldn't help remembering their mad midnight flight from the Temple as they trod the path leading to it. The rough concrete rasped against her feet, bringing back more memories. She'd followed this road before, but this was the first time she'd done so sedately and not hurrying to reach the Temple before its doors shut.

She looked out over the Kepa, which was a dull slate-gray today thanks to the overcast sky. For all they'd spent so much time there, the Jaixante still remained foreign territory. But the east bank of the Kepa, with its myriad small buildings and their tiled roofs, drew her eye and comforted her. Haizea was a lovely city, maybe not as lovely as Aurilien in winter, but for the first time Fiona considered making a home here. Maybe she wouldn't leave when Sebastian did. The thought of him leaving her behind sent another involuntary pang through her.

The Temple doors stood well open, but Fiona and Sebastian were the only ones on the road. Fiona felt a moment's fear that they'd missed the time, that they were late and that would someone guarantee Gizane's victory, but the priestesses at the doors nodded to them with no word of rebuke.

Within, another group of priestesses stood. They wore the same simple garb all the priestesses did, but in rose or pale gold instead of white. One of them took a torch off the wall and gestured to Fiona and Sebastian to follow.

She took them by a different path than the one Fiona remembered from the festival, one with a high, arched ceiling and cool marble floors. The torchlight flickered over the walls and ceiling, giving Fiona the impression of an ancient cave hollowed out by a very tidy river. Ahead, a bluish light gleamed, and shortly they emerged from the cave into a circular chamber that could never be mistaken for anything but manmade.

The domed ceiling was held up by arched ribs of ebony, which stood in contrast to the blue-white walls that gave the light its peculiar tint. Narrow glass windows between the ribs let in that light. The glass was thin and perfect and not thick and bubbly like the glass Fiona was familiar with. The creosote smell of the torches was fainter, diffused through the great space, and mingled with an unfamiliar bitter smell whose source Fiona couldn't see. It was alien, and beautiful, and Fiona hoped they used this chamber for more than just the challenge of faith, because what a waste if people only came here once every seven years.

At the center of the room stood a pedestal of the same white marble as the floor, carved with abstract designs. A marble basin rested atop the pedestal, not circular, but square. It reminded Fiona of a handkerchief someone had put a heavy stone into, making the corners point up and the center sag. She wanted to investigate it, but its alien appearance made her reluctant to approach. No Tremontanan bethel had anything like it, but she was certain it was an altar to ungoverned heaven.

A handful of Veriboldan landholders, all of them dressed in white bodysuits and over-robes like Fiona and Sebastian, stood scattered through the chamber. No one spoke; the room, majestic and overwhelming, made everything Fiona might have said seem frivolous, and she wondered if even the Veriboldans felt that way. She took a few steps away from Sebastian to examine the nearest window more closely. She saw a sliver of the Jaixante through it, too narrow a slice to identify the building, though with the Jaixante's buildings being as uniform as they were, she probably couldn't have identified it anyway.

When she turned back around, more people had entered, among them the rest of the foreign envoys. Morten looked as cranky as always, and Venelda wore the serenity that concealed her disdain for her husband. The Dekerians smiled and nodded in Fiona's direction, and she nodded and smiled back. Stannin looked about him with undisguised delight. It was hard not to imagine him an oversized puppy, though wouldn't it be funny if he was actually a genius in his own land!

The room was filling up, though Fiona noticed the Veriboldans gave the foreigners even more space than they did each other. She and Sebastian ended up some fifteen feet from the altar, with no one standing between them and it. Fiona couldn't help feeling she'd gotten front-row seats to some performance, though she felt a little guilty at the frivolous thought. This was Veribold's most sacred ritual, and it deserved her respect.

The crowd near the door stirred, then parted for a double file of Irantzen priestesses, clad in their simple white wrap-around shirts and trousers. Their bare feet made no noise on the marble floor. They circled the altar, taking up positions at regular intervals around it, bowed their heads, and were still. At the end of the row walked Hien, who didn't join the others in the circle, but stood about five feet away from the little group and on the side opposite the door. She was close enough for Fiona to tug on her shirt, if Fiona had wanted to disrupt the challenge.

Fiona tucked her hands into her sleeves and fingered the soft velvet bag. She hadn't seen any opportunity to conceal the Stones, and no other plan had presented itself. Her heart beat a little too fast, and her palms were sweaty. Hien hadn't looked at her, but she felt certain the woman was as aware of her presence as she was of Hien's.

Hien tilted her head back and said, in a voice that echoed off the ceiling, "*You who would be One among Many, approach.*"

Fiona murmured the translation for Sebastian. He gripped her upper arm, but said nothing. What was Hien's plan? Soon she would have to bring out the Stones, which she didn't have, and then...what next?

The crowd again parted, and the candidates appeared. Unlike the opening ceremony, where they had walked side by side, they now walked in a line: Gizane first, with Bixhor following her, then Alazne, and finally Luken. Fiona was sure it represented the candidates' rankings, and her heart beat even faster. No Stones, Gizane the clear winner...this was a disaster of epic proportions.

"Haran received the vision of the tree, which led her to ungoverned heaven," Hien declared. *"Her faith made it so. Faith means hope in what is not seen, but is so. Faith brings us closer to heaven and to one another."*

Fiona twitched. Hien had glanced her way, just for a moment, nothing anyone but herself saw. *"Each candidate will prove his or her faith on the Jaoine Stones, and heaven will judge that faith."*

Hien fell silent. The silence stretched into an uncomfortable stillness. Fiona noticed Sela, who stood nearly opposite Fiona, glance Hien's way as if waiting for her to do something. Hien's head was held high, and her eyes were closed. Fiona's chest hurt and her breath came in ragged gasps. She only had half a plan. But it was more than anyone else had.

She stepped away from Sebastian and walked toward Hien, dipping into her sleeve. "I have something that belongs to you," she said, and as Hien turned toward her, she dropped the Jaoine Stones into Hien's outstretched hand.

38

---

*G*asps broke the stillness, and a murmur went up as those who were near the back of the room nudged their neighbors, asking what had happened. Fiona had time to realize Hien had anticipated her before Sela said, "*The foreigner has the Jaoine Stones! She must die!*"

"Fiona, what have you done?" Sebastian exclaimed, grabbing her arm and trying to pull her away. Fiona held her ground. She and Hien stared at each other as if they were the only ones in the room. Hien's face was expressionless. Fiona felt strangely calm. She'd faced death once this week; maybe that made it less terrifying.

"*Listen to me!*" she shouted. The din quieted, though not by much. She pressed on regardless. "*I took the Jaoine Stones from the possession of Gizane of the Araton. She stole the Stones to give herself an advantage in the Election. She is the one you should punish, not I.*"

"Fiona—" Sebastian said, in a voice that promised an eruption if she didn't explain herself.

"I told them Gizane is the thief and they should punish her," she said quickly.

"That's not going to matter to them!"

"*Lady North has no proof of her accusations,*" Gizane said. Her cruel smile told Fiona she was enjoying this immensely. *"Take her into custody before her execution."*

"I found them in Gizane's office in the foreign trade building here in the Jaixante," Fiona said. *"You know that place was burgled three weeks ago. You also know no one approached the place where the Stones are kept in the Temple during that time. Gizane stole the Stones and hid them in her office. I took them by accident."*

"She digs herself deeper!" Sela exclaimed. *"She confesses to one crime to save herself from the punishment for another."*

Fiona looked straight into Hien's eyes. *"I claim I did Veribold a service. How could Gizane have affected the Election by stealing the Stones? Consider that, and tell me which of us is the real thief."*

The murmuring grew. "I told them I'm innocent, or at least more innocent than Gizane," Fiona told Sebastian.

"Stop talking," Sebastian said. "We might still be able to claim diplomatic—"

"Gizane of the Araton, you claim you did not steal the Stones," Hien said, her face still expressionless. *"Lady Fiona North, you claim Gizane took the Stones from the Temple, and you took them from her. By law, it is the possessor of the Stones who must die. That is not Gizane."*

Fiona held her breath. She felt certain Hien had something else in mind than presiding over Fiona's execution.

"But heaven cares more for justice than for law," Hien continued. *"This is the challenge of faith. Let us make a test of faith, and allow heaven to decide where guilt lies."* She snapped her fingers, and two of the priestesses came to her side. Hien murmured to them, and they left the room.

Fiona whispered the translation to Sebastian. "What does that mean?" he asked.

"I have no idea."

"We need to leave. I'm not going to abandon you to whatever crazy notion of justice the Irantzen priestesses have."

Fiona grabbed his arm. "We'd never make it out the door. I have to see this through, Sebastian."

Sebastian grimaced, but eyed the door and the Veriboldans

standing in front of it as if assessing his chances and not liking his conclusions. "I won't let them kill you."

Fiona touched his hand. "Do you know," she said, "I have the strangest feeling it won't come to that."

The priestesses returned. One of them carried an armful of the torches, all unlit. The other held a vase in a way that suggested it was full of liquid. They walked through the circle to the altar. The first priestess arranged the torches on the basin into a neat stack shaped like a pyramid. When she was finished, the second priestess poured the clear contents of the vase over the pyramid of wood, drenching it with a pungent substance that was definitely not water.

Hien watched this dispassionately, then held out her hand toward the second priestess, who handed her a matchlighter. It was a Tremontanan Device, Fiona observed, and that struck her as more ridiculous than anything else that had happened that morning. Hien clicked the matchlighter and held the tiny flame to the base of the pyramid. With a *whoomph*, the pyramid went up in blue-white flame, hot enough that it made Fiona take a step back in surprise.

"*Haran taught that with faith, all things are possible,*" Hien said. "*The Jaoine Stones contain the distilled wisdom of Haran. In the challenge of faith, each candidate chooses a stone and interprets its meaning. Gizane of the Araton, Lady Fiona North, choose now.*" She untied the mouth of the bag and held it out toward Fiona and Gizane, who now stood beside Fiona, her beautiful eyes sparkling with anticipatory glee.

Fiona hesitated. Gizane reached for the bag. And Hien, swiftly moving it away from Gizane, upended the bag over the fire. Forty-nine ceramic chips cascaded over the pyramid to lie within the fire.

"*Choose,*" Hien said.

Gizane recoiled. "*This is madness!*"

"Fiona," Sebastian said.

Fiona held up a hand to silence him. Her heart once more hammered in her chest. Hien couldn't possibly know her secret. If this was some deep-laid plan to prove the North family tainted by inherent magic...no, that, too, was impossible. But Fiona absolutely could not put her hand into that fire. All her hiding, all her careful secrecy, gone in a moment.

She looked at Hien, whose expression was as remote as ever. "Have faith in the purity of your intent, Fiona North," she said quietly. "Have faith."

Fiona swallowed. She looked once more at the pyre, whose flames hadn't died down after consuming the flammable liquid. It crackled a welcome at her, beckoning her.

Fiona stripped off her robe and thrust it into Sebastian's hands. She stepped up to the altar and examined it. None of the stones had fallen where they might easily be twitched free of the fire. Of course heaven wouldn't have let that happen. Fiona took a deep breath, let it out slowly, and thrust her hand into the heart of the fire.

The flames tickled her skin and curled the fabric of her cuff, browning it instantly. She scrabbled about trying to get her fingers around one of the slick round tiles, which was harder than she'd guessed. By the time she had a firm grip on one, her sleeve had caught fire, and she withdrew her arm and beat at the flames to put them out.

The room had gone deathly silent. Gizane stared at Fiona with undisguised fear. Hien held out a hand. "*The stone,*" she said. Fiona dropped it into Hien's outstretched hand, realizing too late that it would be searing hot from its time in the fire. But Hien didn't react as if it hurt. She turned it over, examining the rune, which was orange and shaped like a curved triangle.

"*Honesty,*" she said, then repeated herself in Tremontanese. "*What do you say it means, Fiona North?*"

Fiona dusted off her burned sleeve, making a charred bit fall onto the pristine marble. "*I think I just showed everyone what it means.*"

"*Well said,*" Hien said. "*Gizane of the Araton, choose.*"

Gizane licked her lips, a swift, darting motion that didn't seem to calm her. She, too, removed her over-robe, but dropped it on the floor when no one came forward to hold it. She approached the altar sideways, recoiling from the heat as if the fire were a poisonous snake, coiled to spring. Haltingly, she reached toward the fire. Fiona saw her assessing the altar, looking for a stone close to the edge and, as Fiona had done, finding nothing. Gizane closed her eyes, extended her arm—

"*No!*" she shouted, yanking her hand back. "*It's impossible! There was some trickery—*"

Hien grasped Fiona's burned sleeve, making more charred flakes fall. "*No trickery,*" she said. "*Gizane of the Araton, heaven judges you guilty of the theft of the Jaoine Stones. Take her into custody pending execution.*"

Gizane didn't resist as hands closed on her arms. As she stumbled away, Sebastian said, "I swear to watchful heaven I will learn to speak Veriboldan. What the *hell* just happened?"

"I don't know," Fiona said. "Gizane was found guilty. They're going to execute her. She can't become Queen. But—"

"*Extinguish the fire,*" Hien commanded. "*We will continue with the challenge of faith. And may you all witness, this day, that heaven's miracles continue.*" She looked directly at Fiona, and Fiona was sure she was the only one in the room who saw Hien's left eyelid twitch in a faint but definite wink.

She watched the rest of the challenge in a haze, translating for Sebastian absentmindedly, her thoughts circling round and round on what had happened. Hien couldn't possibly have known Fiona could not be burned. She must believe a miracle had occurred. That thought made Fiona feel even worse than before. It was one thing to attend the Irantzen Festival under false pretenses, but to take credit for a miracle—no, Fiona couldn't bear to lie to anyone about that, least of all Hien. But then, why did Hien wink? Maybe that meant she had known, after all—she was a priestess, and in favor with heaven, so maybe she'd had a revelation. But— Her thoughts went spiraling off again.

Finally, Luken completed his challenge, and the three candidates left the room, followed by a trail of Veriboldan landholders. All of them cast sidelong glances at Fiona as they went. Hien wasn't the only one who thought she'd seen a miracle.

Fiona was about to follow the crowd when a hand took hold of her upper arm. "You will wait," Hien said. Her grip wasn't tight, but Fiona felt unequal to pulling free of her.

When the chamber was empty except for Hien, Fiona, and Sebastian, Fiona said, "Why did you do that?"

Hien shrugged. "I knew you would not remain silent. You had the Stones and you knew the right thing to do."

"That's not what I meant. How did you know I wouldn't burn?"

She shrugged again. "Miracles happen."

Fiona bit her lip, fighting with herself. Sebastian startled her by saying, "You know that was no miracle."

Hien eyed Fiona. "No. I imagine you have inherent magic."

She said it so calmly Fiona felt numb. "What are...what will you tell people?"

"Nothing," Hien said. "You want it kept secret. I see no reason to change that."

"You know it's a dangerous secret," Sebastian said. "If people found out the Norths—"

"You mean to ask if I will blackmail you," Hien said. "That would be wrong. You need not fear me."

Fiona, unable to keep still, said, "But everyone thinks it was a miracle! You can't let them go on believing that."

"And why not?" Hien fixed her eyes on Fiona, freezing her in place. "Heaven revealed to me what I should do to regain the Stones and prove Gizane's guilt. That was a miracle. What does it matter if everyone believes the miracle was something else?"

She clasped Fiona's hand in hers. "Fiona North, you have a great gift," she said. "It is unfortunate we live in a world where you must keep it hidden. But do not hide from yourself. Your vision was of change. Embrace that change. Stop being afraid—of your gift, or of your future."

Fiona couldn't help it; she looked at Sebastian and as swiftly looked away. "I don't know how," she admitted. "I dream—"

"You dream of fire. I know." Hien gripped her hand more tightly. "But you just revealed your secret to the world and walked away unscathed. You will not dream that dream again."

Her absolute certainty touched Fiona to the heart. In that moment, she knew it was true. The bands around her heart loosened and broke free, dispelling some of the fear she'd lived with for years. "You're right," she said wonderingly. "How do you know?"

"That you dream, or that the dream is over?" Hien smiled. "I do not share all my secrets with you. Now, go. I am afraid your miracle will overshadow the Election, but it is a small price to pay to have the Stones restored. And…thank you." She bowed. Fiona bowed back.

As they hurried through the corridors of the Irantzen Temple, Fiona said, "I'm not supposed to exert myself, remember? Slow down, please."

"Sorry." Sebastian slowed to a walking pace. "I can't believe it," he said. "Gizane is no longer a threat. We—you—returned the Jaoine Stones without getting killed. You just stuck your hand into a fire in front of dozens of Veriboldans, none of whom have any idea of your true secret. And it's not even noon."

"It should feel like a dream, but I've never felt more awake." Awake, and light enough to float away. "I almost don't care who ends up ruling Veribold."

"Neither do I," Sebastian said. "I'll leave that worry to Mother. We just have to witness the crowning of the new king or queen tonight, and then—"

He fell silent. Fiona's light, airy feeling vanished, leaving her cold and miserable. It wasn't a few more days; tomorrow the Election would be over, and they would return to Tremontane, or not. And that would be the end. Despite her resolve, her heart ached.

She walked beside him in silence through the Jaixante until they reached their carriage. When they were seated inside, Sebastian said, "Where will you go?"

"I don't know. I'm tired of traveling. I was thinking of staying in Haizea for a while. It feels so familiar now."

Sebastian's lips quirked in a smile. "After being chased across it?"

Despite her aching heart, Fiona smiled back. "Maybe because of that."

Sebastian looked out the window, and his smile fell away. "I'll make sure you have enough to support yourself for a while. I owe you that much."

It was a kick to the chest. "This stopped being a business transaction weeks ago," she said.

"I didn't mean owing you because you worked for me. I meant—damn it, Fiona, I can't let you go without knowing you'll be safe."

"I understand." The ache in her chest threatened to overwhelm her. "Thank you."

"We should go on playing the part of the married couple. Anything else would expose you to criticism and mockery." Sebastian turned to look at her. "We'll stop in Haizea tomorrow after leaving the embassy and find you a place to stay. Then..."

"Thank you." She thought about telling him it wasn't necessary, but she knew in her heart he wouldn't forgive himself for simply leaving her on a street corner. This was the last gift she could give him.

When they reached the embassy, Sebastian helped her out of the carriage and escorted her inside, just as if they were actually married. She went to her bedroom without saying anything and stripped off the robe, then stepped out of the ruined bodysuit and wadded it up and tossed it in a corner. Putting on a comfortable shirt and trousers, she lay back on her bed and let her mind wander. Just one more day. She didn't know if that was too soon or far, far too long.

39

The grand pavilion looked even grander in the light of dozens of lanterns, whose golden light reflected off the black pillars surrounding it to reveal specks of glittering mica that hadn't been visible the first time Fiona had been there. The over-grown garden, by contrast, was virtually invisible in the darkness. The golden flowers were indistinct, no more than dim, fuzzy spots of paleness against the dark vines and leaves. Fiona looked up at the evening sky, bright with stars as if heaven knew how momentous this evening was. Or maybe it was just luck. Either way, the night was beautiful, and the assembled people were silent, as if speech would ruin the beauty.

Beside her, Sebastian stood still enough that he might have been a statue, once again clad in his archaic Tremontanan costume as she was. The gold satin gleamed like a living thing, warm and vibrant, and she thought about taking his arm and decided that was a terrible idea. Directly across from them Stannin stood, for once not looking about him with a puppyish eagerness. His eye fell on Fiona, making her feel embarrassed about having been staring at him.

Stannin looked from Fiona to Sebastian and back again. A frown wrinkled his forehead briefly. Then he smiled and tilted his head in

Sebastian's direction, raising his eyebrows slightly. It was so clear an indication that he felt she should take Sebastian's hand that she did so without thinking. Sebastian, startled, glanced her way, then looked down at their joined hands. Fiona blushed, but didn't let go. It might be wrong, it might even be cruel, but she was about to lose him forever and her heart didn't give a damn about the consequences.

Sebastian smiled. His hand closed over hers more firmly. He said nothing, merely went back to watching the crowds, and for a moment the ache that had gripped Fiona all day retreated. When it returned, it was bearable, something she could ignore, and she was grateful for the touch of Sebastian's hand.

The gong at the far end of the pavilion sounded, and Fiona turned to watch the gauzy curtains pulled back. The Queen of Veribold, Ibarhe, stood framed by the curtains, this time clad in a long white robe whose hem trailed several inches behind her. She wore a *toan* jade around her neck, but this one had its edges gilded so it shone in the lamplight. Fiona bowed, mimicking Sebastian, as the Veriboldans all sank to their knees in respect. Ibarhe paused a little longer, then strode across the pavilion to stand in front of the gong. "*Rise,*" she said, and the Veriboldans stood.

"*My time is over, and a new beginning rises,*" she said in a voice that carried the length and breadth of the pavilion. "*You who would be One among Many, come forward.*"

The curtains parted again, and three figures clad in white robes like Ibarhe's entered, side by side as they had done the first day and not single file like that morning. Alazne, Bixhor, and Luken walked forward until they stood at the center of the pavilion. There was no sign that Gizane had ever been meant to take part in this ceremony. Fiona shivered, feeling superstitiously as if Gizane had already been erased from Veriboldan memory. Maybe she had. Fiona didn't know how soon the sentence of execution for theft of the Jaoine Stones had to be carried out. She was just as happy not knowing.

Ibarhe regarded the three dispassionately. It made Fiona wonder if she had a favorite candidate. Surely the ruling Queen had *some* opinion on who a worthy successor should be.

"*The challenges are over*," Ibarhe said. "*One has proven worthy above all others, worthy to rule Our Lady Veribold.*" She paused, Fiona thought for dramatic effect, and said, "*Bixhor of the Triminon, step forward.*"

The hulking Bixhor walked across the pavilion to kneel before Ibarhe, his arms slightly akimbo as if he wanted to wrestle her. Ibarhe said, "*Do you swear to give the next seven years of your life in service to your country, to defend her against all comers, and to prove every day your worthiness to rule?*"

"*I so swear,*" Bixhor said. Fiona had never heard him speak before and was astonished at how beautiful his voice was.

Movement caught her eye, and she turned to see two rows of Irantzen priestesses enter the pavilion, led by Hien. Hien walked forward until she was standing behind Bixhor, and the two priestesses at the head of the lines came to stand immediately behind and to either side of her. One bore a brass bowl wider than her arms were long, the other a length of undyed linen cloth.

From his position, Bixhor couldn't see Hien, but when she held out her hands, he took off his robe and held it up for her to take. Beneath the robe he wore a plain white singlet, and his body was as muscular as Fiona had imagined. Hien handed the robe to the priestess who held the cloth and accepted the cloth from her in exchange.

"*Bixhor of the Triminon,*" Hien said, "*we name you King of Veribold and wash you clean of your mortal concerns, that you may accept the burdens of the country without prior obligations.*" The other priestess came forward and tipped the brass bowl over Bixhor's head. Water poured out in a thin stream, cascading over his dark hair to spill across his face and shoulders and back. Bixhor stared straight ahead without flinching. When the bowl was empty, the priestess stepped back, and Hien draped the linen cloth around Bixhor's shoulders in a gesture like robing a king.

"*Wash away your family commitments. Wash away the ties of blood. Wash away old promises,*" Hien said. Bixhor took the cloth from around his neck and wiped the water from his face and arms. His movements were unhurried, deliberate, and Fiona felt certain they were ritual. When he was finished, Hien accepted the cloth from him and traded it to the priestess for the robe, which she settled around his shoulders.

"*For seven years you are no more Bixhor of the Triminon but Bixhor, King of Veribold,*" Hien said. She nodded to Ibarhe, who removed the *toan* jade from around her neck and placed it around Bixhor's. A sighing sound rose up from the audience as every Veriboldan once more went to their knees, making their silken robes whisper in quiet tribute. Fiona bowed as Sebastian was doing.

Bixhor stood and turned to face the audience. "*I will serve Our Lady Veribold with knowledge, wisdom, cunning, charisma, and faith,*" he said in that beautiful voice. "*We are one.*"

"*We are one,*" the assembled Veriboldans said.

"*Rise, and depart with my blessing,*" Bixhor said.

The Veriboldans stood raggedly, some more agile than others, and made their way through the entrance to the grand reception chamber. Fiona and Sebastian, at the back of the crowd, hung back. Fiona cast a glance at Hien, who was speaking to the new King as Ibarhe listened in. The mystique was gone; the three Veriboldans looked like ordinary people having a chat after some musical performance. Hien looked away and saw Fiona watching. The corners of her mouth twitched, and she nodded, the barest of movements. Fiona nodded back. It was the perfect farewell.

"And so it is over," Dekerian Nikani said, drawing Fiona's attention. Nikani and Salena had also hung back, though Morten and Venelda were already gone. "It was intriguing. Though I think we will not choose to return for the next Election. I am not fond of being an outsider. What do you think, your Highness?"

"I suppose it will be up to Mother who she sends," Sebastian said. His hand closed more tightly on Fiona's. "But I think not. I'm going to recommend she send someone who speaks Veriboldan."

"Ah, but you have such a lovely translator," Salena said with a smile. "I understand, though. It is hard being at a disadvantage."

"Exactly," Sebastian said. He let go of Fiona to offer his hand to Nikani, then Salena. "It was a pleasure meeting you."

Fiona, too, shook hands, then was startled by Stannin's booming voice, saying, "*Is good to here come again. Next we speak Veribold, yes?*" He slapped Sebastian on the shoulder, making him stagger. "*You husband, he good. Much love,*" he added with a grin at Fiona. Fiona blushed.

"What did he say?" Sebastian asked, rubbing his shoulder.

"That next time, you'll both speak Veriboldan," Fiona said. "And that you're a good man."

"If that's how he shows approval, I'm glad he's not my enemy," Sebastian said.

They walked with the other envoys to the outer doors, where they separated to return to their respective lodgings. Fiona had no idea where the others were staying. It made her wonder what Stannin, at home on the windy Eidestal and presumably unfamiliar with a permanent home, thought of Veribold's hospitality. What a story he'd have to tell the kinship.

Sebastian hadn't taken her hand again after shaking Nikani's, and Fiona's hand felt unnaturally cold. It was a bad idea, anyway. She needed to disentangle herself from Sebastian if she wanted to build a new life.

They rode through the streets in silence until they reached the embassy, where Sebastian helped her out of the carriage. "We don't have to leave early," he said. "There's a lot of packing to do, and I was thinking we might go into the city while they're doing that. We could find you lodgings then."

"All right," Fiona said, wishing the ache in her chest hadn't just become a stone in her stomach. "Thank you."

Sebastian nodded. He didn't offer her his arm.

The two of them walked side by side into the embassy, which was quiet and dark except for a few lights shining from beneath doors. It felt to Fiona as if they were miles apart instead of close enough to touch. She went over things she might say and came up blank. But there really wasn't anything to say, was there?

Sebastian held the door to their suite for her, standing close enough that her wide skirts brushed his legs, then closed the door and stood there with his hand on the knob. He didn't turn the lights on. "Good night, then," he said.

"I have to call Georgette," she said. "I can't get out of this gown without help."

"That seems like a design flaw."

It was a joke, but she felt like crying instead. "I don't know why Willow North ever put up with it."

"I don't imagine she did for long." Sebastian straightened and crossed the room to his bedroom door. "I'll see you in the morning."

She heard the click of the latch. "Sebastian, wait," she said, the words tumbling out of her before she could stop them.

He turned. "Yes?"

She could barely see him in the dimness, as if he were already gone, and the ache in her chest threatened to overwhelm her. "I don't," she said, and made herself stop. There was nothing she could do.

Unless there was.

"Don't go," she said. "Please."

Sebastian drew in a sharp breath. "Fiona. We can't. Please don't make this harder."

She shook her head. "I was married for ten years. For seven of those, I was miserable. I never thought—I love you, Sebastian. And now we're going to leave each other, and I'll never see you again, and it hurts so much it's like being poisoned all over again, except it's a poison I chose for myself. I don't want you to go. I don't care if it means I have to be mocked and ridiculed by every well-born man and woman in Tremontane. I want you. I always have."

Sebastian didn't move, didn't speak. Fiona drew in a ragged breath and wiped away her tears. Finally, Sebastian said, "It won't work, Fiona. You said it—love isn't enough to build a marriage on. You'd end up hating and resenting me, and I can't bear that. I love you, and I can't do that to you."

The tears fell more heavily now, choking her. "This is *ridiculous*," she cried. "We love each other. Why can't that be enough?"

Sebastian took a few steps toward her and took her hand. "I don't know," he said, and pulled her into his embrace. She clung to him, crying as if her heart were broken even as his touch soothed her. A fragment of a memory surfaced, of him looking at her wide-eyed in that frigid barn, and it stunned her that she hadn't known then what he would eventually mean to her. She loved him. She didn't want to lose him. There had to be a way.

"I wish you weren't a prince," she murmured into his shoulder. "Just the two of us, living in Veribold...we could have an import business, dealing in Devices..."

"That's appealing," Sebastian said. He stroked her hair, and she snuggled in closer, not caring that it would only make the pain worse when he let her go. "No fancy balls, no awkward dinners with my family, no being snubbed by people with more money than sense..."

His arms went rigid. Fiona lifted her head. She could see him clearly, and he was looking off toward the door. She turned awkwardly in his embrace, but saw nothing. "Is something wrong?" *Other than the obvious.*

"Fiona," Sebastian said, his voice distant. "Fiona, what if we didn't have to be part of Tremontanan high society? That's your objection, right?"

Her heart lurched again. "But that...Sebastian, you're a prince. You can't avoid that."

"I can if we're living in Veribold."

She buried her face in his shoulder again and wished he wouldn't taunt her. "That was just an idle dream."

"It doesn't have to be. Not if I'm the ambassador to Veribold."

That startled her into looking at him again. This time, his eyes were on her, and he was smiling. "You can't," she said faintly.

"I've done enough to save my family that I think I can demand any reward I want from my mother. Think of it, Fiona. We'll live here, away from the court—you already know as much as I do about Veriboldan culture, maybe more—"

"But I still know nothing about high society. I'd make you look like a fool."

Sebastian shook his head. "Noble Veriboldans don't give a damn about other countries' customs or noble ranks. They'll treat you exactly the same as they treat me, with a veneer of politeness over thinly veiled contempt. Fiona—"

"Wait. Just...let me think." The idea had already caught hold of her. Ambassador to Veribold, away from the court and Sebastian's poisonous mother—except... "You don't speak Veriboldan."

"Fiona, my love, no man in the history of the world has ever had so much incentive to learn to speak Veriboldan." He gripped her shoulders. "It's the perfect solution."

She stared at him, at his eyes alight with excitement, and ran over his words in her head, examining them for flaws. Hope threaded its way into her heart, sending out tendrils like a fast-growing vine until she once more felt light enough to fly. "Sebastian," she said, but got no further because his lips were on hers and they were kissing like they'd never have the chance again.

He put his hands low on her hips and pulled her closer as her arms went around his neck, doing the same. The touch of his hands, the feel of his body against hers, filled her with such joy it burned. He let go of her long enough to wrestle his satin coat off and fling it away into the darkness. "Forget about Georgette," he said in a low voice. "Let me help you out of that dress."

She laughed. She couldn't remember the last time she'd had anything to laugh about. "We can't," she said. "We're not married."

"Everyone in Veribold thinks we are," Sebastian said. He buried his face in the crook of her neck, kissing his way along the curve of her cheek and back to her lips. "We shouldn't disappoint them."

It was tempting, but after her experiences in the Irantzen temple, Fiona didn't want to disregard her religious values so completely. "We can wait," she said, withdrawing from him just a little.

Sebastian scowled, but his eyes were alight with mirth, relieving Fiona's heart. "We can wait until morning," he said, "at which point we will take Ambassador Emory aside, tell her the truth about our non-marriage, and get her to witness our vows."

That solution hadn't occurred to Fiona. "And tell her her tenure here will be up sooner than she thought. I don't think she'll be disappointed."

"I think I should receive some reward for having the restraint to not pull the ambassador out of her bed right now," Sebastian said with a smile.

Fiona linked her fingers behind his neck and returned his smile. "Tomorrow," she said. "This will have to do for now," and she pulled him close for a kiss.

40

A week later, they rode into Aurilien to the sound of rain lashing the carriage window. Fiona chose to be grateful it was rain and not snow, but it was still cold, and she couldn't help wishing this was all over and they were back in Veribold. She leaned against Sebastian's shoulder and sighed. They'd been seven days on the road and every morning had felt like a miracle. Seven days traveling. Seven days married. She'd never been happier.

Ambassador Emory had greeted their story with a raised eyebrow, but had asked no questions despite the sketchiness of their explanation. They couldn't explain why they needed to protect Fiona from the Queen's paranoia, so they'd stuck with saying there hadn't been time to marry before leaving Tremontane, and Emory had agreed to help without saying anything about why they'd waited so long once they were in Veribold. Fiona, whose first marriage had been solemnized by Roderick's father as patriarch of the Kent family, had thought the Queen would have to do the honors. She was pleasantly surprised to learn any Tremontanan with a family bond could witness the forming of a new one. And with only a few short sentences, she was Fiona North for real.

She took Sebastian's hand and twined her fingers with his. That first day had passed in a blur, between the marriage vows and packing and saying their goodbyes, that it had seemed like no time before they were rattling along in the carriage away from Haizea. She'd been painfully aware of her new husband all that day, when they sat opposite each other, not touching as if they both knew touching would lead to more, right there in the not-very-private carriage. By the time supper was over, and Sebastian escorted her to their room—one room, no more strange looks from the servants—she felt she might explode if he didn't kiss her, touch her, take her to bed and make her cry out his name. And the night was a blur of a different kind.

Now she cuddled close to his side and closed her eyes. Sebastian would report to his mother, convince her to make him the ambassador, and they could leave again...no, Fiona had sort of promised Sebastian's sister Emily that she could host them a reception. The idea made Fiona cringe, but she liked Emily, and she could put up with one event. Knowing they had somewhere to retreat to, somewhere far from the capital, gave her even greater endurance.

"Strange," Sebastian said. "There are a lot of people in mourning."

Fiona opened her eyes and peered out the window. She'd thought he'd meant people dressed in mourning black, but it was the city that was in mourning. Black ribbons adorned most of the lampposts, many store windows were shrouded in black crape, and even the newspaper vendors' cries were hushed, though they were still doing great business. "I wonder who died?"

"Someone important, but—no, it wouldn't be my mother, someone would have told us even if we were on the road." Sebastian looked out the window past her. "It's all over the city."

"And—there's someone wearing a black band on her sleeve. And two more people. Sebastian, this is unsettling."

"There's no sense worrying about it until we reach the palace. Someone there will know." He squeezed her hand gently. "And then it will be nothing to do with us."

The carriage rattled past the gates leading to the great sweep of the palace drive, then up its curve to deposit them at the front doors. This time, Fiona didn't feel intimidated by them or by the antechamber beyond. They were large, and impressive, but Fiona had seen even larger and more impressive buildings in Veribold.

They stood inside the doors and shook themselves free of the few raindrops that had settled on them during the short few steps between carriage and palace. "Your Highness," someone said, and Fiona looked up to see a stately gentleman in North blue livery approaching rapidly. "Prince Sebastian, Lady North, welcome home. May I give you my condolences on your loss?"

"Ah...thank you," Sebastian said, glancing at Fiona. She agreed silently that this was not the time to admit to ignorance. "Is my mother expecting me? I'd like to speak with her immediately."

"Her Majesty instructed me to ask you to wait upon her in her private drawing room," the servant said. "I will be happy to escort you—"

"That won't be necessary," a new voice said. Fiona remembered the woman who descended the stairs now toward them. Master Thornton. Her face was more careworn than before, her voice rougher, but she carried herself with the confidence of a Scholia Master. "I will escort Prince Sebastian and his lady wife."

The servant bowed. "Of course, Master Thornton."

Master Thornton reached the foot of the stairs and nodded politely to Sebastian. "This way," she said, though Fiona was sure Sebastian knew the way to his own mother's chambers.

The halls of the palace were every bit as disorienting as they had been on her first visit, their architecture so varied it was like stepping backward and forward in time. It reminded her of the Jaixante, though the two couldn't have been more different. Despite their differences, both felt like structures that had been built for the sake of an idea and not for anything so mundane as housing people. Fiona recognized, at one point, the hall leading to the east wing where the royal family lived, and was surprised at feeling relief. It was just a reaction to seeing something familiar in the midst of confusion, that was all.

The queen's private drawing room wasn't in the east wing, as Fiona had expected; it was some distance from those quarters and up another two flights of stairs. Master Thornton opened a door carved to look like a beaded curtain and painted stark white and bowed them inside. Fiona hadn't kept track of the stairs they'd climbed, as they'd gone up and down apparently at random, but it was clear this room was near the top of the palace, though still nowhere near as high as Willow North's tower. The sound of the rain striking the glass, of the wind whistling across the windows, filled the room and made it feel even colder than it was.

Windows of clear, thin glass, very modern, filled two of the walls, beneath which were backless couches strewn with cushions in the style of a hundred years previous. The contrast between the two eras struck Fiona as typically wealthy, because only the wealthy could afford furniture that didn't wear out after five or ten years. To her surprise, it wasn't a dismissive thought. Things were what they were, and how snobbish of her if she turned up her nose at a beautiful room—and it *was* beautiful—because she felt inferior.

A pianoforte in a cherrywood case stood near the corner where the two windowed walls met and the light was brightest, or would be on a less overcast day. Fiona tried to imagine the Queen doing something so ordinary as playing the pianoforte and failed. Maybe it had belonged to some other ruler of Tremontane. Though she couldn't imagine Willow North playing a musical instrument either. Her imagination must be faulty.

Master Thornton stepped inside after them and shut the door. "You may not have heard the news," she said in her gravelly voice. "Prince Douglas is dead."

Fiona gasped. Sebastian turned to look at Master Thornton. "Is he, now," he said without a trace of emotion.

"I realize it must be a shock," Master Thornton said. She sounded as emotionless as Sebastian. "He was riding a green horse. He lost control and broke his neck in the fall. Most tragic."

"And a surprise," Sebastian said. "Doug was an excellent rider."

Master Thornton shrugged. "Even excellent riders aren't perfect. I understand the horse wasn't saddle-ready, but Prince Douglas insisted he knew what he was doing." She bowed, said, "The Queen will join you shortly," and left the room.

Fiona sank helplessly onto one of the couches. Sebastian crossed the room to join her. "Are you all right?"

She nodded. "It's just…"

"I know," Sebastian said grimly. "I hoped Mother would do something about Doug. I might have guessed it would be something permanent."

"What do we do?"

"Nothing." Sebastian sat beside her and took her hand. "It's over. Gizane is powerless—may have been executed already—and Doug can't hurt anyone anymore. The house of North is no longer in danger, and we've done everything Mother commanded. We're free."

The door opened, and the Queen entered. Sebastian and Fiona rose, though Fiona didn't feel much like the pinched, sour-looking woman in front of her deserved her respect. She didn't understand how anyone could cold-bloodedly arrange for her own son to be killed. Though she had to admit, looking at Queen Genevieve, if she had to imagine what such a person might look like, the Queen certainly fit that picture.

It was the first time Fiona had seen the Queen in anything but an elegant gown. Today she wore fitted trousers and a linen shirt with a deep yoke and full sleeves gathered to tight, wide cuffs. Both were dyed black, with some streakiness along the left sleeve that suggested it was a recent dye job. Her clothes, and her black hair pulled tightly back from her face, made her pale skin look almost white, as if the blood had been drained from her body. But her sharp blue eyes were every bit as bright as before. She closed the door behind her and regarded them. "Sit," she said.

Sebastian didn't move, so neither did Fiona. Genevieve arched an eyebrow. "So we have reached the limit of your obedience, Sebastian," she said.

Sebastian said nothing. Fiona wished she could take his hand, but she knew the Queen would see that as weakness.

Genevieve walked away from them, toward the windows, where she stood looking out over Aurilien. Wind blew the rain hard against the window. "I hear Bixhor of the Triminon is King in Veribold," she said. "He is not one to be underestimated, but I believe we will deal well together."

Still Sebastian said nothing. Fiona risked a look at his face; his jaw was tight, his lips compressed in a thin line, and the look in his eyes said he was close to an epic outburst. She didn't dare say anything. This was between Sebastian and his mother.

Genevieve turned to look back at her son. "Say it," she said. "You're wrong, whatever you think, but say it anyway."

Sebastian shifted his weight as if preparing to throw a punch. "You had him killed," he ground out. "You had all the resources in the world and you murdered him."

"Douglas's death was an accident," Genevieve said. "Believe that, or not."

"I don't believe it. Doug was a better rider than either of us. There's no way a horse threw him, no matter how green."

"He was careless," Genevieve said, her thin voice harsher even than Master Thornton's. "And you can believe what you like about me, but don't ever think I'm so stupid as to count on some animal to rid me of a problem."

Sebastian's next words froze on his lips. He closed his mouth, slowly. "You," he began, then seemed to search for words. "What was your plan?"

"Irrelevant," Genevieve said. "Douglas's fortunate accident means we will never know what I might have done."

"But you would have had him killed."

Genevieve pursed her lips. "Douglas was a danger to this family. I argued, cajoled, even threatened, and he laughed and said no one would ever discover what he was capable of. I told you, Sebastian—I *will not* see Willow North's legacy destroyed by a freak magical talent wielded by a foolish boy. I am the Queen. I make the hard choices so you can sleep safe at night."

Sebastian shook his head. "Your own son, Mother—"

"Don't come over moralistic at me, Sebastian. You manipulated things in Veribold nicely, didn't you? I needed Gizane neutralized. You arranged for her death. How different does that make us?"

"It's not the same."

"Douglas and Gizane are dead. To them, it's exactly the same."

"We didn't want—"

"What I *wanted*," Genevieve said in a cold, bitter voice that cut across Sebastian's words, "was a son who respected himself and this family enough not to go raping his merry way through the countryside. But we don't always get what we want. It's over, Sebastian. Let the dead lie."

Sebastian shuddered. "I'll never understand you."

"Then let's thank heaven you will never be King." Genevieve glanced at Fiona as if seeing her for the first time. "And you, Miss Cooper whose fortunes are now tangled with ours. Are you going to be tiresome, and judge me, too?"

"No," Fiona said. "You did what you thought you had to. It's not what I would have done. But you're right about one thing—Sebastian and I are responsible indirectly for Gizane's death, and we did it to save ourselves. So I don't feel I have the right to judge you."

"Very diplomatically said," Genevieve said with a tiny smile. "You would have made an excellent daughter-in-law."

She spoke so placidly Fiona didn't at first understand her. *Would have made*? "I...don't understand."

"What are you talking about?" Sebastian said.

Genevieve's expression was cold and hard. "I know what happened at the challenge of faith. You have inherent magic, and one far more terrifying to the average person than Douglas's."

Fiona sank onto the nearest couch. Her legs shook too hard to support her. "I don't—that was a miracle," she said faintly, feeling like an idiot for saying it.

Genevieve laughed. "As if anyone will believe that. It's only a matter of time before the news spreads, and then everyone will know the truth. And if I was willing to kill my own son to protect my family, you can't imagine I'll be any less ruthless disposing of you."

"Don't threaten Fiona," Sebastian warned. "Everyone at the challenge believed it was heaven's miracle. The Irantzen priestesses swore to that. No one will think inherent magic unless *you* spread the word."

"If that's what it takes to keep this family untainted, you can believe I'll do just that."

"Untainted? You think—"

"Sebastian, no," Fiona said, cutting him off before he could reveal Great-Uncle Sebastian's secret.

Sebastian controlled himself with visible effort. "Mother," he said, "I want you to make me ambassador to Veribold. Fiona and I will never return to Aurilien. It won't be an issue unless you make it one. Please, see sense."

Genevieve shook her head. "Master Thornton is waiting outside to annul your marriage," she said. "We'll provide Miss Cooper more than adequate funds to go wherever she wishes. Say your goodbyes quickly—it will be less painful."

"I refuse," Sebastian said. "You can't force us to do this."

Genevieve tilted her head like an inquisitive hawk that had just seen a mouse break cover. "I wonder," she said, "how well you think you can protect her."

"*Mother!*" Sebastian's cry was anguished, and it made Fiona's heart break. Her week of happiness seemed years in the past. She felt numb, and utterly alone despite Sebastian standing right next to her. Leave him, or spend the rest of her life watching her back for the Queen's assassins—her short life, probably, because the Queen had resources Fiona couldn't even imagine.

She looked at Sebastian, who seemed poised to attack his mother; looked at the Queen, whose fierce devotion to her family had been twisted so completely, and impulsively said, "Prince Landon doesn't know about any of this, does he?"

Both Sebastian and Genevieve looked at her as if she'd gone mad. "He doesn't know about his brother, he doesn't know about me—I haven't spoken to him much, but I get the feeling he's not a subtle thinker, and you couldn't trust him with that knowledge," she went on. "So really, right now the only people who know I have inherent magic are myself, Sebastian...and you, your Majesty."

Genevieve's eyes narrowed. "Do you have a point?"

"I don't have a point. What I have," Fiona said, "is the ability to burn your bedchamber to the ground."

Those blue eyes widened.

"So sad, really," Fiona said, taking a step toward the Queen. "A lamp improperly trimmed, the Queen sleeping so soundly the fire kills her before anyone can rescue her. King Landon will mourn, but life goes on. And my secret...is safe."

The Queen's impassivity cracked, revealing uncertainty and the beginnings of fear. "You wouldn't. You don't have the heart of a killer."

"You mean, a heart like yours?" Fiona smiled. "Maybe. You send us back to Veribold, you leave us alone, you repeat the story the Irantzen Temple spread, and we'll never have to find out."

Genevieve said nothing. Fiona didn't look away. She knew she'd won when Genevieve flinched first. "Ambassador," Genevieve said. "But on condition you renounce your claim to the Crown. I won't take any chances with this lineage."

"I agree," Sebastian said promptly, as if he'd known she'd make that demand.

"Then it's settled. You'll want to leave as soon as the documents are drawn up and the announcement is made."

"Of course," Sebastian said. Fiona couldn't look at him. If she did, everything might still fall apart.

The Queen backed away. She'd regained some of her composure, but the look she directed at Fiona was more appraising than cruel. "I was wrong," she said. "You are a North, after all. Gizane should never have tangled with you."

Fiona said nothing. Genevieve opened the door and let herself out.

The instant the door was closed, Sebastian let out a huge breath and sagged onto one of the sofas. "You know she believes—"

"Don't say it," Fiona said. "She might still be listening." He was right; the Queen clearly believed Fiona's powers went farther than they did. So long as it saved both their lives, Fiona intended her to keep on believing Fiona could ignite fires from anywhere she chose.

Sebastian put his face in his hands and rubbed his temples. "You were very believable. How much of that did you mean?"

"All of it, I think. I'm not sure."

He lowered his hands and looked up at her. "I didn't know you could be so ruthless."

"I never had anything so worth fighting for." She went to his side and laid her hand along his cheek. "I love you. Thank you for kidnapping me."

Sebastian smiled and stood, taking her in his arms. "The best mistake I ever made."

"You probably shouldn't say that to anyone but me. They'd take it the wrong way."

He kissed her, so sweetly she wished they were somewhere warmer. "You're my best mistake," he whispered, "my dearest love, and you will always be the fire in my heart."

Fiona smiled. "I love the sound of that."

ABOUT THE AUTHOR

In addition to the Crown of Tremontane series, Melissa McShane is the author of The Extraordinaries series, beginning with BURNING BRIGHT, as well as The Last Oracle series, COMPANY OF STRANGERS, and many others. After a childhood spent roaming the United States, she settled in Utah with her husband, four children and a niece, four very needy cats, and a library that continues to grow out of control. She wrote reviews and critical essays for many years before turning to fiction, which is much more fun than anyone ought to be allowed to have.

You can visit her at her website www.melissamcshanewrites.com for more information on other books.

For information on new releases, fun extras, and more, sign up for Melissa's newsletter: http://eepurl.com/brannP

The Book of Mayhem

The Book of Lies

The Book of Betrayal

The Book of Havoc (forthcoming)

COMPANY OF STRANGERS

Company of Strangers

Stone of Inheritance

Mortal Rites

Shifting Loyalties

Sands of Memory

Call of Wizardry

THE CONVERGENCE TRILOGY

The Summoned Mage

The Wandering Mage

The Unconquered Mage

THE BOOKS OF DALANINE

The Smoke-Scented Girl

The God-Touched Man

Emissary

Warts and All: A Fairy Tale Collection

The View from Castle Always

www.ingramcontent.com/pod-product-compliance
Lightning Source LLC
Chambersburg PA
CBHW051443260626
47162CB00001B/227